Wicked Games

ALSO BY ELLEN HART

Murder in the Air
The Oldest Sin
Robber's Wine
Faint Praise
For Every Evil
A Small Sacrifice
This Little Piggy Went to Murder
A Killing Cure
Stage Fright
Vital Lies
Hallowed Murder

Wicked Games

ELLEN HART

ST. MARTIN'S PRESS ❦ NEW YORK

Design by Michaelann Zimmerman

Library of Congress Cataloging-in-Publication Data

Hart, Ellen.
    Wicked games / Ellen Hart.—1st U.S. ed.
        p.   cm.
    ISBN 0-312-18680-0
    I. Title.
    PS3558.A6775W53   1998
    813'.54—dc21   98-11576
                                     CIP

First Edition: August 1988

10 9 8 7 6 5 4 3 2

FOR SANDRA SCOPPETTONE
WITH MUCH LOVE

From such crooked wood as that which man is made of,
nothing straight can be fashioned.

—Immanuel Kant

Wicked
Games

Cast of Characters

JANE LAWLESS: Owner of the Lyme House Restaurant in Minneapolis.

CORDELIA THORN: Artistic Director of the Allen Grimby Repertory Theatre in St. Paul. Jane's closest friend.

ELLIOT BEAUMAN: Children's book writer.

PATRICIA KASTNER: Daughter of Virginia and Otto Kastner. Jane's new neighbor.

OTTO KASTNER: Owner of Kastner Construction. Father of Patricia.

VIRGINIA KASTNER: Owner of Kastner Gardens. Mother of Patricia.

EARL WILCOX: Private Investigator.

JULIA MARTINSEN: Doctor. Jane's newest love.

SIGRID LAWLESS: Jane's sister-in-law. Therapist. Wife of Peter.

PETER LAWLESS: Jane's brother. Cameraman at WTWN-TV. Sigrid's husband.

ABBIE KAUFMAN: Potter. Patricia's old girlfriend.

KEVIN TORLAND: Doctor. Patricia's recent boyfriend.

DR. CYRIL DANCING: Psychologist. Professor at the University of Minnesota.

RAMONA DANCING: Cyril Dancing's wife. Judge.

CONNIE MAYVILLE: Grade school friend of Patricia's.

Prologue

When Virginia thought of this night, years later, she was never quite able to shake the sense that she'd failed to see or understand something important. It would become a nagging ache, one that haunted her days and nights just as it would forever destroy her peace of mind. This ordinary summer evening would become the fulcrum on which the rest of her life turned. Was it a chance event? Certainly, she hadn't seen it coming. Nor, for that matter, had her husband.

Driving home from the store that lovely July evening, the scent of summer rain in the air, she was on top of the world. The small floral and garden store she'd opened a few years before was going strong, so strong in fact that she planned to open a second store in the fall, in time for the Christmas rush. And next spring, she was thinking of expanding into a full-service greenhouse, selling everything from house and bedding plants to specialty pots and garden supplies.

As she pulled into the driveway, turning off the motor and sitting for a minute enjoying the cool breeze and the dark, her mind was occupied by thoughts of inventories and plans for the buying trips she would need to make to Mexico and the Far East before the new store opened.

Life was good for Virginia Kastner. Both of her boys were doing well in school, and though her husband was having some trouble finding just the kind of job that suited him, he'd been working steadily as a construction foreman all summer. He loved to work with his hands, especially when it came to carpentry, and Virginia assumed he would eventually end up in the building trades somewhere, probably as the head of his own company.

Hearing the sound of muffled laughter, she slipped out of the front seat, careful to make sure she didn't drop her briefcase. It contained two bone china plates she wanted to show her husband. It was about time they picked a family pattern.

Glancing around to see where the laughter was coming from, Virginia looked up and saw a dark form huddling on the peak of the roof near the chimney. "Otto?" she called, wondering what her husband was doing up there at this time of night.

"Guess again," came a youthful voice.

Feeling a shiver creep down her spine, Virginia stepped away from the car. "My God, Jay! How did you get up there? Get down this minute!" Thinking better of her order, she barked, "No, just stay there. I'll have your dad come up and get you."

"No you won't," he snickered. He tried to stand, but seemed unsteady on his feet. "I been sick, Mom. Don't be mad." He wiped a hand over his mouth.

"Sick? Sick how?"

"I threw up."

"Just stay still!" She felt her stomach clutch. Neither of her sons had ever gone up on the roof before. Not that Jay could entirely understand the danger. He was only ten years old. She set her briefcase down. "Where's your brother?" she asked tentatively. The two of them were always together. Maybe he was up there too, but too afraid to show his face. When they'd moved into the new house, she'd given them separate bedrooms, but since they always ended up sleeping together anyway, she eventually gave up and bought bunk beds.

"Yeah, where *is* Elliot?" said Jay. "That's a good question. Hey, Mom, I'm surprised you can see me." He sounded annoyed now.

"See you? Of course I can see you. Why wouldn't I?"

He let out a snort. "Because you got a wooden eye." His words seemed to strike him as funny and he began to giggle.

"What are you talking about?" Her fear was mixed with impatience now.

"You're as blind as a bat, Mom. That's what Dad said. A blind old *wooden* bat." He giggled again, playing with the sentence. "A blind bat. A blind rat. Are rats ever blind, Mom?"

If she didn't know better, she'd think he'd been drinking. "Just stay still. I'll get your father. You've got some explaining to do, young man."

"Hey, wait," called Jay, standing up and weaving away from the chimney. "This is fun." He hiccupped, then covered his mouth with his hand. "I don't wanna come down. Not ever. I'm gonna live up here from now on. You can put Twinkies and stuff for me to eat on the sun-room roof. You should see the world from this high up, Mom. It's cool. I feel like a king and this is my mountain." He flung his arms out and looked up at the stars. "Really, it's—" Stumbling awkwardly, he lost his balance and tumbled forward.

"Jay!" She held up her hands, realizing the instant she did so that it was useless. Hearing a thud in the backyard, she rushed around the side of the house and lunged through the open gate, but it was too late.

Jay's body lay limp and twisted on the grass, his beautiful dark hair matted with sweat. As she knelt next to him, afraid to breathe, she touched his forehead gingerly, seeing the trickle of blood coming from the side of his mouth, smelling the alcohol, the vomit. She knew she had to run to get help, but it was a moment

5

out of time. Her mind raced, but her body was paralyzed, frozen by a sound she heard somewhere in the distance. It was a high-pitched screech, like the shriek of a siren or a factory whistle. Had someone already called the paramedics? It took a few seconds more before she realized the sound was coming from inside her.

1

Elliot wasn't sure who he should tell. The body was probably still there, though he couldn't be positive. He'd searched in vain through the morning paper hoping to find a story about the murder, something that would put his mind at rest. After all, if someone else found her, he wouldn't need to risk talking to the police. He'd listened to the radio in his car nearly all day. The longer he listened, the more he realized that the provincial, easygoing town of his youth had matured into *Murderapolis*—the murder capital of the Upper Midwest.

Elliot had been away for a few years, setting up residence for most of that time in Pitman, Iowa. Sure, he was used to an even slower pace now; small-town life, the quiet of the country, space to think and to breathe. Yet as he drove back into town last night, the difference jarred him. Elliot was in his late thirties, no longer impressed by what the big city had to offer. As he drove down Hennepin, he could sense that he'd come home to a town in crisis. As a matter of fact, he'd walked straight into the middle of it.

He'd slept in his car last night, hitting the city limits around 2:00 A.M. As a writer—even a widely published children's book author—he hadn't yet made it financially. Every penny counted when you didn't have many pennies to begin with. Tonight, however, he'd reserved a room at the Nicollet Motel in south Minneapolis. Not a palace, but it would do. After unloading the contents of his rented U-Haul into his room, he'd spent the rest of the day driving around town looking for an apartment. Later, he'd found a quiet spot near the Minnehaha creek to have dinner. He sat in the open air with a Mountain Dew and a roast beef sandwich, enjoying the crimson sunset deepening into night. Yet even after only two days, he already missed his rented house in Pitman. And especially, he missed his cat, Cain.

Cain was a wanderer at heart. A free spirit. He loved to roam the cornfields behind Elliot's house. But he was a cat regular as clockwork, always home within two hours of sunset, snuggled next to Elliot on the couch, purring contentedly as Elliot watched TV or read a book. Funny thing was, Elliot had let him out last week and hadn't seen him since. He'd gone out looking for him several times, but with no luck. Of course, Cain could've gotten into a fight with a dog or another cat, crawled into the cornfield to lick his wounds or even to die. But Elliot knew Cain was still alive. He'd simply disappeared. In his prescient cat soul, Cain probably knew where they were headed and even what was about to happen. And smart as he was, he wanted no part of it. Maybe, by taking off, old Cain was trying to give Elliot a last message. Run, friend, run away while you still can.

As darkness fell, Elliot found himself back in his car, driving around town aimlessly, regaining a certain familiarity with the city. Around ten, he climbed into the backseat to take a short nap before heading downtown to catch some of the local night life.

Except, he couldn't fall asleep. Every time he closed his eyes, the same image reappeared. It was like a haunting: indistinct, foggy, and yet each time there was something more—something new and horrific. The air surrounding him grew electric with fear, whispered words, darkness, and the smell of sweating bodies. And a name.

Carrie.

"Carrie, what . . . what happened?" cried Elliot, sitting bolt upright in the seat. He wiped the sweat off his forehead and then rolled down the back window, gulping air into his lungs as if the terror were his own. Pushing open the door, he climbed out, breathing hard as he stood next to the rear fender. After a moment, he slammed the door and looked up at the stars.

The image followed him outside. "No," he said, mashing his hands against his eyes. It was getting stronger. Clearer. Choking him. Carrie was innocent. Nothing like this should have happened to her. He threw open the front door, jumped inside, and started the engine. He needed to get away from the quiet, preferably someplace where there was music, and people, anything to drive away the vision.

Ten minutes later he walked into a crowded Lake Street bar, sat down at the counter, and ordered himself a Coke. Yes, this was better. Mindless. Smoky. Vaguely sexual in an empty sort of way. A good place to sink into invisibility. As he sat staring at a young woman playing a video game, it occurred to him that maybe he should call his sister. She'd moved back to Minneapolis herself three months ago. But what would he say? Hi, sis, guess what? I followed you back. Sure, she'd be happy to see him, but for now it was best to keep a low profile. Find a place to live. Settle in. And then he'd call. There was time for everything he needed to do. The deadline for the next book wasn't until early December. That meant he had two full months left. Piece of cake.

Elliot had always been a loner. But unlike most loners, he wasn't embarrassed by his loneliness. In his current profession, the ability to enjoy spending time alone was actually a plus. All the endless days spent working at his computer, talking to no one but his creations—the animals, the children, the superheroes and the monsters that peopled his books—enriched his life as no human company ever had. He created worlds out of nothing but his own imagination. He could make them as charming and as sweet, or as menacing and dark as he wanted. But the bottom line was, *he* was in charge. He'd already won several national awards for his writing, been praised for the subtlety, beauty, and simplicity of his illustrations. He was in the right profession, all right. If life would simply leave him alone to pursue his interests, he would be a happy man. But life had a way of not cooperating.

The woman sitting next to him at the counter eased over and gave him a boozy smile. "Hey, handsome. Looking for a little company?" She raised her eyebrows seductively.

Elliot cleared his throat, shifting uncomfortably on the stool. "Not really."

"No?" She kept her smile at high beam. "What's your name?"

"Elliot."

She turned toward him, revealing a low-cut dress and far more makeup than he found attractive. He figured she was a hooker. He wasn't interested.

"You here by yourself?" she asked, lighting up a cigarette.

He nodded, then turned away to take a sip of Coke.

"Me too. My old man's gone bowling. Bowling! Instead of staying home to play with me."

Okay, she wasn't a hooker. Elliot looked at her again. This time she just looked sad. Sad and drunk. "I'm sorry."

"Yeah, me too." She blew smoke out of the side of her mouth. "What a life, huh? You get married thinking you're going to be with someone and what happens? He's never home. And when he is, he ignores you."

Elliot remembered now how much he used to like going to bars. He enjoyed the anonymity, the smell of perfume and hot bodies on the make. Then again he never knew how to respond when he got pulled into one of these conversations. "That's too bad," he said weakly.

"Shithead. I hope he drops the ball on his foot. Both feet." She finished her drink and then motioned to the bartender for another. Cocking her head, she said, "I meant that—about you being handsome. I like guys with broad shoulders. And you've got a nice . . . you know, gentle voice. You married?"

He shrugged. "No."

"Well, you're smart. Take some advice from me. Don't bother." Scrutinizing him a moment more, she said, "Hey, you like women, don't you? You're not—"

"If you mean am I gay, no."

"Good." She smiled again. This time, even though it was every bit as boozy, it looked more sincere. "I like you, Elliot."

"Thanks."

"You live in town?"

"I used to. I spent the last three years in Iowa. But my parents are still here."

"Ugh, parents." She picked a piece of tobacco out of her teeth. "That's another subject you shouldn't get me started on. I suppose you like your folks."

The muscles in his face hardened. "Not much."

"Nah, me neither." Her drink arrived. "Put it on my tab."

"No more tabs," said the bartender, a deep scowl on his meaty face. "Cash or no drink."

She glared at him.

"I'll get it," said Elliot, tossing a five on the counter.

The bartender walked off shaking his head. "It's your funeral, pal."

The woman stuck out her tongue at his retreating back. Then, returning her full attention to Elliot, she cuddled up even closer. "Hey, that was real nice of you."

"No problem."

"Maybe this is going to be your lucky night."

Elliot had no intention of staying in this dump for longer than a couple more minutes. And when he left, he was leaving alone. "What's your name?" he asked, picking up his Coke.

"Me? I'm Carrie . . . Lundstrom, although you don't need to know that last part. Some people call me Carolyn, but I prefer

Carrie. You like that name? Say, hon, you look kind of funny. Your face just turned white as a sheet."

Elliot backed off the bar stool and headed for the door. He knew she wasn't the same Carrie, the one he saw so clearly in his mind's eye, but it didn't matter. The name had jarred him. He had to get away.

"Hey," called Carrie. "What's wrong? Where are you going?"

The early October breeze felt bracing against Elliot's hot skin as he burst out of the door. He began to run as fast as he could down Lake Street. Three blocks away, he spotted a police car on the other side of the road. He waved, then dashed up to the front window. "I want to report a murder," he said, resting his hand against the front fender. He needed to catch his breath. "A woman. I'm not sure where, but I can see——"

The officer shot out of the car.

Elliot felt a bright light hit his eyes. "Turn that off," he said angrily, jerking his head away.

The flashlight went dark. "Talk fast, buddy. What about a woman?"

"It happened last night."

"Where were you?"

"Me? No, you don't understand. I wasn't there."

The officer hesitated. "Let's see some ID."

Elliot yanked his billfold out of the back pocket of his jeans and handed over his driver's license.

Switching the flashlight back on, the officer studied it for a moment. "Elliot Beauman. That right?"

Elliot nodded.

"You're visiting our fair city from Iowa?"

"I'm originally from Minneapolis. I'm moving back."

"Right. So, tell me, Elliot, who was murdered?"

"A woman. Her name was Carrie. I don't know any more about her except that she was young. Blond hair."

"And where did this happen?"

Elliot could feel a familiar pounding behind his eyes. "I don't know," he said, mashing his temples hard with both hands. "I think maybe by a water tower. I can see—men with swords. Men with no legs. And eagles." Even though the night air held a chill, Elliot was straining so hard that his face was covered with sweat. "Woods—trees, bushes. And then there was this door . . . and lots of gang graffiti. Cement walls. And . . . and not far away, a school. And houses. Older ones, but nice."

The officer just stared at him. "You say you saw this?"

Again, Elliot nodded. "It was two guys in a van. The license plate—" He closed his eyes and concentrated as hard as he could. "I don't know. There's an M and twenty-three in it. That's all I get. But they live close—I *know* they do."

"You weren't there, but you saw all this? What's the deal here, Mac? You claiming to be psychic or something?" The officer moved aggressively toward him.

"No. I . . . can't explain it. I just . . . had to tell someone." With a speed and a force that surprised him, the officer handcuffed Elliot and then pushed him into the backseat of the squad car.

"I think we better continue this downtown."

Elliot didn't fight. He sat in silence as the lights of the city sped past. One thing he knew for sure, he was in way over his head. He should have kept his mouth shut and not gotten involved. And yet, he had a good reason for what he was doing. It was a calculated risk. He hoped it would pay off.

Elliot was taken downtown to City Hall, a hulking granite structure in the middle of downtown Minneapolis, and ushered into an interview room. He could feel his heart pound inside his chest as he declined the offer of a cup of coffee.

Two burly homicide sergeants interrogated him for the next several hours. Their initial concern seemed to center on Elliot's mental health. After satisfying themselves that he wasn't a "crisis candidate" in need of immediate psychiatric counseling, they began to grill him about his story. They asked the same questions over and over. Elliot figured they were trying to trip him up. After all, if he had information about a murder, that probably pegged him as a prime suspect.

Around 1:00 A.M., both of the officers left. For the next few hours Elliot waited. He paced and read magazines, sat in a chair and studied the ceiling tiles. He knew they couldn't hold him indefinitely without charging him with a crime. Even so, it looked as if it would be a long night.

By three in the morning, his mouth tasted like the floor of a poultry barn. The muscles in his back were sore and his head ached. He'd managed to doze off for a few minutes, though the dark visions inside his brain refused to give him any peace.

Shortly before four, Sergeant Engsdahl, a tall, lanky man with a perpetually disgusted look on his face, reentered the room. "Get up. You can go."

Elliot swung his feet off the coffee table and stood, rubbing the small of his back. "How come? Did you find her?"

"Yeah."

"Where?"

"Over by the Washburn water tower. I used to live in that part of the city. When you mentioned the part about men with swords, it all clicked." As they walked out the door, he added, "It could have been a while before anyone located the body. It's teachers' conference this week—kids are out of school so there isn't as much activity around there. Her body was dumped near the base of the tower."

"What about the guys?" asked Elliot, following him down the hall.

"We spotted a white van parked in a driveway a few blocks away. The interior had been cleaned up, but we could see some stains under the seat. We were pretty sure they were blood. Turns out we were right. The guy inside the house took off out the back door, but we nailed him. In a moment of panic he tried to blame his accomplice for what happened. They're both in custody now. And, lucky for you, neither of them said they'd ever heard of you."

Elliot nodded, yanking on his jeans jacket. "Thanks for the hospitality. It was a pleasure." As he was about to leave, the officer put a hand on Elliot's arm and stopped him.

"Not so fast, friend. As I understand it, you don't have a permanent address in town yet."

"That's right."

"When you do, call me. I may need to talk to you again." He handed Elliot a card: *Sgt. Harold Engsdahl, Criminal Investigations Division, Minneapolis Police Department.* "And second"—his cool blue eyes looked Elliot up and down—"are you really asking us to believe you weren't a witness to that murder?"

"I wasn't there physically, if that's what you mean."

"And nobody told you about it?"

"No. No one."

"So . . . you're telling me you're psychic? You see things? Hear voices?"

Elliot shook his head. "I . . . don't know what I am. But I'm not a psychic. Psychics are all fakes."

Detective Engsdahl's mouth curled, but it wasn't much of a smile. "Seems like there's not much difference between you and some nut case in a mental hospital. They hear voices. See visions."

"Maybe you're right."

He held Elliot with only the force of his eyes. "This kind of stuff happen to you often?"

"Not often."

"Do you get premonitions? You know, before things happen?"

Elliot hesitated. "Sometimes."

"So, did you get any premonitions while you were our guest here?"

Looking away, Elliot said, "No, but I got a strong one yesterday, when I was driving into town." He paused. "I think there may be another murder. In a house this time. Big house. Somewhere near one of the lakes. And it will be a woman again. I wish I could help you more, but that's all I know."

Engsdahl shook his head. "It's a hell of a world if you're a woman."

"Yeah," agreed Elliot. "It is."

2

Jane eased a hand over to the nightstand and switched off the alarm clock before it could ring. She couldn't get up, not just yet. The woman lying next to her in bed would be leaving soon, driving back to her home on Pokegama Lake in northern Minnesota. Jane needed a few more minutes to study her lover's face, to wonder at what was happening between them. Julia slept peacefully, her breathing soft, her arm wrapped casually around Jane's stomach. It was that casual gesture that seemed most intriguing, as if she and Julia had been together for years—as if their affection had somehow become every bit as natural as their passion.

For almost a year, ever since they'd met in a downtown Minneapolis loft, Jane knew she'd been standing at the edge of a precipice. The decision to jump or to turn around and run was, by all rights, hers. For a long time now, life had been safe and simple. She'd poured all her creative energy into the restaurant she owned on Lake Harriet in south Minneapolis. She had her family and friends. And she had the memory of the woman who had shared her life for almost ten years. Christine had died of cancer seven years ago. For Jane, it had been a hard road back from that loss; and yet with the help of her best friend, Cordelia, she'd made the journey. Some of the highs and lows were missing now, but life once again seemed good.

To be fair, Jane had dated here and there, even become involved once for a short time, but she'd never permitted anyone to get as close to her, to touch her as deeply as Julia had. Not since Christine. In fact, it had been so many years since she'd last allowed herself the luxury of these feelings, she'd begun to think of the more romantic part of herself as atrophied.

The problem was, Jane now found herself swept up by a passion long before she'd answered a basic question: Did she want to give up her present stability for uncertainty? She wasn't even sure the decision was hers to make any longer. At this moment, she could feel the gravel starting to give way under her feet. The slide into the unknown had already begun.

Lifting Julia's arm, Jane eased out of bed. She wanted to shower and dress, to feel in control of the day before Julia got up and destroyed the illusion. It wasn't that she was unhappy. On the contrary, she was the happiest she'd been in many years. So happy, in fact, that she had a hard time concentrating on anything other than her happiness.

Right now, however, she had to concentrate on breakfast. If Julia wasn't up by the time they were ready to eat, she'd fix a tray and they could have breakfast in bed. It would be a fitting end to a beautiful weekend together.

As she bounded down the stairs humming an old Leonard Cohen song, she found Bean, her little terrier, asleep in the living room. Her other dog, Gulliver, had died of old age three months before. Bean was all alone now. His sight was far better than his hearing, but he too was aging. Jane gave him a playful scratch and then let him out to do his morning sniff in the backyard.

Entering the kitchen, she put the coffee on, squeezed some fresh orange juice, and then whipped up a quick onion and sausage frittata, placing it in the oven to bake. She'd stopped by the Lyme House yesterday to pick up some fresh pastries, so everything was all set.

Noticing the FOR RENT sign resting next to the back door, she grabbed it, found a hammer, and headed outside. She had some time to kill until the frittata would be ready, so she might as well do a few chores while she waited.

For the past five years, Jane had been renting out the third floor of her home, a large white and brown Tudor. When Christine was alive, she'd renovated the attic and used it for her real estate office. Now, it had become a small yet adequately furnished efficiency apartment. An outside stairway provided a private entrance. Inside, there was an abbreviated kitchen, a full bathroom, and one large L-shaped room that served as living room, dining room, and bedroom. A series of east-facing windows filled the space with brilliant morning sunlight. And in the fall, when the trees finally dropped their leaves, the view of Linden Hills and Lake Harriet beyond was spectacular. The view was one of the major reasons why Jane never had any problems renting the space. The apartment, even though expensive for its size, rented itself.

As she pounded the sign into the grass, she heard a car pull up to the curb. Turning, she saw an attractive young woman sitting behind the wheel. It was Patricia Kastner.

"Morning, Jane." The woman didn't get out. Instead, she let the car idle as she studied the sign. Patricia's mother, Virginia, owned Kastner Gardens, the largest floral and garden store in the state. Patricia worked at the corporate offices in Edina. About two months ago she'd moved into a house on the other end of the block. She and Jane had become friends mainly through the newly established block association. "Time for a new renter, huh?" she called, giving Jane a sunny smile.

"It is," replied Jane, standing back to make sure the sign wasn't crooked. "You know anyone who might be interested?"

"No. But I'll keep my eyes and ears open. You looking for a male type or a female type?"

Jane shrugged, brushing a strand of chestnut hair away from her eyes. "I don't really care. I used to think I'd be more comfortable with a female living upstairs, but then I got burned a couple of times with a couple of different women so I tried a guy two years ago. He worked out just great. I even convinced him to mow the grass."

"By using your irresistible charm?" She flashed Jane a broad grin.

Was she flirting? Since Jane assumed the young woman was straight, she had no idea why Patricia was giving *her* the flirt treatment. Jane didn't hide the fact that she was gay, though in general she was a very private person. And while she and Patricia had become reasonably good friends, their friendship hadn't progressed much beyond a shared concern over neighborhood problems. They'd had dinner together a couple of times, and even attended a weekend seminar given by Community Crime Prevention, but that was about it. "My irresistible charm has seen better days," said Jane, walking up to the car. She folded her arms over her chest.

"Don't sell yourself so short."

"Oh, I'm not. I'm just not sure my brand of charm works on football jocks. I think he mowed the grass because he wanted the exercise."

Patricia laughed. "Hey, don't forget the block meeting tonight. I picked up some flyers on home security I want to pass out. I hope a few more people decide to show up. I'm beginning to think that most of our neighbors are antisocial." Her expression sobered as she glanced up at the house.

Jane looked over her shoulder and saw that Julia had come out on the front steps. "Be right there," she called.

"Remember," said Patricia. "My house. Seven o'clock."

"I'll be there." She stepped back and waved as Patricia sped off down the street. Picking up the hammer from the grass, she walked slowly up the front steps.

Julia stood with a hand on her hip, looking disgusted but amused. "I can't leave you alone for five minutes."

"That's right." Jane pushed her inside the house and shut the door. "I'm in constant demand." She tried to put her arms around Julia, but she resisted.

"You think I'm kidding, Jane, but that young woman out there has a crush on you."

"Oh, please."

"I'm right."

"Because she smiled at me?"

"You know, sometimes you're as thick as a brick."

"It's always good to start off the day with a compliment."

"I mean it."

"Patricia Kastner is twelve years old, Julia. I'm forty."

"She's twenty-eight if she's a day."

Jane stood back and cocked her head. "You're jealous." She began to laugh, knowing as soon as she let out the first chuckle that it was a mistake.

"Actually," said Julia, turning away, "I'm not the least bit jealous. I'm just warning you." She moved off into the kitchen.

"Fine," said Jane to her retreating back. "I've been warned."

As she entered the kitchen, she saw that Julia had pulled out a chair and was sitting at the table.

"So," said Julia, playing absently with a salt shaker, "I wonder where Beryl and Edgar are this morning. London? Lyme Regis?"

They were now going to make small talk. This wasn't turning out to be the morning Jane had imagined. Impatient with the whole interaction, she walked over, bent down, and gave Julia a kiss. Nuzzling up to her golden hair, she whispered, "You're what I want. You know that."

Julia whispered back, "I know."

"Then stop making me squirm."

21

Julia touched Jane's face, tracing the line of her jaw. "I'm sorry. Really. Maybe you're right. I am a little jealous. It's just . . . sometimes I'm afraid I'm going to lose you."

"Don't be ridiculous. Are you hungry?"

"Famished."

Feeling that a small crisis had been averted, Jane opened the oven to check on the frittata. "To answer your question about Beryl and Edgar, I think they're staying with friends in London this week."

Jane's English aunt had come to live with her two years ago. In early September, Beryl had married Edgar Anderson, a retired postman. At Jane's invitation, both of them now lived in the house, an arrangement she felt suited everyone. For their honeymoon, they'd decided to return to England, where Beryl still had a cottage.

"I'll set the table," offered Julia.

"No, let's sit out on the back porch. It's a beautiful morning and it's more comfortable out there." She could have added—but didn't—that they had such a short time left to be together.

In Jane's humble opinion, Julia's decision to set up her medical practice in a small town in northern Minnesota had put a terrible strain on their relationship. Even though Jane tried to be positive, she hated the separation. She didn't understand why Julia hadn't stayed with her original plan to join an already established practice in Minneapolis. One hundred and eighty miles away was one hundred and eighty miles too far. And even more upsetting was the fact that Julia had *chosen* that separation. Jane supposed there was no use in bringing the subject up again; it only caused an argument every time she did. Yet Julia's intransigence hurt and confused her. For whatever reason, Julia seemed unable or unwilling to help her understand anything other than the rudimentary, "It's what I want, Jane. What else can I say?"

"I'll pour the coffee," said Julia, getting down two mugs from the cupboard.

Jane began to cut the frittata into wedges. As she lifted one onto a plate, she heard the doorbell.

"Do you want me to get it?" asked Julia.

"No," said Jane, annoyed at the interruption. She uncovered the basket of pastries. "The blackberry muffins are wonderful. So are the lemon scones. And whoever it is, I'll get rid of them."

Julia smiled. "Of that, dear, I have no doubt. While you're being rude, I'll finish dishing up."

Jane squeezed her arm and then dashed out of the room. Pulling open the front door, she found a scruffy-looking man with a long ponytail standing on the steps. "Can I help you?" she asked, not even trying to hide her impatience.

"I hope so." He cleared his throat. "My name's Elliot Beauman. I saw your sign outside—"

"Oh, sure," said Jane. She glanced back toward the kitchen.

"Is this a bad time?"

"Well . . . actually . . ."

"I could come back, but I have a feeling your place is just what I've been looking for and I'd hate for you to rent it to someone else before I get a chance to see it."

"Yes, well—"

"It's furnished, right?"

She hesitated, then plunged ahead. "It's not luxurious, but the furniture is old and well cared for. The kitchen has most everything you'd need."

"What's the rent per month?"

"Six fifty."

He nodded. "That sounds great. Do you want me to fill something out? I'm sure you'll need to check references."

This was the worst possible timing. Sure, she wanted to rent the space, but Julia would be leaving in a couple of hours and the idea of spending even a part of it doing business was too frustrating for words. "Where are you living now?"

"I'm at the Nicollet Motel. I grew up in Minneapolis, but for the past few years I've been living in a small town in Iowa. I'm a writer. I don't need much space, but I do need peace and quiet. This seems like a pretty peaceful neighborhood."

He'd piqued her interest. "What do you write?"

"Children's books mostly."

"Jane," called Julia. "Are you coming?" She emerged from the kitchen wiping her hands on a dish towel.

"I'm sorry," said Elliot. "I really am interrupting your breakfast."

"Come in," said Jane. She stepped quickly over to a table by the stairs and retrieved a rental application form from a file folder. "When would you want to move in?"

"Right away." He stood somewhat awkwardly inside the door. "I figured I might have to stay at the motel for several more weeks. That will get kind of expensive. The sooner I find a place the better."

Jane handed him the application and a pencil. Turning to Julia, she said, "This is Elliot Beauman."

"That name sounds so familiar," said Julia, narrowing her eyes in thought. "Say, you aren't that children's book writer, are you?"

Elliot nodded. "I'm afraid that's me."

"My cousin's little boy absolutely loves your books! Especially the Danger Doug series. I'm delighted to meet you." She held out her hand.

He shook it and smiled.

Jane was even more intrigued now that Julia seemed to know him.

"I think I've got some copies of the new book with me. Give me a minute and I'll go get you one. I can sign it for your cousin's child."

"That would be incredible," said Julia. "He'd be thrilled."

Elliot ran back down the walk and ducked his head in the trunk of his car. A moment later he returned, inscribing his name on the title page with an expensive-looking fountain pen he took from his shirt pocket. He handed the book to Julia.

Jane looked over Julia's shoulder as she paged through to the end. Sure enough, there was Elliot's picture on the back cover.

"This is really nice of you," said Julia. She tucked the book lovingly under her arm.

"It's my pleasure," smiled Elliot. For the first time, he allowed himself a tentative look into the living room.

Jane watched his dark eyes travel to the fireplace. He'd seemed so reticent about entering, she was surprised to see the intensity with which he now scrutinized every last detail of the room.

"Why don't you take the application with you and fill it out?" said Jane. "Actually, in this case, it's just a formality. If you're really interested, I think we've got a deal."

He turned to her with the same intensity he'd focused on the room. "Great."

"Come by this afternoon. I'll show you the apartment. If you like what you see, it's yours. There's a six-month lease. First and last months' rent up front."

"No problem." He glanced at Julia and then back at Jane. "When can I move in?"

"Well—I suppose—this afternoon, if you want. I just have to check a couple references first."

"Why don't I leave the name of my last landlord with you now? And a check. Just to get the ball rolling."

"Okay, sure. But you may not like the space. As I said, it's small."

"It's perfect," said Elliot. "Just what I want."

"But you haven't seen it," said Julia.

He looked up the stairs. "I've seen everything I need to see." Walking over to the table by the stairs, he took out his checkbook and wrote a check. Then, slipping a business card out of his wal-

let, he wrote a name and address on the back. "This was my landlord in Iowa. He's a farmer, so it's possible he won't be there
when you call. But his wife will be. She can fill you in on my
rental history." He handed the check and the card to Jane. "Could
I come back around two? Would that be too soon?"

"No, it's fine."

"Then, I'll see you later."

As he sprinted down the walk to his car, Jane glanced at the
check. "That's funny," she said, watching him slide into the front
seat.

"What's funny?" asked Julia.

"He made the check out to Jane Lawless."

"So?"

The problem was, she'd never told him her name.

3

After pouring herself a cup of coffee, Jane walked out of the kitchen and sat down in the rocking chair in the living room. She had to be over to Patricia's house for the block meeting in less than an hour, but felt the need to unwind after a hectic afternoon at the restaurant. Not that her house was a safe haven from work. It wouldn't be long before the screens would need to come off and the storm windows would have to be put on, a chore that, because of the size of the home, occupied one entire weekend every fall.

Jane loved her house in Linden Hills, an old section of southwest Minneapolis. She and Christine had bought it together back when huge old houses were still affordable. Christine had actually been the one to find it. She'd just gotten her real estate license and knew it was a good buy as soon as it came on the market. Jane vividly remembered the first time she'd walked through the house alone. She'd relished the feel of the place, the spacious rooms, the large windows and the coved ceilings. She knew she and Christine could be happy here. They were both gone a lot those first few years, building their businesses, but Jane had never felt ill at ease being in the house by herself. That came later. After Christine's death.

These days, with Beryl and Edgar around, something was always cooking, both literally and figuratively. Yet nothing could erase that awful time, the first few years after Christine's death, when the silence made Jane feel constantly on edge and even a little desperate. In retrospect, she realized that she'd held on so tightly to the memory of her former partner that it had almost choked the life out of her. Funny that she should be thinking so much about Christine now. She knew that Christine would have wanted her to move on with her life, to find someone to love, but what would she think of the new woman in her life? No matter how close Jane felt to Christine's memory, it was a question that would remain unanswered.

Julia had packed her bags and left around one. It had been hard saying good-bye, though one way or another, that's what they always seemed to be doing. It had become a pattern. So far, their relationship consisted of intense though brief visits, no longer than a week, and then passionate, tearful good-byes. It made for some great romantic moments, but it didn't do much for Jane's peace of mind. She wasn't a kid anymore, and couldn't quite imagine building a stable relationship on this kind of drama. Still, she was stuck with it. For now. As usual, Julia hadn't wanted to go, but since she had a full patient load tomorrow, she didn't have a choice. Jane was a little surprised at how quickly Julia had built up her new practice, but perhaps in a small town, doctors were in short supply.

A little after two, Elliot Beauman called to say that something had come up and he wouldn't be able to make it over with his boxes and his computer equipment until early evening. Jane explained that if she wasn't home, she'd leave the key to the apartment under the mat on the landing just outside the third-floor door. She'd already called and talked to the owner of the house he'd rented in Iowa. Everything seemed to be on the up and up.

While she had Elliot on the phone, she asked him how he knew her name. She'd been curious about it ever since he'd made the check out to her earlier in the day. He explained that he'd seen it on some mail that was stacked on the table where he'd written the check. It was a simple enough solution. She didn't know why she hadn't thought of it. All that remained now was for him to sign the rental agreement. If they didn't connect tonight, she'd make sure she had his signature on the dotted line tomorrow. She didn't usually allow someone to move in without a signed lease, but Elliot seemed to be a safe enough bet.

Leaning her head back, Jane closed her eyes and for the next few minutes tried to relax. The quiet house had once again become her friend. Until Beryl and Edgar returned from their honeymoon, she had the place all to herself. The emptiness felt delicious. She breathed it in, tasting it as if it were a cool drink of water.

A few minutes later, she was startled out of her reverie by the sound of loud banging. Bean growled and then raised his head. Even he could hear the racket.

"Just a minute," she shouted impatiently.

Racing into the front hall, she pulled back the door.

Cordelia stood outside, a cat tucked under each arm, and one draped around her shoulders. "Trick or Treat," she said, an amused gleam in her eye.

"If you're looking for the Humane Society," said Jane, "you've got the wrong address."

"Cute. Aren't you going to invite me in?"

"Do I have a choice?"

Cordelia Thorn was a large woman, nearly six feet tall and well on the other side of two hundred pounds. She was bombastic, short-tempered, good-hearted, gorgeous, and an amazingly talented creative director for one of the largest theater companies in the Midwest, the Allen Grimby Repertory Theatre. Sometimes, however, when Jane saw her coming, she wanted to hide. She had the feeling that tonight was one of those times.

"I assume there's a reason you've arrived with your cats."

"The suitcases are in the car."

"Suitcases?"

"Four of them. You can help me carry them in when we're done with dinner." She set Lucifer down, then Melville, the youngest, and finally she unwound Blanche DuBois from around her neck. Blanche oiled her way over to Bean, ignoring his low growl, then sauntered off into the dining room. Both Melville and Lucifer bolted up the stairs. Cordelia smiled lovingly at her children, then gave Jane a chuck under the chin as she marched into the kitchen.

"Dinner?" repeated Jane weakly.

Entering the kitchen, Jane found Cordelia with her head in the refrigerator.

"I'll fix us one of my famous omelets, what do you say? Looks like you've got everything I need. Fresh eggs, onions, peppers, salsa, sour cream. And some Monterey Jack. I don't suppose you've got any refried beans? Black or red—I'm not picky."

"Sorry." Jane watched Blanche, the oldest cat, jump up on the counter and make herself comfortable in the sink.

"Well, we'll make do." Cordelia was dressed fairly casually tonight—for her. Black slacks and a long, slinky, black satin blouse. Accessorizing had become Cordelia's passion of late. Tonight, she wore an elaborate turquoise squash blossom necklace, large silver hoop earrings, Zuni and Navaho bracelets and rings, and a matching black satin turban with an exquisite Zuni pin tucked in the center, just above her forehead. Cordelia had become enchanted by the writings of Barbara Kingsolver and Tony Hillerman. So enchanted, in fact, that she'd booked a trip to Arizona in July. She'd come home literally encased in jewelry. Taken alone, each piece was lovely, but when worn together they constituted a fashion travesty of such magnitude, it almost took Jane's breath away. Then again, what was too much for most people was "just a little old-fashioned glamour" for Cordelia.

"I can't stay," said Jane, sitting down at the round oak table.

She knew she'd get an explanation for Cordelia's sudden appearance if she waited long enough, but she couldn't wait. "Not that I'm trying to pry or anything, but . . . are you moving in?"

Cordelia popped her head out of the refrigerator door and grinned. "Do you want the long story or the short one?"

"The short one."

"Okay. You know I'm supposed to move into my new loft this week. The haulers were coming today."

"Movers."

"Whatever."

"And?"

"Well, they came, but the new place isn't ready yet. I *can't* move in. And I can't stay at my old place. I'm no longer wanted."

"You're no longer *paying*."

"Spoken like a true landlord." She swept over to the table and sat down. "Janey, you should *see* what I've done with the loft. It's fabulous. But the painters aren't done yet. And the floor is going to take at least another week, if not more. My friend Michael, the set designer at the Grimby, is doing the frescoes on the walls and ceiling."

"Frescoes? On the *ceiling!*"

"Wait till you see it!" She slapped her hands together in utter rapture. "It's going to be the Sistine Chapel, dearheart. Cherubs and clouds, and gold leaf everywhere you look. Even some of the exposed pipes."

Jane tried not to cringe, but it was a struggle.

"It will be a true home for a diva! You know my theory on decorating, Janey. If there's an empty space, something's missing."

"I'm aware of that, yes."

"So, where else would I come when I needed a place to stay?"

Jane swallowed hard. "Here?"

"Exactly. And with Beryl and Edgar away for the next six weeks, you'll be glad I'm around."

"Why?"

"Because I'm a great house guest. You won't even know I'm here. And my cats? They're quiet as church mice."

Jane turned at the sound of a crash in the living room. A second later, Melville trotted into the room looking guilty but unrepentant.

"And besides," continued Cordelia, "you have to agree these old homes can be sort of scary at night, especially when you're all alone. Like when the clock strikes midnight and you hear a door creak open somewhere down the hall, and you know you're the only one in the house, and you grab the phone but someone's cut the phone line and then the lights go out . . ." As Cordelia continued to weave her Stephen King scenario, she glanced out the kitchen window. "Say, who's that walking up the outside stairs?"

Jane turned to see Elliot carrying a load of boxes. "My new renter."

"When did he arrive?"

"Today."

Cordelia continued to watch until his feet disappeared. "Have you checked him out? He's not a serial killer, is he?"

Jane laughed. "Hardly. He writes children's books."

"As in Dr. Seuss or R. L. Stine? You can't be too careful these days, Janey. Writers are never sane and normal."

"You mean like you?"

"If that's a slur of some kind, may I say that it's not good form to insult a house guest. They can make your life positively miserable, you know." She straightened her turban. "By the way, do you have any Pop Tarts?"

Jane rolled her eyes.

"We'll buy some. They are *ambrosia,* Janey. Absolute heaven. Now back to the renter. His name wouldn't be Norman Bates, would it?"

She smiled, shaking her head. "It's Elliot Beauman. And I was given great references from his last landlord. He was apparently a model renter. Quiet. Respectful. Oh, and Julia's even heard of his books."

"Ah yes, Julia. The phantom girlfriend."

Checking her watch, Jane pushed away from the table and got up. Even if she wasn't already late for the block meeting, she would have devised some excuse to nip this conversation in the bud.

"Where are you going?" asked Cordelia more than a little indignantly.

"To a meeting. Want to come along?"

"Certainly not. I'm going to have a quiet dinner and then take a long, hot bath. It will be nice to have the house all to myself."

The irony of the situation was completely lost on Cordelia.

4

Elliot stood on the doorstep of his new apartment, staring at the locked door. He'd found the key right where Jane said it would be—under the mat. He was sweating, though not simply from the physical exertion of carrying all his boxes up two flights of stairs.

Elliot was anxious. His first experience with the house had been bad enough, but this was bound to be worse. All the boxes were still sitting on the landing right where he'd stacked them. He couldn't bring himself to go in, not just yet. He had to ease into the idea that he was now living on the third floor of 4532 Bridwell Lane. One thing he knew for sure, this pleasant-looking home was filled with uneasy ghosts. He'd felt it strongly this afternoon, the intensity of his reaction taking him by surprise. After what happened at the police station, he thought he had his emotions under control. That was why, when he'd driven past the house and noticed the FOR RENT sign in the front yard, he'd seen it as a stroke of luck. Now, he wasn't so sure.

After stretching a few times to relieve some of his tension, Elliot examined the garage and the neighboring backyards, and then looked up at the sky. It was a clear night. This high up, he could even see the lights surrounding Lake Harriet, though they were just pinpricks. If he squinted just right, the lights and the stars formed a whole. The earth was erased, leaving nothing but the heavens. It was beautiful, mesmerizing, and yet utterly cold. He thought of *Star Trek,* a program he'd once loved. He and his sister had always laughed at the Starfleet Federation's Prime Directive—to visit new worlds, to help, but not to interfere. His family had a prime directive of its own. Put very simply it was, *Interfere constantly, but keep family business private. Protect the family image at all costs. Present a united—happy—front to the world, no matter how much it hurts. To break the code of silence is a mortal sin, punishable by banishment . . . or worse.*

Elliot had solved the problem of his family's code by banishing himself, though he still generally abided by the rules. It was simple expediency. He loved his sister far too much to leave her alone, unprotected, in a family of smiling monsters. But then, as his sister often pointed out, Elliot saw monsters everywhere. He even wrote about them, drew them, making them seem benign, occasionally humorous. What was a monster, really, but an unhappy, misunderstood creature who, if anyone cared to look, was actually quite lovable? In cartoonland, it was always that way. But in real life, Elliot didn't buy it. The reason was fairly pragmatic. Deep down, Elliot knew he was a card-carrying member of his own family, a monster of extraordinary proportions. The feminists were wrong. Biology *was* destiny.

Gripping the key in his right hand, Elliot pressed it into the lock. He was making too big a deal out of this. He simply had to stop thinking and get it over with. Once inside, everything would be fine.

He pushed the door open, shutting his eyes as the warm inside air rushed at his face. For a moment he felt disoriented. Maybe this would be like pulling a bandage off his arm. It would hurt for a few seconds, and then it would be over. Or would it?

"Only one way to find out," he whispered. He took a deep breath and stepped over the threshold.

Inside, it was pitch dark. Elliot fumbled around on the wall until he found a switch. Flipping it on, the room burst into focus. For a moment he couldn't breathe. He took it all in, yet didn't move an inch away from the door. The ghosts were here, all right, their fists clenched, their eyes slits of rage. "I'm not going to listen to this crap," he shouted. "Stop it!"

The room became suddenly quiet. Time fell back into place. "That's better," he muttered walking over to the sofa and bouncing on it a couple of times to see if it was soft enough to sleep on. This was the space he'd rented, and this was the house he'd live in until it came time for him to move on. If he got lucky, he wouldn't have to move for a long, long time.

Right, and the world is flat. As long as he stayed in the Twin Cities, with his parents a twenty-minute drive away, he'd never be happy. Then why had he come back? Again, the answer was simple. His sister.

It took Elliot the better part of the next three hours to get all his stuff unpacked and put away. Jane was right. The furniture was old, but in an odd way it suited him. The desk was perfect for his computer equipment. It was mahogany, and much bigger than the standard college issue. And his drafting table would fit nicely in the living room, directly under the skylight. The galley kitchen, though small, was fine for the kind of cooking he did—mostly microwaving and reheating. The only appliance missing was a good coffeemaker. He'd have to run over to Dayton's and buy one tomorrow. Coffee was a necessity. He often worked late into the night, and without caffeine, he might as well give up his art and his writing and go sell insurance.

Finally satisfied that everything was reasonably well organized, Elliot decided to run to the grocery store for some essentials: cleaning and paper supplies, Chef Boyardee ravioli, Mountain Dew, some bread, milk, lunch meat, and Miracle Whip, coffee beans, fruit, and whatever else he saw that interested him. He might even splurge on some eggs and bacon for tomorrow morning's breakfast. He had a lot to do this week and needed a good meal to start off his Monday. On the drive over tonight from the motel, he'd seen a market in the uptown area. That would do just fine. His needs were simple. He'd also driven past a co-op in Linden Hills, one that wasn't far from the house, but co-ops weren't really his thing. They never carried the food he liked.

Grabbing his car keys, Elliot took one last look at his new apartment: the long living room, the four matching windows facing the street, the sturdy mahogany furniture, the oatmeal-colored carpet, and the deeply slanted ceiling. All in all, the attic had been turned into a pretty reasonable place to live. Remembering that the phone hadn't been hooked up yet, he made a mental note to take care of it first thing tomorrow. Maybe he'd call his sister from the grocery store tonight.

Feeling that his first skirmish with the resident ghosts had been won—by him—Elliot closed the door, felt to make sure it was securely locked, and then began his slow descent down the steps.

37

5

After the block meeting on Sunday night, Jane helped Patricia clear the living room of dishes. The block association's first get-together in August had been held at Jane's house, with about twenty-five people in attendance. Since no one else wanted the job, Jane had been unanimously elected block captain. Tonight, however, only sixteen people had shown up.

In an effort to move things along, Patricia had volunteered to coordinate a November block party. Jane was pretty sure one of the local parks would make their facilities available for the event. In her typical take-charge fashion, Patricia wanted to do it up right. Games for the kids. Prizes, balloons. A pot-luck dinner. Maybe even some live music. This would be the newly established block association's first organized activity—a perfect opportunity for everyone to get to know each other and build some neighborhood solidarity. And after all, as Patricia pointed out, wasn't that one of the primary goals of any block association? If neighbors knew who belonged and who didn't, they'd be far more able to keep an eye on what was happening in the neighborhood—legal or otherwise.

"This party is just what we need," said Patricia, loading some cups into her dishwasher. When she was done, she raked a hand through her glossy black hair, then folded her arms resolutely over her chest.

"I'm not sure you're going to get many volunteers to help organize it," said Jane, putting away the half-and-half in the refrigerator.

"No problem. You and I can handle it."

"Right. In our spare time."

Patricia returned Jane's amused smile. "Oh, and while we're on the subject, I've been thinking we should form a block patrol. I don't know if you realize it, but the number of garage fires in this area has doubled in the last few months. I, for one, don't want to see the tons of important stuff I've got in my garage go up in smoke."

Jane had no trouble believing Patricia had "tons of stuff" in her garage. The interior of her house looked like a floor display from Gabberts. All the furnishings were new, pricey, and beautiful. Patricia's tastes in furniture as well as fashion tended toward the flashy with just a hint of punk. So did her hair—a punk shag with one gold streak. "Did you have a decorator do the house?" she asked, admiring the bright geometric wallpaper.

"If you mean did I have it professionally redone, yes. But I picked everything out myself. I love decorating. It's a hobby of mine. So is food—and wine. When you've got some free time, I'll show you the wine cellar I put in downstairs."

The more Jane got to know Patricia, the more she realized they had a lot of common interests. In a way, it seemed surprising. Patricia was the classic rich kid. The house she'd just bought was the biggest, most impressive home on the block, and as far as Jane could see, Patricia didn't do much of anything herself. She had a cleaning woman, a lawn service, a part-time cook, and a personal trainer who helped her work out in a fully appointed second-floor gym. "Have your parents been over to see what you've done with the place?"

Patricia turned away and began to wipe some crumbs off the kitchen counter. "Dad has. He's sending a crew over to start work on the exterior next week. Some of the stucco is crumbling and the wood around the windows needs to be scraped and repainted. My father owns a construction company. Did I mention that?"

"He's not involved in Kastner Gardens?" Jane stepped into the pantry to examine a series of antique copper molds hanging under the cupboards.

"No, that's Mom's business. She started it with the insurance money she got after her first husband died. But Mom's cut way back on her hours now. It won't be long before she's officially retired. Actually, for the last few months she's been vacationing in Europe. She should be back any day."

As Jane walked out of the pantry, she found Patricia staring at her. Feeling a little uncomfortable, she said, "Well, everything's all cleaned up. I suppose I better get home."

"How about a nightcap first?" Patricia nodded to a bottle of Armagnac sitting out on the counter.

"You must read minds. That's one of my favorites."

"Can I take that as a yes?"

For a moment, Jane thought of Cordelia. She was probably taking a bubble bath right about now, with Vivaldi or Janis Joplin cranked to ear-splitting decibels. As a quiet, unobtrusive house guest, Cordelia was a miserable failure. This, unfortunately, wasn't the first time Cordelia had moved in on a temporary basis, though the cats were a new wrinkle. To be fair, Jane had stayed at Cordelia's home a few times over the years, too. And since Cordelia was very much a member of her family, Jane could hardly turn her away. But that didn't mean she had to rush home just to keep her company.

"Sure, I'd love a drink." She watched Patricia open the cupboard, revealing a set of bar glasses that would rival most restaurants.

Grabbing a sack of pistachios, Patricia led the way back to

the sunken living room. While Jane made herself comfortable in one of the leather chairs, Patricia dimmed the lights and turned on some soft music. Finally, tucking both legs under her, she nestled into one end of the couch. "This is a great room, isn't it? The first time I saw it, I knew I had to have it."

"Did you own a house in Iowa?" asked Jane, taking a sip of the Armagnac. "Before you moved back?"

"No, I rented a town house."

"What part of Iowa was it? If you told me, I've forgotten."

"Des Moines."

"Right. I've never been there."

"You haven't missed a thing. It's pretty conservative."

"What were you doing in Des Moines?"

Patricia shelled one of the pistachios and popped the nut into her mouth. "Well, Kastner Gardens was opening a store in West Des Moines. My mother asked me to go down and supervise the staff, just to make sure everything was done properly. I was also in charge of marketing the new store. That's my specialty."

Jane was impressed. Patricia was young, but her mother obviously put a lot of faith in her business skills. "But you came back. You didn't want to stay?"

Her expression tightened. "The job was done. It was time to come home."

"How long were you there?"

"A few years."

Jane waited for more, but that seemed to be all Patricia was going to say on the subject. After an awkward pause, Jane held her glass up to the light. "It's a beautiful color, isn't it? Sometimes I have a glass at the restaurant before I walk home."

"I know," said Patricia, her smile resuming some of its former playfulness.

"How could you possibly know something like that?"

"One of the bartenders told me."

"It just came up in a conversation?"

41

"No, I asked him what you liked to drink."

Jane was a bit perplexed. "Why?"

"So I could have it on hand for the times when you come over."

Jane nodded. "That's . . . nice of you. Did you talk about anything else?"

"Sure. He thinks you're a great boss, and that you work too hard, but lately he said you've been taking more time off. Because of some new girlfriend." Glancing at Jane over the rim of her glass, Patricia added, "I hope you don't think I'm prying, but you interest me."

Jane wasn't sure what to say.

"Don't look so horrified," said Patricia with a slow grin. She lifted the drink to her lips. "I realize we haven't known each other very long, but I really like you. I think we could be great friends, given enough time. The problem with me is, I get impatient. When I want something, I want it right now."

Jane couldn't help but laugh. Maybe they were more alike than she realized. "If I understand anything, it's impatience."

Patricia stared down into her glass. "If I'm getting too personal, just tell me to back off. It's just . . . that woman I saw you with this morning. Is that her? The girlfriend?"

Perhaps Jane should have seen the question coming, but she hadn't. "Why do you ask?"

"Curiosity. She's pretty. Are you . . . really into her?"

Jane nodded.

"I suppose she lives around here?"

"No. Northern Minnesota."

"Oh." She took a sip of her drink. "I know we've never discussed our personal lives much, but it seems to be common knowledge that you're gay. I'm not blowing your cover or anything, am I?"

Again, Jane laughed. "No, it's not a secret." She decided to ask a question of her own. "Are you dating anyone right now?"

"Me? No. I'm free as a bird."

"But you're straight, right?"

The amused smile returned. "You know, as I see it, my generation has something important to bring to the human table. We're far less hung up on labels. I am what I am, Jane. Sure I date guys, but my first love—in high school—was another girl. Her name was Abbie Kaufman. She was truly amazing. Last I heard she had a small pottery business up near Floodwood. She always wanted to be an artist, create sculptures out of clay—or *mud,* as she called it. Actually, you sort of remind me of her. She had long chestnut hair, just like you, and the same frank expression in her eyes. But, for certain reasons—it didn't work."

"I'm sorry."

"Hey," she said, holding the glass up in a mock toast, "Here's to young love gone wrong. I was only seventeen, right? What did I expect?"

"Maybe more of a chance than you got from the people around you—your friends and family."

Patricia looked up, and then away.

"Are you an only child?"

She shook her head. "I've got a brother. He's ten years older, but we're very tight. He's probably my best friend."

Jane finished her drink and then set the glass down on the coffee table. She wasn't quite sure where the conversation was headed, but wondered if Julia hadn't been right about Patricia's romantic interest. If it was true, it wasn't an interest Jane welcomed. Her life was complicated enough.

"Want some more?" asked Patricia, glancing at Jane's empty glass. She jumped up and headed into the kitchen. "The bottle's still almost full."

"I think I better get home," called Jane to her retreating back. "I've got an early meeting tomorrow over at the restaurant."

Patricia returned to the room looking crestfallen. Resting one knee on the edge of the couch, she said, "But I thought we could . . . you know? Talk a while longer. Get to know each other better."

"Maybe another time," said Jane.

Patricia nodded, though she didn't look happy about it.

"Listen, thanks so much for hosting tonight's meeting. It was nice not to have to do it at my house again."

"Hey, no problem. Say, maybe we can get together sometime soon and brainstorm about the upcoming block party. I've got lots of ideas. You could come over for dinner."

Jane had to admit she was drawn to the younger woman's enthusiasm. "I've got a better idea. Why don't you drop over to the restaurant some evening this week? We can talk about it over a beer."

She gave Jane an appraising look. "I get it. You don't think I can cook."

Jane laughed. "I just don't want you to go to a lot of trouble."

"Believe me," said Patricia with a wry smile, "it would be my pleasure." She slipped her arm through Jane's and walked her to the door. "I'll check my schedule and give you a call. We can do dinner here some other time."

As they stepped outside into the cool night air, Patricia glanced up at a truck parked across the street.

"Something wrong?" asked Jane, noticing that Patricia had become suddenly quiet.

Patricia pushed her hands into the pockets of her red blazer and walked down the steps. "I don't know." Hesitating for a moment next to a pine tree in the front yard, she added, "I've been here over two months and I've never seen that truck parked there before last night. Have you ever seen it?"

Jane walked out to the boulevard to get a closer look. The truck was parked close enough to a street light for her to see that it was a half-ton Ford pickup with lots of rust, especially on the rear quarter panel and around the front grill. There was a topper on the back, with curtains obscuring the windows. "No, I don't remember seeing it, although old trucks don't usually catch my attention."

"No," agreed Patricia. "They're not my style either. Except—"
Again she grew quiet.

"Except what?"

"Well, maybe I'm crazy, but I think I saw the same truck parked outside our offices in Edina this afternoon. I mean, every other car around it was new so it stood out like a sore thumb."

"There have to be lots of rusted white trucks around."

"Yeah," she said, still staring. "I suppose you're right. But . . . see . . . I thought I saw it later too, when I was coming out of Calhoun Square."

"You could always check the plates. Take the number over to the DMV in St. Paul and dig up some information on the owner."

Patricia shook her head. "I'm making too much of this. It's just—I get a little nervous at night sometimes. I'm not used to living alone."

This was the first crack Jane had ever seen in Patricia's carefully projected competent, in-control image. Patricia wore her self-confidence the way some women wore perfume. It was always there in the air, sometimes just a hint, sometimes overpowering. The admission made Jane warm to her in a way she hadn't before.

Looking worried, Patricia said, "I better let you get home, Jane. I'll call you soon."

"You're okay, right?"

Patricia's smile was distracted. "I'm fine. Thanks for the concern."

Jane waited for her to walk back up the front steps. When the door was finally shut and she was alone, she decided it might be smart to examine the truck a bit more closely. If Patricia had a funny feeling about it, for whatever reason, maybe it deserved a little scrutiny.

Hurrying across the street, she looked first into the front cab. Several notebooks were scattered on the seat. One was open and she could see handwriting, but couldn't make out any of the words. A bag of pretzels lay open on the dash, and a tall thermos was on the floor on the passenger's side next to a Minneapolis phone book—the White Pages. As Jane moved around the back of the truck, she glanced at the plates.

"Well, now," she whispered, bending down for a closer look. "What have we got here?"

The truck was from Iowa.

Not everyone who lived in the Twin Cities was a native, but Jane was starting to feel as if she were in the middle of some great Iowan migration.

6

On weekday evenings, the dining room at the Lyme House closed at nine. Though there were still some lingering diners on Tuesday night, Jane decided to shut down the reservation desk and let the evening manager close up. Several times a week, during lunch and especially the evening meals, Jane liked to seat the customers herself. She'd been doing it for years. She felt it was the best way to stay in touch with longtime patrons, make friends with new ones, as well as keep her finger on the pulse of customer opinion, always vital in the restaurant business.

The Lyme House was built on the south shore of Lake Harriet, close to where Penn Avenue dead-ended at the lake. It was a two-story log structure, with a downstairs pub, an upstairs dining room, and a deck facing the water, where guests could sip their drinks while they waited for a table. The interior of the main dining room was rustic, though the table appointments—fine English china, Italian crystal, and Irish linens—were distinctly formal. Jane liked to play with contrasts, in the restaurant's atmosphere as well as the menu, and that allowed diners to dress casually and at the same time enjoy a table service that was pure elegance.

The downstairs pub was really two rooms, one noisy and smoky, where people gathered in groups for a game of darts or cribbage, and another more intimate room, where guests could sit quietly by the fire and sip their lager and lime or enjoy a meal of hearty Irish stew. On weekend evenings, a Celtic band usually entertained.

After a long day, Jane was amazed that she wasn't more tired. She'd arrived at her office shortly before eight, in time to meet with her executive chef and a couple of local produce vendors. From there, the normal work day took over. For a Tuesday, it had been unusually busy, so busy, in fact, that she hadn't had time for dinner. She knew she could stay and grab a bite in the pub—which didn't close until one—but instead, she thought it best to head home. She hadn't had a breath of fresh air since early morning and welcomed the idea of a brisk walk.

Cordelia had promised to feed Bean his dinner and let him out before she left for the theater. That was hours ago now. He probably needed to be let out again. With Beryl away, Jane was beginning to realize just how much she counted on her aunt to hold down the fort while she was at work. Until Beryl and Edgar returned, all the house chores fell to her. She'd grown spoiled these past two years, and she knew it.

Saying a quick good night to the bartender in the pub, Jane headed out the downstairs door and walked through the parking lot on her way to a wooded footpath that circled the lake. Maybe she should have been more frightened, walking home alone in the dark several nights a week, but she wasn't. For the past couple of years she'd been carrying mace, but nothing had ever happened. All the same, she knew that Minneapolis wasn't what it used to be—safe, Scandinavian, and dull. It had joined the ranks of major U.S. cities and was now, if the statistics were to be believed, even more dangerous than New York City, with far more murders per capita than the Big Apple. Minneapolis had come of age, with all the attendant glitter and grime.

Weaving through the parked cars, Jane's thoughts turned to Julia. Jane intended to call her later tonight to discuss the possibility of getting together for another weekend sometime soon. If she cleared her calendar at the restaurant, she might even be able to drive up next weekend. No use in Julia always coming to Minneapolis, especially since Jane was looking forward to seeing Julia's new home on Pokegama Lake.

Nearing the footpath, Jane looked back to see how many cars were left in the parking lot. She was surprised to see a white pickup parked near the entrance. Trotting over to check the plates, she saw that it was the same one she'd first seen on Sunday night outside Patricia's house. She didn't think it came under the heading of jumping to conclusions to assume that the owner must be inside.

Heading back into the pub, she walked slowly through the crowded rooms, looking the customers over. She recognized a few and said hi, though most were strangers. She wasn't sure what she expected to find. Not many people had the word "Iowa" tattooed on their foreheads. And since no one stood out or looked particularly suspicious, it seemed like a waste of time. That's when she got an idea.

Standing near the fireplace in the back room, she cleared her throat and announced, "There's a white Ford truck with Iowa plates in the parking lot. Its lights are on. Whoever owns it might want to check it out before their battery goes dead." She waited, but no one made a move to get up.

Returning to the front room, she leaned on the bar and made the same announcement. Again, people looked at her politely and then went back to their conversations.

Thinking that perhaps she should make an announcement in the dining room upstairs, she raced up the steps and entered through the French doors. After saying her piece, she waited, but just as before, nobody showed any interest in moving.

Feeling frustrated, Jane pushed through the side door onto the deck and walked to the far railing. The truck was still parked in the same spot. Whoever owned it was apparently not going to tip his hand, and that left her wondering why.

As Jane saw it, she had two choices. She could either stay until the pub closed and hope the truck's owner showed, or go home as she'd originally planned. She was probably making too much of this, and yet something about the whole situation nagged at her. Someone was playing games. If a good citizen of the Upper Midwest thought his battery was about to go dead, he'd check on it. Indeed, announcing that headlights had been left on was the equivalent of yelling "fire" in a crowded theater. And yet, nobody had risen to the bait. There had to be a reason.

Sitting down at an empty outside table, Jane let the lake breeze ruffle her hair as she thought it over. The water was calm tonight. Inky smooth. It was a beautiful autumn evening, warmer than the past few nights. Street lights dotted the perimeter of the lake, while moonlight spread across the water in bright yellow ribbons.

Half an hour later she was home, letting Bean out to do his evening duties in the backyard. He was so happy to see her, she knew she'd made the right decision to forget about the truck. The cats were nowhere to be found, but that wasn't unusual. None of them were real "people" cats, except when it came to Cordelia. Jane doubted they provided Bean with very much company. He wasn't used to being alone these days any more than she was. Now that Gulliver, his lifelong companion, was gone, he'd become unusually quiet in a way Jane understood. They had something in common now, and it made her feel closer than ever to her little terrier.

Before leaving for the theater, Cordelia had propped a note against the salt shaker on the kitchen table:

Dearheart,
    I made a pot of my infamous black bean chili this morning. It's in the fridge. I thought you might like a

snack when you got off work. I'll be back around eleven. If you want to wait, we can eat together. By the way, Bean had a good dinner, and since he's turned into such an old geezer, I let him gum part of an apricot croissant for dessert. He told me he loves having his Auntie Cordelia around. The last time I saw the cats, they were in the bathtub. Wait till we move into Mount Olympus and they see their new digs. Aren't you glad you know a diva so you can come visit us there? Oh, by the way, there's black cherry pop in the fridge, but you can only have one.

Ta,

Cordelia.

The idea of drinking black cherry pop was more than Jane could take on an empty stomach, though she was touched that Cordelia had gone to the trouble of cooking. Cordelia's hours weren't the normal nine to five, so her eating habits tended to be rather idiosyncratic. Still, Jane was delighted by the idea of a late dinner, especially since she didn't have to be at the restaurant tomorrow until noon.

After pouring herself a glass of Pinot Grigio and checking on Bean to make sure he was getting down to business, she settled on a comfortable redwood chair in the back porch, switched on a light, and began to peruse the morning paper. Before she got much past the headlines, the sound of footsteps on the stairs caused her to look up. It had to be Elliot. When she'd come up the hill from the lake a few minutes ago, she'd noticed that the third floor was dark. Since he was home now, she figured it was as good a time as any to run up and see if he was done reading the lease she'd dropped off this morning. She needed it back as soon as possible.

Jane let Bean into the house, gave him a hug and a Milk-Bone, and then headed up the back steps. As she reached the landing, she found the door open, but the screen door locked. She bent down and looked inside. One dim light burned in the front room; the rest of the apartment was dark. After another couple of seconds, someone moved in front of the light and began riffling through papers on the desk. She gave a couple of raps on the door.

"Just a minute," came a voice she didn't recognize.

A moment later, a stranger appeared. He was tall—well over six feet, and wearing a light blue sport coat over a yellow polo shirt. His thin, receding white hair pegged him as someone well into his sixties, but the face was strong and weathered, and the body robust, even muscular. It wasn't a gym body. He looked more like a guy used to lots of outdoor activity.

"Can I help you?" he asked brusquely.

"I hope so," said Jane. "I'm the owner of the building. I was hoping to talk to Elliot."

"He's not home." The man waited a moment, then added, "I'm his father."

"Oh, I see." She smiled. "It's nice to meet you, Mr. Beauman. My name's Jane Lawless."

The man stiffened. "Please, call me Otto."

"Of course." She could tell she'd said something wrong, but wasn't sure what it was. "I assume Elliot gave you a key?"

"No."

"Then how—"

"The door was unlocked."

"Unlocked," she repeated, her smile evaporating. She'd have to talk to Elliot about that right away. Inside his third-floor apartment was another door that connected to the main part of the house. Even though the interior door was kept locked at all times, if Elliot left his exterior door unlocked, the security of the entire house was at risk. "When do you expect him back?" she asked, her tone less friendly this time.

"I don't know. Soon, I hope."

They stared at each other through the screen. "Would you give your son a message from me?"

"Sure."

"Tell him I need the signed lease as soon as possible. And also, mention that I'd like to talk when he has a couple of minutes. Tomorrow morning, if possible."

"I'll tell him."

Jane was about to leave when, once again, she heard the sound of footsteps on the stairs. A few seconds later, Elliot puffed his way to the top carrying a sack of groceries.

"Hi," he said with a broad smile. Then, turning sheepish, he added, "You caught me. I'm kind of a junk-food fanatic. I thought I'd check out the co-op in the neighborhood. Jeez, I had no idea you could buy so much healthy, good-for-you junk food these days." Glancing at the interior door and noticing that it was open, he bent down and squinted inside. The muscles along his jawbone tightened when he saw who'd come to call. "Dad." He tried to make his surprise sound light and cheerful, but didn't succeed.

"Evening, son. Thought I'd come by and welcome you back."

"Is . . . Mom here?"

"Nah, just your old man." He thrust the screen door open and caught his son's neck in the crook of his elbow, pulling him close. Otto was a foot taller than Elliot, and outweighed him by a good hundred pounds.

They stood there awkwardly for a few seconds and then Elliot disengaged himself. "You look great, Dad."

"A little worse for wear, but still kicking."

Their interaction was clearly meant to sound friendly, but Jane found it stiff—even forced.

Without being invited, she followed Elliot to the kitchenette where he set the sack down on the counter. "I don't mean to disturb you and your dad, but I need the lease."

"Oh, right," he said, some of the tightness leaving his face. "I'm sorry I didn't get it to you earlier. I guess it slipped my mind." He stepped over to his desk, paged through some of his papers, then handed it over.

She wanted to discuss the unlocked door too, but now wasn't the time. "Give me a call tomorrow. I'd like to talk to you about a couple of things."

"Sure thing." He watched his father move restlessly around the small room.

"I'll be home all morning," she said. She could tell his mind was elsewhere. Reminding him one more time to call, she nodded to his father and then left.

As she made her way back down the steps, waving mosquitoes from her face, she glanced at the patio area in front of the garage. The stone tiles were cracked and overgrown with crabgrass now, but once must have been quite lovely. In the past couple of weeks, she'd contacted several contractors about having the old tile removed. She wanted a new concrete slab laid before winter set in. Next spring, it would become the foundation for a greenhouse. Her aunt Beryl's hobby and passion was gardening. Since she and her new husband were going to be living at Jane's house from now on, Edgar had suggested that he build one. It was a sweet yet practical gesture, very much in keeping with the kind of man Edgar was. Jane wondered how they were getting along in England. She hoped she'd hear from them soon.

As she came around the side of the house, headlights from a car idling at the far end of the drive hit her square in the eyes. She assumed it was Cordelia since it was close to eleven. Waving, she walked toward the light.

Suddenly, the vehicle skidded backward into the street. Jane saw now that it was the white truck. She rushed toward it, yelling, "Wait!" But by the time she got to the end of the drive, it had disappeared around the corner.

7

The darkness in the apartment suited Elliot just fine. The lamp his stepfather had turned on threw a wedge of yellow light across the desk, leaving the rest of the room deep in shadow. "How did you get in?" He rested his back against the kitchen counter and watched the older man sit down on the folding chair Elliot had placed next to the windows.

"You have to ask?"

"You broke in."

"There isn't a lock made that I can't pick."

"Did you damage anything?"

"Of course not."

Elliot moved out of the kitchenette and joined his stepfather in the living room, sitting down on the couch. The visit was un-expected, though not entirely a surprise. Otto liked to drop in on his children unannounced. It was one of his methods of control. But since the encounter had started out politely, Elliot decided to keep up the act a while longer. If he was lucky, he might find out what the old man wanted.

"I hear Mom's in Europe."

Otto surveyed the interior of the apartment, his eyes moving slowly from one end of the room to the other, looking everywhere but at Elliot. "Since you know that, I assume it means you've talked to Patricia."

"Yeah. This afternoon. But just on the phone. I haven't seen the new house yet."

The older man nodded. "It was a good deal. For a house built in the twenties, it's in great shape. I just wish she hadn't picked this neighborhood." His gaze finally settled on his stepson. "Why here, Elliot?"

"You mean me? This apartment? It was for rent. I wanted to be close to Patricia."

"It's that simple?"

"Yeah, it's that simple."

Otto let that digest a moment. "Look, I can understand your sister. There was no use arguing with her. She wanted the house and that was that. But you—I don't get it. I simply don't understand you."

"So what else is new?" Elliot tapped a cigarette out of a pack lying on the coffee table and lit up. After sucking down a lungful of smoke to calm his pounding heart, he said, "Where'd Mom go this time? Italy, France?"

Otto got up. Turning his back to his son, he rested his arms on the windowsill and looked down at the street. "Oh, you know your mother. She's a hard one to keep track of. Last I heard she was in Rome."

"Really?"

"Yeah. She's with that friend of hers, Leslie Janovitch. They're probably getting into a whole bunch of trouble. I'm sure we'll hear all about it when she gets back."

"And when will that be?"

"Soon."

Elliot flicked some ash into a saucer. "That's a nice cover story, Otto, but it won't work on me."

The older man stood up straight, but kept his back to his son.

"What do you mean?"

"Where's she drying out this time? New Mexico? That fancy spa in Houston?"

He whirled around. "I won't have you talking that way about your mother."

"That's not an answer."

Stomping over to the refrigerator, Otto helped himself to a can of Mountain Dew. After taking a couple of swigs, he said, "Why do you buy this crap? It's ninety percent sugar." Opening up one of the cupboards, he pointed to the cans of spaghetti. "You've got the tastes of a four-year-old. This place is a dump, Elliot. You could live anywhere. Are you living out some sort of penance? Would you like it better if we were poor?"

"I'm an artist. And a writer."

"So you need to suffer?"

"I don't tell you how to live," Elliot shot back angrily.

"Fine. *Be* an artist. But that doesn't mean you have to live like a damn monk."

"I don't." He gave his stepfather a smile that was pregnant with meaning.

"You disgust me, Elliot."

"Oh, I'm sorry. Did I do something to upset your delicate sensibilities?" He laughed, sucking in more smoke. "The big difference between you and me is, you cheated on my mother. When I sleep with someone, I'm not cheating on anybody. Now, you tell *me* who's more disgusting."

"That's not what I meant and you know it."

"Oh, right—I remember now. You've turned over a new leaf. Otto Kastner has become a faithful, loving husband. Well, it's *too late*."

Otto held his stepson's gaze. "I love your mother. More than you'll ever know."

"Save it for her eulogy." Elliot pressed his cigarette butt into the saucer with such force that the plate broke.

"Just stop for a second and listen."

"No! This is *my* house. I don't have to listen to a goddamn thing I don't want to." He got up, dumping the plate in the kitchen trash. "You didn't answer my question. Where's Mom?" He drew himself up to his full height and looked his stepfather square in the eyes.

Otto stared at him for a moment, then set the can down on the counter and walked back into the living room. He took up his chair by the windows again. "Houston."

"How long has she been there?"

"She fell apart right after Kevin's suicide. Started drinking heavily. We fought about it for a couple of weeks, but she finally agreed to go."

"You didn't have to commit her this time?"

Pinching the bridge of his nose he said, "No, thank God."

"Does Patricia know?"

He shook his head. "She's got enough on her plate. I can't imagine what it must feel like to have your boyfriend kill himself."

Elliot nodded. Grabbing himself a Mountain Dew, he returned to the couch. "She's doing all right."

"So she says."

"You don't believe her?"

"Look, Elliot, Patricia's very sure of herself, but she hurts just like the rest of us. Actually"—he hesitated—"I'm glad you're back. I know you two are close. I envy that closeness sometimes. A father wants to connect with his children. Maybe it's too late for you and me, but with Patricia it's different. She doesn't shut me out—at least, not always."

Elliot knew this admission cost the old man something, though he had no desire to make it easier for him.

"Do what you can to help your sister, okay? I really liked Kevin. Your mother did, too. And, for a while at least, Patricia seemed happy. She's got to be in a lot of pain."

Elliot leaned back and stretched his arms over his head. He

58

was finally starting to relax. His stepfather didn't know a thing. This was just a fishing expedition. "Of course I'll help her. Any way I can."

"Good."

"One more question before you go."

"I didn't know I was going."

Elliot flashed him an insincere smile. "Isn't it past your bedtime?"

The older man's expression tightened. "Watch your mouth. And don't push your luck."

"Is that a threat?"

"Give me a reason to wipe the floor up with you and I will."

"Gee, I thought you gave up violence right around the same time you gave up cheap women."

Otto knocked the chair over as he stood.

Elliot also stood, matching his stepfather's anger. "Remember, *Daddy,* I'm the one who better not get pissed."

They faced each other, bodies tense, eyes locked straight ahead, but it was the older man who blinked first. "Maybe . . . maybe you're right. I should get home—just in case your mother calls."

As he moved past the couch, Elliot caught him by the arm. "First tell me how you found out I was living here. Was it Patricia?"

Otto yanked his arm free. "No." He removed a newspaper clipping from his coat pocket and threw it at his son. It landed on the floor. "It seems you're famous."

Elliot didn't know what he was talking about. Picking up the clipping, he stepped over to his desk and held it under the light. It was from this morning's *Star Tribune.* The headline said: SON OF VIRGINIA KASTNER A PSYCHIC. The text of the article recounted what had happened on Saturday night.

"I didn't know my son was a psychic."

Elliot glanced over his shoulder. He could read the sarcasm in his stepfather's voice. Now he saw the sneer. "There's a lot you don't know about me."

"What part of the story is true?"

"Shit," said Elliot, reading through the clipping a little more carefully. "I should *never* have called that cop back. They printed my goddamn address!"

"Exactly. That's how I found out you were here. For your information, we've been getting calls at the house all day about that ridiculous article. This is *not* the kind of publicity the family needs."

Elliot picked up his phone and punched in a series of numbers to retrieve his voice mail. "Jeez, I've got thirteen messages."

"Maybe you should hook up with the psychic network. Earn a few extra bucks so you can get a haircut. Ponytails belong on cheerleaders, Elliot, not grown men."

Elliot dropped the clipping on the desk. This wasn't what he'd expected. He turned around to face his stepfather.

"I know you're not psychic. So what happened?"

Elliot ran a hand over his unshaven face, squeezed the back of his neck. "I don't know. I just *saw* it in my mind. I couldn't shake the images. I had to tell someone, so I told the police."

Otto stared at him a moment longer, then laughed. "Right."

"It's the truth." This conversation was going nowhere. "Look, I've got some work to do before I turn in." He glanced around for his stepfather's hat. He always wore one, the Sam Spade variety, even though it made him look years out of date. Sure enough, there it was, next to the sack of groceries on the kitchen counter. He snatched it, pressed it into the old man's hands, then guided him toward the door.

"Nip this psychic shit in the bud, Elliot. I mean it. It's only going to upset your mother when she gets back."

"We can't have that, can we?"

Otto's eyes sharpened. "No, we can't. You know why as well as I do."

60

"The Prime Directive."

"What?"

"Skip it."

"Your mother's health is primary, Elliot."

"My mother's *health* rules the world."

Otto's lips drew together in disgust. "Just be on your best behavior from now on."

"Sure. By the way, I hope you plan to have the same conversation with Patricia."

That stopped him. "Why?"

"Just . . . thought it would be a good idea."

"Do you know something I don't?"

"As you said earlier, it's important for a father and daughter to keep the lines of communication open. A simple reminder from you might go a long way."

Elliot didn't want to get into specifics, but if Otto was concerned about family stress, Patricia was headed in a direction that would make Elliot's psychic revelations seem like a picnic in the park.

8

"Your precious little beast slept at the foot of my bed *all* night," shouted Cordelia from the other room.

Jane quickly braced herself for the morning onslaught. Before noon, Cordelia's persona was generally less than cheerful. Now that she was up and trudging her way downstairs, the day's drama would begin.

Jane had stayed in bed until nearly nine. It felt good to catch up on some sleep, especially after last weekend. She'd always been the kind of person who burned the candle at both ends, though she wasn't as young as she used to be. Not that she felt a day over thirty. Well, thirty-five.

Up until a few moments ago, she'd been enjoying a pleasant, late morning breakfast, sitting at the kitchen table, reading yesterday's *Star Tribune.* Today's newspaper was drip-drying on the porch. The weather outside had turned wet and gloomy, so she'd decided to warm up by fixing herself a stack of wild rice pancakes with maple syrup and some fresh raspberries.

Cordelia entered the kitchen a few seconds later. She walked straight to the counter, tugged her morning robes snugly around her ample curves, and glared. "Well? Any comments on your mini-hound's behavior?"

"You feed him apricot croissants, Cordelia. Cookies. Popcorn. God knows what else. What do you expect?"

"I didn't feed him a cookie, it was a *Power Bar.*"

Jane shook her head. "Look, if he senses a potential food opportunity, of course he wants to stick close."

"I know you think my eating habits are occasionally atrocious, Janey, but I rarely eat while I'm asleep."

"He doesn't know that."

"Well, he *should.*"

"Cordelia, he's just a little dog. And he adores you."

"Well of course he does," she sniffed. "What's not to adore?"

"You know, Cordelia, your cats don't get very high marks, either. Do they always make such a racket at night?"

"I must have slept through it."

"Well, I didn't."

Bean trotted into the room, headed for the back door, and gave it a scratch.

As Jane got up to let him out, she checked to see how much pancake batter was left. Feeding Cordelia was often the only way to brighten her mood.

"And furthermore," said Cordelia, examining her fingernails for imperfections, "he snores."

"Then stop feeding him so much garbage and he won't follow you around like a shadow."

Cordelia closed her eyes and lifted her chin. "I don't see how you could possibly know I fed him popcorn. You weren't even in the room."

"A wild guess."

She opened her eyes and stared at Jane's empty plate. Looking pitiful, she asked, "What were you eating?"

"Breakfast."

"Don't torture me, Janey. It smells wonderful in here. Are those fresh raspberries?"

"No, they're small watermelons."

"You needn't be sarcastic."

Taking a deep, cleansing breath, Jane said, "Yes, Cordelia. They're raspberries."

Cordelia immediately cranked out her lower lip. "So, do I have to stand here like Oliver Twist and beg for my morning gruel?"

Jane couldn't help herself. She began to laugh. "Would you like me to fix you a stack of wild rice pancakes?"

"I thought you'd never ask." She rushed over to the table, sat down, flapped a napkin in the air, and tucked it into her cleavage.

After putting the fire on under the griddle, Jane poured them each some coffee.

"So, did you ever reach Dr. Frankenstein last night?" asked Cordelia. She glanced through the paper, her mood already improved.

Jane ladled on some batter. "If you're talking about Julia, she wasn't home. I tried several times but finally gave up and went to bed around one."

Cordelia snorted. "I thought they rolled up the streets in that town after sundown."

"Don't be such a big-city snob."

"All right, then, where was she?"

Jane shrugged. She didn't want to make a big deal out of it, and yet she'd been wondering the same thing herself. "Maybe she was taking a late night walk. Or out doing some star-gazing."

"Or searching the graveyards for dead bodies," muttered Cordelia under her breath.

"Cordelia!"

"Just trying to be helpful."

"No you're not. You're making some stupid, veiled point."

"I'd hardly call it veiled."

"For your information, I can handle my love life without any snide asides from you."

"Hey." Cordelia held up her hand. "Don't get so hot under the collar. Really, I was just making conversation."

"Fine. Then let's change the subject." The fact was, Cordelia had hit a nerve. Jane knew very little about Julia's everyday life. It hadn't seemed all that important when she still lived in Bethesda and worked in D.C., but now that she was here in Minnesota, it did. It wasn't that Jane was jealous of some unknown someone; at least she didn't think that's what it was. Julia insisted there wasn't anyone else in her life. Even so, Jane's lack of knowledge about Julia's daily existence made her feel . . . uneasy. That uneasiness would translate into serious problems down the line unless matters changed, and soon.

"Listen to this headline," said Cordelia, folding the newspaper to a more manageable size. " 'Son of Virginia Kastner a Psychic.' " She dropped the paper on the table and looked up. "Can you beat that?"

Jane flipped the pancakes over, glad that Cordelia had introduced a new topic. "That's fascinating. I suppose that must be Patricia's brother. What else does the article say?"

"Wait a minute. You know Patricia Kastner?" She raised an eyebrow.

"Sure. She bought the house at the end of the block a couple months ago."

Now both eyebrows raised. "You never said anything about it before."

"It never came up. Why all the interest?"

Cordelia popped a couple of raspberries into her mouth. "Virginia Kastner was just named to the board of trustees over at the Allen Grimby. Since my contract is up in January, she'll be one of five people who'll decide my professional fate for the next three years—if I'm in or out." Looking down, she began to play with the silverware. "You know, Janey, if I promise never to say another snide word about Julia, maybe you'd put in a good word for me with Patricia—since you're friends. That way she could pass all your glowing comments on to her mother and it wouldn't look like a setup."

Jane lifted the pancakes carefully onto a plate, turned off the heat under the griddle, then set the stack in front of Cordelia. "I thought you were almost positive your contract would be renewed."

"I was. Up until last month. One of our long-standing board members retired. And a second had to leave for medical reasons." She buttered the top cake and then doused it with syrup.

"That still leaves three people on your side." Jane sat down across from her, holding the warm coffee mug in both hands.

"I wish. One of the older board members is a complete putz. Homophobic to the core. And he's forever grousing about my choice of plays—and playwrights. Actually, his current snit is over one by Sandra Scoppettone. I want to premiere it in Minnesota next season—if I'm still around."

"I thought she wrote novels."

"She does. But she's also written a number of plays—all of them have been produced off Broadway." Cordelia took a bite, chewed energetically, and then continued, "She was a Eugene O'Neill playwright when she was younger. The one I want to do is a very serious comedy. It's called *Stuck*. I've talked to her a couple of times on the phone and she might even fly out for the opening. Granted, it could be tough having two divas in the same room with each other—the star power would be nearly blinding—but I suppose I could cope . . . if she could."

As Cordelia continued to emote about various problems at the Allen Grimby, Jane picked up the paper and read quickly through the article. Just as she got to the part about Virginia Kastner's son being a well-known children's author named Elliot Beauman—now residing at 4532 Bridwell Lane—the doorbell rang. "What the—Cordelia, look at this. My new renter is not only Pa-

66

tricia's brother, but he apparently helped the police locate two men who murdered a young woman near the Washburn water tower last Saturday night."

Cordelia buttered the last cake. "A psychic, huh? I always check mine out very carefully."

"You mean there's some sort of litmus test?"

"Heavens, no. You're on your own when it comes to psychic credentials. *I* always make mine tell me my birth sign and my shoe size—over the phone."

"That sounds infallible."

Again, the doorbell chimed.

"I better get that," said Jane. "Will you let Bean in the back door? He'll be wet, so dry him off with a towel."

"I have to do *everything* around here," muttered Cordelia, stuffing the last bit of pancake into her mouth.

When Jane pulled open the front door a few seconds later, she found Elliot standing outside, dripping wet.

"Morning." His smile was awkward. "You said you wanted to talk to me today, so here I am."

She backed up. "You better get in here before you're washed away."

"Yeah." He stepped somewhat hesitantly into the foyer. "Not a very nice day."

Cordelia appeared in the kitchen doorway. As she tapped a napkin to her lips, she cleared her throat.

Jane got the message. "Cordelia, this is Elliot Beauman, my new renter. Elliot, I'd like you to meet, Cordelia Thorn. She's an old friend."

Cordelia glided toward him, hand outstretched. "So nice to meet you. I understand you're a psychic."

He glanced at Jane, then back at Cordelia. "Actually, I'm not sure—"

She cut him off. "Tell me," she said, examining him from head to foot. "What's my birth sign?"

"Excuse me?"

"My birth sign, Elliot. Chop chop. I don't have all day."

Again, he glanced at Jane. This time, she could see a smile forming.

"Actually, Ms. Thorn, I'd have to say you're a Leo."

"Ha! You're right! Very good. Now my shoe size. Don't peek!" She held her hand under his chin so he couldn't look down.

He hesitated, then said, "Eleven."

"Eleven and a half. That's close enough." She grabbed his hand and dragged him into the living room.

This wasn't the way Jane wanted to spend her morning off. Leaning impatiently against the arch, she watched Cordelia drape herself dramatically over the couch.

"Now, Elliot," she said, patting a cushion and then waiting for him to sit down next to her, "I understand you're Virginia Kastner's son."

"Why—yes." His expression grew uncertain.

"Then tell me. How do you think she's going to vote—for me or against me?"

He looked over at Jane for help.

All she could do was shrug. He was on his own.

"Well, Cordelia," he said, taking her hand and turning it over so that he could see her palm. "May I call you Cordelia?"

"Certainly."

A slow grin formed. "I see fabulous things in your future. Wealth. Fame."

"I know all that. But what about your mother? Is she on my side, or isn't she?"

"Well, now, that's a little more difficult." He studied her hand, frowning.

"Do you want to look at my feet? I have one reader who swears by foot readings."

"No," said Elliot, coughing to mask his laughter. "I don't do feet. But your palm—I'm sorry. It's inconclusive."

"Then how can I find out?" she demanded impatiently. "Do you read tea leaves? Tarot cards? What about a crystal ball?"

"Oh, I've never trusted crystal balls. They play tricks on real psychics."

"They do?" Her eyes grew wide.

"Absolutely. No, I use waves. You've heard of telepathic waves, haven't you?"

"Well of course I have. I'm not a novice."

"What I want you to do is close your eyes and concentrate."

"On what?"

"Well—the vote, of course."

"Good. Yes." She squeezed her eyes shut.

"Now, I'll just touch my fingers to your temples. Think hard." He waited for almost a full minute and then dropped his hands with a frustrated sigh.

"What? Did you get an answer?"

"Your mind, Cordelia. It's . . . amazing."

"You keep telling me things I already know."

Looking dejected, he continued, "I need more time."

She gave an exasperated squawk. "Oh, all right. I guess I have no other choice but to be Zen about it. Ebb and flow. Yin and yang." She closed her eyes and repeated, "I am a river—or a rip tide, or whatever the hell I'm supposed to be."

"Maybe it's the rain," said Elliot.

"Pardon me?"

"The humidity. Maybe it's interfering with the waves."

She eyed him a moment and then said, "Yes, scientifically speaking, you could be right. We'll wait for a sunny day and try again."

"You're being very patient."

"And you're a very good judge of character, Elliot. It will serve you well." She stood, looking down her nose at him. "What do I owe you?"

"Oh, no. No, this was on me."

She swirled her satin robes and headed for the stairs. "I have to be to the theater in an hour. We'll meet again, Elliot. On a more auspicious day."

"I'll look forward to it," he called, watching her breeze up the stairs out of sight.

Once she was gone, Jane stepped away from the arch into the living room. "Would you like a cup of coffee?"

"No. Thanks. I can't stay."

"Sorry about . . . that." She flicked her eyes to the stairs.

"Hey, she's a hoot. Really, I enjoyed myself. She's like some old movie star. Joan Crawford. Barbara Stanwyck."

"Norma Desmond."

"Who?"

Jane waved the question away.

"Look," said Elliot, pushing his hands into the back pockets of his jeans, "I wanted to apologize about last night. First of all, I should have brought that lease back to you as soon as I'd signed it. I'm sorry. I hope it didn't cause you any trouble. And second, I discovered that the door wasn't locked when I left to run over to the co-op. That's how my father got in. I checked it over this morning and found that it was sticking, so I sprayed some WD-Forty in it. It works fine now. I promise, it will be locked securely from now on."

That seemed to address all of Jane's concerns. "I wondered how he got in. I also wondered why he looked at me so oddly when I called him Mr. Beauman."

Elliot winced. "Yeah, that wouldn't have gone over very well. Art Beauman was my real dad. He died when I was pretty small. Otto is my stepfather. I took my real father's name when I became a writer."

Jane had already assumed as much. "I didn't realize you were related to Patricia Kastner until I saw that article in the paper."

"Oh, that." He squeezed the back of his neck. "So you know about what happened on Saturday night. It's kind of a weird deal, actually. I'm not really psychic, but I . . . I don't know. I got this feeling and I had to tell someone. The police seemed like the best bet. I had no idea it would turn into such a circus."

"How did the paper get your address?"

"One of the homicide cops asked me to give him a call when I finally found a permanent place to live. I called him Monday morning and left him a message. Maybe it got added to the police report and some reporter took it from there."

"Bad luck."

"Yeah. I've already had some calls from local media people wanting interviews."

"Are you going to give any?"

"Absolutely not. Really, Jane. There's no reason for all this fuss. If I were a true psychic, my life wouldn't be such a mess."

She laughed. "Well, if you are, at least you're a modest one."

"I just want to live quietly. Write my books. Take care of the people I love. By the way, I hear you and my sister are pretty good friends."

"We're both part of a new block association."

His eyes shot curiously around the room. "Yeah, she seems pretty stoked about it. Well, I, ah—guess I better hit the road. I've got a lot to do today."

"Still settling in?"

"Yeah. Sort of."

She walked him to the door. "If you have any questions about the apartment, don't hesitate to call. You've got my number."

"Yup, sure do."

As she opened the door to let him out, she noticed the white truck parked by the curb in front of the house.

"See you later," called Elliot, dashing around the side of the house.

Jane watched in silence as the truck's passenger door opened and a middle-aged man in a tan raincoat got out. He hoisted an umbrella over his head and then stood for a moment gazing at her, his face surprisingly solemn. A tiny shiver crept down her spine. This was what she wanted, right? To meet the owner of the truck, ask a few questions. And yet, standing here now, she had a bad feeling about the way he was looking at her, as if his answers might change her life, and not for the better.

9

Ms. Lawless?"

Jane nodded. Up close, she could see that the man was well beyond middle age, more likely in his late fifties or early sixties. His graying brown hair actually looked pretty trendy, though she assumed the shaved sides and longish top had nothing to do with style and everything to do with the way he'd probably worn it since the age of five. The hopelessly out-of-date Madras sport coat under the rumpled tan trench coat confirmed her theory. She had a vague sense that she'd seen him somewhere before, but couldn't quite put her finger on where.

Rain dripped off the edges of the man's umbrella as he stood outside on the front steps. Seeming to reach some sort of conclusion, he continued, "My name is Earl Wilcox. I wonder if I could talk to you for a few minutes? It's important."

Her curiosity fought with her caution. "Well—" She glanced over her shoulder.

"No, not here," he said. "What I have to say to you is . . . private. Actually, you may not remember me, but we met last spring. I was helping your father on the Ferris case. I'm a private investigator."

That was it. She recalled it now. He'd been sitting in her father's law office one afternoon when she'd come by to take her dad out to lunch. Her father spoke very highly of him, said he'd been a great help. "Why don't you come in? There's no one home but a friend of mine."

"You mean, the man I just saw leaving?" His eyes shot right, scanning the walk that wound around the side of the house.

"Elliot? No, he's just a renter. He lives upstairs—on my third floor."

Wilcox gave a slow nod.

Jane could see the wheels turning inside his mind. She wasn't quite sure what he was putting together, but whatever it was, he seemed to grow more confident.

"Look," he said, lowering his voice, "I realize this may sound odd, but I'd feel more comfortable if we met on neutral ground. There's a coffee house a couple blocks away. I'd be glad to drive you over—buy you a cup of Joe."

She was amused by his choice of words, but not so amused that she'd agree to get into a car with a man she really didn't know.

Sensing her hesitation, he added, "I need your help, Ms. Lawless. I don't mean to alarm you, but I'm here on a very serious matter. It concerns a good friend of yours—Patricia Kastner."

Behind his bifocals, Jane could feel his eyes examining every nuance of her reaction. "Actually, I don't know Patricia very well."

"Really?" For some reason, the answer pleased him.

"If it's information you need, I won't be of much use."

"On the contrary, Ms. Lawless. Your cooperation would be very useful indeed. But I don't want to talk any further until I know we're not being . . . observed."

She wasn't quite sure how to take that. "You think someone's watching us?"

"It's possible."

It was also possible that the earth would be hit by a meteor in

74

the next ten minutes, but it wasn't likely. Jane wasn't quite sure how to read Earl Wilcox. All this cloak-and-dagger stuff was a little over the top. And yet by the determined look in his eyes she knew she wasn't going learn what he wanted unless she agreed to get together with him away from the house. "All right. Just let me change my clothes and I'll meet you at the Coffeteria. That's the place you mean, right?"

"That's the one. Thank you, Ms. Lawless. I'll be waiting."

Fifteen minutes later, after saying a brief good-bye to Cordelia and giving Bean a hug and a stern admonition to stay away from any and all junk food, Jane entered the coffee house and quickly spotted Wilcox sitting at a table in the back. At this late hour of the morning, the nervous knot of caffeine addicts who normally crowded the narrow aisles shortly after sunup, waiting for their caffeine fix, had dispersed to home or office, and only a few stragglers were still sitting at the mismatched wooden tables, sated by cappuccinos and lattes, quietly reading a book or staring morosely out the huge picture window at the pouring rain.

Jane quickly grabbed herself a cup of the Jamaica Blue Mountain and sat down opposite him.

Wilcox wasn't a particularly attractive man. His bifocals rested on a deeply pocked, bulbous nose, and with his trench coat tossed over an empty chair and his sport coat open, she could see a thick stomach straining the buttons on his shirt as it spilled over a tired leather belt. Yet when he smiled, as he did now, his face looked kindly. Open. Like a friendly uncle, one you couldn't help but like. Someone you might even trust; not that Jane was that easily swayed by appearances.

"Thanks for making it so quick," he said. He held the butt of a cigarette to his lips, took a puff, and then stubbed it in an ashtray.

"I have to admit," said Jane, removing her raincoat, "you've got me intrigued. If I weren't, I wouldn't be here."

"Fair enough." He slipped a card out of his pocket and handed it over.

Without putting on her own glasses, she had to squint to make out the words, but the letters were bold and black, easy to read: *Earl Wilcox, Private Investigations.* It was a Des Moines address. When she looked up, she saw that his smile was gone.

"Just to give you a little background about me, I used to be a high school English teacher, up until seven years ago. I got sick of teaching kids who couldn't spell, write, think, or do much of anything except whine that the world wasn't treating them fair and square. Not that every kid was like that, you understand, but each year it got worse. So . . . I found myself a new profession." Lighting up a fresh cigarette from a nearly empty pack, he added, "There aren't many PIs in Iowa. I thought I'd be in hot demand. I also thought it would be exciting work—dangerous even, as far from the classroom as I could get." After taking another drag, he smiled again. "Wrong."

"But you're still doing it."

"Yeah, well, it pays the bills. I lost my wife a few years back and it keeps me busy. And every now and then I get a case that makes it all worthwhile."

Jane could see the gleam in his eyes. "Like the one you're on now?"

He nodded.

As she watched him through the smoke, she sensed in him the need to talk, to tell a story, but instead of prodding, she waited.

Studying the burning tip of his cigarette, he gave himself a few moments and then began, "Two weeks ago, a woman came to my office. Her name was Emily Torland, and she was crying so hard I could barely make out her words. It took me a few minutes to calm her down, but when I did, she told me a sad story. It seems her only son, Kevin, had recently committed suicide. He was in his mid-thirties, a successful doctor, and had just broken up with his girlfriend. Emily's husband had been the one to find the body.

Kevin hadn't returned their phone calls for several days, so his father had driven over to the town house where he lived to see what was up. He knocked on the door, and when no one answered, he convinced the manager to let him in. As you can well imagine, it wasn't a pretty sight."

"How did he die?" asked Jane.

"Valium and vodka. A lethal combination. The manager called the police and they arrived, sirens blaring, to check out the apartment. There was no sign of a struggle. The body was in the bedroom, on the floor. The vodka and the pills were mere inches from the young man's hand. His prints and his *alone* were on the vodka bottle. An autopsy was performed simply because it was an unattended death. There was never any doubt. It was ruled a suicide."

Jane nodded. "It seems pretty straightforward."

"That's what everyone thought," said Earl. "Except for the mother. She couldn't believe her son would end his life so suddenly. She explained that sure, he was upset that his girlfriend had just left him, but Emily saw it not so much as sadness but as anger. She didn't know the young woman very well, even though her son had been living with her more than a year. She was rich, and spoiled, and Emily didn't like her one bit, but kept her mouth shut so she didn't alienate Kevin—who, it appears, was wild about the young woman."

It seemed pretty obvious who he was talking about. "The young woman in question is Patricia Kastner."

"You're a quick study—just like your father. That's good." He blew smoke out of the side of his mouth. "Emily asked me to investigate her son's death. She was sure the police had missed something. Her husband thinks she's gone off the deep end now that she's insisting Kevin's death wasn't a suicide."

"I don't understand."

"Emily Torland thinks her son was murdered."

"Murdered," repeated Jane, giving herself a moment to let

that sink in. "But . . . if he died of a drug overdose compounded by alcohol, it seems pretty cut and dried."

"When Emily first came to me with the story, I shared your opinion."

"But you've changed your mind?"

Wilcox nodded.

"Why? Are you saying someone *forced* Kevin Torland to take the vodka and Valium?"

"That's exactly what I'm saying, Ms. Lawless. Someone wanted him dead and to cover his or her tracks, made it look like a suicide."

She thought it over. It wasn't impossible, though it seemed highly unlikely. "Who do you suspect? Or, I should say, who does Emily Torland suspect?"

"Emily thinks Patricia Kastner is responsible."

"Are you serious?" Jane was stunned.

"I'm afraid so."

"But why? What was her motive?"

"I don't know that yet."

Jane shook her head, over and over, resisting the idea. Nothing she knew about Patricia suggested she could do something so horrible. "What made you change your mind? Certainly, all the evidence points to suicide, at least everything you've told me so far."

He tapped some ash into the ashtray. "You're right, but there are a couple points I haven't mentioned. You have to understand, Ms. Lawless, I wasn't at the apartment the night the body was found, so all I had to go on were police photos. But as it turns out, they were enough. I discovered something that the police missed." Taking a sip of coffee, Wilcox continued, "Kevin Torland was left-handed. He wore his watch on his right wrist, and a gold ring with an onyx stone on his left hand. Strangely, in the police photos, the watch and the ring were reversed. I examined the negatives just to make sure the prints were accurate, that they hadn't inadvertently been switched around. I discovered that the photos were correct. Oh, and one other point. The watch was on backwards—the twelve at the bottom and the six at the top. Now tell me, Ms. Lawless—"

"Please, call me Jane."

He smiled. "And you call me Earl." Pressing the butt of the cigarette to his lips, he continued, "Tell me why a man who was about to kill himself would put his watch on backwards, on the wrong wrist, and his ring on the wrong hand. It makes no sense—unless it was a message. Unless he was trying to tell those who would later find his body that something was amiss. Let's say someone was holding a gun on him, forcing him to swallow the pills and the vodka. He had no chance to do anything dramatic, like write a message in blood on the floor, or carve something into the tabletop, the kind of thing you often see in the movies. No, this was a man struggling to find a way to send a message to the world that all was not what it appeared. His options were severely limited. But he did send us a message . . . if we're willing to listen."

It was an interesting argument, but she still wasn't convinced. "Look, Earl, if someone were holding a gun to my head and telling me I could either commit suicide or he'd shoot me, I'd take my chances with the gun. I'd try to fight, because once I'd swallowed the pills, that would be it."

He gave her a long, measuring look. "There's an answer to that, too, Jane. I'm just not sure what it is."

"And also, the watch and the ring—I agree, it's puzzling, but it certainly isn't conclusive proof that it *wasn't* a suicide, or that Patricia was involved in a murder."

"I never said Patricia murdered him. That's Emily's theory."

"What *are* you saying, then?"

"The ring that Kevin was wearing, it had been given to him the month before by Patricia's parents—as a birthday gift. I think that's significant. I believe he was trying to indicate one of them as his murderer, or at the very least, someone in the Kastner family."

"Who? You mean Elliot? Patricia's brother? You think he had something to do with Torland's death?"

Earl ground out his cigarette, then rested his hands on the table and toyed with his coffee mug. "Elliot was seen arguing with Kevin less than a week before Kevin supposedly took his own life. It wasn't just your average shouting match, either. It was much more heated. Elliot took a swing at Kevin, knocked him clean over the hood of his car. One of the neighbors in the apartment complex, an elderly woman, told me all about it. I guess it got pretty violent. Once Elliot was finally gone, the woman who'd been watching from her front window went out to see if Kevin was all right. She said he was hopping mad. She offered to call the police so that he could press charges against the man with the ponytail, but he said no. He'd take care of it. According to the neighbor, his exact words were, 'I'll take care of that sonofabitch—and his whole goddamn family—in my own way and in my own time.' Now tell me, Jane, does that sound like a man who was mere days away from taking his own life?"

Jane had to agree. It didn't.

"Emily Torland said that her son met Patricia Kastner and less than two weeks later he informed his family that the two of them were in love and were going to move in together. Patricia had lots of family money, and Kevin wasn't exactly making peanuts, either. The town-house complex they moved into was pretty ritzy by anyone's standards. Patricia's parents came down to visit at least once a month. Since it was a three-bedroom place, there was plenty of room. From all outward appearances, the Kastners adored Kevin, and he adored them."

"But . . . what? You don't buy it?"

He fingered a crack in the wood table. "I don't know. I do know that the day Kevin died, one of Patricia's parents visited him."

"Which one?"

"I'm working on that."

Jane had to agree, it wasn't as simple as it first sounded. "I guess there's at least some reason to believe it wasn't suicide."

"I thought you'd see it my way. Look," he said, adjusting his glasses, "I've done some checking on you in the past couple of days, and if what I'm told is correct, you've done some investigative work yourself in the past—unofficially."

She nodded, wondering why he'd changed the subject. "So?"

"It's an unusual hobby."

She shrugged.

"If you don't mind indulging an old man's curiosity, why do you do it?"

It was a question Jane had asked herself many times in the last few years. "Actually . . . I'm not sure."

"You're not sure, or you don't want to tell me?"

"No, it's just . . . it's not simple." She turned the coffee mug around in her hands. "You see, when I first opened my restaurant, I was involved in everything. The whole concept, from start to finish, was mine. I even worked as the head chef for a while—until I found a wonderful woman who understood exactly what I was after. I lived and breathed that place, and even though we made a fair splash in the restaurant community, for many years it was a financial struggle. There were times I thought I might have to close the doors. But in the last few years, the restaurant has really come into its own. I'm making money now—more than I ever thought possible. It's just—"

"The thrill is gone?"

"No, it's not that. But . . . you're right, something is missing. The passion I used to feel isn't there anymore. The funny thing is, when I work on these . . . investigations, as you call them . . . I feel engaged in a way I used to feel at the restaurant. And occasionally, it's even gone beyond that. I'm *consumed* by the chase. I used to think it was just simple curiosity, but it goes way beyond that. Am I making any sense?"

He sat back in his chair. "Perfect sense."

Jane couldn't help but smile. "I'm glad it does to one of us." It felt strange talking to Earl so intimately, telling him something she'd never explained to anyone before. Taking a sip of her coffee, she continued, "So, you said you wanted to talk to me. What about?"

His expression sharpened. "I need your help. The fact is, Jane, when I drove up here a few days ago, I was looking for a link, a key, some way to get me inside that family. You're it. You're my way in. That is," he added, folding his arms over his chest, "if you'll help."

"You want me to spy on Patricia Kastner?"

"I want anything I can get. Talk to her. Find out about her relationship with Kevin Torland. Oh, and one other thing. It seems that Patricia's mother, Virginia Kastner, went to pieces after Kevin's death. Find out what you can about her, too. And since Elliot is living on your third floor, see what information you can get out of him—cautiously, of course. You know the ropes. You've done it before. It's for a good cause, Jane. If Kevin Torland *was* murdered, someone should pay for it. If it turns out it was a suicide, then no one will be hurt by a little discreet probing."

"You're a good salesman, Earl." She pushed her coffee cup away. "Maybe you missed your calling."

"Then, it's a deal?" He stretched his hand toward her.

She hesitated, but only for a second. "Sure. I'll help. I can't promise I'll find anything useful."

"Let me be the judge of that."

"How can I reach you? Are you staying somewhere in town?"

He rose from the table, took one last swig of coffee, then grabbed his trench coat. "Don't worry, Jane. I'll get back to you."

10

Come on, Julia, pick up the damn phone." Jane waited, tapping her nails impatiently on the desktop, allowing the answering machine on the other end to record the strained silence. "Are you there? Being coy? In the bathtub?" This was the third time this week Jane had tried to reach her with no luck. She kept regular office hours, at least that's what Jane had been led to believe, so where was she every night? "Look, call me when you get in, okay? It's Wednesday evening. I'm at the restaurant now, but I should be home by eleven. Midnight at the latest. Cordelia's staying with me for a few days, so she may answer the phone if I'm not there. I miss you, sweetheart. And I'd like to plan a time to get together again—soon. If I don't hear from you tonight, I'll call your office tomorrow. I guess . . . you've got me a little worried. This is the third time I've phoned, but the first time I've left a message. I hope everything's all right. Talk to you soon. 'Bye."

She sat back and rubbed her sore eyes, willing the frustration away from her. She had to stop fixating on Julia, on her schedule, on what she said or didn't say. Jane knew she tended to overanalyze, and right now she was driving herself nuts. She simply had to trust that everything was all right——and then get on with her life.

Leaning her head back, she forced herself to think about something else. She was just about to give up and call Julia again with an addendum to her first message when the image of Patricia Kastner floated in front of her eyes. She thought back to the morning, and to her unexpected meeting with Earl Wilcox. Unfortunately, the conversation had left her with more questions than answers. She wished he hadn't been so secretive about where he was staying. She might be able to help with his investigation, but she needed more background, more specifics.

Switching off the desk lamp, Jane made a quick decision to grab a beer in the pub before walking home. The mindless noise would be soothing to her overstimulated brain, and the drink to her overstimulated soul.

After locking her office, she headed down a narrow corridor and entered the pub from the rear. Over the years she'd noticed that on some weekday evenings, customers tended to arrive in waves. Right now, there were only a few stragglers sitting at the long mahogany bar. She crossed to the far end, eased onto a stool, and ordered her usual lager and lime.

Ten minutes later, she caught a whiff of perfume. At almost the same instant she felt a tap on her shoulder. Glancing up, she was surprised to see that Patricia had taken the stool next to her.

"Sorry I didn't call first," said Patricia, unzipping her black leather jacket. Underneath she was wearing a red silk blouse tucked into a tight leather miniskirt. "You mentioned that maybe we could get together sometime this week and talk about that block party. So . . . what do you say? Now's good for me."

Jane thought about it for a moment and then smiled. "Sure. Why not?" Actually, the timing couldn't be better. After ordering herself another beer, and a whiskey and soda for Patricia, they carried their drinks into the back room, where they sat down at a table next to the fire.

"I'm glad you're a spur-of-the-moment kind of woman," said Patricia, making herself comfortable. "I don't like to make too many plans. It's better to live in the moment; that way you're free to explore all the possibilities."

It was an interesting philosophy, thought Jane. She'd come across it before—probably on the back of an old Grateful Dead album. Hiding her distaste behind another smile, she said, "I just found out this morning that your brother is renting my third-floor apartment."

"Yeah, small world, isn't it? I didn't know myself until yesterday."

Jane had a feeling she wanted to say more, but for whatever reason, stopped herself. "I also saw the article in the paper about the murder he solved for the police. Pretty amazing."

Patricia nodded, her gaze wandering to the fire.

She clearly didn't want to talk about her brother, but Jane wasn't going to let the subject drop. "When I talked to him earlier today, he insisted that he's not psychic. I didn't want to press him because I figured it was none of my business. But I have to say, between you and me, I'm pretty curious."

"Do you believe in psychics, Jane?"

She thought about it. "Well, I suppose it's arrogant to assume we know everything there is to know about the universe."

"I'm afraid I'm a hopeless skeptic."

"Has Elliot ever mentioned anything to you before about his psychic powers?"

Patricia sat forward, folding her hands around her glass. "Oh, every now and then he gets what he calls his 'premonitions.' It's a joke, really. Most of the time they mean nothing. Except, well . . . there was one time, when he was a little kid. He got this idea into his head that something terrible was going to happen. And when it did, he blamed himself. He thought he should have been able to prevent it."

"Do you know what that something was?"

85

She shook her head. "Elliot can be pretty close-mouthed when he wants to be. But whatever it was, it upset him terribly." She stared down into her glass. "You don't know Elliot, Jane, but he's a real sensitive guy. He's always been there for me when I needed him. I just wish——" Again, her eyes drifted to the fire.

"Wish what?"

"Oh, just that he got along better with Mom and Dad. I know they weren't around much when he was little. His brother, Jay, had a serious accident when Elliot was seven. Jay spent the rest of his life paralyzed, living in an institution. Mom had a nervous breakdown right after it happened and I think Elliot was left alone a lot. This was way before my time, but I know he's never forgiven either of them for what happened."

"Were they responsible?"

"Mom wasn't even home. Dad was there, but he was in the living room watching TV. How could he know Jay had gone up on the roof?"

"The roof? Why on earth would he do that?"

"Beats the hell out of me. He was probably just being a stupid kid. After Mom recovered from the breakdown, she continued to have some emotional problems. But by the time I came along, both Mom and Dad had thriving businesses and were far more settled. I guess you could say I got lucky." She frowned into her glass. "It's funny. Sometimes I feel like Elliot and I have had different parents, even though ever since he was a small child, they were the same people. Does that sound totally weird?"

"Not at all."

As Patricia looked up, her expression softened. "I knew you'd understand, Jane. I'm not sure why, but I feel like I can trust you—like I can talk to you and you won't judge me."

"I certainly hope that's true."

"Oh, it is. It won't be long before you feel the same way about me."

"Do psychic powers run in your family?"

She laughed. "Yeah, maybe they do."

Jane let her enjoy the joke for a moment and then went on, "Did you date someone special when you lived in Iowa?"

The laughter faded. "Why do you ask?"

"Obvious reasons. I'd like to get to know you better." Jane lifted the beer to her lips, knowing she had to tread lightly. Patricia was smart. If Jane tried to pump her too aggressively for information, she'd demand to know what was going on. Jane didn't want that to happen. At this point, she had no reason to believe Patricia had anything to do with her boyfriend's death. Sure, she came on too strong sometimes, but Jane didn't dislike her—and she certainly didn't want to hurt her for no good reason. She didn't want to admit it, but she felt a little guilty for even entertaining the idea that Patricia had something to do with Kevin Torland's death. Then again, she didn't think a little discreet probing would hurt anyone, especially if Patricia was innocent.

Patricia crossed her legs and leaned back in her chair. "Yeah, I dated a guy while I was there."

"But it didn't work out."

"Actually, he died."

"I'm sorry," said Jane. "You probably don't want to talk about it."

"No, it's okay. It's taken some time, but I've pretty much dealt with it now. His name was Kevin. He . . . well, to be honest, he committed suicide a couple of weeks after we broke up. It just wasn't working between us. I had no choice but to leave. But that didn't mean I wasn't devastated when I heard the news."

"How did you find out?"

"Elliot—he stopped by. He thought he should tell me in person. I was staying at a hotel, trying to tie up some loose ends at work before I moved back to Minneapolis. Kevin had been dead for several days before they found the body. When they did, the news of his suicide was all over the radio and TV. I was so busy right then, I missed it."

Jane realized the next question wasn't particularly kind, but she asked it anyway. "Do you think he committed suicide because of the breakup?"

"Oh, without a doubt."

That surprised her. She would have thought Patricia would waffle about it just a little, if for no other reason than to let herself off the hook. Then again, she seemed to appreciate directness—a quality Jane also valued.

"Kevin was an emotional guy. He begged me to come back to him, pleaded for a second chance. But it was no use. It was over—he just wasn't willing to accept it."

"Had you known him long?"

"We met about a year and a half after I moved to Des Moines. Honestly, Jane, it was love at first sight. But after living together for a while, I knew I'd made a huge mistake. It took me the better part of a year to extricate myself from the relationship. I figured I owed it to him to let him down easily."

Obviously not easily enough, thought Jane. "Since you were living in another city, I suppose your parents never got to know him."

"Oh, no, my parents adored Kevin. Not that anyone is ever good enough for me in their eyes. Even though he was a doctor, he wasn't making much money—by their standards—though I suppose one day he would have. But my parents tried to be supportive. They came down a lot, stayed with us on weekends. Dad likes Des Moines. He even worked up a couple of building contracts while he was down there. He's always looking for ways to expand his business—and, of course, something to get him out of the Twin Cities for a while."

"Same with my father," said Jane, trying to make this covert interrogation sound conversational. "Since he has a pilot's license and owns a small aircraft, he and his wife take trips all over." She shuddered. "Small planes don't do wonders for my nerves."

Patricia's smile was amused. "Then I suppose that means you won't go skydiving with me."

That took her by surprise. "Skydiving?"

"Think about it, Jane. There's a King Air waiting for us at Flying Cloud Field even as we speak."

"I suppose you bungee-jump, too?"

"I don't like bonds or attachments of any kind. When I jump, I want nothing between me and the ground but air—and my skill."

"And a parachute."

Patricia held Jane's eyes. "You always need a parachute. Once the thrill's over, you have to get down safely so you can jump again."

"You sound like you're addicted to thrills."

"You could be too, if you'd just give it a chance."

Jane knew they'd long since stopped talking about skydiving.

Patricia lifted the whiskey and soda to her lips. "I could never get Kevin or Elliot to go up with me. They're both too timid."

"Or sensible."

"It's all a matter of perspective."

Jane realized she was staring, and quickly looked away. She needed to get back to the real reason for this conversation. "Since Elliot lived in Iowa, I suppose the three of you got together a lot."

"Not really. Oh, Kev and Elliot got along okay, but they didn't have much in common. And since Elliot lived out of town, about fifty miles away, he didn't come around all that often. He likes to keep his life simple and quiet so he can work on his books—the opposite of me. As far as I'm concerned, the wilder the ride the better."

Jane was beginning to get a better picture of Patricia Kastner. She had little trouble understanding why Kevin Torland's mother didn't like her—and why Kevin did.

"Elliot just chalked up my relationship with Kevin to my usual impetuous nature, but he made it clear that he would have preferred me to get to know him better before I made any sort of commitment."

"You mean living together?"

Patricia nodded. "Kevin was a nice guy and all, but we weren't really compatible. As soon as we moved in together, Elliot made me swear on my life that I'd talk to him before I did anything dumb."

"Like marry a guy you hardly knew."

She swirled the ice in her glass. "Actually, I think Kevin knew that Elliot was a major sticking point. It annoyed him to no end."

Jane thought back to the angry confrontation Kevin's neighbor had witnessed in the parking lot. Was that what Kevin and Elliot had been arguing about? It seemed not only plausible but likely.

Patricia's gaze drifted slowly around the room. "Well," she said, her eyes finally coming to rest on Jane, "that's the story of my life. Now you know everything."

"Why do I get the feeling that you left out a few important details?"

Patricia laughed. "If you're challenging me to a game of Truth or Dare, I accept."

Man, this kid didn't quit. "I'll think about it."

"You do that. You've got my number. Any time . . . day or night." Leaning into the table, Patricia continued, "Okay, so I gave you a tour of my life, now let's hear all about *your* checkered past."

"I think we talked enough about me the other night."

"No, we didn't." She studied Jane's face. "You're uncomfortable, aren't you? You don't like talking about yourself."

"Look, Patricia—"

"You're a real mystery, Jane. There's a lot more to you than meets the eye; not that what meets the eye isn't enough."

Shaking her head, Jane glanced at her watch. It was almost midnight. "Listen, it's getting late, and there's still the little mat-

ter of that block party——that is, if you think you could stop flirting with me long enough to talk about it."

Patricia grinned. "All right, all right. But you can't say a little
flirting between friends isn't fun."

No, thought Jane, finishing her beer. She couldn't.

11

Shortly before noon on Thursday, Elliot sat at his drafting table studying the illustration he'd begun for the cover of the newest Danger Doug book, the one due at his publishers by early December. The story was complete, as were most of the inside illustrations, but the cover was still giving him problems. He needed something bold, dramatic, scary, befitting Doug the Dog's superhero status—righting wrongs, protecting the weak, generally saving the day wherever possible—but he also needed just the right amount of whimsy. Doug was, after all, a poodle. A macho poodle with bright red and yellow eyes and curly black fur, but a poodle nonetheless.

Picking up his cigarette, Elliot sat back and tapped some ash into a saucer. His sister, who had arrived a few minutes ago bearing chicken soup and other remedies for his incipient pneumonia, was standing at the window looking down at the backyard. "I think that stuff you brought is just about heated." He glanced at the hot plate. The contents of the pan were about to boil over. Patricia was many things, but she wasn't a cook. He doubted she'd made the soup. Most likely, she bought it somewhere. "Patricia?"

"Hum?"

"What are you looking at?"

"What? Oh . . . nothing." With reluctance, she tore her eyes away from the window. Stepping over to the drafting table, she peered down at Elliot's sketch. "Nice work."

"You're going to spoil me with such lavish praise."

She smiled.

"The soup. It's hot."

"Oh, right!" She dashed to the kitchenette. Once she'd switched off the heat, she poured half the pan's contents into a bowl. "Elliot, listen to me. You've got to drink lots of liquids. And eat right—at least for a few days. Do you realize you don't have a single leafy green vegetable in your entire refrigerator?"

He grunted, blowing smoke out of his nose. "I don't eat green stuff."

"If it were *dyed* green, you would."

He grinned. "That's different."

"You worry me sometimes, you really do." She plunked the bowl on a small card table, one she'd already set with a napkin and a spoon, pulled back the single metal chair, and pointed to it. "Get over here."

"Jeez, who's the kid sister here and who's the grownup?"

"I've been grown for many years, in case you haven't noticed."

Glancing up at her, he could see real love and concern in her eyes, and it meant a lot. Relenting, he coughed a couple of times and then said, "I'll turn over a new leaf—as long as it's not green, and as long as it's only for today."

"You're hopeless."

"Take it or leave it."

She shook her head. "I want you to eat this entire bowl of soup, and then I want you to wash it down with a glass of orange juice and a vitamin pill."

His face puckered. Next to him on the desk, the phone began to ring. Sensing a reprieve, he grabbed it, propping the receiver between his chin and shoulder. "Hello?"

"Elliot Beauman, please," came a male voice.

"Speaking." He realized that with his plugged sinuses, his own voice sounded nasal and a good octave lower than normal.

"Elliot, hi. This is Sergeant Harry Engsdahl. We met last weekend."

What did he want? "Right. I remember you."

"I, ah . . . well, I was just wondering how you were doin'. Are you settling in all right?"

Elliot took a quick puff on his cigarette. "I'm settled in just fine, but I have a miserable cold, not that you called to talk about my health."

"No, I didn't. Actually, I was wondering if you'd had any revelations, premonitions—whatever you call them—about that woman you thought was going to be murdered in a house by one of the lakes? You know—the one we talked about the other night at the station?"

Elliot let the cigarette dangle from his lips as he considered the question. The fact was, he knew now that he was the only person who stood between that woman and a deep, dark coffin. Not that he was going to share that small detail with the sergeant. "Sorry. Nothing."

"That's too bad." Engsdahl hesitated. "Listen, Elliot, I've just been assigned to a case in south Minneapolis. I, ah, thought that . . . well, that you might be able to help me. You know—as a consultant."

"You mean a psychic consultant?"

"I know you said you're not psychic, Elliot, but whatever you are, it was pretty useful last Saturday night. Every now and then I need a man with skills like yours. I've worked with psychics before, so I'm not a novice. I don't expect miracles and I know there are limits to what you can do. Just between you and me, some of you people are pretty good, though most aren't. I got a feeling you fall into the first category."

"You've got a *feeling*? Since you've got your own skills, Sergeant Engsdahl, why do you need mine?"

More silence. "Is that a no?"

"Yeah." He stubbed out his cigarette.

"Will you at least think about it?"

"I have. And I'm not interested. And while we're on the phone, you should know that I was pretty pissed you gave my name and address to the local papers."

"Look, Elliot, I had nothing to do with that."

"Save it."

"It's the truth. If you're angry because you think I——"

"Thanks for the call, Harry. You can take my number off your Rolodex now. I'm not interested." He slammed the phone down on the hook.

Patricia stood next to the refrigerator, spooning soup directly from the pan into her mouth. "Considering your past history with the cops in this town, maybe you should be a little nicer."

He shot her a disgusted look.

"Just a thought." She set the pan in the sink and then crossed into the living room and flopped down on the couch. "Whatever possessed you to move in here?" Her gaze wandered lazily over the long room, coming to rest on the skylight above the drafting table.

He shrugged, lighting another cigarette.

"It's bigger than it looks from the street."

"It's perfect for my needs."

"Mom isn't going to be very happy."

He blew smoke out of the side of his mouth and added, "Otto's already been here."

"He has?" She seemed surprised. "He didn't say anything to me about it. Why'd he come?"

"To welcome me home." Elliot could feel his sister's eyes on him.

"I wonder if Mom's back yet from her trip?"

"I don't know. Otto thought it would be soon."

"Why do you call him Otto, Elliot, instead of Dad?"

"Because he's not my father."

"And you take every opportunity to remind him of that fact."

It was an old argument between them; one he had no energy for today. "Otto and I understand each other, Patricia. Let's just leave it at that."

She threw him a disapproving look.

"I'll make you a deal. If you let the subject drop, instead of beating it and me to death like you usually do, I'll be a good boy and eat my soup."

She sighed, tipping her head back against the cushions and closing her eyes. "Oh, all right."

"Thank you." He placed the cigarette squarely between his lips, got up, and ambled over to the chair next to the card table where he sat down with a thunk. "I feel like shit."

"Have you taken your temperature?"

"The only thermometer I've seen around here is the one hanging on the garage."

She let out an involuntary snort. Then, biting a nail, she said, "Say, while I'm here, why don't you show me the sketches for that new concept you came up with? The one that's going to make you a star."

"It's not ready," he said, tasting the soup. "The idea isn't fully formed."

"But it's for a new picture book, right? For kids?"

"Not exactly — or I should say, not precisely."

"Elliot!" She bounced out of the chair.

"Are you *on* something, or what? Diet pills? Too much caffeine?"

"Don't change the subject."

He stared at the vitamin pill, willing it to crawl away. "Oh, all right. See that drawing tablet under the world atlas?"

She nodded.

"Flip it open and tell me what you think."

When she folded back the first page, her mouth dropped open. "It's a . . . cartoon?"

"An action cartoon," he corrected her. "Superheroes are my metier. They're the only subject that interests me now."

"This is amazing," she said, moving to the next page.

Elliot had done some cartoons back in the eighties. After spending a couple of aimless years at the University of Minnesota, he'd entered the Minneapolis College of Art and Design. He'd always admired the cartoon format, but had never found quite the right character to bring his own cartoons to life. Now that he had, it felt like crossing a threshold into a foreign but very welcoming new universe, a place he wanted not simply to visit but to rule. Maybe some of Otto's megalomania had rubbed off on him after all.

"What's this nasty superdude called?"

"Doctor Dart."

"I love it!"

He was delighted by her enthusiasm. She'd always been his most generous audience.

"It's all so dark and creepy."

"Yeah." The vitamin pill was still there, daring him to swallow it.

"You have an incredible imagination."

"I know." If he imagined the pill was a jelly bean, maybe he could actually choke it down. "But I think my imagination's about to fail me."

"Huh?" She didn't look up, but kept paging through the sketches.

Elliot closed his eyes, popped the pill in his mouth, then drank the glass of orange juice down in several quick swallows. "There. I'm on my way to perfect health." He sneezed, blowing his nose on the napkin. "Hey, aren't you working today?"

"I'm taking a long lunch hour." She set the sketch pad back on the desk. "So I can take care of my sick brother."

He figured that was partly true, but certainly not the whole story. From the moment she'd sailed through the door, she'd seemed preoccupied, only partially present. He wondered if she didn't want to talk to him about something specific. He thought he'd try the most obvious first.

"Are you okay about . . . you know . . . Kevin?"

She bent her head and for a moment considered the question. Finally, turning around, she said, "I really would have been up the creek if he'd lived."

"True."

"I found myself almost . . . afraid of him, Elliot. And that really pissed me off."

He looked at her and she looked at him. Both understood the implications and neither said another word on the subject.

She returned to the window overlooking the backyard.

Elliot gave her a few seconds and then moved up behind her, finally seeing what had captured her attention. Jane Lawless and that exotic fat friend of hers were sunning themselves in the backyard. Both were wearing bathing suits, lying on beach towels. "That's what we should be doing," he said, slipping a reassuring hand over her shoulder. "We finally got some warm weather. It won't last."

"Yeah," she said absently.

"I know what's on your mind."

She turned to look at him. "What?"

"Her." He nodded toward Jane.

"What about her?"

"Come on, sis. Have you forgotten all those letters you wrote me before I moved back? If I didn't know better, I'd say you had a crush on her."

"I do," she said, returning her gaze to the backyard. "A bad one."

He'd figured as much. "Are you nuts?"

"I've never been more sane."

"Like you were when you got mixed up with Kevin?"

Her eyes flared at him. "It's nothing like that."

It was like arguing with a wall. When Patricia got something into her head, there was no talking her out of it. He decided to bring out the big guns. "You remember what happened last time, don't you?"

She stiffened. "I never believed any of that mess had to do with my feelings for Abbie."

"Well, take my word for it, Mom was sending you a direct message."

"I don't believe you. She's not homophobic. It was just a bad time in her life and Abbie and I got caught up in it." Her eyes remained fixed on the two women in the backyard. "Besides, Mom's the least of my problems."

"Ah. I get it now," he said, a slow smile forming. "Jane isn't cooperating."

"She will."

"Maybe. Maybe not." When Patricia didn't reply, he knew he'd hit a nerve. He was finally beginning to understand. Saying no to Patricia was like waving a red flag under a bull's nose. She was aroused because she wanted something she couldn't have. "Do me a favor, just this once."

She looked at him over her shoulder, waiting for the request.

"Don't mention anything about her to Mom or Otto."

"Why?"

"Because, with any luck, in a month or two, you'll be on to someone new."

"I may surprise you."

"Just be smart this time, okay? And take it slow."

She flashed him a grin, then returned her attention to the backyard. "Whatever you say. Big brothers always know best."

12

"Do bears eat raw meat?"

Jane lowered her sunglasses and stared at Cordelia. "No, they cook it first. Why do you ask?"

"It just popped into my head. I was curious and I figured you'd know."

"Cordelia, your understanding—or I should say *lack* of understanding—of the natural world never ceases to amaze me."

"I don't *do* nature, Janey." She rubbed more sun screen on her right leg. "Unless it's something like sunbathing in a perfectly manicured backyard." Before lying back down, she flicked an ant off her towel. "If you recall, I *did* the forest once—on a horse. It was a disaster."

Jane grabbed the sun screen back from Cordelia and applied it to her arms, then turned over on her stomach. After the last few days of rain, the weather had turned sultry. Jane wasn't much for lying in the sun, but decided that since this was undoubtedly one of the last days of warm weather, she might as well catch a few rays.

"Sometimes I think I'm part lizard," said Cordelia, stretching languidly. "Just give me a hot rock to wrap myself around and I'm happy. Now then, getting back to my original subject"—she paused to take a swig of chocolate milk—"I've been doing some discreet digging and I'm pretty confident the executive board at the Allen Grimby is evenly divided when it comes to my continued tenure as creative director. That leaves Virginia Kastner as the tiebreaker. Somehow, Janey, I have to get to that woman—impress her with my credentials and my vision for the company."

"Which is?"

"I want to lead this theater into the twenty-first century. The Twin Cities is one of the prime theater locales in America, and the Allen Grimby is a big part of that. The Allen Grimby *must* be innovative—it's not enough to just put on the classics. Movies used to serve as a forum for the examination of ideas in this country, but in the past ten years, Hollywood and to a lesser extent TV have abrogated that function in favor of pure, often mindless entertainment. Theater is the only forum left to us to explore the political, social, and personal forces that shape our lives. But—and this is a big but—we must never forget our audience. Theater *is* that relationship. As the creative director, I have to meld with both: I have to be the visionary for the company and the twenty-five-year-old construction worker who comes to see one of our plays. I'm absolutely committed to this theater, Janey, and passionate about what we've accomplished so far, but I don't want to stop there."

When Cordelia got on the subject of the modern American theater, Jane often felt as if she were having a conversation with a jet engine. "And how do you intend to impress Virginia Kastner with this vision?"

Cordelia balanced the carton of milk on her stomach and looked glum. "I'll get a chance to lay out the specifics of my proposal—I just hope her mind isn't already made up. It would help if I could get to know her a little first, feel out her position on certain matters." Her gaze rose to the third floor. "Speaking of inside information, I haven't seen that Elliot person since the other day."

"I wouldn't count on his psychic abilities to help you."

"It's not raining anymore. Maybe his waves are back on track."

"You're forgetting the humidity, Cordelia. That's almost as bad as rain."

"Really?" She sipped her milk thoughtfully. "I suppose you're right. But he *is* Virginia Kastner's son. Maybe, between Elliot and his sister, they could put in a good word for me."

"That might be possible—if they knew you, which they don't."

"You could remedy that."

Jane raised her head. "How?"

"By giving a party. You're great at dinner parties, Janey. Invite the entire Kastner clan over—and introduce them to *moi*. I'll take care of the rest."

Jane groaned. "Sounds like a fun evening."

"Sarcasm is so unbecoming, dearheart. You might want to do something about it before it becomes a habit."

"You use sarcasm all the time."

"Yes, but I lift it to the level of profundity."

As Jane brushed a mosquito away from her face, she noticed a man walking slowly up the drive. Unless she was mistaken, it was Otto Kastner. In the bright noonday sun, he looked older than he had the other night. His thinning silver-white hair was combed straight back from a high forehead, revealing a deeply tanned, ruggedly handsome face. All in all, he struck an imposing figure.

Seeing Jane, he gave a nod, then turned and started up the stairs. Two steps up, he stopped. "Have you seen Patricia?" he called, taking a handkerchief out of his pocket and mopping the sweat from his face.

Jane sat up. "No, not today."

Continuing to wipe the back of his neck, he came back down the steps and walked through the gate into the backyard. "I've got a crew at her house fixing some of the rotted wood trim. I

102

stopped by to talk to her and one of the workmen said she'd come down here." His eyes rose to the third floor. "So, maybe she *is* up there."

Cordelia cleared her throat, waiting for an introduction.

"That's possible," said Jane. Glancing at Cordelia, she added, "Mr. Kastner, I'd like you to meet a good friend of mine, Cordelia Thorn."

He gave a stiff nod.

"This is a true pleasure, Mr. Kastner," said Cordelia, rising and shaking his hand vigorously.

"Thank you," he said, visibly taken aback by her fervor. His eyes narrowed as he examined the backyard. "You having some work done over there?" He pointed to the old patio area next to the garage. Some of the tiles had been removed and stacked behind a lawn chair.

"Yes," said Jane. "We're going to build a greenhouse where the patio is now. I've contacted a couple of different companies about digging the trench and pouring some footings. We need to lay a cement slab before winter gets here."

He nodded, then walked over to take a closer look.

Jane followed him, throwing on her beach robe to cover up.

"You going to attach the greenhouse to the garage?"

"That's the plan. My aunt's new husband is hoping to build it next spring."

"He do roof repair?"

"No, I don't think so. Why?"

"You got a problem with the garage roof. The stucco is water-damaged. You've painted over it, so, cosmetically, it looks okay right now, but I'd recommend you get that fixed before you build the greenhouse." He righted a ladder that was leaning against the base of the garage and propped it up against the side. A second later he was on the roof, walking around, examining the tiles. "You got three layers of shingles on here, that's part of your problem. And, I suspect, some rotted wood underneath."

103

Cordelia moved silently up behind Jane and whispered, "Don't forget the dinner party."

Otto returned to the ground, slapping his hands together to remove the dirt and asphalt particles. "I understand you're a pretty good friend of Patricia's."

"We're both active in the new block association," said Jane.

"Jane's the new block emperor," said Cordelia with an amused smile. "In Linden Hills, the title comes complete with a throne and a coat of arms."

If Cordelia was attempting to impress Otto Kastner with her rapier wit, it wasn't working. Jane didn't know him all that well, but she'd already determined that he wasn't the jovial type.

Otto studied Cordelia somewhat coldly, then returned his attention to Jane. "You're the block captain?"

"Right. Actually, since nobody else wanted the job, I was elected in a landslide."

He stood back and looked once again at the garage. After walking off the patio area, he said, "I could take care of this for you first thing next week. Have you made a deal with any of those companies yet?"

"Well, they all said they'd try to squeeze me in before the snow flies. I'm waiting for one of them to call back with a specific date."

"But you haven't signed a contract?"

"No."

He smiled at her for the first time. Jane realized she was witnessing a curious transformation. Gone was the serious, almost dour countenance. Otto Kastner was blessed with a wonderful smile, the kind that pulled you in, made you think you were really important to him, that you were being listened to, cared for. He wasn't just a successful builder, he was a salesman, with all the necessary skills—that is, when he chose to use them.

"I could handle all of it for you—the roof, the footings, and the slab—for a pretty good price."

"Well, I—" She wasn't quite sure what to say.

"Believe me, Jane, you *want* this estimate."

"Of course she does," said Cordelia, attempting to be agreeable.

Mopping his face again, he continued, "Here's my best offer. You pay for the materials, I throw in the labor free of charge."

Jane was stunned. "But . . . why would you do that?"

"Simple. I've got a crew in the neighborhood and you're a friend of my daughter's." He removed a card from his wallet and handed it to her. "That makes you a friend of mine."

"I don't know what to say."

"Just give me the word and I'll have a workman here bright and early Monday morning."

"Well, sure. That would be great."

Again, Cordelia cleared her throat.

"Ah, look, Mr. Kastner—"

"Otto," he corrected her.

"Otto," Jane repeated, feeling more than a little uncomfortable. "Actually, I'm quite a good cook—"

"I know," he said, picking up one of the crumbling patio tiles. "I learned a good bit about you recently. Your father is Raymond Lawless, the well-known defense attorney. Your mother died when you were thirteen. Your brother, Peter, is a cameraman for WTWN in Minneapolis—married, no children. And you own a successful restaurant on Lake Harriet. I'm told you're a wonderful chef in your own right, although you employ some hot talent. Oh, and the cookbook you wrote two years ago has been a bestseller here locally." As he straightened back up, he added, "I had you thoroughly checked out."

This was news to her. "By whom?"

"A private service."

"You mean a private investigator?"

He nodded.

"But . . . why?"

He set the tile back down, then brushed some dust off his dark slacks. "I make it a point to know who my daughter's friends are."

"Really," said Cordelia, a hand rising to her hip, her earlier friendliness forgotten. "Does Jane get a letter grade, or do you do it pass/fail?"

"It's just a precaution. My family is worth a great deal of money. There are lots of unscrupulous people out there willing to take advantage of that fact. I simply satisfied myself that you're not one of them."

Jane and Cordelia exchanged glances.

"Thanks," said Jane. "I think."

"You were saying something about being a good cook?" continued Otto.

"Yes—I, ah, was. Actually, I was wondering if you and your wife would like to come over for dinner sometime soon. We'd do it when Elliot and Patricia could join us. And my friend Cordelia here."

By the scowl on Cordelia's face, Jane could tell she still hadn't recovered from the private eye announcement.

Otto's expression sobered. "No, that's not possible."

"What if we let your private investigator check out the menu first?" said Cordelia, scratching the bottom of her chin.

"Sorry. I'm afraid my wife would never agree to come to this neighborhood. Her son was severely injured many years ago when we were living in Linden Hills. The memories are still pretty painful."

"But . . . Patricia lives here," said Jane, pushing her dark glasses to the top of her head.

"I tried to talk her out of buying that house, but—you have to understand, the boy's accident happened before Patricia was born. *Her* experience with the neighborhood was a happy one."

"So you're saying your wife refuses to visit her?"

He nodded. "She returned home a few days ago, but I doubt she'll ever set foot in that house."

"So much for the dinner party," muttered Cordelia with a depressed shrug.

Jane had her own reasons for wanting to get to know the Kastner family better. She wasn't ready to quit on the idea just yet. "What about this? Why don't you come to the restaurant as my guests? Please, you have to let me repay you for the work you're going to do in my backyard. If you like, I could even arrange for the use of our private dining room."

"Wonderful idea," declared Cordelia, slapping Jane on the back so hard that she shot forward several feet.

"Well, I suppose——" Otto still hesitated.

"Ask your wife," said Jane, turning around at the sound of a car pulling into the drive. It was Earl Wilcox's white pickup. "We have a wonderful menu, or I could plan something special."

"I'll talk to Virginia," said Otto. "And then I'll give you a call. Now, it looks like you've got company. I better head upstairs— see if I can interest my kids in some lunch."

"Bon appetit," said Cordelia, grinning. As he walked away, the grin dissolved into a frustrated scowl. "Brother," she said sotto voce, "I hope Virginia is a little more people-friendly."

Jane nodded.

"And, speaking of the badly dressed and the hopelessly peculiar, who's *that*?" She pointed to the short, squat man in the garish Madras sport coat, lighting up a cigarette next to a truck.

"Just go finish your chocolate milk," said Jane. "I'll be right back."

13

Jane ushered Earl Wilcox into a small room off the living room, a den that also served as her home office. The mahogany desk, one that sat next to a window overlooking the rosebushes on the south side of the house, was piled high with books and papers, all part of a new project she was working on, a culinary memoir of her years growing up in England. The antique mohair couch was also covered with miscellany, but she quickly cleaned it off so they had a place to sit.

"Nice house," he said, chewing his gum energetically as his gaze bounced around the room. "And will you look at this." He walked up to a bookshelf that ran the length of one wall. "You must like to read."

"I do," said Jane. She sat down on the sofa and waited for him to do the same.

"You like Fitzgerald." He ran his fingers reverently down one row of books. "And . . . let's see." He repeated some of the names out loud as he moved to the next row. "Alice Walker, Margaret Atwood, Marilyn French, Kurt Vonnegut, Herman Hesse, Edith Wharton, Gore Vidal—you're well read. Mostly fiction. As an ex-English teacher, I'm impressed." He turned around and, still chewing, grinned at her.

"Thanks." He was a funny little man. Most of the time he tried hard to project a tough, Philip Marlowe image, but generally he missed it by miles. Jane figured he was smart enough to sense the failure, but probably enjoyed the charade too much to stop. As he continued to examine her books, she took a moment to examine him. In her opinion, instead of a tough guy, he looked more like the Amazing Mr. Toad from *The Wind in the Willows*. Even with the help of some dark noir lighting, his garish clothing and squat body would never be mistaken for Humphrey Bogart.

Moving over to an end table, Earl bent down to read the spines on a stack of trade paperbacks. "Armisted Maupin. I'm not familiar with him. He any good?" He glanced at Jane.

"Very."

He moved on to another bookshelf, this one along the far wall. "Hey? Are *all* of these cookbooks?"

"Afraid so."

"Yeah," he said, mulling that one over. After several thoughtful seconds, he raised a finger and said, "It fits. The puzzle's coming together."

"What puzzle?" she asked.

"You. People are always a puzzle when I first meet them. The fun part is putting the pieces together to see what you come up with." He finally took the seat next to her. "Books tell a lot about a person, you know. Take me, for instance. I like mysteries. Always have."

"Then you're in the right profession."

"Yeah," he said, turning thoughtful again. "But they never get it right. Most of the time a PI's job's pretty boring. Do you realize I've only been punched once?"

"Really?" She hid her amusement behind a rapt expression.

He lowered his voice. "I thought there'd be lots of danger and action when I first apprenticed with this licensed PI. My wife always told me, 'Earl, you're a real dangerous kind of guy.' " He winked. "I suppose I'm a little too old for the action part now, but I can still handle the danger. That is, if I ever run across any." He tapped his head. "I'd pit my wits against any punk. Criminals are dumb. Most cops will tell you that. Not that I come in contact with very many real criminals. Most of the time I'm staking out some dame because her old man's dead certain she's cheating on him—or vice versa. Not much danger in that—at least, for me." Another wink. "That's why the case I'm on now is so fascinating. Someone in that Kastner family is a bad seed, Jane. And I'm going to nail that sucker or my name isn't Earl Wesley Wilcox."

Shifting a grin, Jane turned to business. "Have you found out anything new?"

"You bet," he said, moving in closer. "Say"—his eyes darted to the open door—"are we alone?"

"Completely."

"What about—" His gaze rose to the ceiling.

"You mean Elliot? He's renting my third-floor apartment, remember?"

"Yeah, but can he get in here?"

"There's a connecting door, but I keep it locked."

This time he winked and nodded at the same time. "Good. You can't be too careful."

"So what did you find out?"

"Well," he said, expanding back against the cushions, "after we talked, I gassed up the old truck and drove back to Des Moines. I had some leads I wanted to run down. Remember that woman I told you about—Kevin Torland's neighbor?"

"The one who saw the fight?"

"You're quick on the uptake, Jane. I like that in a woman."

"I like that in a man, too."

He gave her a quizzical look, then continued, "I talked to her again. Seems she forgot to tell me something the first time we spoke. See, if you recall, Otto and Virginia Kastner would visit Kevin and Patricia on weekends. They always drove up in this big black Lincoln Town Car and parked in one of the two spaces in front of the town house. The car had Minnesota plates on it: KAST-NER-4. It wasn't hard for the neighbor to remember. Anyway, I checked on the plates this morning and the car is registered to Otto Kastner, 298 Red Fox Road, Eden Prairie. That's the Kastner family home."

"It's essentially what Patricia told me the other night."

"You've talked to her?" His eyes nearly popped out of his head.

She nodded. "I didn't learn all that much."

"But you learned *something*, right?"

"Well, mostly, we talked about her family history." Jane briefly covered the high points of the conversation.

As Earl listened, he lifted a pad and pen from his pocket and began jotting down notes. "That's good—very good. Anything else?"

"Just that Elliot doesn't get along with his parents very well, especially his stepfather. Patricia's worried about it. The one real point of interest had to do with Kevin Torland. Patricia said that her parents liked him a lot, but that Elliot wanted her to take it slow, not rush into anything—like marriage. Apparently Patricia and Kevin had only known each other a short time when they moved in together. Kevin was annoyed that Elliot was advising caution. I wondered if that wasn't what the fight in the parking lot was all about. If I read between the lines correctly, it seems that Kevin wanted a commitment from Patricia, but Elliot was advising against it—at least until she'd gotten to know him better."

Earl kept writing. "Excellent." After making a couple of final notations, he looked up. "I knew you were the right person for the job. You've got to keep digging, Jane. We need to get inside that Kastner family and find out what makes it tick."

He seemed so sure of himself. "Earl?" She watched him put away the notebook. "Do you ever have trouble getting your mind around the idea that some normal, average-looking person could commit a brutal murder?" It was a question she often asked herself, especially when she watched the evening news.

He shrugged. "Not really. People are never all good or all bad. And take it from me, doll, what you see isn't always what you get."

"Doll?" She couldn't help herself. She burst out laughing.

He seemed amused by the response. "We're gonna be a great team, you and me. I could tell right off. Now, let's get back to business. Remember I began telling you about that Lincoln Town Car the Kastners owned?"

She nodded.

"Well, it seems that the day Torland supposedly took his own life, that car was parked outside the town house."

"You mean the Kastners were there? Visiting him? Just before he died?"

"So it would seem."

"What time?" asked Jane.

"The neighbor noticed it around three. She was just coming back from a late lunch with a friend and walked right past the car on the way to her apartment. When she looked outside a little after four, it was gone."

"What did the medical examiner say specifically about the time of Kevin's death?" If Earl had mentioned it, she'd forgotten.

"It happened sometime between two and eight P.M. on Saturday, June twenty-sixth. They can't get much more specific than that."

Jane thought it over. This was obviously a key piece of information, but it was frustratingly incomplete. "That neighbor. She never actually saw either of the Kastners?"

"Nope. Only the car. Tantalizing, huh?"

"So it could have been Otto, Virginia, or both of them."

He nodded, snapping his gum.

"Have you formed a theory?"

"Not yet, but I will. The problem is, on that same Saturday night, both of the Kastners attended a reception at the Governor's Mansion in St. Paul. The reception started at five and I have several witnesses that say they saw them arrive around six. If one or both of them were in Des Moines at three, then how did they get back to the Twin Cities, change into formal clothes, and make it to a reception at six? It's two hundred and fifty miles away. Even if they broke all the speed laws, they still couldn't make it in time."

"Maybe the neighbor is wrong. Maybe she saw another car and just thought it was the one that belonged to the Kastners."

"With the name KASTNER on the license plate, there's very little room for doubt."

"Okay. Then, let's assume for the sake of argument that one of the Kastners *was* driving it that day. If you're going to murder someone and attempt to make it look like a suicide, then why park a vehicle with your name on it right outside the front door?"

"Good question. Maybe the murder wasn't planned. It just happened."

"So you're assuming whoever was in the car was the murderer?"

"No, but I think it's a possibility."

Jane took a deep breath and thought it through. "No matter which way we go with this, we're still left with the same question. How did one or both of the Kastners get back here by six?"

"I checked the airlines. No Kastner flew from Des Moines to Minneapolis on June twenty-sixth."

"A fake name?"

"How are you going to fake an ID on such short notice? Remember, if they'd planned to murder Kevin Torland, they wouldn't have parked their car out front. Either something happened that wasn't planned, or Kevin Torland was still alive when they left."

"A charter, then?"

"Maybe, but if that's the case, we may be up the creek. Charters are notoriously difficult to track. Depending on where they flew from and to, there may be no verifiable record at all."

"Don't pilots have to file a flight plan?"

He shook his head. "Not necessarily. And also, if they stay out of restricted airspace, they can do just about anything they want." He got up and walked over to the window. Staring morosely outside, he continued, "Somehow, Jane, we've got to find out who visited Kevin that day and why. My gut tells me it's a key piece of information. We're not going to solve this case without it." After nearly a minute, he turned around. "And there's something else."

She waited, watching him reach into his pocket and draw out a small cardboard box.

"On my way out of town, I stopped by the Torlands' home to talk to Emily. I wanted to give her an update on the investigation into her son's suicide. We sat on the porch and sipped some lemonade together. As I was leaving, she asked me to wait—said there was something she wanted to show me. She went into the house and came back a few seconds later carrying this." He lifted the cover off the box, revealing an eye, crudely carved out of wood.

Jane stood up and took it from his hand. "What's it mean?"

"Beats me. Emily Torland doesn't know, either."

"But . . . I don't understand. Where'd she get it?"

"The day Kevin died, the police found it in his pants pocket along with car keys and a nail clipper. When they returned all of his personal effects to her after the autopsy, she noticed it and it sort of bothered her, but she didn't think more about it until last week. That's when she took it out again and started asking his friends if they'd ever seen it before. No one had. Neither had her husband. It was beginning to really upset her. That's why she showed it to me."

Jane switched on the desk lamp and held the wooden eye underneath the light to examine it more closely. It was about two inches long and an inch high. The back was flat, the front curved.

The entire eye was represented, including the eyelids and lashes. Some dark substance had been rubbed over the surface to highlight the carving marks. "I can't imagine that it has any particular use. It's not heavy enough to be a paperweight. And as a work of art, it's pretty crude."

"It's a mystery all right."

Jane ran a finger over the deep gouge in the center of the eye, an artist's trick to highlight the pupil. What possible meaning could a wooden eye have to Kevin Torland? "Could I keep this for a couple of days?"

Earl shrugged. "Why not? It may mean something—or it may mean absolutely nothing. There could be a million reasons why Kevin Torland had it in his pocket the night he died. Or"—he handed Jane the box—"maybe someone put it there for a reason. This may sound strange, but sometimes murderers like to leave a calling card."

"You really think that's what it is?"

"Possibly. But any way you slice it, it still leaves us with the same problem. We don't know enough about the Kastner family to form any real conclusions. I'm glad you and Patricia had that talk—and I hope you'll have many more. But beyond that, is there any way you could get to know her parents? Do a little discreet fishing?"

"Well," said Jane. She perched on the edge of the desk. "Earlier today, I invited Otto and his wife to my restaurant for a private dinner. If it works out, I hope Elliot and Patricia will join us."

He stopped chewing. "When?"

"Next week, I hope."

"A meeting of the entire clan," Earl said, rubbing his hands together excitedly. "Man, I'd sure like to be a fly on the wall at that dinner party."

"Maybe that could be arranged."

He looked at her skeptically. "How?"

She had to do some checking before she gave him an answer.

"Earl, do you have a number where you can be reached? A hotel you're staying at? A cell phone?"

He narrowed one eye. "Well, I suppose I can trust you with that information—now that we're pals."

She didn't understand his reticence. "Of course you can, *doll*."

He grinned. "Look, the truth is, I often sleep in the back of my truck when I'm on assignment. It saves me a little money—and when you're in my profession, every buck counts."

"You mean—"

"I was in the truck the other night when you came over to look at it. I parked it across the street from Patricia's house so I could keep an eye on her."

"Do you realize that she saw it earlier in the day parked outside the corporate offices? She thinks the truck's been following her."

"No shit." He seemed upset. "I've got to be more careful." He handed her a business card, explaining that his cell phone number was on the back. "Maybe I better move it out of your drive."

The drive! Jane hadn't thought of that. "Patricia is upstairs right now—or at least I think she is."

He bolted for the door. "Sometimes I'm as thick as a brick." Turning briefly, he added, "I really *am* good at my job, Jane."

"I believe you—and I'll call you if I have any news."

" 'Bye," he called, racing off.

Once the front door had slammed shut, Jane placed the wooden eye back in the box and put it away in the top drawer of the desk. As she walked through the kitchen out onto the back porch, an idea began to form. Coming to a quick decision, she shouted, "Cordelia?"

Cordelia raised a limp hand. "I'm baked on this side, Janey. Thanks for reminding me. I better turn over."

"Forget the sunbathing. Get in here right away."

"Excuse me?"

"You need to put some clothes on."

Cordelia propped herself up on both elbows. "Dare I ask why?"

"I've got a hunch about something."

"How exciting. Perhaps we should send out a press release."

"We're going for a drive, Cordelia."

"*We?*" She fluffed her auburn curls. "Where, pray tell?"

"I'll explain everything you need to know in the car on the way."

14

I feel sick," mumbled Cordelia, holding her stomach and staring straight ahead out the front windshield. "Just think about it. The woman who holds the power of life and death over my career is a freaking murderer."

"I said it was *possible*," replied Jane, flipping on her right-turn signal and easing her car onto the highway 212 off-ramp.

"Oh, no. The way my luck is going, she's probably a serial killer."

Jane looked sideways and saw that Cordelia had pulled her straw sun hat down over her eyes. "Stay with me, doll. I'm not finished with my story yet."

"Doll?" Cordelia raised the brim and shot Jane a pained look. "It's finally happened, Janey. You've become a character in a Dashiell Hammett novel. I warned you about this years ago, didn't I? Didn't I!"

Jane let her rant for a few more seconds and then cut in, "Don't you want to know where we're going?"

"What? Of course I do. I'm breathless with anticipation." She tapped her fingers on the armrest.

Jane glanced out the window and saw that they were now on

Flying Cloud Drive. Perfect. They'd left in such a hurry, she hadn't had time to consult a map. "Okay, so back to the story. Remember I told you that the Kastners' car was parked outside Kevin Torland's town house on the day he supposedly took his own life?"

"Right. And you don't know how the driver got back to the Twin Cities in time to for a suck-up session at the Gov's Mansion."

"As far as I can figure it, there's only one way." She pointed to a small plane approaching the highway from the Minnesota River valley.

Cordelia turned to look, watching it zoom across the road and dip almost immediately, landing on a strip of runway on the other side. "Flying Cloud Field," she said, twisting her head around to watch the metal hangars whiz past. "What a hoot. I haven't been out here since I was in high school."

"What were you doing here in high school?"

She wiggled her eyebrows suggestively. "Not that it's any of your business, but I was learning about life."

Jane took the next right and swung the Pathfinder into the parking lot of a charter terminal. She pulled up next to a chain-link fence and stopped. On the other side of the fence was a twin-engine plane, its door open, ready for boarding.

"You think they used a charter?" asked Cordelia.

"Maybe. But before we left the house, I got to thinking about something Patricia said the other night. She was telling me we should go skydiving together sometime—and that there was a King Air waiting for us at Flying Cloud Airport whenever we wanted to use it."

Cordelia did a double take. "*You're* going skydiving!"

"Of course not," said Jane, amused by the horrified look on Cordelia's face. "But what I'm telling you is that Patricia has access to a plane. Maybe her dad flies for fun—like my dad. Or maybe Otto or Virginia has a corporate plane stored out here in one of these hangars. If that's true, then it's possible they employ a pilot, and one way or another, I might have a chance to get the information I want out of him." She looked off in the distance. "The only problem is, how are we going to find out? I can't just walk around and knock on hangar doors. There are hundreds of them—and no central terminal."

"You do have a problem. Seems to me the first order of business is to find out whether Kastner Gardens or Kastner Construction has a corporate plane." Cordelia grabbed her cell phone out of her purse. "Just sit back and relax—let me handle it." After calling directory assistance for the numbers of the two corporate offices, Cordelia punched in the one for Kastner Gardens. When the secretary answered, she used a voice straight out of the movie, *Fargo*. "Yah. This is Mavis Olson of Olson Aviation. I got a mechanic on his way out to Flying Cloud Airport to look at your King Air." She paused. "Ya don't? Not even a cheap little Cessna? What sort of corporation are ya?" Her expression grew indignant. "Well, ya don't have to get huffy. Thanks for your time."

"Strike one," said Jane. "Say, Cordelia?"

"Hum?"

"Try to be a little nicer."

"I'm always nice," Cordelia snarled. She punched in the second number. Several seconds later, in a voice that was far more cultured, she said, "This is Phoebe Carrington of Carrington Aviation. I've got a mechanic on his way out to Flying Cloud Field to look at your King Air." She paused. "Really? Yes, they're terrific planes. I own a fleet of them myself. What?" Another pause. "Well, we think the problem's in the fuel . . . thingie. Anyway, my mechanic called en route and said he'd misplaced the hangar number. Can you give that to me?" She smiled at Jane. "438HPL. Big gray building, flat white roof. East section of the airfield. Great. That should do it. Oh, and your pilot? His first name was"—she waited, closing her eyes prayerfully—"Bob. Bob Johnson. Sure, I realize you only use him when Mr. Kastner doesn't want to fly himself. I always have a spare pilot sit in the back of my plane when I fly, just in case I get tired—or want to devote my full attention to lunch. But you see, Bob's supposed to meet my mechanic at the field. Say, tell me, is Bob a pretty good pilot?" She listened. "No kidding? Well, yes, if you're going to crash-land on a highway it's good to do it next to a Burger King." She shot Jane an appalled look. "How did you find him?" More silence. "Bjornstad Charter Service. I've never heard of that one. Ah, that's why. We only have contracts with the larger companies." She gave a fake titter. "Yes, you're absolutely right, my dear. We were all small once—though some of us were smaller than others."

Jane drew a finger across her throat.

"Let me ask you another question," said Cordelia, removing her yellow sun hat. "It says here on my work order that the fuel problem started back on June twenty-sixth. Do you have any record of where Mr. Kastner was that day? It could be important." She waited.

Jane was amazed not only at Cordelia's gall but at her uncanny ability to wheedle information out of an unsuspecting secretary.

"Is that right? Aberdeen, South Dakota. Lovely spot. Wonderful wine country. You say they left early in the morning and didn't get back until around five? Does that mean that Mr. Kastner had Bob do the flying that day?" Cordelia nodded an affirmative. "Well, you've been very helpful. I'll remember to tell that to Mr. Kastner the next time we talk." She smiled. "Yes, I promise. We'll have that fuel thingie fixed before you can say, 'Sorry, but we sent your luggage to Cleveland.' " She laughed. "Just a little aviation joke. Have a splendid day."

As Cordelia flipped the phone shut, Jane let out a cheer. "Bravo!"

Whipping off her sunglasses, Cordelia took a bow. "You owe me an expensive lunch."

"Done."

"I'm hungry *now*. Something French would be nice."

"First we've got to find Bjornstad Charter Service. I'd like to talk to Bob Johnson."

"Why?"

"Maybe they flew to Aberdeen and maybe they didn't."

"You think old Bob's going to be as easy to get information out of as that secretary?"

It was a good question. "Got any ideas how it could be done?"

"I'd go with thumbscrews. Janey, this is a waste of time. He's not going to talk to you."

She was probably right. Still, she had to try. "Let's just find the office and see what happens." She looked around, adjusting her sunglasses. "That charter terminal is blocking our line of vision. Come on," she said, backing the car up. "Let's drive around."

As they turned onto the highway, Cordelia found an old Benny Goodman tape in the glove compartment and slipped it in the tape deck. "I thought you didn't like jazz."

"I don't like *modern* jazz. And yes, Cordelia, I know it's not cool to dislike jazz."

"I can tell you're truly haunted by your dislike, Jane. You're *so* cutting edge."

"Hey, look. Over there." Jane pointed to a low cement block building next to a line of hangars. On the front a sign said: BJORN-STAD CHARTERS. FLY WITH THE BEST! A newer white metal building sitting directly next to it boasted another sign, this one in tall fire-engine-red letters: PETERSON AVIATION. LEASING. CHARTERS. HOURLY AND DAILY RATES.

Jane pulled into the lot, but unlike the charter terminal, nobody appeared to be around. As she came to a stop a few yards from the front door, she noticed tufts of grass sprouting around the perimeter of Bjornstad Charters. It made the exterior look scruffy and uncared for. Not very good advertising.

"I want to see if anyone's around," she said. Turning off the motor, she eased out of the front seat and walked around the back of the car. There was one window in the front of the building, but the shade was drawn so she couldn't see inside. Walking up to the door, she knocked several times and then waited.

"Nobody's home," said Cordelia, tapping her hand on the car door to the rhythm of the orchestra. "Come on, Janey. I'm wasting away. I need sustenance. Fat grams. Empty calories."

Jane stood back and looked at the other building. A single-engine plane was parked on the tarmac just a few feet from a rear door, but it seemed clear that Peterson Aviation was as deserted as Bjornstad Charters.

"What did you expect?" said Cordelia, turning off the music. "American Airlines?"

Just then, the door of the white metal building opened and a middle-aged man walked out, locking the door behind him. Seeing Jane, he nodded. "Looking for someone?" he asked, pocketing his keys.

"Actually, I am. I was hoping to find a pilot—Bob Johnson."

He eyed her for a moment, then took a Twins baseball cap out of his back pocket and put it on. "He's in Fort Wayne. Flew a party down there a couple days ago. If you want to reach him, just call the main number and leave a message."

Since she'd found an actual human being to talk to, Jane decided to take advantage of it. "I understand he flies for Otto Kastner."

The man rested his hands on his hips. "Yeah, I think that's right."

"Do you know if Mr. Kastner ever uses any other pilots?"

"How come you're so interested?"

Jane had to think fast. "I'm a good friend of his daughter's. She's invited me to go skydiving with her and I just thought I'd check out the plane, the pilot . . . you know. Get the lay of the land."

He grinned. "You're kinda nervous, huh? This your first time?"

"Is it that obvious?"

" 'Fraid so. But you got nothing to worry about. Bob's a great pilot. I should know—I taught him everything he knows."

"You're a pilot too?"

"Going on twenty years."

"I'm curious, Mr.—"

"Peterson. Roy Peterson."

"I'm just curious, Mr. Peterson. If I wanted to find out where a plane had flown on any given day, is there any way I could do it?"

"Well, pilots usually keep a log."

"But I assume that's private information."

"Usually, yeah. Why do you ask?"

Jane knew Cordelia would probably have handled this a lot more cleverly, but she pushed on. "Look, Mr. Peterson, I think I should be straight with you. What I said about Patricia Kastner being my friend is true. But also my father is Raymond Lawless. He's—"

"You mean the defense attorney?"

She nodded, silently thanking the stars that her father was such a local celebrity. "I'm helping him with a case."

He hesitated. "What do you need to know?"

"I'm trying to find out if Bob Johnson flew one or both of the Kastners to Des Moines on June twenty-sixth, or perhaps flew down and picked one or both of them up. I can assure you, Mr. Peterson, Bob Johnson's done nothing wrong."

He poked a finger under the brim of his hat, pushing it back on his head. "But maybe one of the Kastners has?"

"I'm not at liberty to talk about that." She knew she sounded incredibly stuffy, but didn't know what else to say. She also knew she was taking a chance. If Peterson passed this information on to Bob Johnson, and Johnson in turn passed it on to Otto Kastner, she could be in big trouble. But if she was going to make any headway in helping Earl Wilcox with the investigation, she had to take a few risks.

She watched Peterson digest the information, sensing his

growing suspicion. After several uncomfortable seconds, she forged on. She slipped a business card out of her wallet and handed it over. "My name's Jane Lawless. You can reach me at either of these numbers. If you come across anything that you think might be helpful, give me a ring. And . . . if you could keep this conversation just between the two of us, I'd appreciate it."

He stared at the card, then looked back at Jane. "I guess."

She figured he'd toss it in the trash the first chance he got.

After thanking him for his time, she walked back to the car. Peterson crossed quickly to the plane and leaned down to examine part of the landing gear.

Jane watched him for a moment, wondering what he thought of the whole interaction. When she finally returned to the front seat of her car, she immediately saw the scowl on Cordelia's face. "Don't say it. That was dumb, right? I should never have talked to him."

"Well, let's put it this way," said Cordelia, dropping the sun hat back over her auburn curls, "you may lack my clever charm, but you make up for it in earnestness."

"Gee, thanks."

"Just take my advice, Janey. I wouldn't sit by the phone and wait for him to call."

15

When Elliot heard the knock on the door, he quickly put away his newest project and got up to answer it. This was turning out to be his day for visitors. He'd finally gotten rid of Patricia and Otto only to be interrupted by a phone call from his editor, and then another, far more annoying one from his agent. At the rate he was going, he'd never get anything done. Not that he'd found this glorified attic all that conducive to sustained concentration.

Swinging open the door, he squinted into the bright afternoon sunlight. "Oh." He took a drag from his cigarette, letting the smoke float out through the screen. "What do you want?"

"You gonna invite me in?" asked Harry Engsdahl.

"I don't know. Why should I?"

"We need to talk."

"About what?"

The officer ran a hand across the back of his neck, wiping away the sweat. "Look, I already told you about that case I was assigned to."

"And I told you I wasn't interested."

They stared at each other through the screen, the sound of a siren blasting somewhere in the distance.

"This is a bad one, Elliot. Really bad. A fifty-year-old man was stabbed to death in his basement on Monday afternoon. He lived over by Lake Calhoun. Nice, decent family. I'll be honest with you. So far, we're stumped." He hooked a thumb over his belt and leaned closer to the door. "See, his wife came home around two—I guess she'd been shopping at Southdale—and found him lying in a pool of blood on the laundry-room floor. I saw the body. Must have been thirty knife wounds in it, maybe more. He never had a prayer. The wife started screaming and didn't stop until a neighbor came over to see what was wrong. He's the one who called us."

Elliot listened to the scenario with little interest. "Murder-apolis, right? Seems to me the name fits."

Engsdahl's face hardened. "I'm not willing to give up on the city just yet." He hesitated, then continued, a bit more gently this time. "How about it, Elliot? You got any community feeling left, or was that just a fluke last Saturday night?"

Elliot didn't like being challenged, though he knew what Engsdahl was doing. A little bit of well-placed psychological manipulation went a long way—with some people. Not with him. He could see right through the ploy, but he could also see some advantage in playing along. Just this once. "If I agree to help you, I can't promise anything."

"I know. My car's right outside."

Elliot glanced back at his desk. With his headache and his runny nose he felt like shit, but maybe Patricia was right. It wasn't good to antagonize the cops—especially with *his* past. Better that Engsdahl be in his camp. "All right. Let me just grab my keys and switch off my computer."

"Thanks, Elliot. I owe you one."

As they drove north along Sheridan, Engsdahl turned on the air conditioning. "I thought we were done with the heat."

Elliot didn't think the statement required a response, so he just kept looking out the side window. Maybe this was a mistake. After all, what the hell could he do to help?

Engsdahl made a right and headed for the lake. "I should tell you—I did some checking into your background." He paused, glanced at Elliot, then returned his attention to the traffic. "You were kind of a mystery man last weekend. I prefer knowing who I'm dealing with."

"And?" Elliot turned to look at him.

"I hear you had some problems when you were younger."

"Yeah, and I've been clean for years."

Engsdahl nodded. "So it would seem."

"You think I'm lying?"

He shrugged. "I know you're a writer, a pretty successful one at that, so I doubt you break into garages to steal snowblowers anymore."

Elliot had stolen a lot more than a few lousy snowblowers. Thank God the cops never figured out the half of what he'd done, otherwise he would have spent some hard time in jail. With his parents' lawyers playing every card in their very expensive decks, the juvie hall folks never had a chance. It was the psychologists that had really pissed him off. He'd rather be beaten to a bloody pulp than have someone mess with his mind.

"Why'd you do it, Elliot? All the stealing. The fights. Was it the usual crappy childhood?"

Who did this guy think he was, asking so many personal questions? "Something like that."

"I know who your parents are."

Elliot laughed. "Well, then, you know everything."

"Pardon me?"

"I've heard it all before, Harry. I must be crazy, right? I had everything going for me and I still screwed up."

Engsdahl stopped the car at a red light, then turned and studied Elliot for a moment. "Was it hard? Being a kid and being psychic, I mean? I've talked to other people who said it drove them nuts, made them feel weird, different, even abnormal. That's tough—especially when you're young and you want desperately to fit in. Since nobody understood, these kids just stopped talking about it. They ended up feeling isolated—totally alone. Like there was something wrong with *them*. Is that how you felt, Elliot? Alone?"

He needed a cigarette. As he reached for one, he realized his hand was shaking. "Yeah. I suppose."

"So you acted out."

"You a psychologist?"

Engsdahl smiled. "No, but it's a pattern I've seen many times over the years."

The fact was, Engsdahl was right. Elliot not only felt alone, he'd *been* alone ever since his brother Jay had fallen off that goddamned roof. All people ever saw when they looked at his family was the money and the power. It took too much creative effort to imagine that a rich, well-respected couple could also be twisted to the core. That was why, as soon as he felt he could, he'd left. He'd only stayed as long as he had because of his sister. He couldn't leave her all alone, not with *them*. On the other hand, his mother and Otto may have spent their lives ignoring his needs, but it seemed they were going to make up for it by showering Patricia with everything her little heart desired. Everything, that is, except their time and a small word: No. Elliot was the one who'd really raised Patricia—and it had been a struggle.

As a boy and eventually a young man, Elliot had had his own problems to deal with. But he'd tried with Patricia. God knows, he'd given it his best shot. It was hard attempting to rein in such a forceful, headstrong personality. Patricia was all fire and lightning—very different from him. And yet so special, so lovable. Patricia needed a firm hand, that's all. He'd tried to provide that for her, and in her heart, he knew she understood why he didn't always go along with her ideas, didn't always approve of her actions. His mother and Otto were ridiculously overprotective of their

129

only daughter, but they rarely gave her any guidance. Couldn't they see that their behavior was a prescription for disaster?

"There's the house," said Engsdahl, pointing to a Craftsman-style bungalow nestled into a wooded lot.

Elliot was glad they'd arrived. He didn't like discussing the intimate details of his life, especially with a stranger. "Is anyone home?"

"I stopped on the way over to your place. The wife answered the door, but said she was just leaving to go pick up her son from soccer practice. I guess he's a real ace. She said she'd be back in a few minutes. Her daughter was still at school; she's the editor of the school paper, by the way, and probably won't be home until suppertime. She seems like a great kid so I'm sorry you won't meet her. Anyway, I told Mrs. Altman I might bring a psychic by."

"I bet she loved that."

Engsdahl pulled the car up to the curb and cut the motor. Turning to Elliot, he continued, "I was hoping you'd go in and just get a feel for the place. You know what I'm asking."

Elliot nodded.

"Maybe you'll get a sense of who might have murdered the man. I have to say, in a situation like this, we look pretty hard at the family. But the wife wasn't at the house—we have witnesses that put her at JCPenneys at the time of the murder. And both of the kids were at school."

"What about the neighbor? Didn't you say he was the one who called the police?"

"Yeah." Engsdahl pulled a notebook from his pocket and flipped through the pages. "His name is Fergussen. Art Fergussen. A retired bus driver. We got his statement later that same afternoon. Seems he was just finishing his lunch when he heard some woman screaming. When the racket didn't stop, he went outside to see what was up. The screams led him into the back door of the Altmans' home."

"How did he get in?"

Engsdahl nodded, then smiled. "You're pretty good at this. That's the same question I asked. Fergussen said he'd known the family for years, even took care of their dog when they were out of town. That meant he knew where they kept their extra key."

"And that's how he got in."

"Exactly. He raced downstairs and found Eula Altman on her knees, bending over her husband. She was covered in blood, but that was understandable since there was blood all over the floor— the walls, the washer and dryer."

"Did you ask the neighbor specific questions about the family? What they were like?"

"Sure. In a nutshell, Fergussen said the Altmans were just your average, middle-class family. The son, Greg, is in tenth grade. The daughter, Melinda, is a senior—both at Washburn. Also, both were good students and seemed to get along with their parents. Well, Fergussen said there was the occasional fight, but nothing out of the ordinary. The marriage seemed solid enough. Frank Altman was a salesman for Varani's Pasta Products. His hours were erratic, but according to his wife, he didn't have any enemies, at least none she knew about."

"Could the neighbor have done it?"

"He's pretty old. In his late seventies. Altman was a fairly big man, and much younger. It's not impossible, but it would have been difficult."

"Does the neighbor have a wife?"

"Nope. He lives alone."

Elliot thought about it for a few seconds and then asked, "Was anything stolen from the house?"

Engsdahl shook his head. "Not a thing."

"So you're looking for a motive."

"And a suspect. Right now we've got zip."

Elliot opened the car door and got out. As he leaned against the front fender, looking the house over, Engsdahl joined him.

"You want to go in?" asked the sergeant.

131

He didn't want to go anywhere but home. "The wife and son are inside?"

"As far as I know."

Elliot nodded, then took a deep breath. "Okay. Let's do it."

Engsdahl led the way. After ringing the bell, they both waited on the front steps. When no one answered, Engsdahl rang again. This time, the door opened almost immediately. Behind the screen, Elliot could see a large, disheveled woman holding a cigarette in one hand, a glass in the other. Even a few feet away, he could smell the liquor. "Home sweet home," he whispered under his breath.

"Mrs. Altman?" said Engsdahl, taking off his shades, "This is the man I was telling you about. Elliot Beauman. He's here in an unofficial capacity. I'd appreciate it if you'd let us come in."

She took a quick, nervous puff on her cigarette. Wiping a tear away from her cheek, she said, "This is a very bad time for me and my family, Sergeant Engsdahl."

"I realize that, ma'am. We're simply trying to find out how your husband died. I know you want that, too."

"Of course I do." She ran a hand through her hair, almost as if she were trying to wake herself up. "He's the psychic?" She eyed Elliot with distrust.

"That's correct," said Engsdahl. "So . . . can we come in?"

After several seconds of strained silence, she relented. "Oh, all right. But I hope you can do this quickly. I need to get dinner started." She continued to scrutinize Elliot as he moved into the front room. "It kinda feels funny having someone like him in here. I feel . . . I don't know. Sort of naked. Like he can read all my thoughts."

"It doesn't work like that," said Elliot, amused that she wasn't able to address him directly. He walked between the couch and the coffee table on his way to the fireplace.

"What's he doing?"

"Just give him some space, Mrs. Altman," said Engsdahl.

After glancing at the photos on the mantel, Elliot closed his eyes for a few seconds.

"What's he doing now?" she asked, studying him with a worried expression.

Engsdahl held a finger to his lips. "Why don't we go in the kitchen, Mrs. Altman? Give him some privacy."

Elliot continued to move about the room, running the tips of his fingers over various knickknacks. Finally, he crouched down, placing both hands flat on the carpeting.

"I didn't run the sweeper this week. Tell him that. Tell him I'm usually a good housekeeper." She brushed some dust off an end table. "But I . . . I—" She started to sniff, then broke into tears. "What's the difference anymore? With Frank gone, who's going to notice?"

"I know this is hard on you, Mrs. Altman, but if we could just give Elliot a few minutes alone."

"I'd like to see the basement now," said Elliot, standing up.

"But . . . it's not cleaned yet," said Mrs. Altman, a shocked look on her face. "I couldn't do it myself . . . I called a service . . . I want it done but it's not . . . not yet. Nobody can go down there until—" Again, she burst into tears.

Elliot and Engsdahl exchanged glances.

"It's through the kitchen and down the back steps," said Engsdahl, pointing the way.

Elliot took it as his cue to leave. Moving quickly into the messy kitchen, he descended the steep wooden steps. The basement below was damp, cluttered with years of accumulated junk. In one corner he could see a workbench surrounded by tools and an electric saw. The laundry room was directly to his left. Rounding the corner, he came face to face with horror. The bloodstains were dark now—in the dim light they almost looked black. Engsdahl had been right. Traces of the sticky liquid were everywhere; so was a faint odor of decay. Mrs. Altman would want to get it cleaned up and *soon*—before the smell became permanent. Not that she'd stay here. Elliot couldn't imagine why any sane person would want to live in a house after a loved one had met with a violent death inside its walls. She'd probably want to move right away. Then again, Elliot had been forced to live in the same house where his brother had been murdered. He'd survived.

The intensity of his memories made him momentarily dizzy. He reached out and steadied himself against the dryer. There wasn't as much blood with Jay's death, but there was every bit as much anger. That's what this room reeked of. Hate. And it didn't take a psychic to figure that out.

Fifteen minutes later, Elliot returned to the living room. Engsdahl and Mrs. Altman were sitting on the couch, talking quietly. The golden liquid in Mrs. Altman's glass had miraculously increased. She'd obviously poured herself another.

"All done?" asked Engsdahl.

Elliot nodded, stuffing his hands into the pockets of his jeans.

"Ask him if he learned anything," whispered Mrs. Altman, pulling her skirt down primly over her knees. She was trying to appear normal, though the slurred speech and the bobbing head spoke far more loudly than any attempt at fake propriety.

Elliot was about to respond when he heard a loud, rumbling noise behind him. A second later, Mrs. Altman's son reached the bottom of the stairs and burst into the living room. He was an athletic-looking young guy. Fresh-faced, even handsome.

"Greg, come and sit by your mother." Mrs. Altman patted the couch.

As Greg looked from face to face, his expression grew sullen. "Who are *they*?"

"You remember me, Greg," said Sergeant Engsdahl. "We talked the other day down at the police station."

"Oh." He looked down at his hands. "Sure."

"This man is a psychic, Greg," said Mrs. Altman, nodding to Elliot. She acted almost pleased with the situation, though Elliot

134

figured she simply liked to show that she knew stuff her son didn't.

Greg didn't look up. "That's nice. I'm . . . ah, gonna go fix myself a sandwich."

"That's fine, honey," said Mrs. Altman, waving him away with an expansive gesture. Glancing at Sergeant Engsdahl, she added, "He's such a good boy. He and Frank were very close." Sniffing into a tissue, she added, "He's taking his father's death very hard."

Engsdahl nodded and then rose. "Is there anything else you want to look at while you're here, Elliot?"

"No, I'm finished."

"Good. Well, then, thank you for your time, Mrs. Altman. Don't get up. We'll show ourselves out."

"But what did you learn?" asked Mrs. Altman.

Elliot was already to the door. Turning around, he fixed her with a serious look. It was the first time she'd spoken to him directly and he figured she deserved an answer. "Not much, I'm afraid. I'm sorry."

She nodded. "Thanks for being so honest."

Once they got back out to the car, Engsdahl said, "You didn't learn *anything*?" He unlocked the door, looking deeply frustrated.

Elliot shrugged. "Like I said, I'm sorry." Glancing back over his shoulder, he saw that Greg Altman had come through the side gate and was watching them from behind a clumped birch. For a split second, their eyes met.

Turning away, Elliot slid into the front seat and rolled down his window.

Engsdahl walked around to the driver's side and did the same. After starting the motor, he pulled into the street and headed back to Linden Hills.

Neither of them spoke for several minutes.

When they finally reached Lake Harriet, Elliot said, "Check out the son."

"What?" The sergeant looked over at him.

"He did it."

Engsdahl hit the brakes, nearly missing a stop sign. "You're . . . sure?"

Elliot tilted his head back and closed his eyes. "I'm sure."

16

It was late Friday afternoon. Still no call from Julia. After driving back from Flying Cloud airfield, Jane dropped Cordelia off at the house and then walked over to the restaurant. With so much weighing on her mind right now, she had a terrible time concentrating on her work. Around four, she decided to call it a day.

Returning to the house, she found that Cordelia had already left for the theater. She'd scribbled Jane a note saying she wouldn't be back until late—if at all. She was having dinner with her newest love—Neva Moore, a gorgeous African-American set designer—and would probably spend the night at her place.

Jane luxuriated in the unexpected peace and quiet by pouring herself a glass of iced tea and sitting for a few minutes on the back porch. She'd already retrieved the hand-carved wooden eye from her desk drawer so that she could look at it again, study every inch of it in an effort to form some conclusion about what it might mean.

Touching the rough surface with the tips of her fingers, she couldn't help but wonder what a psychic would make of something like this—if there *were* such people as psychics. Maybe it gave off vibrations. If it did, Jane was oblivious to them. To her, it just looked like someone's pathetic attempt to whittle an eye out of a small block of wood. Nothing to write home about. Certainly the artist couldn't have had any pretensions about what he'd done. The fact that it was so poorly made, almost childlike in its crude simplicity, gave it a kind of primitive energy, but so what? What, if anything, did it mean? Why had it been in Kevin Torland's pocket on the day he died? There could be a million reasons; but if it was put there by his murderer, as Earl suggested, it was a vital clue, something they would need to understand to solve the mystery of how Kevin really died.

Finishing her tea, she glanced at the crumbling patio, wondering what the new greenhouse would look like—once it was built. With Kastner Construction starting on the cement slab bright and early Monday morning, everything would be ready for Edgar and his own construction plans first thing next spring. Jane couldn't believe her good luck. Not that she felt completely at ease with the situation. Otto Kastner had been incredibly generous, and yet here she was, trying to find information that might prove he—or someone in his family—was a murderer. It didn't seem right. Then again, if she waited for the other construction companies to come through with an actual work crew, she might still be waiting for them next June. Besides, Earl Wilcox could be wrong about the Kastner family. Maybe Kevin Torland *had* committed suicide. Since Jane didn't know anything for an absolute fact, there was no particular reason to turn down Otto Kastner's offer. At least, that was the rationalization she'd picked to assuage her guilty conscience.

Checking to make sure all the doors were locked, Jane poured herself a glass of wine and went upstairs. A few minutes later she stepped into the shower, leaving the door open so she could hear a Chopin étude. The cool water felt wonderful against her hot skin. And the music reminded her of the times she'd spent here, in this house, with Christine. She wasn't quite sure why she'd selected that particular CD, but now she knew. On nights like this, she ached to touch Christine again. To talk to her. To sit on the back porch together and just watch the sun set. Sometimes she missed her so much it almost took her breath away.

Jane returned to her bedroom a few minutes later feeling an intense melancholy. It was always there somewhere inside her, though most of the time it stayed beneath the surface. And yet, in a way, she welcomed these moments. After many years she finally realized that *this* was her connection to Christine. In that place of wistfulness her memories were still alive and vivid.

Switching off the CD, she sat down on the bed, closed her eyes, and for a few seconds listened to the silence. Not the quiet without, but stillness within her own soul. It never lasted very long. Tonight was no exception. She picked up her wineglass and took a last sip, and then the moment was gone.

As she was about to get dressed, she was startled to hear a noise downstairs. It was a low, grating sound, as if someone were opening and then closing the kitchen drawers. She walked to the edge of the stairs and looked down, noticing that a light was on in the kitchen. She didn't remember turning on the overhead light, but that didn't mean she hadn't. A second later, she heard another noise. This time it sounded as though someone was in the dining room. "Cordelia?" she called. "Are you back?"

The noise stopped.

"Cordelia?"

No one else had a key to the house—except Beryl and Edgar, and of course their next-door neighbor, Evelyn Bratrude. But why would Evelyn come over? "Mrs. Bratrude?" she called. "Is that you?"

She listened for another couple of seconds, but when no more sounds were forthcoming, she shrugged it off. It had to be the cats. She would never get used to them. At the same time, she refused to become some jumpy female upset by every unexplained sound.

After slipping into a clean shirt and cutoffs, she went downstairs. She checked all the doors again, and then walked through the rooms, even looking into some of the closets. Everything was quiet and secure. Blanche and Melville were sitting on the kitchen counter, so that no doubt explained the noise in the kitchen. Lucifer was nowhere to be found, but that was normal, too. So much for her momentary fright.

Jane knew she should probably think about making herself some dinner, but she wasn't in the mood, not just yet. Instead, she put on a pot of coffee to brew. She hadn't been able to get any work done at the restaurant, but maybe she'd have better luck here where there were fewer distractions.

When she entered her den a few minutes later, she found Bean asleep on the rug in front of the sofa. Sitting down behind the desk, she felt a welcome breeze pass through the open window and gently rustle her wet hair. The rosebushes on the south side of the house smelled incredibly sweet this year. It was a moment she should be savoring, and yet, as her eyes found the framed photo of Julia, the one that rested next to her desk lamp, she knew it was impossible. It had been five days since they'd last spoken. Julia had returned none of her calls. Something was wrong.

Picking up the phone, Jane tried Julia's home number again. When the answering machine clicked on, she hung up. Leaving another message was pointless.

Grabbing her personal phone book from the top of a black metal filing cabinet, she looked up the number for Julia's office in Earlton. Julia had instructed her not to call the clinic unless it was an absolute emergency. Well, damn it. This felt like one to Jane.

She punched in the number. After a couple of rings a woman's voice answered. "Earlton Clinic. May I help you?"

"I'd like to speak with Julia Martinsen."

"Dr. Martinsen is out of the office until next Wednesday."

"Wednesday?"

"She's only here two days a week."

This was news to Jane. "Does she work someplace else? The hospital maybe?"

"I think she does some private medical consulting."

Jane didn't have a clue what that meant. "Well, do you know how I can reach her?"

"Are you a patient?"

"No, a friend. I'm calling from Minneapolis."

"Oh, hi. Well, Dr. Martinsen has been out of town all week."

"She has?" Jane tried to hide the surprise in her voice.

"Let me check her schedule to see when she gets back." The woman rattled some papers. "Yes, her flight got into Twin Cities International at three forty-two this afternoon. She had a layover and then the connecting flight to Grand Rapids was due to arrive there shortly after five. I'd say she should be back to her house sometime this evening. Do you have her home number?"

"I do."

"If she stops in here first, would you like to leave her a message?"

"No," said Jane. "I'll catch her at home. Thanks." So, Julia had been in Minneapolis today and hadn't called? Jane couldn't understand it. "Say, I wonder if you could tell me where Julia's flight originated from?"

"Sorry. All I have is the carrier and the flight number. It's Northwest, flight five seven three."

Jane wrote it down. "I appreciate the information." After saying good-bye, she hung up and then leaned back in her chair feeling totally confused.

Okay, she thought to herself, let's take it one step at a time. If Julia had been out of town, maybe she hadn't checked her voice mail—although, when Jane left town, she always checked hers. Most professional people did. Next, why hadn't Julia said anything to her about going away? Was this just one more of her little secrets? Like her consulting business—whatever the hell that meant.

The more Jane thought about it, the angrier she got. She was about to leave an angry message on Julia's machine when she heard the front doorbell chime.

"Damn," she muttered, nearly falling over Bean on her way out of the room. "Sorry, kiddo," she said, patting him on the head. She raced into the front hall and pulled back the door.

Outside stood her sister-in-law, a suitcase resting next to her on the steps. "Sigrid! Hi." She glanced over Sigrid's shoulder out to the street. "Is my brother here too?"

"No." Sigrid touched a tentative hand to her sunglasses.

Jane couldn't quite fathom the need for the shades since what light there was was fading fast. "What's up? You need a ride to the airport?"

She shook her head.

"But you're going somewhere, right?"

"In a manner of speaking. Can I come in?"

"Sure," said Jane, stepping back from the door. She was always glad to see her sister-in-law, though Sigrid rarely just dropped by.

Setting her suitcase down, Sigrid continued, "If you're smart, you'll offer me a drink."

"All right," said Jane. Something was up. She was fairly confident that if she waited long enough and didn't push, she'd find out what was on her sister-in-law's mind. By the grim look on her face, it wasn't good news. "What do you feel like?"

"Bourbon and soda. Go light on the soda and make it a double."

Jane retreated into the kitchen and returned a few minutes later with two glass tumblers: a double bourbon for Sigrid; a brandy for her. In the interim, Sigrid had removed her sunglasses and made herself comfortable on the couch, though perhaps "comfortable" wasn't the right word. Jane's sister-in-law was a woman who expected a great deal from herself and those around her. She was a marriage and family therapist, and a good one, but she wasn't always an easy person to be around. Tonight, her usual self-confidence seemed to be absent.

Jane handed her the glass and then sat down on the old rocker next to the fireplace. It was too hot for a fire tonight. Bean hunkered down next to her foot and promptly fell asleep.

They sipped their drinks in silence for several minutes. By the preoccupied look on Sigrid's face, Jane knew she had a lot on her mind. She hoped her sister-in-law was gathering up the courage to explain why she'd come.

Finally, after downing half her drink in record time, Sigrid's eyes slowly shifted from the glass in her hand to Jane's face. "When do you expect Beryl and Edgar back?"

It wasn't the opening she'd expected. "Mid-November, last I heard. They may stay a little longer, but I'm sure they'll be home by Thanksgiving."

Sigrid nodded, her gaze drifting away. After another couple of seconds, she leaned forward, set her drink down on the coffee table, and then rested her elbows on her knees. "Look, I might as well just come out and tell you. You're going to hear about it soon enough—from Peter." Her eyes dropped to her hands. "We've separated."

Jane was stunned, and let it show. "But . . . I don't understand. I thought—"

"You thought we were in love. That we were the original happy couple."

"Yes. Something like that."

"We do love each other, Jane. I'm totally devoted to your brother. He's everything I want—all I'd ever need."

"Then why—"

She picked up her drink and swirled the ice in the glass. "He doesn't feel the same way I do."

Jane had a hard time believing that. "Siggy, all he ever does is tell me how much he adores you."

"Maybe. But I'm not enough."

"Are . . . are you telling me Peter's found someone else?" She knew it was none of her business, but she couldn't help it. She loved these two wonderful people—she needed to understand.

Sigrid's face hardened. "I just can't talk about it right now. Give me a little time, okay?" She got up and walked to the windows. With her back to Jane, she continued, "It was crazy to come here. I knew you'd take Peter's side."

"I'm not taking *anyone's* side, Siggy. I care about you both. Besides, you haven't given me enough information to form an opinion."

Sigrid lowered her head. "And I won't. At least not now. I'm too confused myself." She put a hand up to her face.

Jane could tell she was wiping away a tear. "Just tell me what I can do to help."

Still brushing away the tears, Sigrid turned around. "Let me stay here tonight, Jane. I promise, I'll find somewhere else to go tomorrow. I just couldn't check into a hotel. It seemed—too cold. Too foreign."

Jane got up. Sigrid wasn't the kind of person who gave or received affection easily, but tonight, she allowed Jane to give her a long and reassuring hug. "I'm really sorry."

"Yeah. Me, too." She sniffed, then pulled away. "I know I'm putting you in a terrible position. Peter's not going to like it that I came here."

"Then he knows where you are?"

Sigrid walked a few paces away, seeming to need some distance between them. "We had a terrible fight. I'd just gotten home from work. He was cooking dinner in the kitchen. Things . . . I don't know. They just got out of hand. We've been arguing for weeks, but this was the worst. When he saw me take my suitcase down from the top of the closet, he left."

"So he doesn't know where you've gone."

Sigrid shook her head.

"He's going to worry, kiddo. Maybe you should give him a call. Let him know you're safe."

"He doesn't care."

"Of course he cares."

She shook her head and then kept shaking it. "No. *Let* him worry. If I'm not there, maybe he'll do some thinking for a change. And maybe, just maybe, he'll see my side of it. If he wants to call me tomorrow, he knows he can find me at work."

Jane wanted to ask for more details, but since Sigrid had already made it clear she didn't want to talk about it, Jane had to respect her privacy. "Why don't you take the room next to Beryl and Edgar's? Cordelia's staying in the front bedroom."

Sigrid cocked her head. "She is? How come?"

"The floors in her new loft are being redone." Jane was glad she had a couple of spare rooms. Otherwise, someone would be bunking on the sofa in the living room, most likely her. "And Siggy, you don't have to leave tomorrow. Why don't you wait a couple of days? See what Peter has to say."

She nodded. "Thanks, Jane. You're a good friend." Picking up her suitcase, she crossed to the stairs. "I think I'll take a shower."

Jane's smile was gentle. "Are you hungry?"

"Not really."

"Well, you should eat something. I'll fix us a salad. When you're done, come back downstairs and we'll sit on the porch."

"You're a lifesaver Jane. And . . . thanks for not pushing. I'm sorry I can't talk about any of this right now, but I just couldn't be alone."

"I understand," said Jane. And she did.

For the next half hour, Jane busied herself in the kitchen. Since she had a fresh tuna fillet in the refrigerator, she whipped up a salad niçoise. She always had capers and olives on hand; she even had a couple of hard-boiled eggs in the fridge. And thankfully, she'd bought some beautiful greenleaf lettuce and a box of homegrown tomatoes at the farmers' market just the other day. When the potatoes she'd put on to steam were almost done, she tossed in several handfuls of fresh green beans. Everything was just about ready.

As she turned off the flame under the steamer, the phone rang. If it was Peter, she wasn't quite sure how to handle it, but assumed she'd figure it out as she went along. "Hello?" she said, lifting the green beans into a bowl of ice water and then dumping the potatoes into a colander to cool.

"Jane, hi."

Her heart skipped a beat. It was Julia. "Hi." She sat down at the table. "I assume you finally got my messages."

"Jane, I'm so sorry. I had to go out of town unexpectedly and I've been so busy, I never checked in. Not once. Please say you forgive me."

Jane wasn't going to let her off the hook so easily. "I was really worried, Julia."

"You were more than worried, honey. You were angry and you had every right to be. All I can say in my defense is that my mind was elsewhere. My Uncle Chester—he lives in Boston—suffered a severe heart attack last Monday morning. I got the phone call late Monday night and left first thing on Tuesday."

This was the first Jane had ever heard of Uncle Chester; not that she knew all of Julia's relatives. "Is he all right?"

Julia was silent for a moment. "No, Jane. He died Wednesday afternoon. I was there. So was his wife and one of his kids. The funeral was earlier today. I took a cab from the church and went directly to the airport."

Now Jane felt like a complete toad. "God, that's awful. Were the two of you close?"

"Yes. But he's been sick for years. We all knew it was coming."

"That doesn't make it any easier."

"No. You're right. It doesn't."

"How's his wife taking it?"

"She's doing okay—under the circumstances." Another pause. "Listen, Jane, when can we get together? I really need to see you. I've missed you so much."

Jane closed her eyes, allowing the words to wash over her. Julia's voice felt like a cool drink in the parched desert heat.

"Jane? Are you still there?"

"Yes, I'm here. What would you say to my driving up tomorrow?"

"Really? You wouldn't mind?"

"Mind? I've missed you every bit as much as you've missed me. Besides, I'd welcome the chance to get out of the city."

"That's fabulous! What time can I expect you?"

"Well—" She had to think about it for a second. "I've got a few loose ends to tie up at the restaurant in the morning. I've also got some business in Floodwood. I could do that on the way."

"Floodwood? What on earth could you possibly do in *that* tiny town—other than fill your car with gas?"

"It's a long story. I'll tell you all about it when I get there, which should be sometime in the late afternoon."

"How long can you stay?"

"I'd have to leave on Sunday. I've got a workman coming to the house first thing Monday morning."

"Oh, all right. I'll take what I can get. See you tomorrow then, hon. And Jane?"

"Yes?"

"I love you."

Before Jane could respond, the line clicked.

17

Cordelia boogied up the front walk and breezed through Jane's front door, bursting into song as soon as she hit the foyer. It was a Whitney Houston tune, one about undying devotion—not a personal fave. But since she was thoroughly smitten with her newest love, the sappy melody and the equally sappy sentiment seemed to take on a rare poignancy. "I–e–I–e–I–" she crooned.

Et cetera. Et cetera.

There was nothing but magic air beneath her feet as she danced her Ginger Rogers moves into the living room, dropped her overnight bag on the couch, and flung her sun hat into a chair. She then swirled through the dining room, where the magic air failed her as she stepped on a dog toy and stumbled into the kitchen.

"Good morning," said Sigrid, looking up from her bowl of cereal.

Cordelia yanked her clothes into place and glowered. "What are *you* doing here?"

"It's nice to see you, too."

"Huh? Oh . . . right." She cleared her throat and started again. "I'm truly delighted to see you, Siggy my dear. You're looking splendid. Spiffy as ever in that ratty gray sweatshirt and baggy jeans. You're the picture of Saturday morning relaxation." Raising an eyebrow, she added, "Actually, if you don't mind a bit of truth telling, you look like roadkill."

Pulling the morning paper in front of her, Sigrid glanced down the front page and said, "I moved in for a few days. Want some coffee? It's fresh."

"Moved in? Why?"

"It's personal."

Cordelia smelled a story. Walking around behind her she said, "Where's Peter?"

"Beats me."

"Do I detect the faint growl of a lover's quarrel?"

"Don't be patronizing." She folded the paper in half and continued to read.

After subjecting Sigrid's back to a penetrating gaze, Cordelia ambled over to the coffeemaker and poured herself a cup. "All right. You don't have to hit me over the head with a two-by-four. You don't want to talk about it."

"Right."

"Because Cordelia Thorn understands *boundary* issues, dearheart."

"That's good to hear."

"If you and Peter are having problems, it's none of my business."

Sigrid shifted her gaze from the paper to Cordelia's face. "I knew I could count on your sensitivity."

"Sensitive to the core. It's the curse of all artistic people."

"And it's good to know you'll respect my privacy."

Cordelia held up her hand. "Absolutely. You can count on me." She'd wheedle the details out of Jane later. "Where's Janey?"

"Gone."

This taciturn act was becoming tedious. Sitting down at the table, Cordelia folded one leg over the other and then took a slow, contemplative sip from her mug. Using her most patient voice, she continued, "Gone as in abducted by aliens? Raptured into the heavens to await the Lord's return? Kidnapped by foreign terrorists? Or perhaps she's merely left us to join the circus."

"Why would she leave *here* to join a circus?"

"Good point."

Sigrid returned her attention to the paper. "She drove up to Grand Rapids to spend the weekend with Julia."

"Will wonders never cease." Under her breath, Cordelia added, "Dr. Jekyll strikes again."

"Excuse me?"

"Nothing. Nothing at all." She sipped her coffee in silence for several seconds. "Well," she said finally, slapping her legs and pushing out of her chair, "nice talking to you, but I think I'll head upstairs and take a shower. I've got to be at the theater by noon."

"I hope you don't mind—I washed out some of my things and left them drying in the bathroom."

Welcome to dorm life, thought Cordelia sourly. She wondered how the floor sanders were doing at her loft. Gritting her teeth, she smiled. "Mind? Why would I mind? But you know, Siggy, there's a laundry room in the basement."

"Oh, I never put delicate fabrics in a washing machine."

"Heavens, no. What was I thinking?" Cordelia looked away and then rolled her eyes. "By the way, which room are you in?"

"The one right next to yours. Hotel Lawless, huh?" Sigrid laughed. "Oh, by the way, I saw that you'd left a lot of your clothes in my bedroom. I moved them into your bedroom last night. Oh, and not to change the subject, but Jane got a call from a man named Kastner shortly after she left this morning. Actually, the guy said I could pass his message on to either of you."

"And the message was?"

"He said he'd talked to his wife and they'd be happy to join the two of you for dinner at the Lyme House next week. Tuesday or Wednesday night would work best for them. He also thought that one of you should invite the other members of his family. He left his home number so you could call to confirm the date and time."

Cordelia's eyes lit up.

"I take it it's good news?"

"Good? This is the best news I've had in weeks!" She had to do some heavy thinking, devise a plan to impress Virginia Kastner not only with her skills as a creative director—which were unassailable—but with her wit and charm. One way or another, she was going to dazzle that woman. And when it was all over, if she played her cards just right, Virginia Kastner would be eating out of her hand.

Glancing at her watch, Cordelia smiled. "Deary me, the time is getting away from me." She patted Sigrid's hand. "Don't expect me home tonight."

"I won't wait up."

As Cordelia got to the door, she turned around and said, "Aren't you just a little curious to know where I'll be?"

"Do I look like your mother?"

Without skipping a beat, Cordelia continued, "Her name is Neva Moore. She's a set designer. This time, I'm really in *love*, Siggy. Hearts and roses all the way."

Sigrid blinked, then started to laugh.

"What's so funny?"

"You don't find anything amusing about your new friend's name?"

"Neva Moore?"

"Quoth the raven."

A disgusted look passed over Cordelia's face. "I will *not* stand here and listen to you insult Neva by making Edgar Allan Poe jokes. Besides, she's heard them all."

"Later," said Sigrid, giving her a dismissive wave.

Cordelia glared, then turned on her heel and fluttered out of the room.

18

You must be Jane," said Abbie Kaufman, stepping out onto the front porch of her ramshackle farmhouse. The back of the structure was nestled under several ancient oak trees. Most of the branches were bare now, the leaves scattered over the dry grass. A row of white pine divided the yard from a field where two horses grazed lazily on some hay, their tails whipping the flies from their haunches. Shading her eyes from the midday sun, Abbie walked down the rickety wooden steps and stuck out her hand.

Jane shook it, taking in the young woman's dusty overalls and faded plaid workshirt. "Thanks for letting me come. Sorry it was such short notice."

"You were in the neighborhood, right?"

Jane smiled. "Not exactly. I have a friend in Grand Rapids. I'm on my way up to see her."

Abbie studied her for a moment, then said, "Come on. Let's go out to the pottery shed. I might as well work while we talk."

Jane followed her through the yard, amazed at how cool and crisp the air was even a hundred and fifty miles north of the cities. The Kaufman/Munoz farm was located several miles east of Floodwood. On the phone, Abbie had explained that her partner,

Maria, owned a combination gas station and baitshop in town. It was their main source of income, although Abbie's pottery business was finally beginning to show a profit. She said she'd be happy to talk to Jane—she'd eaten at the Lyme House many times, and knew from reading the Minneapolis paper who Jane was. When Abbie pressed to know something more about Jane's unexpected visit, Jane said she'd rather wait and discuss it in person.

After sitting down on a bench in the corner of a new brick building located directly behind the barn, Jane watched Abbie remove plastic wrap from around a lump of grayish clay. She was a small woman, olive-skinned and pretty, with thick dark hair pulled back into a ponytail and tied with a bright red scarf. Her eyes were quick and intelligent as she sat down at the wheel and centered the lump, making sure it was just where it belonged. "So," she said, looking up, "I assume you're here for a reason."

Jane knew there was no point beating around the bush. Abbie would either give her the information she wanted, or she wouldn't. Removing a small box from the pocket of her leather jacket, she lifted off the cover and then held up the carved wooden eye. "Have you ever seen anything like this before?"

Abbie stared at it for a moment, then shook her head. "No, not that I recall. Why? What is it?"

Jane looked at it herself for a few seconds, then put it away. "I'm not sure. I thought you might be able to tell me."

"Sorry."

Leaning forward, Jane clamped her hands between her knees. She wasn't quite sure how to begin. "I understand you knew Patricia Kastner in high school."

Abbie's eyes widened slightly. The statement had obviously taken her by surprise. "That's right."

"The two of you dated."

"We were lovers."

Jane nodded, grateful for the woman's candor. Since she had nothing to lose, she decided to try some candor of her own.

"Look, just so you know where I'm coming from—a man showed up at my house last week, a private detective. He told me that Patricia, or someone in her family, might be mixed up in another man's death. Patricia and this other man had been living together, but had recently broken up. He committed suicide shortly after she moved out, but his mother is convinced it was murder."

Abbie took it all in without responding. After several seconds she said, "And what do you want from me?"

"Well, actually, Patricia's a friend of mine, but we haven't known each other all that long."

"I see." An amused smile tugged at the corners of her mouth. "You want me to tell you if she's capable of murder—before you get too involved."

Jane held up her hand. "No, that's not it at all."

"It's all right. I understand."

"No, really—"

Humor creased Abbie's eyes. "You know, I thought after I took off that Patricia would see the error of her ways and choose the straight and narrow—well, at least the straight. Actually, I kept track of her for a while in college—from a distance, of course. We both attended the U of M. By our sophomore year, it became pretty clear that we lived in different worlds. She'd joined a sorority; I was living in a three-room dump just north of the campus. She was a business major; I spent most of my time in grubby jeans and a sweatshirt over at the studio arts building. But from what I could tell, she dated only guys after we broke up. I gave up following her illustrious academic career during our junior year."

"Any particular reason?"

She hesitated for a moment, then said, "Ever heard of Dr. Cyril Dancing?"

"Doesn't ring any bells."

"Patricia had an affair with him. At the time, he was a well-respected psychiatrist, an author, and a past president of the American Psychiatric Foundation. Married; several kids. In his late fifties. He had an extensive private practice, but also taught a class in business psychology at the U. That's supposedly how they met."

"So, what happened?"

Abbie shrugged. "He committed suicide. From what I understand, Patricia was really broken up about it. I was surprised that she didn't try to hide it better. I mean, sleeping with a professor is really stupid, not that it doesn't happen, but why be so open about your grief? She missed several weeks of classes—even took a couple of incompletes."

"Did she get in trouble?"

"Not that I ever heard."

"Do you think he was pressuring her to sleep with him?"

"This may not be the politically correct thing to say, but if I know Patricia, it was probably the other way around. Normally, I'd take a student's side against any professor. It's such an unequal power relationship it's hard to tell what's happening, even if the woman says she's doing it of her own free will. But with Patricia, I don't buy it."

"So, why did Dancing do it? Kill himself, I mean."

"I never heard a definitive reason. If I recall correctly, he didn't leave a note, so it was all speculation. Some people thought it was overwork; others suggested his marriage was on the rocks. Just because he was a trained therapist doesn't mean he could solve his own problems. Frankly, I thought the whole thing was pathetic—that Patricia had sunk to a new low. After that fiasco, I simply lost interest in her. I mean, what was the point?"

Jane thought about it for a few seconds. "Abbie, do you remember any of the details of how Dr. Dancing died?"

She thought about it for several seconds and then replied, "Alcohol and pills, I think. It was a fairly easy matter for him to get his hands on just about any prescription drug." She glanced pointedly at Jane. "I will say that it's encouraging to know that the young woman I once knew is still alive and kicking. I'm glad she's dating a woman again, Jane. I think she lost an important part of herself when she knuckled under to her mother's pressure. Maybe with you she can find that part of herself again."

Jane glanced down at a deep gouge in the wooden bench. It was probably dishonest of her not to address this misunderstanding. She wasn't involved with Patricia, nor would she ever be. Abbie had jumped to an erroneous conclusion, and yet, maybe it was for the best. It certainly gave her a plausible reason for wanting such personal information, particularly when the truth might very well put Abbie off. She would hardly have opened up so readily about a past love affair if Earl Wilcox were the one doing the questioning. "Just out of curiosity, what did you think of the Kastner family?"

Abbie thought about it for a minute, kicking the wheel a couple of times. "They seemed nice enough—at first. Patricia informed them I was a lesbian before I ever met them."

"When was that?"

"At a pool party at their house. It was the summer before our senior year. Patricia had invited a bunch of her friends over for the afternoon. If I recall, Mr. Kastner grilled burgers and Mrs. Kastner tried to impress everyone with her great body. She sat around the pool in a swimming suit and made conversation—mostly with the guys. Patricia told me later that she didn't figure my sexuality would be a big deal since her mother had lots of gay friends."

"But it was?"

"Yeah, though at the time, the Kastners were both nice to me. Then again, they didn't know Patricia and I were falling in love. You better watch your back, Jane. I wouldn't get mixed up with that family again for all the money in the world. I hate it when people smile and act friendly and then undermine everything you do."

Jane had so many questions. She decided to start with a very personal one. "Why did you and Patricia break up?"

Abbie stared at the lump of clay in the center of the pallet, waiting for the wheel to stop. "Patricia didn't tell you?"

"No. All she said was that it was a case of young love gone wrong. As I think about it, I did get the impression that her family wasn't all that supportive."

Abbie's eyes rose to Jane's. "That's putting it mildly. When Virginia Kastner found out that Patricia and I were sleeping together, that we loved each other and planned to rent an apartment close to the U so we could live together while we went to college, she hit the ceiling—not that Patricia or I knew about it at the time. I was still invited to the house for dinner. Virginia still had her warm conversations with me, just as if nothing was wrong."

"So, what happened?"

She smoothed the top of the lump, giving herself a moment to collect her thoughts. "First, about a month into our senior year, Mr. Kastner began dropping little concerned comments about our relationship—like, had Patricia considered my background? My mother and father were divorced and I'd been raised by my grandmother. He told her it was inevitable that I had lots of emotional scars, and that I probably wasn't a very good bet for a long-term relationship. Also, I was Jewish. Christians and Jews didn't mix—it was just a fact of life. And, since Patricia wanted a career in business and I was the original artistic flake, he didn't think we'd be particularly compatible once the romantic glow wore off. Given our fundamental differences, he felt we'd end up hurting each other, whether we wanted to or not. I had to hand it to him. He was very clever in the way he went about it. He never once attacked us because we were gay."

"But I thought you said it was *Mrs.* Kastner who had the problem with you two being together."

"It was. Quite honestly, Jane, I think Mr. Kastner liked me—certainly far more than his wife. Oh, there was some initial resistance to the notion that his daughter was dating another young woman, but when it came to Patricia, anything she wanted was okay by him. As long as she was happy. No, Mrs. Kastner put him up to it; probably primed him with the exact words to say. You had to know her, Jane. She never said anything directly. She always used emissaries. In this case, her husband and her son."

"Elliot? What did he have to do with it?"

Abbie hesitated, chewing her bottom lip. "When Virginia Kastner saw that her husband wasn't getting anywhere with Patricia, she sent her son to talk to me. Elliot came over to my house right after Christmas vacation started. He brought an ultimatum with him; If I didn't stop dating Patricia, he'd tell my grandmother what I was. I told him she already knew, which was true. I was never very good at keeping secrets. My grandmother and I loved each other. Nothing would come between that. So, next, he threatened to tell my teachers. I told him to go ahead. He could announce it on the ten o'clock news for all I cared. I wasn't ashamed of who I was. Finally, he brought out the big guns. He explained that his mother had a drinking problem, but that it had been under control for years, ever since Patricia was born. Recently, however, he'd become concerned that the longer this 'situation' went on, the harder it would be for her to stay sober. Patricia had never seen her mother drunk. He said Virginia was a totally different person when she was drinking. Loud, abusive, deeply angry."

"Did he mention what she was angry about?"

Abbie shook her head. "But he did tell me that I had no right to screw up Patricia's life, to subject her to a kind of family turmoil she'd never known."

"You mean her mother's drinking."

"Exactly. Elliot kept insisting that Patricia deserved better. If I loved her as much as I said I did, I'd put her needs before mine. Again, it was a smart tactic, but it didn't work because I didn't believe his story. If I had, I might have acted differently. The thing is, I thought it was just one more of Virginia Kastner's manipulations.

I told him in no uncertain terms that I wouldn't knuckle under to his mother's emotional blackmail. I knew she'd sent him to my house, and I wasn't buying what she was selling. I asked him to give Virginia a message from me. Patricia and I loved each other and we planned to be together, no matter what stumbling blocks she threw our way. When he saw that I wasn't going to budge, he told me I was making a mistake. He was really furious—as angry as I'd ever seen him. But eventually he just gave up and left."

"Did you tell Patricia about the conversation?"

She shook her head. "It wouldn't have mattered. I didn't realize it at the time, but when it came to Virginia Kastner, I'd met my match."

By the look on Abbie's face, Jane could tell that the admission wasn't an easy one. "How so?"

Placing a hand over the lump on the wheel, Abbie dug her fingers into the clay. "Virginia won. It's as simple as that."

"But . . . how?"

"She got stinking drunk one night when her husband was out, climbed in the bathtub, and slit her wrists."

Jane was horrified. "But—she lived. Someone must have found her."

"Sure. Patricia did. Virginia planned it that way."

"You think . . . it was calculated? That she set the whole thing up?"

"What's the difference? She got the result she wanted. Patricia was so freaked by the whole experience that for weeks she didn't know if she was coming or going. I tried to be there for her—to stay strong for both of us, but after it happened, we started seeing less and less of each other, mostly because Patricia was busy keeping her mother company in the evenings. I don't know if you fully comprehend the kind of power someone has when they attempt suicide, fail, and then teeter on the brink of doing it again. She had everyone in the family tied up in knots. I mean, the woman couldn't blink without someone taking her emotional temperature. And then, to top it all off, two months after the suicide attempt, Elliot paid me another visit. This time he brought a threat of his own. He said if I didn't get out of Patricia's life and *stay* out, he'd hurt me. Bad."

"He threatened you *physically?*"

"He didn't go into specifics, but he didn't need to. Have you ever met Elliot?"

"He's renting my third-floor apartment."

Abbie stared at Jane for a moment. "Lucky you."

"He seems like an okay guy. He's a writer, you know. And an artist."

"He's a *freak*. He spent most of his teenage years in and out of therapists' offices. It was either that or wind up in jail."

This was news to Jane. "But why?"

Abbie sat back and folded her arms over her chest. "Among other things, he used to take orders from his buddies. If someone wanted a new bike, he'd steal one—for the right price. If a guy wanted a snowblower to give to his dad for Father's Day, or a set of wrenches, or a fishing rod, he'd find a garage, pick the lock, and steal what he needed. He did it for years before he got caught. And he kept doing it even after he was busted."

"Surely he didn't need the money?"

"Of course not. He liked the thrill. Or maybe he liked pissing off his parents. Whatever the case, he was in trouble all the time. Eventually he stopped stealing, but he still seemed to enjoy an occasional fight. He was always beating the crap out of some poor jerk. Otto Kastner paid off a lot of people to keep Elliot out of jail. I knew, if I provoked him, he wouldn't think twice about beating me to a bloody pulp."

Looking down at the clay, Abbie went on, "But that's not what stopped me from seeing Patricia. I guess, after a while, I simply began to see the writing on the wall. You can fight indifference, or even hate, but you can't fight something as invidious and demoralizing as constant manipulation. It wears you down. Patricia and I did love each other. She was an amazing woman. I still think about her sometimes and wish things had gone differently."

Jane could see a wistful sadness pass across Abbie's face, but for whatever reason, the emotion didn't last long.

Picking up the piece of clay, Abbie tossed it on a table behind her, then got up and walked over to a series of shelves along the far wall where the bisqued pots rested, waiting to be glazed.

"How long had you known Patricia?"

"You mean before we dated? About a year. If you want a character analysis of her prior to that, I'd get in touch with Jessie Holman. She and Patricia were best friends from grade school through high school. She married a guy named Dave Strom. Last I heard, they bought a house in Richfield."

Jane made a mental note, though she couldn't imagine why she'd need to do that much digging into Patricia's background.

"Getting back to your original question," said Abbie, lifting one of the fired pots over to the work table and examining a crack in the base. "I don't think I ever really answered it. You wanted to know if Patricia was capable of murder." After setting the pot down, she picked up the lump of clay she'd just ruined and began kneading it back into a smooth ball. Her movements were quick and experienced, her attention fully drawn to the ball of mud in her hands.

Jane waited. She had a pretty good idea what Abbie would say, but needed her own impressions confirmed.

After several thoughtful seconds, Abbie wiped the back of her hand across her forehead, then rested the hand on her hip. "This may surprise you, but Patricia was a deeply giving lover. I don't regret a moment of our time together. I suppose you think that since I'm the one who identified myself as gay, I was the one who pursued her. The truth is, she came after me. I'd never met anyone like her before—and I haven't met anyone like her since. She's special, Jane. And very smart. She knows how to get what she wants. If she wanted something badly enough and something or *someone* stood in her way, she'd be capable of just about anything. But then," she added, slapping the clay down hard on the table, "so would every member of that godawful family."

19

The woods filtered out most of the early evening light as Jane drove up the gravel road toward Julia's house. This was only the second time she'd been here. The first was shortly after Julia had closed on the place five weeks ago. Walking up from the drive, Jane observed that the house looked both impressive and expensive as it sat perched on a bluff overlooking Pokegama Lake. It was a modern structure—lots of vertical lines, high vaulted ceilings, and bold angles. The interior had been empty of furnishings at the time, but even then, Jane could see how beautiful it was going to look. A wraparound deck stretched from the living room to the dining room. Indeed, the entire west facade was nothing but beams and glass.

Jane rang the front doorbell, but when no one answered, she walked around the side of the house to the stairs leading up to the deck. She could see lights on all all over the main floor, so she assumed Julia was home. Pausing for a moment, she looked through one of the side windows and saw a fire burning brightly in the living room fireplace.

Taking the last four steps two at a time, Jane found Julia standing on the deck watching the sunset. She looked so trim and healthy in her red wool shirt and jeans, her short blond hair ruffled by the breeze. Since she was standing at the railing with her back to the stairs, Jane's approach went unnoticed. It was a perfect fall evening. Cool. Windy. Above them, the clouds were dark and ominous, but in the distance they'd cleared, revealing a golden evening sky. Streaks of yellow light touched the tops of the trees. Jane was so transfixed by the beauty, she didn't move for almost a minute.

Finally, hearing the deck creak behind her, Julia turned around. "You made it!" She brushed a hand quickly across her face and then moved away from the rail, reaching out and pulling Jane close.

Jane wondered if she'd been crying. "Are you all right?"

"I am now that you're here."

"But—the tears."

She didn't respond.

"Julia, tell me what's wrong."

"It's been a bad week."

Jane assumed she was talking about the death of her uncle. "I know, sweetheart. I'm so sorry."

"God, you look great." She touched Jane's hair. "I'm so glad you made it before dark. Another hour and I would have begun to worry."

Jane could see the genuine concern in her eyes, and it warmed her. "It seems like a year since I last saw you."

"Two years."

As they kissed, Jane realized she wanted nothing more than to stay here like this forever. Finding someone like Julia, after all this time, seemed like a miracle.

Finally, drawing back, they each examined the other's face.

Lifting Jane's hand up to her cheek, Julia said, "I made us dinner. It's nothing special—well, I mean, I slaved on it all afternoon, but I freely admit I'm not in your league when it comes to cooking."

"Don't apologize," said Jane. She hated it when the people in her life were afraid to cook for her. If someone went to the trouble of making a homemade meal, she was hardly going to critique the effort—especially when so many people never made any effort to cook at all, for themselves or anyone else. "I'd be happy with a hot dog." She sniffed the air. "Although it smells more like chicken."

"You have a good nose," said Julia. "Come on. Let's go inside. I've already got a fire going."

"I saw that," said Jane, following her through the glass doors into the living room. "Wow, this place is incredible. I knew it would be." The furniture was mostly modern, with a few of Julia's antiques scattered here and there to break up the severity. In the center of the polished wood floor rested a large geometric rug—all tans and mellow grays with a few touches of burnt orange. Matching tan and gray pillows were stacked by the fireplace. Jane was intrigued by the sculpture and the paintings, but figured there would be time tomorrow to examine all of it. "How did you furnish the place so quickly?"

"I had a professional decorator do it. Chaz Monroe. He's an old friend. He flew in from D.C. two days after I bought the house. You'll meet him one day soon. The second floor isn't finished yet, but down here it's mostly complete. He knows my tastes, so I gave him a budget and he did the rest."

"You had a budget?"

Again, Julia grinned. "Hey," she said, hanging her arm around Jane's shoulder, "I make a pretty good living, you know. And a dollar goes a lot further around these parts than it does on the East Coast. I like to live well."

From what Jane had been able to observe—both here and in Bethesda—that was an understatement.

"Come on," said Julia, heading up the open staircase. "I'll give you the fifty-cent tour. Master bedroom. Guest rooms. Exercise room. Library. You can get the full tour in the morning."

Half an hour later they were back downstairs, this time in the kitchen. Jane pointed to a closed door directly opposite the back door and asked, "Where does that lead?"

Julia pulled her head out of the refrigerator. "Oh, that. It takes you down to the lowest level. Mainly, it's just storage down there. Nothing very interesting." She handed Jane a bottle of wine, a corkscrew, and two glasses. "Are you hungry?"

"Famished."

"Why don't you take the wine into the living room and I'll join you in a minute?"

After making herself comfortable on the pillows in front of the fire, Jane uncorked the bottle and poured them each a glass. Noticing that it was a 1995 Château Mandagot Montpeyroux, she called, "This is a pretty obscure wine, but it's fabulous. How'd you hear about it?"

"From my friend Chaz," called Julia. "He brought two bottles with him when he came. We only drank one." A moment later she entered the room carrying a tray of French brie, champagne grapes, and crackers. "We can nibble on this until dinner's ready." Dimming the track lighting, she tossed another log on the fire. "I see you got your ring back."

Jane glanced down at the scarab Julia had given her last summer. The stone had come loose from the setting so she'd taken it to a jewelers to have it fixed. "I got it back yesterday."

"I missed seeing it on your hand." Julia touched her glass to Jane's, then eased down next to her. After a moment's reflection, she said, "To us—to a happy future together."

They each took a sip. Leaning back against the pillows, Julia tugged Jane down next to her. "That's better." They kissed and then, arms entwined, watched the flames dance over the new log until the bark caught fire.

"The woodsmoke smells wonderful," said Jane. "Everything smells wonderful up here. It's so fresh—so lush."

"You don't miss the delicate scent of car exhaust?"

Jane smiled. "I'm not Cordelia. I love the north woods."

"Maybe I should be the one pressuring you to move up here, instead of you always pressing me to move to Minneapolis."

"Do I do that?"

"Oh, not more than four or five times a week."

Jane shook her head. "I'm sorry."

Stroking Jane's arm, Julia said, "Don't be. Actually, I think this arrangement is just about perfect—for now."

"You do, huh?"

They bantered easily for another few minutes. Finally, feeling the need to resolve what still felt unresolved, Jane sat up. She spread some cheese on a cracker and handed it to Julia, then made one for herself. "Did you really mean that—about our having a future together?"

Julia gave her a frustrated look, and then sat up herself. "Of course I did. Why do you always doubt my love for you?" She drained her glass, then poured herself another. "I know I have a complex life, but I've tried to make it clear how much I care about you. Have I failed that miserably?"

"No, of course not, but—"

"But what?" She traced the line of Jane's jaw with her fingers. "Tell me why you look at me with such uncertainty."

It was hard to concentrate when they were so close. "It's . . . little things. Pieces of your life you don't talk about, or pieces you . . . simply leave out. Like, why didn't you tell me you only worked two days a week at the clinic? I thought you moved up here so you could pursue your practice full time."

"I did."

"Then where are you the rest of the time? The receptionist I talked to yesterday said you did some kind of medical consulting."

Julia withdrew her hand from Jane's face. "That's right."

"Do you think I'm not interested in your life, Julia? Is that it?"

"No. Of course not." She fingered her gold necklace. "But tell me the truth, Jane. Are you really interested in blood disorders? If I talked to you about standard versus experimental treatments, wouldn't your eyes glaze over?"

Jane reflected a moment, then relented. "All right, probably; but on the other hand, I like to know what you're doing with your days—what you think about, what's important to you."

"*You're* important to me."

How could a person be so frustrating and at the same time so incredibly endearing? Jane wondered. Maybe it was just her own insecurity talking; not that she'd ever been particularly insecure. Then again, she hadn't fallen this hard for someone in a very long time. She hated to think she was turning into some ridiculously critical, hopelessly demanding shrew.

"Look, I know what this is all about," said Julia, helping herself to some of the grapes. "I didn't call and tell you I'd be in Boston. And then, when I didn't return your calls, you got worried. I promise, Jane, I'll never do that again. I explained why it happened, but it's still no excuse. Please, honey, say you forgive me. I repent in dust and ashes."

Jane drew her close. "There's nothing to forgive."

"Are you sure?"

"Absolutely."

"Good," Julia said, smiling broadly, "because that means we can now move on to blood disorders. I've got lots of interesting theories I know you'll be fascinated to hear."

Jane laughed. "I can't win with you, can I?"

Julia's face sobered. "I don't want anything ever to come between us, Jane. You believe that, don't you?"

"Well . . . sure."

"Maybe I don't deserve someone like you—"

"What a silly thing to say."

"I'm thirty-six years old and I've only recently discovered

what I really want out of life. In my book, that's pretty pathetic. I've wasted a lot of time, Jane, but now that I've found you, I'm going to hold on tight for as long as I can."

There it was again—that tentative way of expressing herself that always threw her. "You make it sound like we're doomed to failure."

Julia's eyes drifted to the fire. "I love being with you—touching you, talking to you, taking walks with you, having breakfast with you. Just the simple stuff's enough for me. And if the gods will only smile on us, I'd like to grow old with you."

Maybe it was the setting, or the second glass of wine on an empty stomach, but Julia had never said anything this demonstrative before.

"I've never been more sure of anything in my entire life, Jane."

The phone interrupted them.

"Damn," said Julia. "That's my office line." She squeezed Jane's hand, then scrambled to her feet. "To be continued," she said, gazing at Jane for a moment and then dashing into her study.

Jane couldn't see her pick up the phone, but she could hear the conversation.

"Dr. Martinsen." She was silent for several seconds. Then: "What's her BP?" A pause. "No, that's not good." More silence. "I see. Yes, I'll leave right away. Tell her husband I'll meet him at the emergency-room entrance at St. Gervais in fifteen minutes. Right. Thanks, Sal."

Returning to the living room, Julia moved quickly now, slipping into her shoes, finding a coat. "Jane, I'm so sorry. I've got to leave."

"Sounds like someone's pretty sick."

"Yes, she's the patient of a colleague of mine—Dr. Stewart Saari. I'm covering for him this weekend because his son's getting married."

Jane admired Julia's professional competence as well as her

commitment to her patients. They'd talked about it many times. Julia loved being a doctor. She'd gone into medicine not only because she was fascinated by the human body but because she truly wanted to help people. Tonight, however, Jane could see that her professional concern was at war with her own—far more personal—frustration. "Do you know how long you'll be gone?" She followed Julia into the kitchen.

Grabbing a set of keys from a series of hooks hidden inside one of the shelves, Julia said, "Could be half an hour, could be more. Can you take care of dinner?"

"Whatever it is, I'll keep it warm until you get back."

"You're a doll." She gave Jane a quick kiss. "Have I told you recently that I love you?"

"It's been at least a minute. I'm beginning to feel neglected."

Julia smiled and waved as she shot out the back door. It was the quickest route to the garage.

Jane watched from one of the dining room windows as Julia backed her car into the drive, turned it around, and then sped off down the dirt and gravel road, the same one Jane had driven up less than an hour ago. Once the car was out of sight, Jane spent a few seconds surveying the woods surrounding the house for signs of life, but eventually gave up and returned to the living room.

The house seemed huge and empty now that Julia was gone. Spreading some cheese on another cracker, Jane picked up her glass of wine and went into the kitchen. She wanted to check on the food before it burned to a crisp. After lifting the cover off a delicious-looking chicken concoction, she turned the oven temperature down to warm. As long as Julia returned before midnight, their dinner might be abused, but it would still be edible.

Walking around sipping from her glass, Jane examined the pots and pans. Tomorrow would be her day to cook; or perhaps they'd take a drive to Deer River and have a late lunch at a favorite restaurant. Whatever the case, she'd have to hit the road by evening. But she wasn't about to dwell on that now.

Hearing the phone ring again, she hesitated, wondering if she should answer it. After all, it wasn't her house. Thinking that it might be Julia with an update, she grabbed the one on the wall in the kitchen. "Hello?" she said, immediately aware of a cacophony of background noise.

"Janey? Is that you?"

It was Cordelia. "Where are you?"

"At the theater—on my cell phone. Look, I've only got a minute."

People were shouting and laughing, and someone was playing a trumpet—badly.

"Here's the deal. Otto Kastner called this morning. Virginia accepted the invitation. We're on for dinner next week."

"That's great news," said Jane. "Did they say which night worked best for them?"

"Tuesday or Wednesday. Either's fine for me. Now, do you want me to call Patricia and Elliot and invite them too?"

"I'll talk to Patricia when I get home tomorrow," said Jane. "But if you see Elliot, you might as well mention it."

"Will do."

"By the way, in case you're interested, I had an intriguing talk with an old friend of Patricia Kastner's this afternoon. The two of them were lovers in high school." She heard a door slam, and then quiet on the other end.

"Give, Janey. I'm always up for a good dish."

Jane quickly hit the high points of her conversation with Abbie Kaufman, ending with what she'd learned about Dr. Cyril Dancing's death by suicide.

"You mean," said Cordelia after a long pause, "that Patricia was sleeping with a professor?"

"So it would seem."

"How did he kill himself?"

Jane sat down at a large glass kitchen table. "This is the most interesting part. Booze and pills."

"Amazing," whispered Cordelia. "Just like old Kevin Torland. So, Janey, what's your theory? Is it irony, or is it a modus operandi?"

It was a good question, one she couldn't answer.

"And hey, while we're on the subject of hot dish, how come your sister-in-law's moved into our house?"

"*Our* house?"

"I know there's a story, Janey. Come on, give."

Jane sipped her wine. "Honestly, Cordelia, I don't know. She wouldn't talk about it."

"Not even to you? Sister Mary Jane of Our Lady of Perpetual Prying?"

"I beg your pardon."

"Ooops—gotta run. I think someone's about to shoot the trumpet player. And if they don't, I will. Later, dearheart." The line clicked.

Jane finished her wine out on the deck, listening to the waves crash against the rocks and thinking about Patricia Kastner. She wasn't an easy person to get a handle on. One minute she was being extolled for her virtues, the next, pegged as a potential killer. But this new piece of information was enough to give anyone pause. If two men in her life—both lovers—had committed suicide in exactly the same way, it might be coincidence, bad luck, or it could be a pattern of murder. As soon as Jane got back to town tomorrow night, she'd call Earl Wilcox and tell him what she'd learned. Maybe he'd have some thoughts on the subject— ideas on how to follow it up. Come to think of it, she had a few ideas of her own. But for tonight, she'd made herself a deal. She wouldn't spend even one more minute thinking about the Kastner family. Why on earth would she when she had far more pleasant matters to occupy her thoughts.

Leaving her empty glass on a table in the living room, Jane returned to the kitchen and spent the next few minutes looking through some of the high-tech black laminate cupboards. Chaz Monroe hadn't changed or added much to this particular room—with the exception of a butcher block table and a hanging pot rack. Jane recognized most of the dishes from Julia's old place in Bethesda. Walking over to the door leading down to the lower level, she tried the handle, but found that it was locked. It might be fun to take a peek at the storage area downstairs, so she returned to the cupboard where Julia kept her keys. Sure enough, a full set hung from the last hook.

Jane quickly found the right one and unlocked the door. She flipped on a wall switch and began her descent. At the bottom, she found herself standing in a long hallway, one that led to a pair of double doors which in turn opened on to a family room. Pulling back the curtains, Jane saw that the it faced the lake, though there was no exit, as there was upstairs. The room was beautifully appointed with expensive leather furniture and a state-of-the-art entertainment center—if anything, even nicer than upstairs.

What had Julia been thinking to suggest this was simply storage space?

Directly off the main room was a bedroom and bath, again, richly appointed. After examining some of the bureau drawers and finding them empty, Jane walked into the bathroom and opened one of the cabinets. Inside was a tube of toothpaste, several small bottles of shampoo, a razor, shaving cream, and a couple bottles of aftershave. All of them were new and unopened. It reminded her of a hotel.

What was going on? Did someone live here besides Julia? And if so, where were his clothes? It seemed fairly obvious from the toiletries that it was a man. Jane felt the muscles in her neck tighten as she contemplated what this new revelation about Julia might mean.

Dashing back into the hall, she tried another door, but again it was locked. She fumbled through the keys until she found one that worked. Switching on a light, she saw that this room was smaller—filled with storage boxes and a series of gray metal filing cabinets. Okay. So Julia hadn't entirely lied about using the lower level for storage. But once again, she'd failed to tell the whole story.

Pulling back one of the metal drawers, Jane saw that the files were numbered. She slipped one out and looked at it, but it didn't make much sense. Lots of numbers—codes, probably. A few notes full of medical terminology. Feeling more frustrated than ever, she dropped it back into the drawer.

Only one door remained. Moving back into the hall, Jane walked resolutely to the opposite end. Retrieving the keys from her pocket, she pushed a few into the lock until the door opened. She found the light switch, flipped it on, and then stepped inside, startled into silence by the sight that met her eyes.

It was a doctor's office, complete with examining table, cabinets full of drugs, cotton balls, bandages, syringes, blood pressure cuffs, even some larger, more ominous-looking medical equipment—everything a physician might need to examine and treat a patient. "What gives?" Jane whispered out loud, walking slowly through the room.

Was this what Julia did with her time off—treat patients in her home? Did some of them stay here? Was that why there were no clothes in the bedroom? Maybe this was all part of her consulting business; but if so, why not just tell the truth? What was the big deal? Then again, perhaps Jane had jumped to another conclusion. Julia hadn't *refused* to allow her down here; she'd merely said it was used for storage and wasn't particularly interesting. Not a terribly precise description, but not entirely a lie, either.

Walking over to the desk, Jane picked up a photo frame next to the phone. It was the picture of a dark-haired man, someone she'd never seen before. He was reasonably young—probably in his thirties, and nice-looking— except for the dark mustache, which made him look sort of seedy.

Hearing a car engine, Jane felt a moment of panic. It had to be Julia. She'd come back sooner than Jane had expected. Setting the picture back on the desk, she turned off the lights and then raced around to make sure everything was put back exactly the way she'd found it. She shot up the steps without a moment to spare, closing the kitchen door behind her. The cupboard where Julia kept her keys was standing open, just the way Jane had left it. Rushing across the room, she heard a voice call, "Are you hiding, honey?" A second later, Julia was in the room.

"What have you got there?" she asked, her eyes dropping to the keys in Jane's hand.

Jane smiled, desperately hoping she didn't look as guilty as she felt. "I, ah—" She glanced down, flailing around in her mind for something to say, anything to get her out of this tight spot. She couldn't tell Julia she'd been snooping; not that any part of the house was off limits, but good taste probably dictated that she ask before she went downstairs. Damn, she cursed silently. She was growing more confused—about herself and Julia—with every passing minute. "Well, I . . . I saw these in the cupboard and—" One of the keys now caught her eye.

Julia walked a few paces closer. "And what?"

"Well, I know this sounds crazy, but it looked to me like you had one of my backdoor keys." She held up the blue metal one.

"I do. You gave it to me."

"I did?"

"Sure." Julia took the key ring and hung it back up in the cupboard. "We were sitting in your study one night—it must have been last spring, right after Easter. You found it in the top drawer of your desk and tossed it to me."

Jane had no recollection of that, though it could have happened. "Oh, sure. I guess it just slipped my mind."

"You better watch that," said Julia, turning around, a mischievous grin on her face. "I thought I was so *incredibly* fascinating that you never forgot even a moment of our time together."

"Well, it was only that once. It won't happen again."

"See that it doesn't," she said, easing her arms around Jane's waist and nuzzling her hair.

20

When Jane pulled into her garage shortly before ten the following evening, she thought she saw someone standing in the backyard looking up at the house. She couldn't tell who it was because the exterior security light must have burned out while she was away. She made a mental note to replace the bulb first thing in the morning. Grabbing her overnight bag, she slid out of the front seat and crossed through the gate into the backyard, but whoever it was had already gone—if anyone was there to begin with. Thinking no more about it, she carried her bag onto the back porch and stood for a moment stretching her sore muscles. Four hours in the car had turned her body into a pretzel. She needed some time to work out the kinks.

Leaning against the screen door, Jane looked up at the stars. Once again, her thoughts turned to Julia. Their time together had gone by all too quickly. Jane wondered now if she hadn't been a complete wimp by not mentioning her foray into the lower level of Julia's house. Earlier in the day, her reasons had seemed logical enough. First of all, she didn't want to start an argument when they had such a brief time together. Second, she wasn't entirely sure she hadn't overreacted—again. Right after breakfast she'd mentioned that she wanted to take a look at the storage area downstairs. Julia hadn't batted an eye, but merely suggested they look through some of her old family photographs first. The snapshots—and the history they documented—had been so fascinating that Jane never did make it downstairs. One thing led to another, and before she knew it, the day was gone and it was time to hit the road.

Leaving was always hard, and yet so incredibly bittersweet. Julia promised she'd drive down on Friday. The best part was, she wouldn't have to return home until Monday evening. A long weekend, as she pointed out, was just what they both needed.

Watching a cloud pass over the moon, Jane wondered what Julia was doing tonight. She'd tried so hard to make this a wonderful visit. It *had* been wonderful. Yet Jane could tell that Julia had been struggling with her grief over her uncle's death. Only once before had Jane seen Julia so quiet and pensive—right after the death of her mother. Julia had tried to hide her sadness, but every now and then, especially when things quieted down, she would get a faraway look in her eyes and Jane would know she was somewhere else. No doubt her thoughts had returned to her uncle, to the good times they'd shared, and most likely, to the last day they'd been together. Jane had pressed her only once to talk about it, but Julia had refused, saying it was too painful.

Putting her thoughts of Julia aside for now, Jane checked the time, remembering that she had some important matters to take care of before calling it a night. First on the agenda was Patricia Kastner. Jane wanted to invite her to the dinner party before her schedule filled up. Since she knew Patricia never went to bed before midnight, she decided to go over to her house and invite her in person. After being cooped up in the car for the last four hours, a short walk sounded like a tonic.

Ten minutes later, Jane was seated in Patricia's second-floor exercise room, sipping a glass of Armagnac. She'd arrived during her evening workout. "I'm glad Tuesday night works for you. I apologize for the short notice."

"Actually, I already knew about it," said Patricia, wiping the sweat from her neck and shoulders, all the while keeping up a brisk pace on the treadmill. She was wearing a shiny black Spandex body suit, one that highlighted every curve. Jane could tell that she enjoyed being watched. Even the way she touched the towel to her body was meant to be seductive. "Elliot called this morning. He said he'd run into your friend Cordelia and she'd invited him. He also explained about my father doing some work for you at your house."

"I wanted to thank him," said Jane. "He's only charging me for materials. Dinner at my restaurant seemed the least I could do."

"Yeah, Dad's great like that. Cordelia also mentioned to Elliot that you were going to invite me as soon as you got back to town. I assume that means you were visiting your girlfriend."

Jane nodded. She didn't feel like talking to Patricia about Julia, so she returned to the subject of the dinner party. "Will Elliot be able to make it?"

"He hates stuff like that, but I twisted his arm. He'll be fine, as long as he doesn't have to wear a tie—or eat anything green."

Jane laughed. "We'll dye the romaine, just for him."

"He'll be thrilled." She nodded to a bowl of nuts. "You're not eating."

"I stopped for dinner in Cambridge. I'm still stuffed."

"Want some more Armagnac?"

Jane glanced at her glass and saw that it was just about empty. "Why not? When I'm done here, all I'm going to do is go home and fall into bed."

Patricia grinned. "Why walk all that way when you could do it right here?"

It was the first time Patricia had ever flirted so openly. Jane returned the grin, but shook her head. "Thanks. But no thanks."

Switching off the machine, Patricia stepped down. "I'll go get the bottle. Maybe after your second drink, you'll change your mind." She tossed Jane her towel on the way out the door.

Jane wasn't quite sure what to do with this new, more sexually aggressive Patricia Kastner. She couldn't help but be a little flattered, and yet she was also wary, with good reason.

Dropping the towel on an end table, she noticed two dog-eared paperbacks resting next to a cold cup of coffee. One was *Frankenstein* by Mary Shelley, the other *Dr. Jekyll and Mr. Hyde* by Robert Louis Stevenson. Odd books for someone like Patricia Kastner to be reading. Leafing briefly through Stevenson's thin volume, Jane found many sections underlined or starred. Several were highlighted in bright yellow. "If I am the chief of sinners, I am the chief of sufferers also." And: "My devil had been long caged, he came out roaring." Absently grabbing a peanut, Jane continued to read.

"What are you doing?" said Patricia sharply.

Jane looked up. "I, ah——" She saw now that the younger woman was smiling at her.

"You said you weren't hungry, and there you sit, eating."

Jane relaxed back against the chair. "I guess you caught me."

"You think I've got a wooden eye, huh?"

Her head shot up. "What did you say?"

Patricia poured more brandy into Jane's glass—enough to put three people under the table. After retrieving her towel and hanging it around her neck, she continued, "Yeah, that did come out of left field, didn't it? It just popped into my head." She sat down at a workout bench, then reached up and pulled the crossbar down.

By the strain in her face, Jane could tell she had it set for heavy tension.

"It's an old German saying. Dad and Elliot use it occasionally." She did fifteen quick reps, then stopped to catch her breath. "Roughly, it means, 'I see you, so don't think you can get away with anything.'"

Jane couldn't believe her ears. Was it a coincidence?

"You know," said Patricia, doing ten more reps, "I wrote a short paper on eyes once. It was for a philosophy class I took my freshman year of college, something on morals and ethics—I forget the exact title of the course. In a way, I suppose you could say it was my introduction to the subject of good and evil. My parents aren't very religious; we never attended church. What can I say? The subject fascinates me."

"But . . . what about *eyes* interested you?"

Patricia shrugged, wiping the sweat from her face. "Oh, you know. Stuff like how no other body part so directly represents the forces of good and evil. The eye being the 'window of the soul'— that kind of thing. If I recall correctly, the word 'fascination' comes from a Latin word that refers to an enchantment or spell cast by a look—usually a bad look. That's where we get the 'Evil Eye.' " She thought for a moment. "Then, there's the Eye of God stuff. Ra, Atom, Osiris, Jehovah; it doesn't really matter because, with all of them, the eye is central, a sign of power and omnipresence. Actually, the eye is a universal symbol for good luck."

Jane decided to take a chance. "Do you have one yourself? Say, some sort of carved eye you use as a charm?"

Patricia popped a couple of nuts into her mouth. "I said I was interested in moral philosophy, Jane, not ancient superstition." She nodded to the books. "Ever read either of those?"

"A long time ago. I don't remember them very well."

"They blow me away—both of them." She stopped for a moment to remove the sweatband from her hair. "Sometimes I wish I understood people better."

Since she was in the mood to talk, Jane decided to go along for the ride. "In what way?"

"Every way. It's like those books. To me, they're both making the same point. As humans, we try to separate our good selves from our evil selves. Except, we can't. We want to be good and do what's right, but sometimes we fail. We suspect that we have the potential to be *really* destructive given the right set of circumstances, and hope that, when the time comes, we do the right thing. But like Dr. Jekyll and Dr. Frankenstein, we refuse to accept who we really are. Jekyll is torn between his good self and his evil desires. He calls it his 'dual nature.' The bottom line is, it's impossible for one part of our nature to exist without the other. I mean, literature is full of warnings about people who've tried to separate the two. Dorian Gray. Peter Schlemihl. Even Hans Christian Andersen wrote a story about a dismissed shadow that comes back with a new body and reduces the former owner to a shadow—and then kills him. You can't be too careful about the shadow part of your personality, Jane. It's very complex. The thing is, everyone reads Robert Louis Stevenson's book and thinks Jekyll is good and Hyde is bad."

"You don't agree?"

"No, I don't. I think Dr. Jekyll is far more evil. He sets the whole experiment up—and all the way along, he's in charge. Hyde is just doing what comes naturally, and Jekyll is getting his kicks from watching Hyde behave badly—it's what he'd really like to do himself. That is, until one day when Hyde crosses a line. He kills someone."

"That's a fairly dramatic line."

"Sure, but Hyde has no moral sense. It's all the same to him. He merely wants what he wants. See, he's missing what the Bible calls 'the knowledge of good and evil.' Without it—without that inner sense of right and wrong, without true guilt—you can become a terrible person. Actually, I've got a theory. There are some real freaks out there, but they're hard to identify, mainly because it's not something, but the *absence* of something that makes them behave so badly. And how can you ever know when you're staring at nothing?"

Patricia's question and the sound of a door slamming somewhere downstairs startled Jane out of the conversation.

Patricia crooked her neck around and glanced toward the hallway. "Elliot, is that you?"

A moment later, Elliot sauntered into the room, a Coke in one hand, a chicken leg in the other. "I stopped for some KFC on my way over. And I borrowed a soda from your fridge." He stopped when he saw Jane. "Oh. Hi."

"I think I better get going." Jane sensed that he wanted to talk to his sister alone.

"But . . . you don't have to leave just yet, do you?" Patricia shot her brother a frustrated look. "It's still early. Besides, Elliot will only be here a minute or two."

"I will?" He stopped chewing.

"Really, it's getting late," said Jane, rising from her chair. "I'll talk to you tomorrow."

"Oh . . . all right," she grumped, clearly unhappy with this turn of events.

"See you on Tuesday night," said Elliot, taking a swig of Coke and waving at her with the chicken.

Patricia led the way down to the front door.

Stepping outside into the cool night air, Jane said, "I'd like to continue our conversation some evening soon."

Patricia grasped the towel around her neck with both hands. "I'd like that, too. Say, before you go, I wanted to ask you a question." Shutting the front door behind her, she stepped outside. "The other day, I was over at Elliot's apartment and I saw a white Ford pickup parked in your drive. Was it the same one that was parked outside my house last week—the one I thought might be following me?"

Jane should have seen this coming and prepared some sort of answer. Now she was caught off guard. "Actually, yes it was."

"So, did you talk to the driver?"

She nodded.

"What did he want?" Patricia was all business now. Every shred of friendliness was gone.

"Well, first he asked if Elliot lived in my house. I told him he was renting my third floor."

"And then?"

Jane shrugged. "He asked if I knew Elliot very well. I said no, not really. He'd only been renting my apartment for a few days. Then he asked if I thought Elliot was home. I said yes."

"Did he tell you why he wanted to know?"

"I assumed they were friends."

"Right," muttered Patricia. "Some friend." She walked a few paces away, standing at the edge of the steps and looking toward the dark street. The white truck was conspicuously absent tonight. "For your information, he's a private investigator. I'm telling you this so that you won't allow yourself to be used by him. I told Elliot what you said about checking the license plate, and that's just what he did. That man is following me, Jane, and now it seems he's following my brother, too. He hasn't made any attempt to contact either of us directly, but I'm sure he will." Her mouth set angrily.

"I had no idea," said Jane.

"Of course not. How could you?" She looked down. "Elliot's going to do some more digging. If he doesn't find out what that guy is after, I *will*."

"You mean—you have no idea?"

Patricia turned to face Jane. "How would you like it if someone started prying into your life? This is harassment, plain and simple. You believe me, don't you?"

"Well, sure." Jane moved back to put some distance between them. With each passing second she could see that Patricia was growing more and more angry. "I'm sorry this is happening to you."

"Yeah, sorry. Someone's going to be sorry all right." Coming forward and gripping Jane's arm with unnecessary force, Patricia said, "If that man ever tries to contact you again, tell me right away. Promise you won't listen to any of his lies."

184

"No, of course not."

She held Jane's eyes for a long moment, then let go of her arm. "You're right. It's getting late and I need to talk to my brother."

"That's a good idea."

"Catch you later," murmured Patricia as she turned to go.

Jane would have said good night, but the door had already slammed in her face.

21

A workman arrived at Jane's house shortly before 8:00 A.M. After introducing herself, Jane listened as he explained that he was the only one who'd be working today. He expected to remove all of the patio tile by noon, and then after lunch, he'd start digging the trench. If everything went as planned, he'd pour the footings tomorrow. He hoped to have the entire job done by the end of the week.

Jane didn't much care for having someone at the house when she wasn't home, but with Beryl and Edgar away, it couldn't be helped. Both Sigrid and Cordelia had to be at work by ten, and so did she.

After giving the man her office phone number and asking him to call if he ran into any problems, she spent the rest of the morning at the Lyme House in a meeting with her head chef about the restaurant's proposed holiday menu. By two, she'd made all the arrangements for tomorrow night's dinner party. In between other matters, she'd placed several calls to Earl Wilcox's cell phone, but for whatever reason, hadn't reached him. She wanted to fill him in on everything she'd learned since their last conversation. Her most interesting bit of news centered on the talk she'd had last night with Patricia. The fact that she'd brought up that old German saying made Jane wonder if there actually *was* some connection between the carved wooden eye found in Kevin Torland's pocket and the Kastner family. Dr. Cyril Dancing's suicide was also an important lead, one that needed to be pursued.

By three, Jane had finished her most pressing work and decided to run home to check on the workman's progress. Pulling her car into the drive next to the house a few minutes later, she noticed that the man she'd talked to earlier in the day had been replaced by a younger man. All of the old patio tile was piled next to the fence, so he was making good progress.

Stepping across the drive into the backyard, she could see that the new man had just begun work on the trench. "What happened to Harlan?" she asked, snaking her way in between a wheelbarrow and several sacks of cement.

The man stopped digging. Wiping the sweat from his forehead, he gave her a friendly smile. "You must be Ms. Lawless."

She nodded.

"The crew foreman took Harlan to the hospital. I think it might be his appendix. He was complaining all day yesterday about a pain in his lower stomach. Anyway, since my work was done over at Ms. Kastner's house, I offered to come up here and finish out the day. I didn't think anyone would mind."

"No, I'm happy you're here. But—do you know if Harlan's okay?"

"I expect I'll hear something before the day's out. I'll let you know before I leave."

"Thanks," she said, moving off toward the house. She was sorry the older fellow had been taken ill, but if it really was his appendix, the hosptial was the right place to be.

It was exciting to see a change happening in the backyard. Jane stood on the porch for a few minutes and watched the man dig. There were lots of tree roots that had to be hacked away or sawed in half before he could make any headway removing the dirt. It was hard, physical labor. At one point, Jane had considered doing the job herself, but as she watched him struggle to saw through a particularly nasty root, she was glad she'd changed her mind.

When she finally went inside, she found Blanche lying on the kitchen table, licking the side of a jar of apricot jam, one some-one had left sitting out. Bean, as usual, was asleep in the living room. Instead of waking him, she left him to his rest and ran upstairs to change into something more comfortable. She had a couple of hours before she had to get back to the restaurant and wanted to spend it reading. On her way back downstairs a few minutes later, she heard the phone ring. She answered it in the kitchen. "Hello?"

"Jane? Wilcox here."

"Earl, hi!"

"I've got to make this fast. I'm meeting a guy any minute."

"Where are you?"

"I'm back in Des Moines—at my house. I've been following up a lead. If I'm right about it, this new information could blow the case wide open."

"Right about what?"

"I'll fill you in when I get back to Minneapolis."

"When will that be?"

"On Wednesday afternoon—I hope."

She opened the refrigerator door and took out the carton of orange juice. "Wednesday. That's too bad. The Kastners are coming to my restaurant tomorrow night. You said you wanted to be a fly on the wall when we got together."

"I doubt they'd want to have dinner with someone like me."

"But you could always be part of the wait staff. I talked to my headwaiter today. He said he'd be happy to give you a short training session, that is, if you could make it back by four tomorrow afternoon."

"A waiter?" Another laugh. "You've got a devious mind."

"Thank you—I think."

"But I'm afraid I'll have to pass. Business will keep me here until Wednesday morning at the earliest. Can I count on you to give me a full report when I return?"

"Absolutely." She opened a cupboard and removed a glass. Thinking she heard the floor creak in the front hall, she walked to the door leading into the dining room, stretching the phone cord as far as it would go. She thought perhaps Bean had finally discovered she was home. Covering the mouthpiece, she called, "Here boy!" She quickly removed her hand. "I've got a lot to tell you, too. I think I've found some important leads of my own."

"Great," said Earl, rushing to get off. "Sorry, Jane, but my appointment's here."

"When will I see you?"

"How about Thursday night? Late, just in case I don't make it back on Wednesday. Say . . . around midnight?"

"Thursday's great. But you can't come here again. Last time Patricia spotted your truck in the drive."

"I was afraid that had happened. I hope you were able to cover. She doesn't know you're helping me, does she?"

"No. Everything's fine."

"Good. So—where should we meet? You pick the spot."

She thought for a moment. "What about the Lake Harriet bandshell? It's deserted at that time of night, but it's a pretty safe area."

"Fine. See you then."

After hanging up, Jane clapped her hands, hoping Bean would hear and come racing into the kitchen like he used to. "Here, Beany," she called, crossing into the dining room and then into the front hall. But there he was, still asleep on the rug in front of the fireplace. So, if he was *there,* what had made the floor creak? She glanced up the stairs. "Anybody home? Cordelia, Sigrid?"

No response.

Jane scratched her head, then walked slowly back into the kitchen to get her glass of orange juice. It had to be those stupid cats. Last night she'd been awakened by Lucifer chasing Melville back and forth through the upstairs hallway. Never, *ever,* would she willingly live with something that nocturnal.

Just to be on the safe side, she spent the next few minutes walking around the house, examining all the rooms. She even checked the door leading to Elliot's third-floor apartment, but found it locked tight, just the way she'd left it.

A knock on the front door drew her back downstairs.

Much to her surprise, she found her brother standing outside on the front steps. He wasn't smiling. "Hey there, kiddo. Come in."

He peered cautiously over her shoulder. "Is Sigrid here?"

Of course. This wasn't a social call. He'd come to talk to his wife. "No, I'm afraid she's not. But she left me her schedule. I could go check it, but I'm pretty sure she works until nine."

He nodded. "Yeah. Monday's her late night." He attempted a smile, though not a very convincing one. "I guess you've heard the news."

"I'm not taking sides, Peter. She just needed a place to stay. She didn't want to be alone."

"It's all right," he said, giving her a quick hug.

Growing up, Jane had been very close to her brother. People always said how much the Lawless kids looked alike. Both of them had inherited their mother's quick smile and lush chestnut hair. And both were tall and slim, though Jane had to fight a lot harder to stay thin than Peter did. Their father's gifts were less physical. Peter and Jane had been blessed with his analytical mind, his intellectual bent, and a certain bullheadedness that pervaded the entire Lawless clan. After Peter's marriage to Sigrid several years ago, Jane had begun to see less and less of him. She assumed it was a normal life passage. He was busy building a marriage with the woman he loved. She was busy building a business. Since she knew he was happy, she didn't worry. At least she hadn't until now.

Leading him into the living room, she offered him something to drink. He declined, saying he couldn't stay long.

Jane was angry with herself now for not trying harder to contact him before she left town. "You have to understand, Peter, I don't even know what any of this is about."

"You mean Sigrid didn't tell you?"

She shook her head.

"And of course you didn't want to push."

"No, I didn't. I assumed one of you would offer some explanation sooner or later. Or maybe you wouldn't. I guess it's your call."

He nodded, then looked down, fingering the wedding ring on his left hand.

"Have you told Dad about the separation?"

"Not yet."

She could tell he was struggling with himself over just how much to say. "Peter, is this . . . final? Are you two finished?"

"I don't know. But I'll be honest with you. This is a pretty tough one. We may not survive."

"Do you want to talk about it?"

He rubbed the sides of his temples. "Yeah, I guess I should talk to someone. Not that it would change anything. Sigrid and I have to make some hard decisions. Nobody can make them for us. And no one, not even you, sis, can make this any easier."

Seeing him in such pain was hard. She wished she weren't so totally in the dark, but until one of them cared to enlighten her, all she could do was offer an ear—and her love. "I'm here for you, Peter. Anything you ever need——"

He squeezed her hand. "I know." He glanced at his watch. "Listen, Janey, I didn't come here to talk about Sigrid."

Now she was confused.

"I called the restaurant hoping to find you, but they said you'd left for a few hours. So I decided to stop by. Technically, this is a business call."

Peter had been a cameraman for WTWN-TV for many years. "You want to film me making dinner?" She laughed at the absurdity.

Looking around the room, his eyes came to rest on the coffee table directly in front of him. "Have you read that yet?" He nodded to the morning paper.

She shrugged. "No. Why?"

He picked it up, pointing to a short article at the bottom of the front page.

The headline immediately caught her eye: PSYCHIC SOLVES SECOND MURDER. Slipping on her reading glasses, she read silently:

> Elliot Beauman, children's book author and resident of Linden Hills in south Minneapolis, offered the police a tip last week which led to the arrest of Gregory Altman, 16, for the murder of his father, Frank Altman, a salesman for Varani's Pasta Products.
>
> Sgt. Harry Engsdahl of the Criminal Investigations Division of the Minneapolis Police Department issued a statement late yesterday afternoon saying that after receiving the tip from Mr. Beauman, Altman was interrogated for several hours. Against the advice of his lawyer, he admitted to beating his father to death with a claw hammer in the basement of their family home.

Jane looked up. "That's—amazing! I had no idea Elliot had helped the police again." The more she found out about him, the harder it was for her to know what to think of him.

"Carol Lowry, one of the producers at the station, called and tried to convince Beauman to go on camera about it, but he refused. This is a hot story, Jane. And this guy's totally media-shy. Whoever finally gets the interview will really grab an audience. I had no idea he was living here until I saw his address in the police report this morning. When I mentioned it to Carol, she suggested

I come talk to you. We hoped that maybe you knew him, that you might even be friendly with him, and that you'd be willing to talk to him about it—as a favor to your favorite brother."

"My *favorite* brother?"

He grinned. "We could do an interview here at the house, Janey. Very low key. Just a Betacam. No special lights. We could even discuss the questions first—make sure he's completely comfortable. And he could stop at any time. See, we would have explained all this to him on the phone, but he hangs up on anyone who calls. Even a ten-second sound bite from the guy would be worth its weight in gold. We're hoping to build an entire story around psychics and how they help the police. If I could get Beauman for the station, it would mean a lot."

He seemed so eager she could hardly say no. "Sure, I'd be happy to talk to him. But don't count on anything."

"Could you do it now?"

She smiled at his impatience. "Sure. But I don't know if he's home." She got up and crossed to the front windows. "Yeah, his car's outside. Unless he's gone for a walk or something, he should be around."

"Great." Peter stood. Hooking his arm through hers, he walked her into the kitchen. "I'll make myself a sandwich while you run upstairs."

"I'm not sure what I should say."

"You'll think of something. Just be your normal charming persuasive self."

"Right."

Before she could make it to the back door, she heard a man's voice call, "Ms. Lawless? Are you in there?"

Stepping onto the porch, she saw that the workman was standing by the screen door. "Can I help you?"

"I hope so. I think you better come look at something."

"What is it?"

He took off his cap and scratched his head. "Bones."

Jane turned around and saw that Peter was listening, too.

"Better check it out, sis."

She nodded. Following the workman out to the patio, she watched as he bent down, pointing to some dirty chunks.

"They're human bones, ma'am. The skull's right here." He brushed some dirt off a large lump. "It's face-down. I didn't move it because——" He pointed to a deep crack.

Jane bent down to get a closer look. The skull had been badly damaged. "You didn't hit it with your shovel, did you?"

"No, ma'am. When I found the other bones, I was real careful. I took the dirt away with a hand trowel. At first I thought it was a dog, but then I saw the skull."

She touched it, then drew back her hand. "The pieces seem awfully small."

"Right. I think it was a kid."

"A child," she whispered, looking back at her brother.

"You better call the police, Janey," said Peter.

"The bones are old, ma'am," continued the workman. "I don't know what happened, but my guess is it was a long time ago."

She straightened up. Turning toward the house she was surprised to see Elliot standing on the small landing just outside his door. He was smoking a cigarette, flicking ash over the railing. She wondered how long he'd been there. This was no time to think about interviews. Dashing into the house, she grabbed the phone and called 911.

Fifteen minutes later she was seated on a small wicker loveseat on the back porch answering a homicide investigator's questions. Peter sat next to her. Outside, she could see the workman being questioned by another officer.

"How long have you owned the house, Ms. Lawless?" asked Sergeant McKay.

She felt the muscles in her neck tighten. "Since nineteen eighty-three."

"And who did you buy it from?"

"A man named Seymour Getty."

He jotted it down. "Do you know how long he lived here before he sold you the place?"

She shook her head.

"Was the patio here before you moved in?"

"Yes, it was quite new."

"But you don't know if Mr. Getty put it in."

"I'm sorry, I don't."

He wrote for a minute more, then continued, "Do you have any idea what happened to Mr. Getty? Where we might locate him?"

"Well, I think he bought a house out on Lake Minnetonka. I only talked to him once—at the closing. My partner handled most of the details. She was a real estate agent."

The officer looked up, narrowing his eyes at her, but made no comment.

"I believe Mr. Getty said he was retiring. He'd bought a boat and wanted to kick back—do some fishing."

"Do you recall anything else he said?"

Jane shook her head again. Waiting until he finished writing, she asked a question of her own. "What do you think happened out there?"

"We don't know yet."

"But the bones. They're pretty small."

He got up, placing a hand over his gun. "For now, we're treating this as an unexplained death. But we're going to have to stop your workman from digging—at least for now. A couple of forensic investigators will be dispatched shortly. Hopefully, they'll be done with their examination by the end of the day. If not, we'll have to treat this as a crime scene. In that case, we'll tape it off. No one, not even you, will be allowed inside the tape."

"Of course," said Jane. "But . . . can't you just give me your opinion?"

He adjusted his hat. "It wouldn't be worth much."

"Give it to us anyway," said Peter, putting his arm around his sister's shoulder.

The officer studied him for a moment, then returned his attention to Jane. "I could be wrong, but from what I saw out there, I think we may have a homicide on our hands. I'm sorry, Ms. Lawless. I know that's not what you wanted to hear."

"You're right," she mumbled. It wasn't.

22

On Tuesday morning, Jane sat at her kitchen table reading the morning paper. She was searching for an article on the bones that had been discovered in her backyard yesterday afternoon.

Behind her, Cordelia leaned against the counter munching on a bowl of Cap'n Crunch. "Nothing, huh?"

"It's probably too soon. Or maybe it's not a big enough story."

Cordelia shuddered. "I am so *incredibly* horrified to think someone could do something like that." She shuddered again, then went on eating.

Jane glanced up as Sigrid breezed into the room. She was dressed in a tailored navy blue suit and carrying a briefcase. "Off to work?"

"Afraid so," she muttered.

"Say," said Cordelia, setting her empty bowl down in the sink, "you're our resident psychologist. You tell us what kind of sicko would murder a child and then bury the body in someone's backyard."

Very patiently, Sigrid replied, "I'm a marriage and family therapist, Cordelia. I don't deal with sociopathic personalities—at least, not very often." She opened up one of the cupboards and rummaged around until she found a box of chocolate chip granola bars. "I should be home pretty late tonight, Jane. Peter and I are getting together to talk."

"I'm glad to hear it," Jane said, watching her sister-in-law stuff two bars into her briefcase. "I hope everything goes well."

Sigrid paused for a moment, then pressed a thumb and forefinger to her eyelids. "This is so ludicrous. How am I supposed to counsel people all day about their marital problems when my own marriage is a disaster?"

"It's called *life*," said Cordelia, patting Sigrid's shoulder.

Sigrid glared, then relented. "I suppose you have a point."

"You'll make it through," said Cordelia. "Listen to your Auntie Jane and Uncle Cordelia. Just tell that husband of yours that he's got himself one hell of a good woman."

"I wish it were that simple," Sigrid whispered, picking up her briefcase. "I'll see you two later." As she got to the door, she stopped. "There's a cop in the backyard."

Jane quickly rose and went out onto the porch. Waving goodbye to Sigrid, she watched the officer, the same one she'd spoken with yesterday, step up to the partially excavated patio. He stood just outside the taped-off section, looked around a minute, then turned and headed for the house.

"What's he doing here?" grumbled Cordelia, moving up behind Jane. She was now eating one of Sigrid's granola bars.

Jane looked back at her, her eyes moving from the bar to the Coke in Cordelia's other hand. "You know, you and Sigrid are certainly children of the nineties."

Cordelia smirked. " 'Time is just a stream I go a-fishing in.' " At Jane's questioning look, she added, "Thoreau. This has been a literary moment, brought to you by Cordelia M. Thorn. For a copy of today's quote—"

"Zip it," muttered Jane, waiting for the officer to reach the porch door. "Can I help you?"

198

"Morning, Ms. Lawless."

She nodded.

"I've got something I'd like to show you."

"Sure. Come in," she said. As she stepped back, she bumped into Cordelia. "Give me a little room, okay?"

"I do not *hover*," said Cordelia indignantly. Smiling beatifically at the police officer, she said, "And I am, of course, Cordelia Thorn." She extended her hand, looking for all the world like the Queen Mother accepting the obeisance of a loyal subject.

They all sat down.

Pulling a small plastic bag out of his pocket, the sergeant handed it to Jane. "I need to know if you've ever seen this before."

The bag contained a gold cufflink in the shape of an oak leaf. She examined it carefully, turning it over in her hand. "No, sorry."

"Me neither," said Cordelia, nearly crowding Jane off the loveseat in her eagerness to look at it.

"We found it yesterday," said McKay.

"With the bones?" asked Cordelia.

"That's right."

"Then whoever dropped it was probably responsible for burying the body," Cordelia continued in the same excited tone.

"Well, that's one theory." He switched his attention back to Jane. "A determination will be made later today about the crime scene. Since we've pretty much sifted through the dirt surrounding the victim, my guess is you'll be able to resume your work out there tomorrow."

"Thanks." She could tell he was in a hurry, so she got up and walked him to the door. At least she had one piece of good news. She could pass it on to Otto Kastner this evening at dinner. Hopefully, his workman would be able to return in the morning. Not that Jane's excitement about the greenhouse was what it used to be. "Have you learned anything new about the person who died?"

He paused next to the door. "It was a girl. The cause of death was severe head trauma. That's all I know for sure. They're estimating her age at somewhere between eight and ten, but that could change."

"And how long ago did she die?" asked Cordelia.

"We'll know more when we find out who laid that patio. It was a perfect spot to hide a body. We're checking our records to see if there was a report of a missing child in the area—going back as far as the late sixties."

Jane shook her head. Cordelia was right. This was incredibly ghoulish. "I hope you find out who did it."

McKay tipped his hat. "Thanks for your time."

After he'd gone, Jane sat down on the wicker rocker across from Cordelia. She couldn't hide her frustration, or her revulsion.

"I know this is rough on you, Janey."

"That's an understatement."

Waiting a moment more, Cordelia added, "I hope you won't think I'm a rat leaving a sinking ship, but—"

Jane glanced up.

"I realize it's a poor metaphor. I look far more like a rooster, but somehow rooster doesn't work. Anyway, I'm leaving. Tonight's my last night at Hotel Lawless. The work is finished at my loft. And the haulers are delivering my stuff tomorrow morning."

A week ago, Jane would have cheered. Today, Cordelia was right. She felt as if she were being abandoned. She knew she didn't have the right to insist that Cordelia stay, but it was tempting. "I'm really happy for you."

"And you know what that means, Janey." Cordelia wiggled her eyebrows meaningfully.

"The cats are leaving too." Jane said a silent thank you. At least she got something out of the deal.

"Yes, that's true. But more specifically"—Cordelia's arms shot triumphantly into the air—"you get to help me unpack. In fact, I'll even let you cater the party."

Jane's enthusiasm wasn't overwhelming. "Who all is coming?"

"Oh, well . . . there's you . . . and there's me. That's about it." She grinned, then turned serious. "You know, Janey, I can't ask just anyone. It's the sort of thing one loses friends over."

"But you're not afraid of losing my friendship?"

"Of course not. We're family—in every way that counts. Which means, we can abuse each other with impunity, and we're still supposed to love each other."

"What a sick view of family life."

"Listen, Janey. Without twisted family dynamics, there'd be no comedy, no drama. And without *that,* I'd be out of a job."

"So, in a sense, you see human dysfunction as the source of your employment?"

"Precisely. And don't give me that Quaker stare of yours. I merely speak the truth. Now, I've got to run upstairs and slip into my work duds. In between all my meetings today, I have to prepare my game plan for tonight."

"Just remember, Cordelia. We'd like to talk about something other than your brilliant career."

"But, of course, Janey. We'll talk about *your* brilliant career, too. But in your case, there's not as much to say." She patted Jane's knee and then hurried back into the house.

A few hours later, Jane walked up the front steps of a large Victorian home in the Merriam Park neighborhood of St. Paul. She'd called Ramona Dancing, Cyril Dancing's widow, late yesterday afternoon and asked if she could come by today to see her. When Mrs. Dancing asked what the visit was about, Jane sidestepped the issue the same way she had with Abbie Kaufman. She said she preferred to talk about it in person. Mrs. Dancing was clearly dissatisfied with her explanation, but agreed to meet at three. Checking her watch, Jane saw that she was right on time.

After ringing the bell, she waited, wondering how she was going to get Cyril Dancing's widow to open up to her. The door finally opened and a tall, prim, white-haired woman peered out. "Ms. Lawless?"

"That's right."

"Please, come in." She unlocked the screen and then walked back into the house.

It was a cold, blustery fall day. Jane was glad to be inside out of the wind. As she followed Mrs. Dancing into a rear room, she noticed a series of portraits on the walls in the hallway. Some were of children, some adults.

"Please," said Mrs. Dancing, motioning to a chair, "sit down. Would you like something to drink? You look cold."

Jane smiled. "No thanks."

"I would have built us a fire, but my arthritis is particularly bad today." She eased down onto a small sofa. Books and papers lay all around her.

From the look of the room, Jane decided it was a study—or perhaps a library. If she wasn't mistaken, several sets of law books adorned the deep oak shelves. "Is someone in your family a lawyer?"

"Yes. I am. In these litigious times, every family needs at least one, don't you agree?"

By the smile on her face, Jane wondered if she wasn't referring to her father. "Do you know my dad?"

"Of course. Everyone in this town knows Raymond Lawless. He's a very fine man. That's one of the main reasons I agreed to see you. I knew he had a daughter named Jane. I assumed that was you."

She nodded. "What sort of law did you practice?"

"The right kind, I hope. I served on the District Court of Appeals for fifteen years."

"You're a judge?"

"You seem surprised."

"No . . . I mean——"

"I'm retired, Ms. Lawless. Though I keep busy. Sometimes busier than I'd like."

Jane glanced up at an oil portrait of a handsome, middle-aged man hanging above the fireplace.

"Yes, that was my late husband. A real stud, wasn't he?" She said the word with a twinkle in her eye, but Jane also detected a note of sarcasm.

"How old was he when the portrait was done?"

"Fifty-five. He died the following year."

"I'm truly sorry."

"Thank you. Now, tell me, Ms. Lawless, why are you here? Something tells me it has to do with Cyril."

"Well, yes, it does."

Her eyes rose to the painting. "What have you done now?" she mumbled. Returning her gaze to Jane, she folded one arthritic hand over the other and waited. "Come on, Ms. Lawless. I won't bite."

"No, of course not."

"Don't misunderstand. I *do* bite. I was just assuring you that in this instance, I would refrain."

Jane smiled. She liked Ramona Dancing—liked her clarity. "Thank you."

"You may continue."

Jane cleared her throat and then said, "Have you ever heard the name Patricia Kastner?"

The older woman narrowed her eyes. "Ah, I see now where this is leading. You've heard the story about Patricia and my husband."

Jane blinked, but kept her expression even. "Yes, some of it. But I was hoping you'd tell me about it in your own words."

"I don't know why I should. You've explained nothing about why you're here. I was curious when you called last night, so I indulged my curiosity by inviting you here today. But I'm not a patient woman, Ms. Lawless. I suggest you get to your point."

Knowing she had only moments before being tossed out on her ear, Jane reached into her coat pocket and drew out the wooden eye. "Have you ever seen anything like this before, Mrs. — "

"I prefer Judge Dancing."

"Of course." Jane handed the wooden piece over.

The judge examined it briefly and then handed it back. "Where did you get this?"

"It was in the pocket of a man who recently committed suicide. There is . . . some . . . reason to believe he didn't die by his own hand."

"You think it was a homicide?"

"I do."

"And that" — she nodded to the wooden eye — "was the murderer's signature?"

Jane nodded.

Judge Dancing stared at her long and hard. "What's your interest in the matter?"

"Well, I'm unofficially looking into it."

"Unofficially."

"That's right."

"You're not a licensed investigator?"

"No. Actually, I own a restaurant."

The judge leaned her elbow on the arm of the sofa, touching her fingers to the bottom of her chin. "You know, Ms. Lawless, normally the police handle matters like this. That's why we have them."

"I understand. But the police consider it a closed case. They believe the death was a suicide."

She thought a little before going on. "Well, I have to be honest with you. I've never had one moment's doubt that my husband committed suicide."

Jane felt her heart sink.

"That is . . . until now." With some difficulty, Judge Dancing got up and walked over to the fireplace. Removing a small red box from the mantelpiece, she handed it to Jane, then sat back down. "Open it."

Jane pulled back the cover. Inside, she found a wooden eye, almost exactly like the one she'd brought with her.

"Cyril's body was found in a hotel room at the Maxfield Plaza in downtown St. Paul. The official cause of death was an overdose of drugs and alcohol. The police found Valium and several bottles of vodka in his possession. It was enough to kill a man several times over." She paused, adjusted her skirt over her knees, then continued, "After his body was released to me for burial, his belongings were also returned. That carved wooden eye was among them. It puzzled me, Ms. Lawless, particularly because I'd never seen it before. After the funeral, I put it in that box and forgot about it. Oh, every now and then I'd take it out and wonder what he was doing with something so strange. It reminded me of the amulets one sometimes sees in West Africa. Cyril and I took several trips there during our marriage."

"But you said you were sure your husband's death was suicide. At the time, was he upset over something specific?"

Judge Dancing's gaze drifted to the cold fireplace. "Yes."

When she didn't continue, Jane prompted her. "His relationship with Patricia Kastner?"

She pressed her lips together. Leaning forward, she said, "You see, my husband was in the middle of what we used to call a midlife crisis. He wasn't sure he wanted to be married to me any longer. Our children were grown and out of the house, and Cyril was . . . restless. That's when he met Patricia. She was a student of his at the university. In time, she also became a patient. I remember his saying that she was a very troubled young woman. He felt he could help her. I'm ashamed to say this, Ms. Lawless, but Cyril did something he'd taken an oath never to do. He slept with her."

Jane knew this was undoubtedly a difficult admission for Ramona Dancing, and yet she said the words with little emotion. "From what I was told, Patricia didn't hide their affair."

"That's because, in her eyes, it was more than an affair. She claimed she loved my husband—wanted to marry him. I'll be honest with you, Ms. Lawless. All I know is what Cyril told me. He came to me one night and confessed to his infidelity. He said that Patricia's parents had found out about their *relationship* and were threatening to make it public. You have to understand, if the story had become public, Patricia Kastner wouldn't have been the only casualty. It would have ended Cyril's career—and left him in total disgrace. In the final analysis, whether it was some truth about himself he couldn't face, or the fear of professional censure, he took his life. He left no note. If his death was meant to placate Otto and Virginia Kastner, it served its purpose. It put an end to the rumors and the threats, but it also put an end to Cyril."

There were no tears in Ramona Dancing's eyes. She must have come to terms with her husband's suicide long ago. And yet now, Jane had presented her with a new possibility.

"Tell me, Ms. Lawless. If Cyril didn't die by his own hand, how did someone get him to drink all that vodka and swallow all those pills? He was a strong man. He would have fought like a tiger to save his own life."

"I don't know," said Jane.

"There were no marks on his body—except where he fell and hit his head when he passed out."

"I understand. But if it wasn't murder, how do you explain the presence of that wooden eye?"

Ramona Dancing considered the question. "I'd say we have ourselves an old-fashioned standoff. I can't answer your question and you can't answer mine. On the other hand, if you want to know who had a motive for wanting my husband dead, you need look no further than Otto or Virginia Kastner." Rising from her chair, she added, "Come back and see me again, Ms. Lawless, when you do have some answers."

23

The Lyme House had several large banquet rooms, all on the ground level behind the pub. Jane's favorite place to hold a private gathering, however, was upstairs, a section of the main dining room the staff referred to as "the Lake Harriet Room" because it had a beautiful view of the lake and could be closed off by shutting two sets of French doors. It had the same table appointments as the main dining room, and was often reserved for special occasions when only a small area was needed. This was the space she'd reserved for tonight's dinner.

The Kastners were due to arrive at seven. By six, the room was already being prepared. Jane entered from the kitchen and spent a few moments talking to the wine steward. She needed to make sure the wines she'd ordered earlier in the day were ready to be served. Walking around the table, she saw that the flowers had arrived: a delicate bouquet of white and ivory. The lights would be dimmed shortly before seven, and the candles lit.

The preparation was going so smoothly that she decided to run down to the pub and talk to the assistant manager about the poet who would be reading on the pub's stage later tonight. Less than a month ago, she'd begun a series of poetry readings at the Lyme House. Since they'd been so well received, she was thinking of doing some other literary events—as soon as she had some time to brainstorm with her staff.

Just as she finished her conversation, she noticed Elliot come into the bar and sit down at the counter. He glanced through the menu briefly, then waited for the bartender to take his order. Easing down next to him, she smiled a greeting. "You're early."

He looked over at her somewhat blankly. "Oh, hi. I've never been here before. I guess I wanted to check the place out. Get the lay of the land."

She was glad for the opportunity to have a private moment with him before dinner. "I've been wanting to talk to you."

"About what?"

The bartender arrived.

"Just some mineral water," said Jane. "How about you? We've got some great beers on tap."

"I don't drink," said Elliot curtly. He glanced at the menu again, then put it away. "A Mountain Dew please."

Jane couldn't help but notice that he wasn't in a particularly good mood tonight. He'd put on an expensive-looking suit for the occasion, but the lack of a tie and the wrinkled shirt spoke more loudly. "I've got a favor I want to ask you," she said, leaning away from him.

He turned to look at her. "And that would be?"

"My brother is a cameraman for WTWN-TV. He came by yesterday and asked if I'd talk to you."

The light dawned in Elliot's eyes. "He wants you to beg me for an interview."

"I'm not sure I'd use the term 'beg.' "

He laughed, looking around the crowded room. "Boy, these people never quit."

"That's because you're news, Elliot. You and your psychic

abilities helped the police solve two recent crimes. Who knows? Maybe you'll help them solve another."

The smile faded.

Based on his reaction, she decided to ask him a question. "Have you . . . come up with some thoughts on another local crime?"

"No," he said, a little too quickly. "I'm done with all that. I told the police to leave me alone."

Their drinks arrived.

Elliot didn't taste his. Instead, he leaned morosely on the bar, his eyes drifting to the bottles behind the counter. "I just want it all to go away."

"All of what?" she asked, pouring her bottled water over the ice in her glass.

"All of this *psychic* crap."

He was obviously upset. "Look, Elliot, I told Peter I'd ask you, and I have. If you don't want to do the interview, no one can force you."

He drummed his fingers on the bar. "Where would we do it?"

She was surprised by his response. She had felt certain that his answer would be no, no matter how hard she pushed. "Well, Peter said they could tape it at the house. In my living room, if you like."

"Would I get a chance to look at the questions first? There's some stuff I refuse to talk about."

"Sure," said Jane. "And you could stop the interview any time you want. The people at WTWN want to make this as easy for you as possible."

"*Easy,*" he grunted. "Right."

She waited a few seconds before continuing. "So, what do you say? Will you do it?"

His gaze shifted to the door. Something had caught his eye. Stiffening suddenly, he said, "It's a deal. As long as it's soon. This week."

"I'll call Peter when I get home tonight. He'll phone you in the morning."

"No, not him. You. I want to handle this all through you."

"Well . . . sure."

"Good. Just let me know when and where."

He seemed almost eager now. Wondering what had captured his attention, she turned to find Otto and Virginia Kastner standing in the lower hall, removing their coats. She quickly moved off her stool. "If you want to bring your drink, I'll show you where we're having dinner."

"I can hardly wait," he said, his tone oozing sarcasm.

Fifteen minutes later, everyone except Cordelia was seated at the large round table. Jane listened with great curiosity to the family banter. Even Elliot's sour mood improved slightly with the arrival of his sister. Jane knew these people weren't about to betray their deepest, darkest secrets over a casual dinner, and yet she thought it important to get a feel for who they were as a group. How they interacted. She didn't *want* to like any of them, but the longer they talked, the more she found herself enjoying the conversation.

For one thing, Virginia Kastner was far more friendly and engaging than Jane had imagined she would be. She was a small woman, with a quick smile, a shrewd gaze, and dyed platinum blond hair pulled back into a perfectly smooth French twist. Tonight she was wearing a tasteful linen dress, almost the same color as her hair, and a single strand of cultured pearls. Taken as a whole, the Kastners were reserved—no belly laughs or raucous humor—but still friendly. What struck Jane most about them was their intelligence. Each one seemed not only well-read but culturally aware, even astute. An outsider looking in would see an attractive American family; and yet after her visit with Ramona Dancing this afternoon, Jane was convinced one of them was a murderer.

"Isn't Cordelia Thorn joining us this evening?" asked Virginia. She'd refused the wine offered her and instead sipped from a glass of Perrier.

Jane glanced at her watch. "She should be here any minute." No sooner had she said the words than Cordelia swept into the room. Jane found herself staring when she saw what her friend had chosen to wear: a black top hat, black tie and tails.

Cordelia winked at Jane, removed her hat, and bowed to Virginia Kastner. "I'm delighted to finally meet you," she said, looking for all the world like a glamorous version of Luciano Pavarotti. Her hair was drawn back severely from her face and tucked into a smooth bun. Bright red lipstick and tiny gold earrings completed the look.

Jane couldn't imagine why Cordelia had opted for something so blatant. If Virginia was indeed homophobic, arriving in drag was a sure way to court disaster. Then again, if Cordelia was about to go down, she would want to do it as herself, in a blaze of sartorial glory, so to speak. Cordelia was a true iconoclast and rarely did anything that was expected of her. Many years ago, she and Jane had been invited to an all-lesbian dance. In the face of tradition, Cordelia had donned a slinky, low-cut evening gown, and decked herself out in jewels, fake fur, and feathers. The clothes and the makeup had caused more than a few eyebrows to rise, and dozens of comments afterward. If Jane recalled correctly, Cordelia had loved every minute of it. She wasn't going to be stuffed into *anybody's* box.

After Cordelia had pulled out a chair and made herself comfortable, Virginia gave her a broad smile. "I just want you to know that I'm behind you one hundred percent. I can't imagine why the Allen Grimby is even *thinking* of replacing you."

Cordelia's eyes, already sparkling from her dramatic entrance, registered surprise. "That's . . . fabulous!"

"*You're* fabulous," continued Virginia, taking another sip of her Perrier.

Patricia beamed at Jane from across the table. "You mentioned the other night that Cordelia was nervous about how my mother would vote. I asked her to address it early in the evening so that everyone could relax."

Jane nodded her thanks, touched that Patricia would show such concern for someone she barely knew.

"Tell me again how you met my daughter," said Virginia, glancing at Jane.

"Actually, it was——"

"——at our Grand Avenue store in St. Paul," said Patricia, quickly finishing her sentence.

"Are you a gardener then?" asked Virginia, touching a napkin to her lips.

"My aunt is." Jane felt a bit uncomfortable with the lie, but she couldn't exactly contradict Patricia without causing problems.

Relieved of the need to sell herself, Cordelia tucked into her appetizer—the Lyme House's famous salmon Beasley, a chilled salmon in a light vinaigrette with capers and a garnish of quails' eggs. "They also belong to the same block association. Jane's the new block emperor."

Jane kicked her under the table.

"Ouch." Glaring down her nose, Cordelia said, "You should have warned me I was sitting next to you tonight. I would have worn my shin guards."

"Excuse me?" said Virginia, looking up.

"Jane may throw a great dinner party," said Cordelia, rubbing her sore leg, "but she has a tendency to attack my lower extremities given even the slightest provocation."

Jane smiled, trying to blend into the wallpaper. She could have kicked Cordelia—if she hadn't already. As the wine steward walked around the table pouring more wine, Jane gritted her teeth and whispered sideways, "Don't talk about Linden Hills."

"What?" said Cordelia. "Stop mumbling."

Again, Jane smiled.

213

"What did that mean about you being a block emperor?" asked Virginia, taking a taste of the soup that had just been served to her.

"It's nothing, Mother," said Patricia. "Cordelia's just being silly."

"Would someone please pass the rolls?" said Otto, attempting to change the subject. "They're wonderful, by the way. Do you make them here?"

"We do," said Jane, handing him the basket. As he reached across the table, her eyes dropped to his cufflink: a gold rectangle with the letters OAK stamped into it. She immediately thought of the cufflink the police had shown her that morning.

"Is something wrong?" asked Patricia, noticing Jane's stare.

"What? No, nothing."

"About this soup?" said Elliot, pushing it around with his spoon. "What's in it?"

"Pumpkin," replied Jane. "Cream. A few herbs and spices."

He gazed at it suspiciously.

"This is a lovely restaurant," said Virginia, glancing around. "We don't usually visit this part of town." Giving her daughter and son sharp looks, she added, "I can't for the life of me understand why my children would move back to this area of the city."

Jane saw a worried look pass over Otto's face. "Let's not talk about that tonight, honey."

"Property values," replied Cordelia between mouthfuls. "Jane got her house for around fifty thousand. It's worth four times that now. Patricia made herself a sound investment, Virginia, take my word for it."

"Cordelia just bought a loft in downtown Minneapolis," said Jane, hoping to avert a small crisis. Hearing a noise behind her, she turned as two police officers pushed through the French doors. She recognized Sergeant McKay.

"Sorry to interrupt, Ms. Lawless," said McKay. Grasping one wrist with his other hand, he stood rigidly next to the door. "I'm

214

afraid this couldn't be helped. We're looking for Otto Kastner."

Otto finished chewing. He appeared to be in no particular hurry. "I'm Otto Kastner."

"We'd like to talk to you, sir. It shouldn't take long."

"What about?" He didn't get up.

The officers exchanged glances. McKay then said, "Did you once own the house at 4532 Bridwell Lane? The one Ms. Lawless now owns?"

"What?" said Jane. She blinked back her surprise. "*You* owned my house?" Turning to Virginia, she saw a similar look of shock.

"Yes, I owned it," said Otto. "Many years ago. Why?"

"Were you responsible for putting in the patio in the backyard?"

"Sure, I put it in. And now I'm taking it out. As far as I know, there's no law against it."

"But . . . Elliot," said Virginia, looking across the table at her son, "you told me you're renting Jane's third floor."

"I am."

"But"—her shock had turned to horror—"how could you go back *there*? After what happened—"

"It's a house, Mother. That's all."

"Elliot!"

"I'm sick to death of having to tiptoe around you. I've spent my entire life being hushed whenever I brought up our old home. None of us talk about it, not even the good times. We also don't tell you if we've gone to Southdale because you used to take Jay and me there to watch the birds in the courtyard. We stopped eating at Murray's because it was Jay's favorite restaurant. Jay's favorite color was blue; you won't even allow that color in your house now. Life goes on, Mother. Sometimes it feels like . . . like you're trying to *erase* him—to wipe him out by never talking about him, or that time in our lives."

She stared back at her son, dumbfounded.

"Please, Mr. Kastner," said McKay. "Let's take a walk outside."

Rising very slowly from his chair, Otto said, "Is this about the bones my workman found?"

"Yes, sir. It is."

"What bones?" demanded Virginia. "Whose bones?"

Otto shot Elliot an angry look. "Take your mother home. And stay there with her until I get back. Patricia, you go with him."

"Dad," pleaded Patricia, "there's no reason to let this ruin our evening. Take care of whatever it is these men want and then come back inside."

He shook his head. "I never should have agreed to come tonight. I only did it to make you happy—and look what's happened. Do as I say, you two. Take your mother home." Glancing warily at his wife, he tossed his napkin on the table and followed the men out of the room.

After they were gone, one of the wait staff appeared. "Ms. Lawless? Should we give you a few minutes before serving the main course?"

Jane wasn't sure what to say.

"Waiter," said Virginia, staring blankly at the cold soup in front of her, "bring me a double vodka on the rocks."

"Mother, don't," said Elliot.

"Bring it!" She looked up defiantly.

Jane nodded to the waiter, then looked over at Patricia. It was the first time she'd ever seen the younger woman at such a loss for words.

"I refuse to stay and watch this," said Elliot, tossing down his own napkin.

"Fine," said Virginia coldly. "Do whatever you want. You will anyway."

Patricia watched her brother leave, then gazed at her mother with uncertain eyes. "Elliot's probably right. You shouldn't drink. You've had a bad shock tonight, Mom. Maybe . . . maybe we were wrong, keeping Elliot's address from you the way we did. But if

216

you could just try to understand. This neighborhood has good memories for me. I was happy here. Jane's third floor was for rent and Elliot wanted to move some place close to me. Can't you understand—we didn't do it to hurt you."

"You've all *lied* to me."

"We did it to protect you."

Virginia's eyes shot to the door as the waiter returned with her drink.

"Mom, let me take you home."

"I don't need your help. I don't need *anyone's* help." She took several quick gulps, set the glass down, then picked it up again and finished it. Rising from the table, she said, "I'll find my own way home."

"But, Virginia," said Cordelia, "I was hoping we could . . ."

"Another time." She gazed down at Jane. "I think you did me a favor. At least now I know what my family thinks of me behind my back."

"It's nothing like that," insisted Patricia. "We all love you."

"Funny, but it doesn't feel that way." Without another word, she picked up her purse and left.

After making sure Virginia got safely into a cab, Jane said good night to Cordelia and then walked Patricia home. Before they left, they'd received word from Otto via one of the restaurant staff that he'd agreed to go downtown to answer more police questions. Jane had some questions too, and hoped she could convince Patricia to answer them before they called it a night.

On the way up the hill from the lake, Jane could tell Patricia was worried, though the source of her concern seemed to fluctuate. One moment it was her family, the next she seemed bothered by something far more personal. Jane made several stabs at getting her to talk about it, but gave up when they reached her front door.

"I've got a question that I really need answered," Jane said finally, leaning against the wrought-iron railing. "Why didn't you tell me you'd lived in my house?"

Patricia's eyes drifted toward the street. "It's what Elliot said. We don't talk about it."

"Because of what happened to your brother?"

"Yeah. And also . . . I wanted to protect you from knowing what had happened there. I mean, I'd never want to know if something tragic had happened in my home. It would make me feel too weird. I suppose it was stupid, right? I should have said something right away. I'm sorry, Jane."

"There's no need to be sorry."

"But you're angry with me now."

"No. Not at all. I'm just trying to understand."

"But you're still not satisfied. I can tell."

Jane hesitated. "It's just . . . if the house held such bad memories for your mother, why didn't your parents move right away? Why did they stay until you were ten?"

Patricia looked up at the moon. "It's complex, Jane. See, first, Mom thought she'd bring Jay back home—that he'd recover there. He did come back for a while, but it was too much for her. I think I told you she had a nervous breakdown. While she was recovering, one of her therapists told her it was best to deal with her problems, not run away from them. Dad said she took that to mean she should stay in the house, confront her demons head-on. So, when she got home, they locked the door to the upstairs and no one ever went up there again. I'd never even seen the space until Elliot moved into it. And then, all I remember is that one day, my dad up and said we were moving. And that was that." She opened her purse and took out her keys. "Are you sure you're not mad at me, Jane? For not telling you?"

"No. Of course not."

"Then, would you like to come in for a drink?"

Patricia's front light wasn't on, but the moon was full. The soft light filtering through the bare branches was enough to illuminate their faces.

"Not tonight," said Jane. Patricia seemed so depressed by her response that she asked, "Are you okay?"

"No. I'm not."

"Is there something I can do?"

"Yes, but you won't."

Jane stared at her a moment, then said, "You know I'm involved with someone else."

"I know." She pressed a finger to Jane's lips, then leaned close and kissed her.

Jane pulled back, but it took her a moment to regain her bearings. "Patricia, I don't want to hurt you."

"You could never do that. You're on my side."

"That's very important to you, isn't it?"

"Yes, it is." She leaned close again, her lips almost touching Jane's. "Come inside."

"I can't."

"Nobody would ever know."

"Patricia, please."

She held Jane's eyes. "That girlfriend of yours . . . she's a lucky woman. Then again, who knows? Things can change." She brushed her lips one last time against Jane's, then said, "I guess I'll see you around." Turning away, she pressed her key into the lock and disappeared into the house.

Jane stood for a moment on the steps, contemplating the closed door.

24

Sigrid was upstairs listening to music when Jane finally returned home. Switching on the front hall light, Jane stood for a moment and flipped through her mail. Mostly bills—a few junk advertisements. The last item in the stack was a letter from Julia. Carrying it into the den, she turned on the desk lamp and sat down. She sliced open the envelope, then drew out several snapshots and a handwritten note.

> Monday morning
>
> Jane:
>
> I wanted to get these off to you right away. The ones we took down by the dock were the best—especially the one of you standing by the boat house. I had such a great time this weekend—and I look forward to next. I'll call you later in the week. By then I should have a better idea of my schedule. Hopefully, I'll see you early on Friday. Maybe we could have another picnic by the Minnehaha creek—if it's not too cold. We had a hard frost last night, so it's getting pretty chilly up here.

There was a break in the writing. The next part looked different. More of a scribble. Jane wondered if Julia hadn't been rushing to finish:

> I've got something important I need to talk to you about. I'm glad we'll have lots of time.
> Till Friday, sweetheart.
>
> All my love,
> Julia.

Jane held the photos under the light. Julia hadn't sent the one mentioned in the note—she'd undoubtedly kept that for herself. But she had included several of the two of them being silly on the deck. They'd set the camera on the railing, pressed the time release, and then raced to form a pose, laughing as they arranged themselves around each other in ever more ridiculous ways.

Jane closed her eyes and breathed in the sweetness of that beautiful autumn afternoon. It was a memory she'd carry with her always. Only two more days and they'd be together again.

"Oh, you're home," said Sigrid, passing by the den door on her way to the living room. She was eating a sandwich, her hair wrapped in a towel.

Jane put down the photographs. "I got back a few minutes ago."

"How'd your dinner go?"

"Don't ask. How about your talk with Peter?"

Sigrid sat down on the couch and stared gloomily at her sandwich. "It was . . . about what I expected. Nothing's changed."

"You're not moving back in with him, then?"

"We talked about it. But I'm not ready. Neither is he—though he insists that I come back."

"I'm sorry." And she *was,* but selfishly, she was also glad of Sigrid's company, at least for a few more days.

"Yeah. Even though it wasn't a surprise, it's still depressing."

"You want to talk about it?"

She chewed thoughtfully. "To be honest, I'd like to talk about *anything* else."

Jane nodded, then smiled. "I hear you."

"So . . . how about those Vikings?"

They both laughed.

"Actually," said Jane, putting away Julia's note and the photographs in her top desk drawer, "I do have a question for you. Something you might be able to answer, based on your intimate knowledge of the human psyche."

Sigrid raised an eyebrow. "Is this one of those 'moments of our lives' we should celebrate with coffee?"

"Brandy might be better."

"Done." Sigrid stuffed the last bite of sandwich into her mouth, then dashed out of the room. A minute later she returned with the brandy bottle, two glasses, and a bag of pretzels. "Brain food," she grinned, dumping it all on Jane's desk. "You pour. I'll crunch." She ripped open the sack and took a handful. Once she was back on the couch, drink in hand, she said, "Shoot."

"All right," said Jane. "Let me think how to put this." She paused for a few seconds to collect her thoughts. "I had an interesting conversation the other night with a friend of mine. We talked about good and evil—Dr. Jekyll and Mr. Hyde, to be exact. The pressure we put on ourselves as human beings to conform to a moral code. Now, I know psychologists don't like to place human behavior in a moral context, but it seems to me that when we're talking about murder—about killing someone in cold blood—we can call that evil. Would you agree?"

Sigrid bit off a piece of pretzel. "Sure it's evil. I can say that as a human being, and as a psychologist."

"Okay, then take it a step further. Since murder is such a horrible, repugnant act, shouldn't it leave a psychological mark on the person who's committed it? And shouldn't we—as creatures

222

whose evolutionary survival has depended on our superior ability to read and make intelligent use of information about each other's state of mind—be able to detect a murderer in our midst? Shouldn't they look different? Smell different? Sound different? If we get close enough to one of them to touch or be touched, shouldn't bells ring or flags wave? I guess what I'm saying is, can the veneer of civilization be that thin? Can these people walk among us and we don't even recognize who they are?"

"You don't need a psychologist to answer that, Jane. Sure. They're here, and most of the time, they're invisible." Sigrid paused, taking a sip of her drink. "What's this about, anyway? The child's bones that were found in your backyard?"

Jane closed her eyes and looked down. "God, I hope not. But yes. Partly. I'm just a little . . . confused tonight."

"About what?"

She shook her head. "It's a long story." Pouring herself another inch of brandy, she asked, "What do your psychology books say about murder, Sigrid? About murder*ers*?"

"Well," Sigrid said, eating another pretzel, "I don't think anyone is born with the compulsion to kill. I'm always impressed by the evidence that links poverty, brutality, and lack of love to crimes of violence, but I think it's safe to say that no one really knows what makes a murderer. For every person who ends up killing, there are hundreds with the same relative background— or worse—who don't."

"So what's the answer?"

"I don't think we have one. Oh, we do know a few things. Take serial murderers, for instance. Psychopaths really don't have any kind of inner being. When you talk to them, they'll tell you they don't *feel,* not the way the rest of us do. They're like actors—they adopt the right gestures and attitudes to create the impression of normality. They *portray* sanity. But they're not sane. Then again, that's not true of everyone who commits a violent act. Some people kill for what we might term 'the greater good.' In a sense, that's what we do when we go to war. But we're getting into the realm of philosophy here, Jane, not my expertise."

"What about the way a person is parented? You've talked about lack of love—brutal parents. But what about too much love? Could that create a murderer?"

Sigrid reflected a moment. "I'm not sure any one thing *creates* a murderer, Jane, but it might be a factor. Either one of those extremes could easily be a prescription for disaster. Look, you have to understand, violence in the family is a huge topic—emotional, physical, or otherwise. Actually, it's so common that it's *at least* as typical of family relations as love. The problem is, we become violent toward our intimates—our lovers, friends, spouses, children—because few other people in our lives can anger us so much. Families may be the main source of our pleasure, but they can also be the main source of our pain. Also, I think you could say that our urge to kill is at least partially situational. The home is where we spend most of our time. It's the same reason why most car accidents occur within a few miles of a person's house. That's where we and our cars most often *are*. The fact is, murder may fascinate us, but we have only the most rudimentary understanding of who kills whom and why. I'm sorry I can't be more specific."

Jane was sorry, too.

It wasn't enough.

25

I just talked to Dad," said Patricia, tossing her coat over one of Elliot's kitchen chairs. "You won't believe what the cops told him."

Elliot closed the door, locked it, then moved back behind his drafting table and sat down. He wasn't up for company tonight, but couldn't exactly throw his sister out. He'd taken the long way around the lake on his way home from the restaurant, going east, then north, and eventually west along the footpath, past the bandshell, and up the hill. The dinner had upset him. The fresh air felt good, helped him clear his head, but it wasn't enough to settle him down. He'd made a mistake allowing his sister to talk him into going. And if this visit was intended to be some sort of postmortem on the evening, he'd have to pass. "Okay, Patricia. What did the cops say?"

"They found something buried with those old bones."

"Really? What? A treasure map? A pirate's doubloon?"

"Don't be so goddamn cynical all the time. It's tiresome." She moved over to the window and looked down at the street. "It was a metal cufflink. An oak leaf." Glancing over her shoulder, she added, "Ring any bells?"

"You mean—" He poked the end of a colored pencil into his mouth, then remembered his cigarette resting on the saucer. "Are you telling me—"

"I am. It was one of Dad's cufflinks."

Elliot tapped some ash into the saucer. "That bastard!"

She whirled around. "You think he murdered the girl?"

"Come on, Patricia. If he didn't do it, what was his cufflink doing buried there?"

Raking a hand through her hair, she walked over to the coffeepot on the kitchen counter and poured herself a cup. "I don't know. Maybe . . . maybe it came off accidentally when he was working on the patio. It could happen."

"He didn't usually dress formally to dig in the dirt, Patricia."

"I knew you'd take that attitude. You always think the worst of him." She glared, gripping the cup with both hands.

Elliot's eyes dropped to her white knuckles, then he returned his attention to the drawing on the drafting table.

"We don't even know who the little girl was," she continued.

"Maybe the police do."

"No. Dad said they hadn't identified her yet."

He added a bit of yellow to Danger Doug's tail. "I guess that means they didn't arrest him."

"Of course not. When he called, he was on his way home." Her eyes narrowed in thought as she stepped away from the counter. "Elliot?"

"Hum?"

"You don't know who that girl was, do you?"

"Me? How would I know?"

"Maybe you sensed it . . . psychically."

"Cut it out, Patricia. If you're going to make fun of me, you can leave."

"I'm serious."

He glanced up at her, noticing that she seemed terribly agitated.

"Don't you remember . . . you know . . . about those cuff-links?"

"Remember what?"

"Well, that Dad gave them to me? I kept them in that pink and gray jewelry box under my bed."

"He let you *play* with them, Patricia. That's all."

"No! They were mine. He still wore them, but he said I could keep them—for ever and ever."

"You sound like you're six years old." Elliot set his yellow pencil down and picked up a blue one. "What I do remember is that you were the only little girl I ever knew who liked to wear men's cufflinks. Maybe you *are* a dyke."

"Oh, just . . . just shut up."

"Look, sis, I'm sorry. I guess we're both a little edgy tonight." He watched her pace in front of the couch. "So tell me. You still having trouble with the resident dyke downstairs?"

"I don't like that word, Elliot. It's nasty."

He gave her a lecherous grin. "All I'm saying is that you seem kind of . . . frustrated."

"And you've never been frustrated? Oh, I forgot. I'm talking to a rock."

"I'm no rock, Patricia. I just don't set my sights on people I can't have."

"I wouldn't jump to that conclusion just yet."

"Face it. She's not interested. Leave her alone."

"Since when do you issue edicts?"

He stubbed the cigarette out angrily. "She's bad news."

"Maybe," muttered Patricia, dropping down onto the couch. "That remains to be seen."

"She talked to that private investigator. Who knows what was really said? Doesn't that worry you?"

"No, it doesn't. Besides, it's all taken care of."

"Really? How?"

"I talked to Dad. He's on top of it."

Elliot laughed. "I hope he does a better job with Wilcox than he did burying that body in the backyard."

She glared at him, then looked away.

"Okay, so Otto's taken care of him. Bought him off. Scared him off. Does that mean you told Daddy the truth?"

She stared down into her mug. "Of course not."

"So your trust only goes so far."

"Trust is a tricky subject, Elliot. Once it's broken, it's hard to get back. But . . . I mean, we've got to forgive, haven't we?"

He lit up another cigarette, blowing out the match and tossing it on the plate. "I don't."

"Sure you do. You forgive me all the time."

"That's because I love you."

"So, it's not trust that's important, it's love."

"Listen," he said, tapping some ash into the saucer, "I'm not going to play these philosophical mind games tonight. I'm too tired."

"I'm not the least bit tired," Patricia said, pushing out of her chair.

She looked like a caged animal, thought Elliot. A cliché, perhaps, but dead accurate. "Patricia, listen to me. When it came to Kevin, you were playing with fire—and now you're playing with fire again."

"According to *you*."

"Yes, according to me!"

"I can handle it."

"No, you can't. Just look at what happened tonight. One stressful situation and Mom starts drinking again."

She set her mug down next to a stack of comics. "I know she sometimes drinks too much, but who doesn't?"

"It's more than that. You didn't grow up with a drunk for a mother—I did. She got it together before you were born, and she kept it together all during your childhood. But when you started dating that girl in high school, you got a glimpse of what she can

228

be like. I'm not saying it's her fault. Whatever she is today, Otto made her that way."

"Why do you always blame him, Elliot? What did he do that was so awful?"

"I refuse to be drawn into another argument about that old man. All I care about is you. Listen to what I'm saying, Patricia. I'm not trying to hurt you, I'm trying to help."

She moved sullenly around the room.

He could tell she was mulling it over. She was twenty-eight years old, for chrissake—she *had* to make decisions based on something other than her hormones.

"So," she said, stepping up to the drafting table and folding her arms over her chest, "you're saying I have to live my life in a box so I don't cause my family any stress."

"No, that's *not* what I'm saying. I'm telling you to use the brain God gave you."

"I know I've got flaws, Elliot, but I'm not a bad person. Dad believes in me. So does Mom."

"And so do I. I love you more than any other person on this earth."

"I know," she whispered. "I realize I've asked a lot of you over the years, but right now I need to ask one more favor."

He could tell by the look on her face that she was scared. "What?"

She returned to the window. Turning her back to him, she said, "You were right about the police thinking Dad had something to do with that little girl's murder. He said he's sure the men who questioned him view the cufflink as a vital piece of evidence. They think they've got him; they just need to fill in a few blanks. So . . . he did the only thing he could do. He lied. Since he's innocent, he didn't think it was wrong. I, for one, agree. But, he also did it partly for me. What if the truth had come out? What if the police find out the cufflinks belonged to me?"

"That's crazy, Patricia. You were a child. A child doesn't kill

229

a child. Besides, if the cufflinks were in the house, we all had access to them."

She hesitated. "Okay, I suppose you have a point. All the more reason to back him up. None of us wants to be unjustly accused of a murder. We've all got to tell the police the same story."

Elliot looked down at the saucer, watching the cigarette burn itself into a snake of gray ash. "You don't know what you're asking."

She turned around. "What do you mean?"

"You really expect me to lie for *him*?"

"We have to. If you can't do it for him, then do it for me."

He felt completely flattened. He couldn't take much more of this. Woodenly, he replied, "What's the story?"

"Just . . . tell the police that you recall those cufflinks being sold at a garage sale. We used to have one every summer. We can't be expected to remember who bought them. For all we know, it could have been a neighbor—someone who watched our backyard being dug up."

"And that unnamed person was the child's killer?"

"Exactly."

"It's . . . fairly convincing, and basically unverifiable. It might even work on a jury, though I doubt the police will buy it."

She dropped the blinds. "So, you'll do it?"

"I'll think about it, Patricia." Even in the shadows, he could tell she was smiling.

"You won't let me down."

"You're awfully sure of yourself."

"No, bro. I'm sure of you."

Patricia unzipped her leather jacket as she entered the bar a few minutes later. She liked the atmosphere at Della's. It was a pickup joint catering to a liberal crowd—both hets and gays. Sometimes there was entertainment. One weekend a month there was a drag show. Being Tuesday, it was a pretty slow night.

Snaking her way through the tables up to the bar, she eased down next to a tall, butch-looking young woman. "Hey, handsome." She smiled. She hoped this wouldn't take long.

"Hi," said the woman, returning her smile. "I'm Sandy."

"Patricia."

"You go by that name? Or do people call you Pat, Patsy—Patty."

"No, just Patricia."

"Kind of formal." She popped a few peanuts into her mouth. "You . . . ah, live around here?"

"Near Lake Harriet."

"Nice area."

"How about you?"

"Over by the U. I'm in med school. One more year."

"Your parents must be proud."

"My parents?" The woman laughed. "Yeah. They are."

"So . . . you wanna dance?"

"Well, I—" She looked around, then down at Patricia's thigh pressing against hers. "My girlfriend's gonna be back any second."

Patricia withdrew her leg. "Too bad. Another time, maybe."

Feeling more thwarted with every passing minute, she stepped over to the dance floor, closing her eyes and moving to the deep, rhythmic beat. It seemed to be Melissa Etheridge night tonight, and that was fine with her. The song matched her mood. It was the title cut off Etheridge's latest album—something about secrets. Patricia breathed in the smell of hot bodies, booze, smoke, the muscles in her back finally beginning to relax.

"Hey, pretty lady."

She felt a hand touch her arm. Opening her eyes, she saw a broad-shouldered man, blond hair, nice smile.

"Would you like—"

"I would," she said, putting her hands on his hips and pulling him toward her.

They danced for a while, touching and teasing, not talking much, except to exchange names.

"Like a drink?" he asked finally.

"No." She hooked her fingers onto the front of his belt, playing with the buckle.

"But you'd like something, right?"

"Right."

"I like a woman who knows what she wants."

"If you're going to be trite, I'd prefer you didn't talk."

He laughed.

Her hand inched up his stomach, unbuttoning his shirt and moving slowly inside.

"Do you always get what you want, Patricia?"

She smiled. "Always."

26

I promise, Cordelia. This won't take more than a few minutes. As soon as we're done, we'll go back to your loft and I'll help you unpack." It was Wednesday morning. As Jane rang the doorbell, she tried hard to ignore her friend's snarl. "Just play along, okay? And suck it in or you'll scare the poor woman."

"My visage, as always, is the picture of composure." Cordelia's hands rose to her hips as she looked around the neighborhood. "You should have warned me that our breakfast date would include a tour of the slums." She nodded to a planter filled with plastic geraniums.

"You can always go sit in the car."

"That car of yours is still overrun with deer ticks from last weekend's foray up north."

"That's ridiculous." Jane heard a noise inside the house. "Shhh, she's coming."

A stocky, dark-haired young woman holding a little boy in her arms opened the door. "What do you want?" she asked, a cigarette dangling from her lips.

Jane felt Cordelia's elbow poke her in the ribs. "Hi. My name's Mary Bishop. And this is Bertha Lake."

"Yeah?"

Jane tried a friendly smile. "I was wondering . . . I understand you used to be good friends with Patricia Kastner."

"So?" The woman removed the cigarette, blowing smoke out of the side of her mouth.

"I was hoping you'd have a few minutes to talk."

"I'm busy." She started to shut the door.

Not everyone was as friendly or curious as Abbie Kaufman and Ramona Dancing. Jane resisted the urge to stick her foot in the door. She'd been wrestling with a difficult question for several days now, one she was almost afraid to pursue, and at the same time, a question she couldn't ignore. This woman was her best— perhaps her only—hope to help her find the answer. "If you could just give me two minutes."

"We're reporters for *City Beat*," said Cordelia, giving Jane a sideways smirk.

The woman stopped.

"We're . . . ah, doing some research for an article on Patricia and her family."

The woman eyed Cordelia with newfound interest. "And you came to talk to me?"

"So it would seem."

She set her child down, sent him back into the house with a pat on his seat, then gazed out the screen, thinking it over. "Do I get paid?"

"Sorry," said Jane, picking up the conversation. They'd prepared this little deception in advance, knowing the woman might not cooperate without it. "But we'd quote you in the article."

"That's right," said Cordelia. "Ms.——"

"Strom. Jessie S-T-R-O-M."

"Of course. What a charming . . . ethnic name. So Minnesotan."

"It's Swedish."

234

"How truly *wonderful* for you, my dear."

"Can we come in?" asked Jane.

"Well, I don't have much time. My boy's sick. I've got a doctor's appointment for him at eleven."

"This will just take a minute," said Cordelia, brushing past her into the living room.

As Jane entered, she saw that the interior of the small house was cluttered with knickknacks and toys. A clothes basket full of clean but unfolded laundry sat next to the couch.

Jessie switched off the game show she'd been watching and then sat down. "So, what do you want to know?" she asked, tapping some ash into an ashtray.

Jane and Cordelia made themselves comfortable on the matching La-Z-Boys in front of the picture window.

"Tell us about Patricia Kastner," said Jane, hoping that a general question would put her at ease.

"Well . . . gee. Where do I start? We were best friends in grade school, and stayed close all the way through high school—that is, until I left to have Dave Junior." She handed her son a ball. The little boy immediately walked up to Cordelia, dropped the ball, and kicked it at her legs.

Cordelia bared her teeth in an imitation of a smile. "What a nice little lad."

Jessie glanced up at a picture of an older boy hanging on the wall. "That's Dave Junior up there. He's in school today. And this one's Brandon." She nodded to her other son. "Anyway, after Dave and I got married, Patricia and I sort of lost touch. But when I was little, I lived right across the street from the Kastners. You know the Linden Hills area?"

Jane nodded, watching Brandon crawl onto Cordelia's lap, look up at her, and sneeze.

"Well, she lived in this big stucco and brick Tudor, and I lived in what my mom used to call a Dutch Colonial. If you ask me, it looked more like a glorified barn. When Patty and I were little and would get mad at each other, we'd sit in our driveways and shout bad words at the top of our lungs. Things like 'idiot,' 'dummy,' 'stupid jerk.' " She laughed, shaking her head at the memory.

Brandon stuck his thumb in his mouth and eyed Cordelia's curly hair. "My mommy's got a wig too."

Cordelia swallowed back her revulsion and looked over at Jane. "Perhaps I should have taken my chances with the wood ticks."

"Hey!" said the little boy eagerly. "We got lotsa ants in the kitchen. Wanna see 'em?"

"Thank you, no." She tugged on her sweater.

"How come? They're way cool."

"Shouldn't you be in school?"

"He's only four," said Jessie.

"I'm this many," said Brandon proudly, holding up four fingers. Using the same fingers, he removed a sticky mass of gum from his mouth and set it on the back of Cordelia's hand. "I'm all done chewing." Ignoring her look of horror, he crawled out of her lap.

"Does Patricia have any kids?" asked Jessie.

"She's not married," replied Jane.

"Doesn't surprise me. Every now and then I hear things about how well she's doing with her career. That doesn't surprise me either. If you ask me, she came from one heck of a family."

"So, you liked the Kastners?" asked Jane.

"Yeah, they were great. Mrs. Kastner used to make us popcorn all the time, she'd even butter it."

"This is going to fascinate our readers," said Cordelia, flicking the gum into the back end of a toy truck. "What else?"

"Well, I remember one time, Patty and I were playing with this jump rope in their kitchen. Mrs. Kastner got kind of wound up in it. Somehow or other, we yanked on it and she went spinning around and fell against the refrigerator and landed on the floor. God, if I'd done that to my mother, she would have grounded me for a month. Mrs. Kastner thought it was hysteri-cal. She laughed and laughed. She rarely ever got mad at Patty. I guess I kind of envied that 'cause I was always in the doghouse over at my place."

"When did the Kastners move away?" asked Jane.

"When Patty was ten. But they made sure we still got to-gether. They had a really cool pool at the new house—and a lake, just a few hundred yards from their front door. It was sort of an English-style country house. Mr. Kastner built it himself, and Mrs. Kastner landscaped it. The front lawn sloped down toward the lake. The gardens were a real showpiece. She'd always walk her guests past the lilacs and the beds of lilies. Everything was carefully manicured—it was moneyed elegance both inside and out. I remember that Patty and I would stand for hours in that funny tall grass behind the lake and watch the ducks quack at one another. We got pretty good at imitating them. I haven't done a duck call in years, but I could try one—so you'd know what we sounded like."

"I don't think we'll cover *quacking* in our story," said Cordelia, her expression completely serious.

Jessie seemed disappointed.

"You were talking about the Kastners' new house," said Jane.

"Right. Well, Mr. Kastner would drive into town on weekends and bring me out. Sometimes I'd spend the night, which is really how we stayed friends. In junior high, I remember Mrs. Kastner used to take us shopping at Dayton's downtown. We'd have lunch at the Sky Room and then just wander around. She was so cool. The whole family was great—well, except for Elliot."

"You didn't like him?" asked Jane.

As her son ran past, headed for the kitchen, she grabbed him and gave him an affectionate squeeze, then told him to go get a tis-sue and wipe his nose. "Elliot—well, to be honest, he scared me. He was always getting into trouble. Once, when he was sixteen or seventeen, Patty was sure he was going to be arrested. But then he wasn't. Mr. Kastner talked to the police and they must have dropped the charge."

"What had he done?"

"Stolen something, I think. And he was always getting into fights. I tried to stay away from him as much as possible, which was hard, because he and Patty were pretty tight." She gave Jane a quizzical look. "Say, don't you have to take notes or something?"

Cordelia smiled serenely. "I have a fabulous memory, Ms. Strom. Worry not."

"Okay then, remember this. Don't quote me about Elliot. I don't want him to read your story and give me and my family any trouble."

"Of course not," said Jane. Taking the carved wooden eye out of her jacket pocket, she held it up. "Have you ever seen this before?"

Jessie shrugged. "Not that I recall." She glanced at her watch. "Say, I don't mean to be rude or anything, but I've got to get Brandon ready to go."

"One last question," said Jane. She couldn't leave without asking it. "When you and Patricia were kids, did any children at your school ever disappear?"

Jessie looked down at the *TV Guide* resting on the coffee table. "Yeah, now that you mention it, there was a kid who disappeared. Her name was Mattson. No . . . Mayville. Connie Mayville. She was the same age as Patty and me, but I think she was in Mrs. Hemple's fourth-grade class that year. We'd all been in the same room the year before."

Jane felt her pulse quicken. "Do you recall her parents' first names?"

"Sorry."

"What else do you remember about her?"

"Well, she disappeared in the fall, right before Halloween. I remember 'cause our parents wouldn't let us go trick-or-treating alone that year. It was a real big deal. We even had some assemblies at school about it—you know, the teachers telling us not to get into cars with strangers. That sort of thing. We all assumed she'd been kidnapped."

"Was she ever found?" asked Jane.

"Not that I ever heard."

"Were you good friends with this girl?" asked Cordelia.

"Hell, no. She was horrible. A regular little torture master. Patty hated her guts. See, Connie used to tell Patty that her hair was too long. If she didn't get it cut, Connie would cut it for her. She was a big kid—bigger than most of us. And mean. I figured she was jealous because Patty was so pretty and popular. Patty wasn't afraid of anything—well, except Connie Mayville. Connie would walk by Patty in the halls and make a scissor out of her hand, just to remind Patty she was being watched and she better do what she was told. She was terrorizing the poor kid."

"Patty never tried to fight back?" asked Cordelia.

"She was way too scared. She got her hair cut four or five times that year, but it was never short enough for Connie. Mrs. Kastner didn't understand what was going on. She saw how unhappy her daughter was, that she was fixated on her hair, but she just went ahead and did what Patty wanted. Every few months she'd take her to a hair stylist to get more and more of her beautiful hair hacked off. It was awful to watch. Kids can be really cruel, you know. Sometimes Patty would come to school with a scrape on her arm, or a cut on her face. She wouldn't tell me what happened, but I knew it was Connie. She'd wait for Patty somewhere near the school and then beat the crap out of her. So, in a way, when she disappeared about two months after school started the next year, I wasn't all that upset about it. Neither was Patty."

"Did you ever talk with her about what might have happened to Connie?" asked Jane.

"I don't remember. I suppose we must have."

"Did Connie live close to you?"

"I think her parents' house was on the other side of the lake."
Again, she glanced at her watch. "I'm really sorry, but——"

"We're going," said Jane, getting up. "You've been incredibly helpful."

Walking them to the door, Jessie asked, "So, where's Patty living these days? I haven't talked to her in ages."

"She's back in Linden Hills," said Cordelia. "Where the huddled masses still yearn to breathe free."

"Huh?" Jessie cocked her head, then turned around as her little boy burst into the room. "Brandon, slow down!"

Ignoring his mother, he raced up to Cordelia and handed her a dead bug. "That's for you."

"Heavens!" Cordelia's hand rose to her chest.

"It's an ant."

"I can see that."

"I told you we got lots of 'em." He gazed at it with a rapt expression. "When he gets alive again, you can play with him."

"What a . . . thrilling prospect." Patting him on the head, she added, "Brandon, I shall treasure it always." When he wasn't looking, she flipped it over her shoulder.

"Thanks again for your time," said Jane.

"No problem," said Jessie, ejecting her cigarette butt onto the front lawn. "Just be sure you spell my name right."

27

After stuffing the last handful of leaves into a plastic lawn bag, Sigrid tied the end securely and then dragged the heavy load around to the back of the house. She'd already piled six other bags next to the garage. Since she'd taken the day off, she thought she might as well help out around the house by raking the leaves in the front yard. It was funny, but she'd been living in an apartment for so long, she'd almost forgotten how many outside chores there were to do in the fall.

By this time tomorrow, she'd be home—back with Peter. She'd talked to him shortly before noon. It had been a stiff conversation, but they both agreed that they would never solve their problems by running away from each other. Sigrid missed her husband terribly, couldn't imagine a life without him. And yet, that's just what she might be facing—if certain things didn't change.

Crouching down next to the garage, she was overwhelmed by a feeling of despair. She covered her eyes with her hand, hoping with all her might that she wouldn't cry, but it was a losing battle. She'd been crying a lot lately. She'd tried to keep a lid on it—especially at work—but when she was alone, she couldn't pretend. She was miserable. It wasn't fair. Why did Peter have to be so—

"Are you all right?" asked a voice from behind her.

Turning and looking up, she saw that Elliot Beauman was bending over her. She'd seen him a couple times from a distance, but they'd never actually been introduced. "I'm fine," she said, brushing the tears off her cheeks.

"You don't look fine."

"No, really . . . I'm okay."

"Been doing some raking, I see." He nodded to the sacks. "That always makes me cry, too."

In spite of her mood, she found herself laughing. She knew he was just being nice—making conversation until he felt sure she was all right. "I'm Sigrid Lawless. Jane's sister-in-law."

"I've seen you around. Elliot Beauman." He stuck out his hand.

She straightened up and shook it. "You're Jane's new renter." He nodded.

She could feel him watching her, so she said the first thing that came into her head. "Cordelia tells me you're a psychic."

It was his turn to laugh. "She did, huh?" He shook his head. "Actually, she brought a crystal ball up to my apartment last Saturday afternoon. Demanded I give her a reading."

"And?"

"I'd already told her I didn't like crystal balls, but she insisted. What could I do? I'm a full service psychic, you know—at least according to Ms. Thorn. I went into a trance, rubbed the ball meaningfully a few times, and then gave her my best shot. I told her stuff like she'd be coming into a huge fortune in the near future. Oh, and that she'll live to a ripe old age and die in her sleep."

"Not terribly original."

"Like Cordelia said, it was a cheap crystal ball."

"Garbage in, garbage out."

"Exactly."

Again, she found herself smiling.

"Feeling better?" he asked, straightening the sacks next to the garage.

"Yeah, a little. Maybe . . . maybe you should give me one of your psychic readings."

"Be happy to." He opened the gate and walked into the backyard, then paused next to the fence. "See, the thing is, people sometimes think other people are psychic when they're merely being observant. Take you, for instance. I'd say you've got some major marital problems."

She was a bit startled.

"I don't mean to speak out of turn, you understand, but every time I've seen you, you've seemed upset. I know your husband lives in town because he's coming over here tomorrow afternoon. His TV station is doing an interview with me and he's the one filming it. So I ask myself, why aren't the two of you together? The answer seems fairly obvious."

He held the gate open for her as she entered. "You're right about the marital problems," she said, perching somewhat awkwardly on a stack of cement sacks. Sometimes it was easier to talk to a stranger—and right now, she felt like talking. "Except . . . I'm going back home tomorrow."

"You don't seem all that happy about it."

"No, I am. I miss Peter. But I'm not sure our problems can ever be resolved."

He leaned back against the fence, slipping a pack of cigarettes out of his jacket pocket. "Would you like to talk about it? I've got a good ear. And I sure as hell understand problems."

As he lit up, she took a moment to study his face. He was an attractive man. Dark, soft brown eyes, a sensitive, almost intellectual face, and full, sensual lips—a lot like Peter's. His clothing was rugged, working class, even a little unkempt. Jeans, fraying at the bottoms. Heavy black boots. A chambray shirt with a missing button. A black T-shirt underneath. A watch with a thick leather

243

strap. The ponytail completed the redneck image. But she was struck by a dichotomy. Here was a man who tried hard to look rough and tough, and yet he so obviously wasn't. Had they been in therapy together, she would have brought it up.

Blowing smoke out of his nose, Elliot flicked the match into the deep hole next to him. "So? What's the big sticking point between you and your husband?"

She glanced down at her diamond ring. "Children," she said softly. "Peter wants to have a child. I don't."

He nodded, and then kept nodding. "Not much room for compromise there."

"No."

"You got something against kids?"

"Oh, I forgot. You write children's books. You must love children."

"Well, I appreciate their readership, but I'm not interested in having any of my own." He tapped the cigarette over the dirt, then added, "I respect the fact that you've given it some serious thought. Believe me, a kid knows when he's not wanted, when the parents think he's in the way, preventing them from having the kind of life they really want. Was that your experience?"

She shook her head. "No. My parents were great. But they divorced when I was in my early teens. My mother eventually remarried, but for about four years, I was in charge of the other kids while Mom was at work. I was the oldest. My dad lived about two hundred miles away, so he wasn't much help. Don't get me wrong, I love my brothers and sisters, but taking care of a bunch of screaming kids is not how I want to spend my life. I know how much time they take, how much time they *deserve,* and I'm simply not interested. What I am interested in is my career—and my husband. But Peter thinks that to be a real family, we've got to have one or two children—or five or six." She shuddered. "God, it makes my sinuses throb."

He smiled. "At least you're honest."

"Yeah. Honest to the core. That's me. The problem is, when we got married, I was more or less undecided. We talked about it a few times, but since I was in school, it wasn't an immediate issue. Now it is. If I'd had the sense then, I would have given it a lot more thought, but I was so happy—so in love. I just didn't realize that it would become such a problem. I don't know . . . maybe . . . maybe I thought I'd get into the mood after I was married awhile. But with my educational background, my knowledge of marriage and family problems, I should have known I was flirting with disaster."

"What is it they say about hindsight?"

Covering her wedding ring with her other hand, she looked away. "Peter would make a great dad. He loves kids. But if I give in, I know I'll be miserable, and I'll probably take it out on him *and* the child. If Peter gives in, he'll never have the family he wants so desperately. As far as I can see, there's no way out except to get a—" She couldn't finish the sentence.

"But you're going back to him," said Elliot, dropping his cigarette into the excavated hole.

She watched the burning tip glow and then fade in the damp earth. "I have to. We need closure. We can't live in limbo." As she got up, she turned for a moment to look at the huge pile of dirt the police investigators had removed. "I guess . . . I better get going. Thanks for listening, Elliot."

"Sure. I hope everything works out."

She nodded, then started for the house.

"Say . . . Sigrid?"

Stopping, she turned back to him. "Yeah?"

"I had something I wanted to talk to Cordelia about. Do you know if she'll be home tonight?"

"Last I heard, she was supposed to move into her new loft today, so I doubt she'll be back at all, at least not to stay. Jane went over there this morning to help her unpack."

"Well, I guess I'll just have to catch her some other time."

"If I see her, do you want me to give her a message?"

"Nah, I'll take care of it."

When she reached the porch door, she turned to wave, but saw that his attention was elsewhere. He'd crouched down next to the hole—right where the bones had been discovered—one hand scooping up some dirt. He was concentrating so hard, it made her wonder what was going through his mind. Suddenly, squeezing the dirt into a solid mass, he hurled it against the side of the garage. He stared for a moment at its muddy imprint, then stood, his eyes rising to the roof of the house. And that's when Sigrid saw it. The look of pain that spread over his face was so heartbreaking that, for a moment, it almost took her breath away.

28

Thursday afternoon had finally arrived. Jane leaned against the arch and watched the WTWN-TV crew set up the living room for the interview. Elliot hadn't arrived yet, but Marian Sturbach, one of the station's best known reporters, had. She and Peter were busily whipping the place into shape.

Jane had spent most of Thursday morning at the restaurant, but came home right after lunch. She wanted to watch the interview firsthand. She still couldn't believe that Elliot had agreed to talk to the reporter. She assumed he had his reasons and hoped that today she'd find out what they were.

"Move that table over here," Peter called to Marian's assistant, an energetic young woman with bright red hair. He placed the Betacam on the tripod, then adjusted the focus.

"Where's Beauman?" asked Marian, glancing at her watch. "It's nearly three. Wasn't he supposed to be here by now?"

Peter looked over at Jane. "Could you go call him, sis? See if there's a problem?"

She backed out of the room and went straight to the kitchen. Picking up the phone, she glanced out the window, then put the phone back on the hook. Elliot was in the backyard, standing next to the remains of the patio, staring down into the pit. She was about to shout to him, when she got an idea. "Peter?" she called. "Will you come in here a sec?"

Half a minute later, Peter breezed into the kitchen carrying a can of Sprite. "Problems?" He tipped the can back and drained it, then tossed it in the recycling bin.

"No. Elliot's right outside."

"Good. Then what do you need?"

Her eyes shifted from Peter back to the window. "Listen, do you know if Sturbach is planning to ask Elliot about Connie Mayville—the young girl who was buried in the backyard?" Thanks to a tip from Jane, both the morning papers had carried the story, reporting not only the girl's name but the details of the supposed abduction back in the sixties.

He shrugged. "She doesn't clear her questions with me, Janey."

"Well, tell her she should ask. I've got a feeling she might get an interesting response."

"Will do."

When Jane glanced back outside, Elliot was on his way up to the house.

"In case our audience doesn't know this," said Marian Sturbach, smiling at the camera, "Mr. Beauman is the author of the Danger Doug picture book series. The newest book is—" She looked over at him.

"Danger Doug Saves the Universe."

Before Marian had begun the interview, she'd explained to Elliot that the videotape would be edited back at the station. Depending on his responses, she might choose to rephrase some of her questions, but for now, she would stick to what they'd agreed on. "Do you do the story or the artwork?"

"Both."

"Really. Isn't that somewhat unusual?"

"Well, I suppose most of the time the publisher does like to choose the illustrator, but in my case, it was a package deal. They could either take it or leave it."

"And much to many children's delight, they took it." She glanced down at her notes. "Now, Mr. Beauman, tell me, how long have you known you were psychic?"

He blinked into the camera. "All my life, I guess."

Jane heard the screen door open and then shut softly. A moment later, Patricia Kastner walked into the rear of the living room. Jane was surprised. She had no idea Patricia even knew about the interview. She smiled as the younger woman moved up next to her.

For the next few minutes, Elliot answered questions politely but with very little enthusiasm. Yes, he'd helped the police solve a couple of local crimes. No, he wasn't interested in doing it again. No, he didn't do private readings. Yes, he liked to help people when he could, but most of the time he sensed nothing. It didn't work like that, at least not for him.

Jane could feel him going through the motions. All of his answers sounded plausible, but rehearsed. It occurred to her that he might even be lying—except, if he was, how had he helped the police solve those crimes? It seemed more likely that he was simply a private person doing something uncomfortably public.

"I find it interesting, Mr. Beauman, that you're renting space in a house where you once lived as a child."

Jane saw the muscles tighten along his jawline.

"That's right," he said, clearing his throat. "But . . . I don't think that was on the list of approved questions."

"It wasn't?" Again, she glanced at her notes. "Hum. I thought for sure . . . well, let's just explore it a second more, if you don't mind. The skeletal remains of a young girl were found in the backyard of that house earlier this week. From what the police forensic experts have been able to piece together, the girl probably died shortly before you and your family moved away."

He glared at her, sitting forward in his seat.

"One of your father's cufflinks was found buried with the child's bones," she continued.

He gave a stiff nod.

"What do you make of that, Mr. Beauman?"

Why didn't he stop this? thought Jane. He was obviously upset that Marian wasn't sticking to the script. If he didn't want to talk about it, why didn't he just get up and walk out? The answer seemed plain enough. He stayed because he had something he wanted to say.

"Have you gone out to the site, Mr. Beauman? Touched the dirt?"

He looked down at his hands. "Yes."

Next to her, Jane felt Patricia stir.

"What did you sense? Do you know who murdered her?"

"No," whispered Patricia. "Elliot . . . *don't!*"

Marian's assistant walked up to Patricia and tapped her on the arm. "Shhh," she said, touching a finger to her lips.

Patricia pushed her hand away. A look of intense concentration passed over her face. She watched her brother without blinking, without moving a muscle.

"Mr. Beauman?" said Marian Sturbach. "Can you answer my question?"

"I don't know," he said, clearing his throat nervously.

"But you see something."

"I . . . maybe."

"What? Is it a person? Someone you know?"

"Elliot, please!" said Patricia, louder this time.

Peter's head popped up from behind the camera.

"Keep going," ordered Marian. "Mr. Beauman, please. Tell us what you see. Help the police and this community solve a very important crime."

"No," groaned Patricia. Her voice was softer this time but more plaintive.

She seemed so upset, Jane touched her sleeve. "Are you all right?" she whispered.

Patricia pulled her arm away. "Elliot . . . stop. For me!"

"Remove that woman," said Marian, motioning to her assistant.

Elliot's eyes grew fierce. "That woman is my *sister.*"

"Of course," said Marian. "I meant no disrespect. Why don't we all just take a moment and calm down."

Elliot ripped the tiny lav mic off his shirt. "This interview is over."

"But—"

"I see *nothing,* Ms. Sturbach. Is that clear enough for you? Nothing!" Without so much as a backward glance, he shot off the couch and disappeared out the front door.

29

Elliot eased back into the shadows near the grandfather clock and watched Otto come into the living room. Waiting as his stepfather switched off the lights, it occurred to him, more strongly than it ever had before, that this father figure he'd been so frightened of as a child was an old man now. Old and worn out. But there was no pity in Elliot's eyes tonight, only resolve. "Getting ready for bed?" he asked softly, feeling a certain satisfaction when the old man jumped.

"Who's there?" Otto squinted into the darkness.

"I thought maybe you'd be expecting me."

"Elliot?" He switched the track lighting near the fireplace back on. "What are you doing here?"

"Don't you know what day this is, Daddy?"

Otto stiffened. "Don't call me that."

"No? But you used to insist."

"Look, I don't have time for your games tonight. Your mother's not . . . feeling well."

"Euphemistically speaking, of course."

Otto's lips drew together angrily.

"It doesn't surprise me. I'm sure she's in the same depressed mood I'm in. Since you killed her son, Otto, I'd think you'd have some memory of it."

"Shut up!" he hissed, looking over his shoulder to make sure they were alone.

"Yeah, the truth hurts." Elliot stepped out of the shadows. "Did you get my present? My annual . . . commemorative gift? He died ten years ago today, you know."

The old man gave him a hard look. "It went into the trash with all the others."

"You mean you don't save them?" Elliot feigned a pout. "That hurts. I work very hard to carve those eyes. You should have a spectacular collection by now."

"I don't need any reminders."

Elliot's expression darkened. "I think you do. You need to be reminded that you *do* have a wooden eye. You never understood Jay, and you never understood me. It took too much effort."

"That's not true."

"It is!"

"Look, Elliot, I've told you before, I'm not interested in your pathetic little art projects. Stop sending them. It's harassment. In case you're interested, your mother found the last one in my office wastebasket where I'd tossed it. It upset her."

"And we can't have that."

"Look, we agreed to keep quiet about what happened—for her sake." His voice softened, though only slightly. "I . . . I know I've made mistakes—"

"Damn right you have. Jay stood up to you, but I cowered in the corner. Even after the accident, I was still afraid of you. I went along with your self-serving *deal*. Thank God I was smart enough to make one of my own."

"You mean Patricia? I told you I'd never hurt her."

"And if you did, I'll kill you with my bare hands."

"I kept my promise!"

"Did you? Look at her, Otto!"

"I do. As often as I can. She's beautiful. Smart. Talented."

"But she's also spoiled. Headstrong. Self-consumed. You and your goddamn guilt made her that way. The damage is there; it's just harder to see."

They stared at each for several long moments. Finally, Otto said, "You think I don't understand you, is that right? That I made a mess of everything? That I'm a selfish bastard with no heart? Well, think about this for a minute. You've never made any attempt to understand me either—what it was like back when your mother and I were first married."

"I remember it vividly. I was there, in case you've forgotten."

"You were only a little kid, seeing everything through a little kid's eyes." Wearily, Otto sank into a chair by the cold fireplace. Rubbing the back of his neck, he added, "Look, you and I are never going to be friends. It's too late for that. But . . . for your mother's sake, can't we call a truce? This animosity between us is hard on her, and right now, she needs both of us. She's in a bad way tonight, Elliot. She's been drinking again."

"Where is she?"

"Watching TV in the den." He hesitated. "Listen, why not give me five minutes of your precious time? Let me explain a few things to you that you might not understand."

Elliot didn't figure Otto had anything new to tell him, but he sat down anyway. He wasn't in a hurry. What he'd come for could wait.

Otto folded his arms over his chest and studied Elliot for a moment. "All I ask is that you listen to me with an open mind for once in your life. Will you do that? You're not a kid anymore, so I'm not going to talk to you like one."

"That'll be a switch."

"Look, by now you should understand a bit more about life, know that things aren't always black and white. You have to believe me, when I married your mother, I was deeply in love with her. I was also dead broke. Most of my buddies, the ones I worked with on construction, thought I'd married her for her money. I didn't see it that way, but in my darker moments, I sometimes wondered if your mother didn't secretly agree with them.

"When I was a young man, Elliot, I never wanted for female attention. But with your mother, everything was different. It was more than physical. She listened to me—seemed to reach inside me and bring out qualities I didn't even know existed. Everyone told her I was a dead end—a big mistake. But when I proposed, she accepted, and that was that.

"After the honeymoon, we all moved into our new house in Linden Hills. That's when I found out what it was like to live with kids. I tried to be a good father to you and Jay, I really did, but it didn't come naturally. You boys resisted all my attempts at discipline and that made me furious. I felt you needed a strong hand, not just the coddling you got from your mother. We fought about it a lot, which frustrated me even more.

"Virginia was away at her garden store a lot that first year, and since I wasn't working regularly, most of the child care fell to me. I won't lie to you—the constant commotion in the house drove me nuts. I tried, Elliot, I really did, but all my attempts to win you and Jay over, to make you accept me as your new father, fell flat. And then, the busier your mom got at work, the more depressed I became. I even started to wonder if my buddies were right. Maybe I *was* a gold digger. After all, I couldn't seem to find a job that lasted more than a few weeks. Your mother was supporting the entire family and it made me feel like a failure. But if chasing two kids around the house was what my new life of wealth and privilege was all about, I didn't want any part of it.

"The second year of our marriage was when everything fell apart. I insisted that I couldn't be responsible for you boys and look for a job at the same time—especially during the summer months when you were home all day. We solved the problem by hiring a housekeeper."

"I remember her," said Elliot with a sneer in his voice. "Inga the Awful."

"She was young, and granted, not very good with kids, but she was *there,* and she saw that you were fed and monitored. She also let me know in no uncertain terms that she was available—if I was ever interested."

"And boy were you interested!"

Otto shot Elliot an angry look. "Look, I'm not pulling any punches here. I'm telling you the truth and I expect you to listen like a man, not some sniggering boy."

Elliot held up his hand. "Fine. But get to the point—if you have one."

"The point is, I didn't want to become the bastard my buddies already insisted I was. I hadn't slept with another woman since I'd married your mother, and I didn't intend to. But when my best buddy kept calling me a 'little poodle on a leash'—well, one afternoon, I just snapped. I jumped in my truck, drove home, ordered you boys to go play outside, and nailed the housekeeper right there on the kitchen table. I kept nailing her, several times a week for the next year. And . . . there were others."

"That's not news."

"I'm aware of that. But you have to understand, your mother and I . . . well, we weren't together much during that time. She was so involved with her new business, she didn't notice much of anything that second year. Sometimes, late at night, I'd catch her looking at me and I'd wonder: does she know about the other women? And if she does, does she care? On those occasions I wanted desperately to make a clean breast of things, to try to get the marriage back on track. But then the moment would pass. Virginia would turn off the bedside lamp and we'd turn away from each other. I'd close my eyes and sink into despair."

"You're breaking my heart," said Elliot, wiping a fake tear off his cheek.

Otto's eyes grew fierce. "Can't you put yourself in my shoes for even one miserable minute? This was a hard time! I was confused, depressed—angry at the world, myself, and at Virginia. I know I took that anger out on you kids, and for that, I'm sorry. But there's nothing I can do about it now. What's done is done. By the third year of our marriage, your mother and I had become strangers to each other, in every way that counted. Oh, we went through the motions, but nothing had much meaning. That's when the tragedy with Jay finally happened. And then, against my wishes, your mother insisted on bringing him back from the nursing home. After six months of taking care of him nearly night and day, no wonder she had a nervous breakdown and had to go to that sanitarium. You were about eight, right? I tried to reach out to you, but it was no use. I'd hurt you too many times and you couldn't trust me. So, you shut me out.

"And then came 'sixty-nine—the worst year of my life. When your mother finally came home from the hospital, I wanted it to be a fresh start for all of us. By then, Virginia knew about the other women in my life, so I promised, swore on everything I held sacred, that from then on out, I'd be a faithful husband. And I have been. I truly love your mother, Elliot, and I wanted a second chance. But though Virginia tried, it just wasn't in her anymore. Her spirit was broken. Even after all that goddamn therapy, the spark that had drawn me to her so many years before was gone. Finally, not knowing what else to do, she went back to work. Work had always been her way of coping with stress at home, and so the same pattern that had driven me into the arms of other women began all over again.

"Your mother was hardly ever home during that period. I'm sure you remember that when she was home, she was medicated. And she'd begun to drink, sometimes heavily. And yet for me, there was one big difference. I'd begun building my own construction company—bidding jobs all over the metro area. The fact that she was absent didn't bother me as much since I was absent myself, absorbed in my own business. I know we left you alone a lot during that time. All I can say is, if I had it to do over, I'd do many things differently. Ultimately, it was your sister who brought your mother and me together again. Our love for her was a tonic. I'd tried to bond with you and Jay, but I'm ashamed to admit that deep down I always knew you were the children of another man. I knew it was some hideous character defect that made me care, but I did. Patricia, on the other hand, was mine. She was so beautiful and sweet, and she brought the life that was missing for so long back into Virginia's eyes. Even you fell in love with her. Nobody could resist.

"We had a few good years in the late seventies and early eighties, at least I thought we did. But by the time Jay died in 'ninety-two, your mother was addicted to booze and all kinds of prescription drugs. Most of the time she wouldn't admit she had a problem. She tried to hide it from Patricia, but I knew you understood what was going on. Sometimes at night she'd cry and I'd try to comfort her, but she said I would never understand what it meant for a mother to lose a son. Maybe she's right."

"She had *two* sons," whispered Elliot.

"What?" said Otto, looking up.

"Nothing. It's not important."

Otto stared at Elliot a moment. "So . . . can't you see? You've got to stop blaming me for everything that doesn't work in your life. Nobody has it easy. Everybody has to live with pain, one way or the other. That's the way life is."

Elliot stared back at him, incredulous. "That's it? That's the moral of that pathetic, self-serving story?"

Otto shook his head. "I bare my soul to you and what happens? You insult me. I've gone to a lot of trouble over the years to salvage this family, Elliot, but you're never going to forgive me, are you? No matter how hard I try to explain, to apologize, you're always going to hate me."

"*That* was an apology?"

Otto heaved a deep sigh, shook his head, and then got up.

After glancing at his stepson for one last moment, he turned away. "Shut the lights off when you leave."

Elliot waited until he was almost out of the room, and then said, "You haven't heard *my* news yet. I was interviewed this afternoon by WTWN."

Otto stopped, but kept his back to his stepson.

Elliot allowed himself a small smile of triumph. "They wanted to talk to a real-life psychic. And wouldn't you know, the interviewer asked about Connie Mayville. As a matter of fact, she pleaded with me to use my psychic powers to help the police find the little girl's murderer."

Very slowly, Otto turned around. "You're not fooling anybody. You're not psychic." He hesitated, but only for a moment. "So . . . what did you say?"

Elliot didn't answer right away. Instead, he took some time to savor his stepfather's fear. The tables were turned now and it felt good. Better than good. It felt just. "I came mere inches from telling the whole world that you murdered her."

Otto's eyes opened wide. Steadying himself by holding onto the back of a chair, he replied, "But . . . you didn't?"

Elliot shook his head. "To be honest, I haven't made up my mind what I'm going to do yet. I may still turn you in."

"But—why?"

"Because I hate you!"

"But I didn't murder that girl!"

"You're a liar, Otto. You've lied your whole life. Do you think you'd still be married to my mother if she knew what really happened to her firstborn son?" Hearing a noise behind him, Elliot whirled around. His mother was standing just inside the dining-room arch. One hand held a drink, the other gripped the side of a wing chair. "What *did* happen to my firstborn son?" she asked, her eyes searching her son's face for an answer.

Otto rushed to her side. "It's nothing, sweetheart. We were just arguing. Nothing new in that."

She backed up. "I'm not talking to you, I'm talking to *him.*" She returned her gaze to Elliot. "I demand that you tell me what you meant."

"Virginia, this isn't the time," pleaded Otto.

"I agree with my mother," said Elliot. "On the tenth anniversary of Jay's death, she deserves to know what you did. That's why I'm here tonight."

"What?" Otto's face turned ashen.

"Shut up, Otto!" snapped Virginia. "Let him talk."

Otto stared at his wife in stunned disbelief. Finally, his surprise fading to defeat, he sat down, leaning his elbow on the arm of the sofa and cradling his forehead in the palm of his hand.

Elliot got up from his chair and walked a few paces closer to his mother. "Maybe you should sit down, too."

"I'll stand."

"Sure. All right." He'd prepared what he wanted to say, but it was harder than he imagined it would be. Clearing his throat, he wiped a hand over his mouth. "Well, see, it all started about two weeks before Jay fell. He came to me one night with a bottle of Otto's scotch. He'd taken it out of the liquor cabinet downstairs while nobody was looking. We opened it, poured some into a glass, and then laughed ourselves silly making faces. God, but it tasted awful. I couldn't understand how anybody could drink that stuff. Otto used to bring it out when his women friends came over. You were always at work, Mom, but let me tell you, Jay and I got an eyeful. Otto would order us outside to play, but you can't count on kids to do what they're told. God, we hated him for what he was doing behind your back. We wanted to tell you but figured we'd get in big trouble if we snitched. So we kept quiet. I'm sorry, Mom. I really am."

"I don't need your pity," she said, her voice stiff and cold.

He nodded. "All right. So, anyway, after everyone was asleep that first night, we crept back downstairs and returned the scotch

to the cabinet. For the next week or so, I'd see Jay with the bottle every now and then. I think he was drinking some, just to try
it out, to be cool and daring. You remember what he was like. And
whatever he drank, he replaced with tap water.

"The night he fell from the roof was the same night Otto figured out what was happening to his precious booze. He was furious. Jay and I were playing upstairs in the attic. Remember, we had
our toys up there? It was our fort. Sometimes we arranged bat-
talions of plastic soldiers in war zones under the rafters. Other
times Jay would crawl out the back window and climb up on the
roof. I was too chicken, but I always encouraged him. I thought my
older brother was the bravest guy that ever lived. It was the two
of us against the world—essentially, that meant Otto. As long as
we stuck together, we could handle anything.

"That night, I remember hearing Otto's footsteps on the
stairs. He burst into the attic with the bottle in his hand, demanding to know who'd been messing with his scotch. Well, we
denied it, of course, but he knew we were lying. He bellowed
something about punishing us both, getting out his strap. That's
when Jay admitted he'd done it. It was the truth, but he was also
protecting me. He was like that—always looking out for his kid
brother." Elliot pressed a hand to his temple. The last thing he
wanted was to let his stepfather see him cry.

Gritting his teeth for a moment, he continued, "Otto was . . .
totally out of control. He screamed at Jay. Pushed him against the
wall. Slapped him. And then he hit me. Jay lunged at him, which
only made him more furious. He grabbed the bottle of scotch, un-
screwed the cover, and said something like 'So you want to drink
my liquor, huh? Wanna be a big man? Well, that's just fine with
me.' And then he ordered Jay to drink it all. The whole bottle—
or what was left of it. I'm sure part of it was water, but it was still
a lot, especially for a ten-year-old kid. I just sat in the corner and
watched. Jay thought it was funny. He even winked at me a cou-

ple of time when his stepdaddy wasn't looking. Finally, Otto ordered me downstairs. Before he came down himself, I heard him tell Jay that he had to stay upstairs—he couldn't come down until Otto said so."

Elliot bent his head. "You know the rest. He climbed out on the roof and fell off. For years, I thought it was my fault. I thought, if only I'd done something different. If I'd just snuck back upstairs instead of cowering in my room, maybe he wouldn't have done it. Maybe he'd still be alive." He glanced at his mother. She'd remained still through the entire story. "I know it's hard to hear," he said softly. "But you had to know."

Otto remained on the couch, his arms crossed defiantly over his chest, rocking. He didn't look up. And he didn't speak.

Virginia stared straight ahead.

Elliot waited for almost a minute. The silence in the room was beginning to press on him. He didn't like it. It made him feel itchy, like something was jumping up and down inside him. Every muscle in his body was filled with the need to run. If only he *could* run—as fast and as far away from this place and these people as his legs would carry him. He'd never look back. Except—it was impossible. He couldn't leave Patricia alone the way he'd left Jay. "Mom, are you all right?"

His words seemed to bring her back from some dark, inner landscape.

"Yes," she replied, her voice flat, listless, wooden. "But nothing's changed. It was all my fault."

"No, you're wrong! It was *his!*" He pointed to Otto. "Don't make the same mistake I did. Don't blame yourself! I finally realized I wasn't protecting you by keeping the truth from you—I was hurting you. That's why I told you, so you could see what really happened. So you could finally be free of your guilt—free of *him!*"

Virginia looked at her son as if he'd lost his mind. "But there's no one else *to* blame."

262

"You're not making any sense!" He didn't understand her re-action. He'd rehearsed this moment a thousand times in his mind. His revelation was always received with shrieks of anguish, tears, and rage. She should be screaming, swearing, beating on Otto's chest, breaking dishes, railing at the cold, indifferent universe.

Instead, she lifted the drink to her lips and drained the glass.

Elliot turned his fire on Otto. "Look at her! Look at what you've done to her. She's not even human anymore. She's just some goddamn drunk."

"That's right," said Otto, matching his wife's flat tones. "And the drunk's been drinking all evening."

"I refuse to stay and watch this," cried Elliot.

"Fine. Come back tomorrow, Elliot. She'll need all of us to-morrow."

"She won't need *you* ever again. Not after tonight."

"That's where you're wrong, son."

At the sound of shattering glass, Elliot's eyes shot back to his mother. She'd dropped her drink on the terrazzo floor.

"Stop talking about me as if I'm not here!" she commanded.

"Mother——" Elliot walked closer. He realized now that she had a purse slung over one shoulder. "Where . . . where are you going?"

"A bar. Where I can drink in peace." She moved unsteadily into the front hall.

"Virginia," said Otto, rising from his chair and turning around, "I won't allow it. You've had too much to drink already."

"Don't wait up," she called, slamming the door on her way out.

30

By the time Jane finally arrived at the bandshell on Thursday night, it was almost midnight. She stood for a moment gazing up at the magnificent building—probably her favorite in all of Minneapolis. In the moonlight, it looked like some crazy Disney castle, with its turrets, its Robin Hood flags rippling in the breeze, its curved, whimsical lines. The stage was open in the front, but a huge wall of Plexiglas windows faced the lake. The building was constructed in the mid-eighties, modeled after a pair of historically significant bathrooms just a few yards away. At night, when the sky turned into a canopy of stars and the park across the way grew deserted, it was Jane's favorite place to think—to examine the world and her own life.

Once she'd finally ensconced herself on the stage, she glanced up at the moon hanging just above the trees in the distance. Behind her, she could hear the faint sound of water lapping against the dock. The sailboats that were usually moored in this part of the lake were all gone now. The band concerts had ended for the season. Winter was in the air, and for a moment, Jane felt the same excitement she felt every autumn. In Minnesota, October was a month for transitions. Tonight's chilly air felt exhilarating. She could think better in the cold, when the air felt thin. Light. Fresh. It didn't weigh on her the way the heat and humidity always did.

Holding her watch out to catch the lamplight, she saw that it was midnight on the dot. Her eyes quickly surveyed the darkness, coming to rest on a couple of cars in the parking lot. Neither was Earl's Ford pickup.

After this afternoon's interview, she'd gone back to the Lyme House, placing Peter in charge of making sure the house was returned to normal and then locked up tight. She needed time to prepare, to organize her thoughts before she met with Earl; but as soon as she'd walked into the restaurant, a crush of problems had descended on her. She'd spent the evening working in her office, taking only half an hour off to run home and let Bean outside. She'd been expecting a call from Julia, but for whatever reason, it hadn't come. Jane tried calling her place a couple of times during the late afternoon, but got her machine. Given Julia's erratic schedule, it worried her a little that they hadn't connected by phone before this weekend's visit, but it didn't worry her a lot. She had more immediate concerns on her mind.

She'd come to an important conclusion this afternoon after the interview. After listening to Elliot, and seeing Patricia's reaction, it seemed apparent to her that both of them knew what had happened to Connie Mayville. If Patricia hadn't been present during the interview, Jane was almost positive Elliot would have blown the whistle on someone, and from Patricia's reaction, it seemed likely that it was a member of the Kastner family. Okay, so if they both knew the truth about the little girl, then perhaps it wasn't a stretch to also assume they both knew everything. Whether it was planned or not, Patricia had shown up in the nick of time to force Elliot to close ranks, to protect whoever had murdered not only the little girl but probably Torland and Dancing as well.

265

Jane desperately wanted to talk to Patricia after Elliot had taken off, but she'd been sidetracked by her brother. When she looked around, Patricia was gone. Jane was beginning to wonder if Patricia knew that she'd lied about her involvement with Earl Wilcox and his investigation, though she couldn't imagine how she'd found out. Whatever the case, Jane knew she had to be careful. It might not be smart to have come to the bandshell alone tonight. She'd made the date on Tuesday and hadn't had any luck getting in touch with Earl since, so in some ways she felt she had no choice but to show up. Under other circumstances, she might have asked Cordelia to come along, just to be another pair of eyes and ears, but tonight was the opening performance of one of the fall plays at the Allen Grimby. By now, Cordelia was probably celebrating up a storm, dancing on a table at Scotties, the famous theater bar at the Maxfield Plaza, or doing one of her infamous imitations at a cast party. Warmed by those thoughts, Jane folded her arms over her chest and waited.

Half an hour later, she was still waiting. Had Earl forgotten? It didn't seem likely. He had important information to pass on, and knew Jane did, too. If he couldn't come, he would have called, right? He'd said as much on the phone. No, she just had to give it more time.

By one-fifteen, Jane was not only chilled to the bone, she was also forced to face the fact that he wasn't going to show. If something had indeed prevented him, he had her phone number. He'd get in touch. When she got back to her house, maybe there'd be a message waiting.

She jumped down off the stage and started for home, careful to look over her shoulder every few minutes just to make sure no one was following her. By the time she reached her front yard, she was convinced nobody was. She stood on the steps for a moment, looking around, but saw nothing unusual. The night sounds were all familiar—the bark of the little schnauzer across the street, the wind chimes tinkling on her back porch, the rustle of dry leaves blowing across her dying grass.

This was the first time she'd come home to an empty house since early last week. Pushing the key into the lock, she felt a moment of trepidation, but it passed as soon as she saw Bean scuttle into the front hall wagging his tail. She gave him an enthusiastic scratch, then let him out into the yard to do his nightly duties. Back in the kitchen, she put on the teakettle, knowing she was too keyed up to sleep.

The first order of business was to check her messages. Dashing down the hall into her study, she found the red light blinking on her answering machine. She hit the playback button and then sat down, switching on the desk lamp for a little light. After a couple of clicks, she heard Julia's voice:

"Jane, hi. I tried calling you at the restaurant, but you'd gone. I didn't leave a message—I thought I'd catch you at home. I know it's late, but I took a chance that you'd still be up. I . . . guess you're not there." She paused, then started again. "Look, Jane, I'm afraid I've got some disappointing news. It looks like I won't be able to make it down tomorrow. I'm really sorry, honey. Believe me, I want to see you as much as you want to see me. It's just, something's come up. I have to stay here this weekend . . . actually, kind of indefinitely. I'll be busy tomorrow, so I won't call, but I'll get in touch sometime during the weekend. Jane, really, I'm *very* sorry about this. It's—a patient. Not entirely unexpected." Another pause. "As I said in my letter, I really need to talk to you. I didn't want to wait, but now it looks like I'll have to. Please don't be upset with me. You've hooked yourself up with a doctor now. Maybe . . . you want to reconsider." She gave a nervous, rather high-pitched laugh. "Assuming that's not the case, I'll talk to you soon. I love you, Jane. 'Bye."

That was the only message.

Sitting back in her chair, Jane felt a wave of depression hit her.

This was her day for disappointments. She would've spent more time dwelling on it if the teakettle hadn't started to whistle. Rushing back to the kitchen, she turned off the fire and set about preparing the Earl Grey. Problems always called for tea. Maybe somewhere inside she was still half English after all.

After letting Bean in the back door and giving him his nightly Milk-Bone, she carried her cup into the living room to survey the damage from the interview. Everything was basically back where it belonged, though nothing that had been moved looked quite straight. Tomorrow would be soon enough to deal with it. She simply didn't have the steam tonight. She was about to sit down on the couch, put her feet up, and decide how to handle the situation with Julia, when she heard the doorbell. The only person who ever came by this late at night was Cordelia.

Jane wasn't exactly in the mood for one of Cordelia's nocturnal visitations, but she could hardly turn her away. Fortifying herself with a sip of tea, she went into the front hall, checked through the peephole to make sure she'd guessed correctly, and then drew back the door.

Cordelia leaned against the door frame, grinning broadly. "Did you miss me?"

"Well, actually—"

She held up a bottle of champagne, wiggling her eyebrows. "I knew you were still up because I saw the light." Erupting into the hall with characteristic vigor, she headed straight for the living room. "Where's the roaring fire? I count on you for *ambiance*, Jane! Especially this time of year." She gave the room a critical once-over. Raising an eyebrow, she said, "Have I entered some sort of alternate universe? The room feels slightly . . . off."

"It's a long story," sighed Jane, picking Bean up and giving him a hug.

"You know, Janey, since I'm in the process of turning my loft into Trump Tower—"

"I thought it was about to become the Sistine Chapel."

268

"All of the above, with elements of Versailles and the Empire State Building thrown in. You know, you could use a little decorating help, if you don't mind my saying so. Of course, I'm not into the Ozzie and Harriet style of decorating you practice, but—"

"Spare me your insults."

"No, no. Primitive Americana is good, dearheart, it's just not *me*." She smirked, then peeled the foil off the bottle and popped the cork. "But you're right. My ideas for the renovation of your cozy little hovel can wait. It's time to celebrate."

"I take it the opening went well?"

"Much more than *well*, Janey." Cordelia crossed into the dining room, shouting over her shoulder as she removed two champagne flutes from the china cabinet. "The cast was *inspired*. They hit every note with such sensitivity that it created a single, thrilling chord. Oh, there are some rough edges we need to smooth out, but that will come. The audience was entranced. I watched the reaction from the wings, hoping I'd see Virginia Kastner leap to her feet. But, alas, I don't think she came. A pity, too. We did six curtain calls, Janey. Six!"

Lowering herself into a chair, Jane sat Bean in her lap, then waited as Cordelia returned to the living room and poured the wine. "What's the play about?"

"It's called *Saving Grace*. The playwright is an old friend. Leonard Quartermaine. It's his third play: very dark humor, and lots of social commentary. In several scenes, it almost approaches melodrama—which I love. It's tastefully handled, and a real hoot."

Again, the doorbell sounded.

"Ah, right on time," said Cordelia, setting the champagne down and then charging out of the room.

Jane couldn't see who it was, but she could hear Cordelia's delighted cry.

"Oooooh! Fabulous. The Yuppie special, right? Goat cheese,

fresh tomatoes? Free-range chicken to assuage our guilty little carnivore consciences. Wonderful. Here. That should take care of you." After shutting the door, she returned to the living room and plopped the box on the coffee table. "I took the liberty of ordering us a midnight pizza. Well, that is," she said, glancing at her watch, "a two A.M. pizza, to be exact. What a delicious time of day to be alive."

"Cordelia? What if I'd been in bed?"

She waved the question away. "It's from Luigi Lobello's, that great new place uptown. And come on, Janey. Who could sleep with fresh baked pizza and *moi* in the house? The night is young. *We're* not, but hell, after a bottle of champagne, who cares?" She opened the box and began to pull the wedges apart. "So, I was telling you about my play. See," she said, licking her fingers, "it has a fascinating story."

This time, instead of the bell, the sound of pounding on the door interrupted her.

"He must've forgotten something," she said, scrambling to her feet and trotting back into the front hall.

Jane set Bean down on the floor and followed her.

Cordelia continued to talk. "The play's set in the late forties. It's sort of a cross between *Mildred Pierce* and"—as she drew back the door, her eyes opened wide in surprise—"*The Days of Wine and Roses*," she mumbled, looking the woman up and down. She swallowed hard. "Virginia, what a surprise. You look terrible. I mean, terribly—" She glanced back at Jane for help.

Jane was too tired to be creative. "Great?" she offered.

"Right," said Cordelia, plastering on a smile. "Terribly *great*, As usual."

"What was that you said first?" asked Virginia, her voice slurred. "About the wine?"

"Why don't you come in?" said Jane, noticing that the older woman's freshly applied lipstick was badly smeared.

Virginia stood in the doorway, draped in mink, her dyed blond hair done up in a cream-colored scarf, considering the request. Hesitating, she peered cautiously into the interior. "Coming here was a mistake."

It took Jane a minute, but she finally realized what was going on. This was probably the first time Virginia had set foot in the house since she'd left it back in the mid-seventies.

"Do I smell food?" she asked, allowing the scent to draw her into the front hall.

"Ah, well, actually," said Cordelia, shooting Jane her best "she-may-hold-the-power-of-life-and-death-over-my-career-but-I-refuse-to-share-my-pizza-with-her" look.

"Why don't you come into the living room?" said Jane. She helped Virginia off with her coat as Cordelia scurried ahead and hid the pizza box under a chair.

Squaring her shoulders, Virginia made a valiant stab at a dignified entrance. "I came here for two reasons," she began in an overly precise manner, weaving her way over to the couch.

"I hope you made a list," muttered Cordelia.

Jane caught the sarcasm, but was pretty sure Virginia hadn't.

Fixing Jane with a freezing stare, Virginia continued, "I've never been one to beat around the bush, so I'm just going to say it. Keep your grimy hands off my daughter! Don't think I didn't see the way you were looking at her the other night at your restaurant. It was disgusting."

Jane didn't know what to say. She stared back at Virginia, dumbfounded.

Picking up Cordelia's wine flute as if she'd been drinking from it all evening, Virginia downed half of the champagne in one quick gulp, then added, "Patricia isn't gay, she's just being rebellious. She's always been rebellious when it comes to her lovers." She gave a bitter laugh. "She thinks her father and I didn't know what was really going on with that Kevin Torland—but we did. I

271

thought he would listen to reason. I tried . . . I did everything in my power, but it was no use. For your information, Jane, other people have tried to hurt my family before, and they didn't succeed. Neither will you. With money comes power—and I'm not afraid to use it!" She finished the champagne, then poured herself another glass, spilling part of it on the coffee table. "Do I make myself clear?"

Jane and Cordelia exchanged perplexed glances.

Holding the flute between her thumb and forefinger, Virginia began to wander unsteadily round the room. "I didn't know if I could stand coming here tonight. I hate this place. My son . . . died here, you know." Her head teetered backwards as she gazed at the stairs leading to the second floor. "Well, he didn't die exactly, but he as good as died. He left me. I've been alone ever since. I'll never hold him again—never touch him. Jay was my beautiful boy. My only, sweet loving son."

"But . . . what about Elliot?" asked Jane, noticing that Cordelia had inched her way toward the champagne bottle and was about to stash it behind a pillow.

Virginia lurched around. "Don't touch that," she ordered. "I'm not finished with it."

"Of course not." Cordelia smiled. "Silly of me to think you were."

Shifting her eyes back to Jane, Virginia continued, "What were we talking about?"

"You called Jay your only son. Aren't you forgetting about Elliot?"

"Certainly not," she said indignantly, her slurred speech making her sound a little like Daffy Duck.

"But," said Cordelia, "you just said—"

Jane shot her a cautionary look. There was no use arguing with a woman in her condition.

Virginia ran a polished fingernail around the rim of the glass.

"I've put up with a lot in my life," she muttered, easing over to the sofa and then falling onto it. She reached for the champagne bottle. Bean hopped up next to her, sniffed her hands, and then moved on to her purse. While she was otherwise occupied, Jane whispered to Cordelia, telling her to go into the kitchen and call Patricia. She'd find her phone number on the side of the refrigerator.

As Cordelia slipped discreetly out of the room, Jane sat down in the rocking chair across from Virginia and listened while she continued to mutter about her hard life, her pain, her disappointments, and her loneliness. One way or another, the monologue always returned to her dead son. It didn't matter whether Jane was in the room or not—Virginia would have talked to a bartender or a wall. The picture of a mother who blamed herself for her son's death began to emerge. She insisted that having a drink every now and then was the only way she could relax, let her true feelings out. And what was the harm in that?

Finally, as Virginia spilled the last of the champagne into her glass, Jane heard the front doorbell chime and got up to answer it. Patricia stood outside looking fairly disheveled herself, though for different reasons. She'd undoubtedly been awakened from a sound sleep, only to be told that her mother was dead drunk and annoying the neighbors. Cordelia had probably painted a gruesome picture.

"Thanks for calling me," she said, her manner cool, even a little distant.

"I'm sorry," whispered Jane. "I assume Cordelia explained everything?"

"Yeah."

Patricia didn't say a word as she walked into the living room. Bending down next to her mother, she looked up into her face, trying to make some sense of the situation. "Mom, what are you doing here?"

For several seconds, Virginia seemed unable to focus. When she finally did, she grabbed Patricia's hand as if it were a lifeline. "I knew you'd come," she whispered, closing her eyes and pressing the hand to her cheek. Her speech was almost unintelligible now. "You're my child," she mumbled, or something resembling that. "You won't . . . disappoint me." The last few words were more distinct, as if she understood that she had to try harder.

"No, of course not, Mom," said Patricia, squeezing her hand. "Come on now. I've got to take you home."

Suddenly, Virginia's face filled with terror. "You love me, don't you?"

"Of course I do. You're a great mother."

"You really think so?" She seemed desperate for confirmation.

"Absolutely. I always felt lucky to have you and Dad as parents. Look at me, Mom. I'm telling you the truth."

Thinking they deserved some privacy, Jane moved back into the hall, bumping into Cordelia, who was standing just outside the study door.

"Mom, please," coaxed Patricia. "Let's go. It's late. Jane wants to get to bed." She kept tugging her mother's arms until she teetered to her feet. "Put your arm around my shoulder."

"But . . . you don't hate me?" When it came to reassurance, Virginia appeared to be a black hole.

"Mother, let's talk about this some other time."

She stopped dead in her tracks, such as they were. "Answer me."

Looking exasperated, Patricia said, "No, Mother, I don't hate you."

"Even . . . even if I've killed someone?"

"Don't be ridiculous."

"Answer me!"

Patricia gave up trying to drag her into the front hall. "You didn't kill anyone, Mom. And I want you to stop this nonsense, do you hear me? Not another word!"

Virginia gazed at her for a long moment, then gave a wobbly nod. "I understand," she whispered. "Too many eager ears around here." With no further protests, she allowed herself to be led away.

31

By noon the following day, Jane still hadn't heard from Earl Wilcox. Now she was worried. After last night's fiasco—both at the bandshell and then later at the house with the arrival of the inebriated Virginia Kastner—she felt physically tired and more than a little weary of the whole situation. Even so, she'd managed to drag herself out of bed at a ridiculously early hour, shower and dress, and then make it to the Lyme House by seven. Every half hour on the dot she'd called Earl's cell phone. She left several messages, but once again he didn't call back. Out of total frustration, she finally tried phoning Kevin Torland's mother in Des Moines. She figured she had nothing to lose and everything to gain. Perhaps Mrs. Torland knew what was happening with the elusive Mr. Wilcox.

After Jane explained who she was and how she was connected to Earl, Emily Torland told her that she'd talked to him yesterday morning. He'd stopped by on his way out of town. He didn't have much time because he said he was meeting someone in Minneapolis at one. Jane asked who it was, but Mrs. Torland didn't know. She did say he seemed happy and upbeat, even excited. He had told her he was hot on the trail of Kevin's murderer: he'd narrowed it down to two people, but didn't want to say anything else until he had more proof. Jane thanked her for the information. She didn't see any point in passing on her anxieties, so she simply wished her a good day and said good-bye.

And that was that. As of yesterday morning, Earl was alive and kicking and following new leads. So what the hell was going on? Had he decided he didn't need her help any longer? Unless he'd been in a car accident on the way to the Twin Cities, he was here, somewhere. So why hadn't he shown up last night? When it came right down to it, she didn't know him all that well. She'd formed her opinions of him based on her father's comments and a couple of personal conversations, but that wasn't all that much to go on. Maybe this disappearing act of his was normal behavior.

The more she thought about it, the more she realized she had to get her mind on something else for a while. This really wasn't her battle. Sure, she'd grown to like Patricia Kastner more than she had a few weeks ago, but certainly not enough to risk life and limb to prove her innocence. She wasn't even sure Patricia *was* innocent. Sometimes it might be better to simply leave well enough alone and stick to what she knew how to do best—run a restaurant. Of course, that was easy to say now, when she was in this mess up to her eyeballs.

She sat back in her chair and tossed her pen on top of the desk. And as usual, her gaze came to rest on a photo of Julia. What a perfect solution. When you need a break from one problem, why not move right along to the next? At least she wouldn't have to switch emotional gears. Frustration seemed to be the order of the day.

Jane had listened to Julia's message again this morning. Okay, so she said she was going to be busy today all day—but surely, she'd have time to talk just for a second. Nobody could be *that* busy.

Checking her personal directory, Jane picked up the phone and punched in the number of the clinic. Since Julia had informed her that she worked in the office on Thursdays and Fridays, she expected to find her in. Waiting for the receptionist to answer, Jane pulled Julia's photo closer.

"Earlton Clinic. May I help you?"

From the sound of her voice, Jane could tell it was the same woman she'd spoken with last week.

"Yes, I hope so. I'm calling for Dr. Martinsen."

"This sounds like her friend in Minneapolis."

Jane smiled. "Yes, it is."

"What's the weather like down in the cities? We got our first snow this morning. It really surprised me to wake up and find my yard covered with it."

Weather was always a hot topic with Minnesotans, especially this time of year. "It's sunny and cool. No snow."

"We might get more tonight. I'm not ready for winter yet. Anyway, back to Dr. Martinsen. She's not here today, though I expect you know that. She drove down to the cities yesterday."

Jane leaned forward, gazing intently at the photo in front of her. "Yesterday. Ah, that's right."

"I suppose she's staying with you?"

"Yeah," she said, feeling her throat tighten.

"So, how can I help?"

She had to think fast. "Do you know where she's supposed to be this afternoon?"

"The airport, I assume. She's picking up that friend of hers."

"Oh . . . right," said Jane. "But I mean, do you know the flight number? I was supposed to meet her out there, but I've lost all the information she gave me."

The woman laughed. "You sound about as organized as me. No, I'm sorry. All I know is the flight was coming from Miami—sometime around one, though I could be wrong."

"What airline?"

"Well, I saw a notation she made on her desk calendar—Northwest, I think. Yes, I'm almost positive."

"Thanks," said Jane, checking the time. "You've been a big help." She cut the line, gave herself a moment to regroup, then switched off her computer and headed out the door. She had a flight to catch.

Entering Twin Cities International Airport half an hour later, she checked the Northwest arrival and departure screens. Sure enough, there was a flight arriving from Miami at one-fifteen— gate 24 on the red concourse.

Since it was almost one-fifteen now, she pushed as fast as she could through security and then raced through the crowded central courtyard toward the concourse entrance. Bumping her way past a crowd gathered in front of a McDonald's, she saw the gate about thirty yards away. She walked quickly, staying behind a tall man carrying a bag of golf clubs.

As she got closer, she slowed her pace and grew more watchful. She didn't want to run into Julia, she merely wanted to observe. She'd been lied to again and again, but this time she had proof. Julia said she had to stay in Grand Rapids for the weekend. She couldn't come down. But unless the receptionist at her clinic was mistaken, she'd been here last night—somewhere. That meant she'd made last night's phone call from somewhere in town. The more Jane thought about the lies and the deception, the angrier she got.

Glancing up at the signs, she saw that the gate was just ahead. She stopped at a food kiosk and ordered herself a cup of coffee. From this vantage point, she could observe without being observed. The gate was just across the aisle. After paying the young woman behind the counter, she studied the sandwiches, secretly surveying the sitting area. Julia was standing alone by the far windows. She was dressed casually—jeans, a sweater, and hiking boots. This was no business meeting and she wasn't waiting for any patient. Outside, the plane had already landed and taxied to the gate.

Jane felt like hell—like someone had dropped a lead weight on her from a second-story window. How could this happen? How could she have *let* it happen? The kicker was, some part of her still couldn't believe it had.

Standing behind a pretzel warmer, she watched as people began to trickle down the ramp from the plane. Julia had moved closer to the exit door. Did she look nervous, or was it just Jane's imagination?

As the minutes ticked by, Jane kept her eyes glued to the doorway. Finally, bobbing down the ramp behind two Asian men, she saw him, the dark-haired man with the seedy mustache. She recognized his face from the photo in Julia's office—the office that was part of the house tour they never quite got around to.

Jane's hand closed tightly around the cup as she watched Julia throw her arms around him, holding him tight. They didn't kiss, but then they didn't need to. There would be time enough for that later. They stood locked together for what seemed like minutes. Then they began to talk, smiling at each other, laughing, arms entwined, walking slowly away from the gate. Julia's face was flushed with happiness, and yet there was something else there, too. Some emotion Jane couldn't quite identify. She wondered if it was guilt, but knew that was probably just wishful thinking.

As they walked past the kiosk, Jane heard Julia say, "No, I'm going to drive you up. My car's right outside. That way, we'll have more time to talk." And then they stopped again. This time, he put his bag down, drew her into his arms, and kissed her hair. Jane couldn't see Julia's face, but she could see his. She understood what he was feeling—she'd felt it herself. For one brief moment, she almost pitied him. He was probably as ignorant of her existence as she'd been of his. In a very real sense, they were both Julia's victims. What a modern way to live your life, thought Jane, realizing that she truly understood hate for the very first time.

She dumped her coffee in the garbage and then headed the

other way down the concourse. She didn't know where she was going and she didn't care.

For the next hour, Jane walked aimlessly around the airport, weaving through the crowds, trying to find a way to calm down. She couldn't go back to the restaurant and pretend nothing had happened, and she didn't want to talk to anybody, not even Cordelia. She felt angry, confused, hurt, betrayed, but mostly she was furious with herself for allowing something like this to happen.

Her life had been working just fine before Julia. She was happy. Content. She had the restaurant, her family and her friends. From the very beginning, she'd had doubts about this new relationship, but she'd ignored them. Sure, she'd jumped in way too fast, but it seemed so perfect. Julia said all the right words, made all the right moves. It had taken Jane almost a year to see those words and moves for what they really were—lies and manipulations.

Since her late teens, Jane had lived fairly consistently by a simple rule: she didn't date heterosexual women. She'd be damned if she was going to be some straight woman's *gay* experience—as if her life was a theme park, put there for the general amusement. During the first few months of their relationship, she and Julia had talked a lot about sexuality. Julia maintained she'd always been attracted to women, but simply found it easier, given the way modern society operated, to date men. It really didn't matter all that much to her because her career came first, last, and pretty much in between. She explained that she'd never had a good relationship with a guy—that Jane was just what she'd been looking for all along but never dreamed she would find. Okay, so if that were true, then what the hell was she doing in the arms of Mr. Mustache? When it came right down to it, Jane didn't give a damn about labels, they were too easily blurred. People didn't always stay put in their neat little boxes—sexual or otherwise. But she did care about commitment. And honesty. And on both counts, Julia failed miserably.

For the next few hours, Jane drove around the city just blowing off steam. She composed a few blistering letters to Julia in her mind, relishing every scathing syllable, but by five, she was becoming weary of the whole exercise. Noticing the highway signs, she realized she was only a few miles from the Lawless family lodge on Blackberry Lake. She'd been on automatic since she left the airport, thinking so fast and furiously that she couldn't say exactly where she'd gone. Perhaps some unconscious part of her brain had brought her here. Sunset wouldn't come for another few hours, so she decided to sit on the dock and try to put her world back into some kind of perspective.

Parking her car next to the tool barn, she spent a few moments standing at the edge of the water contemplating the cool late afternoon sunshine. Depression had settled into her bones now, making her wish she could rev up some of the rage she'd felt just a few short hours ago. She still loved Julia—loved her intelligence, her quickness, her competence, her commitment to her patients. And when the world quieted down, she loved Julia's tenderness. She couldn't turn off her emotions just because her intellect dictated it. Besides, somewhere inside her, she still believed Julia loved her. So what had happened? Twice, Julia had said she needed to talk about something important. Did she want to come clean about her relationship with this guy? What *was* that relationship? My God, thought Jane suddenly. Were they married?

Walking out to the end of the dock, she sat down on the familiar, rough wood planks, the same spot where she'd spent many nights as a child wrapped in her father's arms, gazing up at the stars. And for the zillionth time today, she went over the message Julia had left on her answering machine last night.

She said she had to stay in Grand Rapids for the weekend. She didn't say she was there at the time of the call. So, technically, she

hadn't lied, she'd merely omitted part of the truth. She also explained that the reason she had to dump their weekend plans was
because of a patient. Was Mr. Mustache ill? He sure didn't look
that way to Jane, though appearances could be deceiving. Since
they obviously knew each other on a personal level, he was more
than a patient, but technically, it could still be true.

Once again, Jane found herself second-guessing her conclusions. Was she just being jealous? Unreasonable? Part of being
with someone you loved was the enjoyment you received from
how that person made you feel about yourself. And yet with
Julia, Jane often didn't like herself at all. She constantly swung
back and forth between feeling like a stupid chump for missing
the red flags that would alert her to Julia's lies and feeling like a
supercritical, hotheaded jerk, someone who had no business calling herself committed when she was incapable of simple trust.
When Jane looked at those two extremes, she didn't even recognize herself. She'd never behaved this way before. So, what
was going on?

As darkness fell, she still hadn't found any comfortable answers, only more uncomfortable questions. Glancing back at the
dark lodge, a log structure set about twenty yards back from the
beach, she wondered for a moment if she should spend the night,
but quickly nixed the idea. Walking back up the dock, she took
one last breath of the pine-scented air, then got in her car and
headed home.

By eight, Jane was seated behind the desk in her den, going
through the day's mail. There was still no word from Earl Wilcox.
She would have welcomed the opportunity to switch gears, but no
matter how hard she tried, her thoughts always returned to Julia.
She'd calmed down some since this afternoon, but not enough to
concentrate on anything else. The empty house provided her with
no distractions at all. Bean was asleep in the living room. And
without Cordelia's cats sneaking around corners, making their

nightly racket, the house seemed almost morbidly quiet. The perfect accompaniment to depression.

Organizing a bunch of unpaid bills into a pile, Jane felt a wave of exhaustion hit her. She'd gotten little rest last night, and now here she was, facing another long, potentially sleepless night. She stared at the photo of Julia on her desk, wishing they could talk, but knowing she needed more time to think things through. Or maybe she was just putting off the inevitable. Maybe she should just let go and admit they were finished.

On that desolate note, she opened the top drawer looking for some stamps. Instead, she found the notation she'd made about Julia's flight from Boston last week: Northwest, Flight 573.

On a whim, she picked up the phone and dialed Northwest information. It took a few minutes but she was finally connected to a reservation agent.

"Hi," she said, removing a pen and then shutting the drawer, "I wonder if you could tell me what time Flight five seven three from Boston gets in tomorrow afternoon?" She felt a pang of guilt, but she needed to check, just to make sure Julia was telling her the truth about something.

"Sure," said the agent.

Jane could hear the woman tapping on a computer keyboard.

After a couple of seconds, she came back on the line. "Five seven three doesn't come from Boston. That's the number of a Miami flight. It gets in at three-forty-two P.M."

Three-forty-two, thought Jane, glancing down at her notes. Yes, that was the correct time according to the woman at the clinic. Julia had arrived at 3:42 on Flight 573. But it was the wrong city. It was, however, the same city Mr. Mustache had flown in from today. A coincidence?

"Perhaps you're thinking of another airline," said the agent.

"No," replied Jane, drawing a circle around the number with such force that the tip of the pen ripped the paper. "That's the information I was given."

"Well, maybe you should check with the person you're picking up. You might have written the number down wrong. Would you like me to check the numbers for the Boston flights?"

"No," said Jane. "Thanks for your time." As she hung up, anger once again boiled over inside her. Was this just one more lie? Julia didn't have an uncle in Boston—she was never even *in* Boston. She'd been in Miami, visiting her boyfriend. It all fit.

In one lightning-swift movement, Jane picked up Julia's photo and slammed it hard against the desk, shattering the glass into a million pieces. Damn her! How many lies was she supposed to swallow before she threw up? She took what was left of the frame and the photo and dumped it in the trash. She had to get out of here. Before she could change her mind, or come to the conclusion that she didn't see what was right in front of her face, she grabbed her coat, switched off the light, and left, never noticing the dark form standing in the shadows just inside the kitchen door.

32

When Patricia entered Della's bar late Friday evening, dressed to kill—or at least to wound—she gazed dispassionately around the room for a few seconds, examining the clientele, guaging how best to handle her next move. She wasn't interested in going home with anyone tonight; she just wanted to forget about her problems for a while and have some fun. She recognized a few of the people from the other night. Thank God the stud she'd gone home with wasn't around. She must have made quite an impression because he'd called five times in the last two days, twice at her home and three times at the office. He'd left messages everywhere asking her to call, but she hadn't. Nor would she. He was pretty, and briefly useful, but stupid. Not her type.

Weaving her way through the tables, she stood for a few seconds at the edge of the dance floor, soaking up the sound. She loved a tune with a deep, driving bass, like the one that was playing right now. It was body music, and her own body responded. She'd been in a bad mood all day and hoped that tonight she could cut loose. From the looks of the crowd, she wasn't going to have any problems.

As she turned back to the bar, her attention was drawn to a

woman sitting at the far end. It was the darkest part of the room, the farthest point away from the dance floor, the smoke, the heat, and the seduction. This woman clearly wanted to be alone. And yet she'd come to Della's. Interesting, thought Patricia, moving slowly through the smoky haze toward her. Even in the dark she would have recognized her, not that she wasn't a little surprised to see Jane at Della's.

Easing down onto the stool next to her, Patricia waited until Jane looked up from her drink. When she did, Patricia tilted her head inquiringly and said, "Slumming?"

Jane stared at her a moment. "I guess you could say that." She caught the bartender's attention and held up her glass, ordering another.

There was no smile of surprise. No friendliness. But then, what did Patricia expect after the chilly way she'd treated her last night. "What are you drinking?"

"Irish whiskey. Doubles."

"Can I assume that wasn't your first?"

"You can assume anything you want. It's a free country."

Patricia unzipped her tight leather vest, then turned away and smiled to herself. This was the first time she'd seen Jane even remotely high. Kind of pleasant, really. Patricia had always found smart, straight-arrow types to be a fascinating challenge—especially when they were a little damaged, like Jane appeared to be tonight. She would never have had any luck *getting* Jane drunk; it had to be her own idea. But here she was, as vulnerable as she was ever going to be. The next drink might just open the night up to a world of possibilities.

When the bartender brought the double whiskey, Patricia ordered a vodka martini. She might as well go with the flow, as long as it was flowing in her direction. "I can hear it all now. You're about to tell me you need to be alone, right? You want to suffer in silence."

Jane eyed her briefly. "Would it do any good?"

"Probably not. Look, you may not believe this, but I'm your friend. You look like you could use one tonight."

She studied the ice in her glass. "I'm not sure what I need. Probably a lobotomy."

"Sounds serious."

"It is."

"Does . . . this have something to do with you and Julia?"

"It's not something I'm going to talk about, Patricia."

Bingo. She'd hit a winner on the first try. "Okay. Consider the subject dropped." Pulling a bowl of pretzels in front of her, she tried a different subject. "I should thank you for calling me last night—about my mom."

"Did you get her home safely?"

Patricia nodded. "Dad was really angry when he saw the condition she was in, but he said he'd take care of her. Yesterday was the anniversary of Jay's death. I knew it would be a rough one for her—I just didn't know how rough. As far as I'm concerned, she's entitled to a bender every now and then. Everyone is."

Jane took a sip of her drink. "I didn't realize—about Jay. I just knew she was upset."

"Yeah, it seems to be going around these days, kind of like the flu."

Jane glanced over at her, but said nothing.

"It's some coincidence, our meeting here like this. I didn't know you liked Della's."

"I don't. I just needed a place to think."

"Right," said Patricia, glancing around the room with an amused look on her face, "there's a lot of that going on in here."

Jane finally laughed. "Okay, so it was a poor choice."

"Yeah, but if you hadn't come in here, we wouldn't have hooked up. Say, I've got an idea. You need to get your mind off your problems, and so do I. Here's what we're gonna do. It's a game. You tell me a secret—something you've never told another living soul. I promise," she said, holding up her hand, "I'm as discreet as the day is long. Then I'll tell one too."

Jane grinned. "I don't think I'm drunk enough to play that."

"Nah, it's easy. Come on. Take a big sip. That's right. Now, one more. Good, good. Now, you go first."

"Why me?"

"You're older. And wiser. You can set the tone for just how honest we're going to be. Besides, you like to take risks every bit as much as I do."

"I do, huh?"

"Yes, Jane. You do." As Patricia watched her wrestle with the whole idea, she realized for the first time that she wasn't just attracted, she'd actually grown to care about Jane as a person. There was some quality in Jane—some intensity—that matched her own. If she told Jane the real secret of her life, would she understand? Patricia wanted to touch her so badly right now, to make her pain go away, and yet Elliot was more right than she cared to admit. Jane could cause big problems in her life. The thing was, she was almost positive that Jane was attracted to her, at least a little. Both of them were used to being in control. And here they both were, poised on the edge of potential chaos. It was a frightening—and intriguing—thought.

Patricia waited, watching Jane tip the glass back and drain it. When it came time for Patricia to tell her secret, would she have the guts to tell the truth? This was no silly child's game any longer. Maybe she should wait until after they'd made love. As the bartender finally set her martini down in front of her, she noticed Jane stir.

"Okay," said Jane, folding her hands over her glass. "But you've got to promise. You won't tell anyone about this."

Patricia held up two fingers, making a victory sign. "Scout's honor."

Jane laughed, then paused for a few seconds to collect her thoughts. "When I was nine years old, my family moved back to the States."

"Where were you living before that?"

"England. My mother was English. My dad's family was originally from Illinois, although his parents moved to Minnesota, which is where he grew up. Anyway, we took a trip down to Springfield that year to visit a great-aunt who was dying. I'd seen her maybe four or five times before, so I knew her better than some of my other relatives. She even visited us once in England. I thought she was an amazing woman. She loved to read—and talk, and laugh, and tell stories. Every now and then my father would make some veiled comment about her drinking, but all I knew was that I was her favorite niece. At the time of the visit, she was still living in her house with round-the-clock nursing help. I think she must have been pretty wealthy. She never married. Nobody ever talked about that much.

"Anyway, one evening, I peeked into her room. I thought she was sleeping so I snuck up to the bed. I remember thinking she looked like a walnut—sort of brown and wrinkled, but still, a rather imposing, regal walnut. She had such frail hands, with lots of silver rings on them. I studied them for a few minutes, and when I looked back at her face, she was smiling at me. 'You've inherited my eyes, you know,' she said. I assume she meant the blue-violet color. Lots of the Lawless kids have them. And that's when she did something I've never been able to forget.

"I don't know why, but I asked her what it was like to be dying. Remember, I was only nine. I didn't realize it was such a personal question. Well, she just laughed. 'I understand the world in a very different way now,' she said. 'Would you like to see something I've learned?' I said sure. You have to understand, her bed was in the corner of the room. She raised her arm, with some difficulty I think, and as I watched from just a few feet away, she pushed her hand clear through the solid wall. It just passed right through it, like it was made of nothing but air. And then she removed it, held it up for a few seconds, wiggled the fingers, and smiled again. 'See,' she said, winking. 'There's a lot we don't know about this universe of ours. Don't let anybody ever tell you they've got a corner on the truth market. You go find your own, child. And when you do, remember me.' A few seconds later my dad came in and shooed me out."

Jane shook her head, pushing her glass away. "For years I convinced myself it never happened. It was just a dream. But it did happen. I saw it with my own two eyes. I've never told another living soul about it before because it's so crazy. Do you . . . believe I really saw that happen, Patricia? Do you think I'm crazy?"

"Absolutely not," Patricia said, without even a moment's hesitation.

"And now, you can tell me your story about being abducted by aliens."

Patricia laughed. "I might just do that," she said, running her finger around the rim of her martini glass. "But first—let's dance."

Jane seemed startled by the suggestion. "Hey, are you trying to get out of your part of the bargain?"

"Certainly not. But we need to lighten up a little first."

"I don't know—"

"Oh, come on." She motioned to the bartender to bring them each another drink, then tugged Jane onto the floor. "It won't hurt, I promise. You do dance, don't you?"

"I'm a good dancer."

"Good. This number isn't exactly the Beatles," Patricia teased, "but it's slow—it won't injure your old bones."

"You think I'm past my prime, huh?"

"No," said Patricia, pressing her body against Jane's, "I don't think that at all."

* * *

Since Jane was in no condition to drive, and Patricia had taken a cab to the bar, Patricia drove them both home in Jane's car around one. On the way back, Jane talked for a while about her mother. It was somewhat stream-of-consciousness by now. Jane wasn't in the best shape, but Patricia was still interested and learned some important details she hadn't known before.

Jane's mother, Helen Lawless, had died when Jane was just thirteen. It was a hard loss—and if tonight was any indication, one she still had difficulty talking about. Patricia didn't press, she just kept driving and listening, asking a question here, making a comment there. After a few minutes Jane switched the subject to her first partner, Christine. Christine had also died—ten years into their relationship. If there was a theme to Jane's life, it seemed to be loss.

And now it appeared Jane had lost again. Over the course of the evening, it became clear that she and Julia had either broken up or were about to. Patricia was delighted with the news—not for the pain it caused Jane, but because Julia wasn't the right woman for the job. Patricia, on the other hand, was. Jane needed someone younger, sexier, more alive—more dangerous—not some old doctor who spent her days suturing wounds and setting broken bones. It was a necessary but disgusting profession, and Patricia wasn't shy about letting her feelings be known. Jane just listened, and then changed the subject.

But now, as Patricia helped her into the house, the conflict she'd felt for the last few days raged once again. Being anywhere near this woman might be totally insane. And yet here she was, about to crawl into bed with her.

They walked slowly up the stairs, arm-in-arm, until they reached the bedroom door. Once inside, Jane dropped onto her bed. "I guess," she said, running her hand through her hair, "I must have needed that."

Patricia sat down next to her, switching on the light and then switching it back off. Darkness was better, especially since she hadn't made a decision yet about what she was going to do.

"I . . . didn't expect to find you at the bar tonight," said Jane. "I'm sorry you had to get mixed up in my screwed-up life."

"I'm not sorry," whispered Patricia. This was the moment she'd been waiting for. She bent and kissed her. This time, Jane didn't resist. Instead, she pulled Patricia down next to her.

Even in the dark, Patricia could see the tears in her eyes. "You don't want this."

"I do," said Jane, running a hand along Patricia's shoulder, caressing her neck, and then slowly unbuttoning the top of her blouse.

Patricia closed her eyes and for a moment, gave in to the sensations. It would be so easy just to stop thinking. To let it happen. And yet tonight, for some reason, it seemed too easy. When it came right down to it, Patricia wanted more. She wanted love. She needed what Julia had but threw away. Pulling away, she said, "Jane, it's okay to feel sad."

"I don't feel anything right now," she whispered, more forcefully than necessary. "And that's how I want it to stay."

"You're a liar," smiled Patricia, gently brushing the tears from Jane's cheeks.

"Maybe . . . you're partially right. But I do feel *something*." She eased her hand under Patricia's blouse. "I can't stand . . . to be by myself tonight. Do you understand at all what I'm saying? I've been alone so much of my life. Sometimes it's just . . . too much. Too hard. I feel like I can't breathe. Like I'm drowning in the silence."

"I won't leave for a while," whispered Patricia, "unless you tell me to. Don't misunderstand, I want you. But not like this. Not as a stand-in for Julia."

"You're not."

"Of course I am."

"I hate her," said Jane, turning her face away.

293

Patricia held on to her for a long time as she cried. When the clock finally struck two downstairs, the worst of the storm seemed to have passed. Patricia stroked her hair for a few more minutes and then laid down next to her. "Try to sleep now."

Jane nodded, closing her eyes. Just before she drifted off, she whispered, "You never told me your secret."

"I know," said Patricia, their lips almost touching. "And I probably never will."

33

Jane awoke to the sound of whining. Disengaging herself from the blankets, she looked over and saw Bean standing in the doorway. Sunlight filtered in through the partially open blinds, so it was morning, though all she could concentrate on for the next few seconds was her throbbing head. She closed her eyes and pressed her temples, trying to make the pain go away, but she blinked her eyes open again when she felt Bean hop up onto the bed and snuggle his nose under her arm. She scratched him absently, trying to bring last night into focus.

She remembered the call to Northwest Airlines, then the bar, the whiskey, and Patricia. Somewhere in there the two of them must have come home together, though she wasn't quite sure how. Glancing down, she saw that she was still wearing yesterday's clothes, even her suede boots were still on her feet, so it was fair to assume she and Patricia hadn't slept together. It gave her a moment of psychic pain to think she could have forgotten something like that, though in her current condition, it wasn't difficult to understand. As soon as she'd seen Patricia in the bar last night, the idea that they might get together had crossed her mind. And yet she knew it was not only a dumb idea, but a dangerous one as well.

Lying back against the pillows, Jane covered her eyes with her arm. What a great beginning to another great day. Last evening was starting to come back to her now in little dribs and drabs. Kissing Patricia—and then crying. God, she felt like such a fool, falling apart in front of someone she barely knew. As much as she was loath to admit it, she hated being out of control, and yet given the mood she was in last night, it would have been a miracle if she hadn't lost it.

So, if Patricia had come back to the house with her, where was she now? And what exactly had they said to each other? The big picture was in focus, but the details were still missing.

Jane decided to try sitting on the edge of the bed for a few seconds, just to see if her head could manage not to crack off and roll out the door. As she flipped the tangle of blankets off her legs, the phone on the nightstand gave a sudden, ear-splitting ring.

Grabbing it before it could ring again, she mumbled a quick hello.

"Is this Jane Lawless?" asked a male voice.

Pinching the bridge of her nose, she said, "I think so."

"Sorry. I know it's kind of early for a Saturday morning."

She glanced at the time. It was almost ten. "Who is this?"

"My name's Roy Peterson. We met a while back at Flying Cloud Airport."

She tried to recall the name. "Oh, right. You're the pilot."

"That's me. Listen, I was wondering if we could talk. I've got some business in your neck of the woods around noon. I thought maybe we could meet first at that restaurant on your card—say, in an hour?"

She wondered if she had any aspirin in the house. "What's this about?"

"That investigation of the Kastners you're working on for

your father. I got some information I think you might find interesting. Buy me a cup of coffee. What have you got to lose?"

Good question. "You said eleven o'clock?"

"Yeah."

She'd have to get cleaned up first, but she figured she could do that in an hour. "Okay. I'll be there."

Jane stumbled into the bathroom and gulped down a couple of aspirin, then took a quick shower. She would have called Cordelia to see if they could get together later in the day just to talk, but right now, other matters took precedence. She also wanted to speak with Patricia, to apologize, but wasn't quite sure what she'd say, especially since she couldn't exactly remember how she'd behaved last night.

By the time she'd slipped into some fresh clothes and pinned her hair back into a modified French braid, the world was pretty much back in focus. As she pulled on her boots, she realized that she hadn't thought about Julia once. Perhaps last night had been the catharsis she needed, though it may have come at Patricia's expense. Jane didn't like feeling indebted to someone—especially when that someone might turn out to be a murderer—though she was inclined more and more to think of the other members of the Kastner family as the primary suspects. She wondered briefly if she'd come to that conclusion based on the facts as she currently knew them, or on her emotions. She felt strangely close to Patricia this morning, in a way she hadn't before. The scent of her perfume still lingered in the bedroom, making Jane wish once again that she had a clearer picture of what had happened last night.

As she was about to head out the door, the phone rang again. "Hello," she said, hoping just a little that it was Patricia.

"Jane, hi. I'm so glad I caught you before you left."

It was Julia. Her voice sounded strained—and a little too cheerful.

Jane could instantly feel her emotions do a flip flop. Suddenly, she was angry.

"Honey? Are you there?"

"Yes," said Jane curtly, cupping the phone between her ear and her shoulder. "What do you want?"

"Is . . . something wrong?"

"What could be wrong?"

Julia was silent for several seconds. "Look, I ah . . . just phoned the clinic in Earlton. The receptionist told me you'd called yesterday. I guess she mentioned I was in Minneapolis. I just . . . well, I mean, I thought I should explain."

"Oh, goody. You haven't lied to me in several hours, Julia. You better talk fast before you forget how."

"Jane?"

"I was at the airport yesterday. I saw you and your *friend*."

More silence. "Please. Let me explain."

"Why should I? So you can feed me more garbage, like the story about a dying uncle in Boston? Do you enjoy making a fool out of me, Julia? Do you!"

"No, of course not. I never meant—"

"You never meant what? To hurt me? Well, you have. You were in Miami last week, weren't you? Not Boston. You were visiting the same guy you met yesterday."

"Just give me a chance to—"

"Answer me! Tell me the truth, just once in your life."

Another silence. Then, "No, Jane. I wasn't in Miami, but I did fly through there on my way to Jamaica."

Jane flung her arms in the air. "Oh, great. You and your boyfriend were vacationing. How idyllic."

"He's not my boyfriend!"

"Then who is he?"

"He's my *best* friend."

"Ah, now we're splitting hairs."

"Just stop for a minute and—"

"Does he live in Miami?"

She hesitated. "No, he lives in D.C."

"Then what the hell was he doing in Miami?"

"It's . . . a long story." Her voice was beginning to tremble.

"Is he sick? Is he a patient of yours?"

"No."

"Then what?"

"I can't talk to you about it on the phone."

"Oh, that's just peachy, Julia. You torpedo our weekend plans so you can spend time with him, and now you tell me we can't talk on the phone. How are we going to conduct this discussion? By carrier pigeon?"

"Look, I know you're angry—"

"Oh, sweetie, that doesn't even *begin* to cover it."

"Jane, just stop a second!"

"Why? After all the half-truths and outright fictions you've told me in the past year, give me one reason why I should believe you're telling me the truth now."

A long pause. "Because I love you."

The words felt like a knife twisting inside her stomach. "Right. Have a nice weekend, Julia. As a matter of fact, have a nice *life*." She slammed the phone down, then willed herself not to come apart at the seams, as she had last night. As far as she was concerned, as of this moment, she and Julia were finished. Grabbing her car keys, she headed out of the room, hoping the scent of Patricia's perfume would still be there when she got home.

"You got great coffee at this restaurant," said Roy Peterson, waiting as the waitress warmed his cup. He smiled up at her, then switched his attention back to Jane. "Do you manage the place?"

"I own it," she said, watching him shovel more food from the special Saturday morning buffet into his mouth.

She'd arrived late for their appointment. As she entered the dining room, she spoke briefly with the manager on duty, explaining that she'd only come by for a short time, then spotted Roy sitting by the windows, reading the morning paper. She sat down at his table and ordered a cup of tea. She would have preferred to get right down to business, but she could tell by the way his eyes kept straying to the buffet table that he was hungry. Figuring that she'd get more cooperation out of him if he was happy, she told him to go get himself something to eat.

Jane was barely able to tolerate the smell of her own tea, let alone the Belgian waffles, ham, eggs, potatoes, sausage, fresh fruit, crumpets, gravlax, ginger cakes, berry tarts, and whatever else he'd managed to cram onto the elegant bone china plate. "So, getting back to your story," she said, prompting him.

"Right," he said, wiping his mouth on the linen napkin. "Okay, so here's the deal. You wanted to know if Bob Johnson flew Otto Kastner—or someone in his family—down to Des Moines on June twenty-sixth."

She nodded.

"Well, he didn't."

"You talked to him?"

He shook his head. "I didn't need to. I did the Des Moines flight. See, Bob had flown Mr. Kastner to South Dakota that day. They left around eight and got back to Flying Cloud by four."

"You're positive?"

"Oh, absolutely." He spread one hand over the top of his coffee cup and leaned forward. "About eleven that same day, I got a call from Virginia Kastner. She sounded pretty upset. She needed a pilot to fly her down to a small, unattended airstrip near Bentonville—that's northwest of Des Moines. I said, sure, I could do it—for a price. Since it was such short notice, I added on an extra hundred bucks, but she agreed to it, so I thought, hell, great. I had her there by two. I was kinda surprised when she said that the car parked next to the only building on the property was hers, but then she explained that she and her husband always flew in to this strip and then drove the car into the city. They just left it there when they weren't using it. They'd arranged it all with the guy who owned the strip—turns out he was also the local coroner. There was a pay phone outside the building where a pilot could place a call to get him to come out and gas up the plane, or do whatever minimal maintenance might be necessary. It was a pretty slick little operation. And very private.

"Anyway, so Mrs. Kastner stays gone about an hour and a half. When she gets back, she's driving like a bat outta hell. The front end of the car is banged up, and I could tell she's had a few too many drinks. All the way back to Minnesota she never says a word. Except for one thing: As I was helping her up into the plane, she muttered something like, 'It wasn't my fault.' Or, 'I didn't do it.' I assumed she was referring to the damage to the front end. But maybe not. I got to thinking . . . what if someone got hurt while she was down there? Maybe even killed. Am I close?"

Jane hesitated. "Possibly."

"So this information helps, right?"

"I hope so." She couldn't wait to tell Earl Wilcox. She was still convinced he'd call, unless something truly terrible had happened to him. The longer she went without hearing from him, the more likely that seemed, though she wasn't willing seriously to entertain the possibility of foul play just yet. "Really, Mr. Peterson, this might just turn out to be a key piece of evidence." So Virginia Kastner was the one driving the car on the day of Kevin Torland's death—the car the neighbor had seen. It was all coming together. It also explained how Virginia could be at Kevin's apartment in the late afternoon, and still make it back to attend that fund-raiser at the Governor's Mansion by six. "Tell me, Mr. Peterson, why did you wait until now to tell me?"

He shrugged. "I just got pissed off. I'm usually scrupulous about maintaining my client's confidentiality. That's part of the deal, at least for me. But when Mrs. Kastner and I landed back at Flying Cloud, I asked her how she planned to pay me. She pulled out a hundred-dollar bill and pressed it into my hand. I told her

301

that wouldn't even begin to cover it, so she mumbled something about sending a bill to her office. I knew she owned Kastner Gardens, so I said fine. I figured she was good for it.

"I sent the bill and I waited, but nothing happened. I called her secretary a couple of times but got the standard runaround. She couldn't cut a check without Mrs. Kastner's approval and Mrs. Kastner wasn't in the office. When I finally called the Kastners' home in late August, I got a housekeeper who said she was in Europe and wouldn't be back until early October. I explained what I needed and the woman said she couldn't help. I was really angry by then, but what could I do? So, I waited some more. I finally reached Mrs. Kastner a couple of weeks ago. She apologized profusely for holding me up and said she'd send a check right away. But then she never did. I'm sick of waiting, Ms. Lawless. I called her house this morning and told the housekeeper to pass on a message to her from me. I'm taking her to Small Claims Court. You were my next call."

Jane nodded, her mind jumping ahead to just how this new piece of information would fit into her theories.

"But I gotta get moving if I'm going to make my next appointment." He took a last sip of coffee and then pushed away from the table and got up. "If she did something wrong, Ms. Lawless, I hope you and your father nail her knees to the floor."

"Thanks," said Jane, rising and shaking his hand.

"I hate it when rich people stiff small businessmen like me."

She gave him a sympathetic nod.

"And thank *you* for the breakfast. Since you were late, I had a chance to read the paper." He nodded to it. "Should I leave it there or take it with me?"

"I'll take care of it," said Jane, smiling at him. She watched him disappear out the front door, and then sat back down and gathered the newspaper into a more manageable pile. As she did so, a headline caught her eye: DES MOINES PRIVATE INVESTIGATOR FOUND DEAD.

Feeling her pulse quicken, she drew the paper directly in front of her, slipped on her reading glasses, and scanned the article.

Earl Wilcox, 58, a longtime resident of Des Moines, Iowa, and a former English teacher, was found dead in his truck late Friday evening, an apparent suicide.

The body was discovered by Officer Clifford Sande-gaard, after receiving a tip from a jogger. The woman indicated that she'd run past the truck four or five times in the past couple of days. Several times, she heard a ringing cell phone in the back of the truck. When nobody answered, she became suspicious and alerted the police.

A police spokesperson said that Mr. Wilcox had been dead for several days, though the official time of death has yet to be determined. The truck was parked on the 4600 block of Blaisdell Avenue in south Minneapolis. Mr. Wilcox was a widower with no children.

Jane put the paper down. "My God," she whispered, feeling her entire body shiver. "He's—dead!" A wave of panic washed over her. *Breathe,* she ordered herself, her eyes bouncing wildly around the room. For a few intense seconds, she felt as if the bottom had dropped out of her world.

She finally focused on the cup in front of her. If someone had gotten to Earl, she could very well be next. Except—the Kastners didn't know anything specific about her connection to the investigation. How could they? Patricia was aware that Earl had come to Jane's house to question her, but that was it. And after last night, Jane felt confident that she and Patricia were still friends. If Patricia thought she was helping someone investigate her family, that wouldn't be the case. No, she was safe. For now. And she was going to stay that way if she had anything to say about it.

The first order of business was to give all the information she had to the police. Jane had one big ace in the hole, something

Earl didn't have when he'd gone to the cops in Des Moines. Jane could prove that Earl's death wasn't a suicide—at least she thought she could. There was no better time than now to see if she could turn that theory into fact.

34

Hurrying out to her car, Jane drove straight to City Hall. After talking to a receptionist through a bulletproof glass wall, explaining why she'd come and what she needed, she was ushered into an interview room where she waited for Sergeant Ranfelt, the detective assigned to Earl's suicide, to join her. She hoped she could present her case clearly and succinctly, but she also needed something in return. She wanted absolute confirmation that Earl's death was linked to the murders of Kevin Torland and Cyril Dancing. Not for one moment had she entertained the thought that his death was anything other than a murder, but she needed specific information. She was saddened, angered, and terribly frightened by what had just happened, but she realized now that she was in way too deep to simply let go. She had to know the truth—one way or the other. Especially about Patricia.

The room they'd put her in was depressingly bland—empty beige walls, a plain round table, and simple office chairs. Nothing else. The entire Criminal Investigation Division looked less like a *Cagney & Lacey* set than a renovated warehouse, one that had been turned into some nondescript corporate office.

After a good ten minutes of drumming her fingers on the

table, a burly, middle-aged man wearing a tan business suit entered and took the chair opposite her. He introduced himself as Dan Ranfelt, then pulled out a package of gum and offered her a piece. When she refused, he unwrapped a stick and folded it into his mouth. He seemed mildly curious about her, though mainly he just looked tired, as if he figured this was a complete waste of his time.

"Now, Ms.——"

"Lawless," she said, taking some notes out of her backpack.

"Right, Ms. Lawless." He stopped. "I don't suppose you're any relation to Raymond Lawless?"

"He's my father."

He nodded, examining her with a little more interest. "I'm told you wanted to talk to someone about the Wilcox suicide."

"It wasn't a suicide."

"Is that right?"

"It was a murder."

He continued to nod. "And I assume you've got some proof of this allegation?"

"Have you released the details of his death yet? How he supposedly killed himself?"

"No, I don't believe we have."

"Then, let me tell you how it happened. He killed himself with booze and drugs——most likely, Valium and vodka."

He sat up a bit straighter. "Okay, you've got my attention."

"It probably looked fairly straightforward. No obvious marks on the body; only a bump on the back of the head."

He held her eyes. "Is this a wild guess, or do you really have some inside information?"

"It's happened before——twice."

"Well, now, lots of people kill themselves with booze and drugs, Ms. Lawless. They pass out and hit their heads. It's nothing unusual."

"In a truck? Lying on a mattress?"

The corners of his mouth turned down. "What's your point?"

She reached into her pocket and drew out the wooden eye. Pushing it across the table, she said, "How many suicides have *that* in their pocket?"

He glanced at it, touching it lightly with the tip of his finger. "Where did you get it?"

"First tell me if I'm right. Did Earl have one of those in his pocket?"

He stared at it a moment longer, then looked up. "All right," he said, nodding. "Yes. He did. Now tell me where you got it."

"It was found in the pocket of a man who supposedly committed suicide in Des Moines last June. His name was Kevin Torland. His mother hired Earl Wilcox to find out who murdered him. That's why Earl was in town."

"You said there were *two* suicides."

"The second was a man named Cyril Dancing—he was a psychologist, and a professor over at the University of Minnesota. He died in nineteen eighty-seven, in a hotel room in downtown St. Paul. One of those wooden eyes was found in his pocket, too. If you don't believe me, you can talk to his wife. She's an ex-judge. I think you'll find her credible."

Ranfelt bit his lower lip and thought for several long moments. "What else have you got?"

Jane told him everything. How Earl had come to her with his suspicions about the Kastner family, seeking her help. That Elliot Beauman, the son of Virginia Kastner and her first husband, was currently renting part of her house. She explained about the little girl who was buried in her backyard—how Otto Kastner's cufflink had been found buried along with the girl's bones. Some of the information he already knew; most of it he didn't.

Next, she briefly detailed the information she'd learned about the Kastner family, how their lives touched these two men. She explained that Elliot was a psychic, and that he'd helped the police solve several recent crimes, though he was personally somewhat ambivalent about his psychic powers. Jane said that she was sure he knew who'd murdered the little girl in the backyard, but had stopped short of giving that information to the public during a recent TV interview. She felt that his knowledge had less to do with his psychic abilities than it did with his own family's involvement, though she didn't know that for a fact.

In discussing Patricia, Jane explained that she was something of an enigma, though a well-respected businesswoman and—a personal friend. Some people spoke highly of her, others didn't. Jane said that her personal experience with her had led her to believe that although Patricia was young and headstrong, she was not a murderer. She addressed Patricia's involvement with the two men, but added that she hadn't found a strong enough motive to conclude that Patricia was the guilty party.

Finally, she told Sergeant Ranfelt that Earl had expressed the opinion before his death that the murderer was one of two people. Her gut instinct told her that he was referring to Virginia and Otto, though again, she didn't know it for a fact. But Earl was definitely on the trail of some piece of information that he thought would blow the case open wide. Unfortunately, she didn't know what that was, but she assumed he was getting close to the truth and that was why he was killed.

Throughout her account, Ranfelt asked an occasional question, but pretty much just let her talk. When she was done, he sat back in his chair, crossed his arms over his chest, and chewed his gum. "That's all very interesting."

"So, now do you believe Earl's death wasn't a suicide?"

"Oh, there was never any doubt about that."

She didn't even try to hide her surprise. "You mean—"

"We suspected it was a homicide from the very beginning, but we didn't know any of the stuff you just told me."

"But, how—"

"Look, Ms. Lawless, I'm taking a chance by telling you this, but I think we may need you. You've obviously got a better handle on this case than we do; at least right now. See, Earl had some strange marks on his body—and on his clothes. First of all, he had duct tape residue on his jacket and pants—like he'd been wrapped in it so that he couldn't move. It wasn't real obvious, but it was there, and we had to wonder about it. Second, he had that bump you described on the back of his head. We couldn't quite figure out how he got it when he was lying down in the back of his truck. Now, if he'd been standing somewhere and had taken all those pills and drunk all that vodka, then he could easily have fallen and hit his head. The bump was nasty enough to send him to dreamland for a while, but in conjunction with the suicide, it made no sense. So we looked at his body very carefully. We found some scrapemarks on the inside of his throat—like someone had shoved something down it."

"Like what?" asked Jane, feeling the muscles in her neck tense.

"Well, we're not exactly sure, but when I was in Nam, I saw a guy being force-fed once. It wasn't pretty. They stuck a long metal funnel down his throat. I didn't get a good look at it, but then, I didn't really want to. I assume something like that happened here. Maybe the police in Iowa didn't look carefully at the victim's throat. Same for the people who did the autopsy on Dr. Dancing. But we had some red flags on this one. We couldn't ignore them."

"So, how did it all happen?" asked Jane. This had been the question she'd had all along.

"Well," he said, scratching the side of his face, "we figure someone must have snuck up on him, hit him on the back of the head hard enough to put him out—temporarily. When he came to, he was bound around the shoulders and the ankles by the duct tape so he couldn't move, and the feeding funnel was probably already in his mouth, so he couldn't talk. But he could listen. I think the murderer probably talked to these guys. He probably got a charge out of telling them they were about to die. To save time, I assume he'd already ground up the drugs and dissolved them in the alcohol. After he'd administered the mixture, he simply waited for them to pass out. When they did, he removed the funnel and the tape, and that was that. He took off, leaving them to die. Except, this time, the murderer was rushing. He made mistakes—left us some clues."

Jane had a question she hadn't yet asked. Now seemed the right time. "You said Earl's shoulders and arms were probably wrapped in duct tape, so he couldn't move. What about his hands? Would they have been free?"

"Possibly."

She thought of Kevin Torland—of what he'd done to his watch and his ring to alert those who would later find out from his body that his death wasn't what it appeared. "Did anyone take note of Earl's watch?"

"Why do you ask?"

She explained about Kevin.

"Was Earl left-handed?" asked the sergeant.

"I don't think so."

"Well, his watch was on his right hand. We wondered about that, too."

She closed her eyes and looked down.

"I'm sorry, Ms. Lawless."

"Thanks."

He rose and walked her to the door. "One last point before you go. If what you told me today proves to be accurate, we've got a dangerous killer out there, probably someone you know. For reasons of your own, you've put yourself right in the middle of this mess. I wouldn't agree to help any more private investigators if I were you. But for now, let *us* proceed with our investigation. Stay out of it, for your own sake. If you learn anything new—and believe me, I'm not telling you to go out and seek that knowl-

310

edge—call me. If you need me for any reason, just pick up the phone." He handed her a card. "One last word of advice. Don't be a hero, Ms. Lawless. Not unless you want to end up like your friend Earl Wilcox."

35

Since Jane was already downtown, she decided to drop by Cordelia's new loft to see how everything was going with the move. She'd helped her unpack on Wednesday, though the place was still piled high with unopened boxes when she left. Hopefully, Cordelia had dug herself out by now.

Linden Lofts was a massive six-story building located in the northeast corner of the warehouse district. It had been renovated by a man name Heywood back in the eighties but was now owned by Julia, part of the inheritance she'd received from her mother. Julia didn't handle any of the building maintenance or rent collection—she left that to a management company—but she continued to maintain Heywood's sixth-floor loft for her personal use. It was where Jane and Julia had first kissed, so it held special memories for them both.

The first three floors of the Linden building contained businesses. Cordelia's apartment was on the fifth floor, with an extraordinary view of downtown Minneapolis and the Mississippi River. It was just the kind of inner-city ambiance Cordelia loved. Except for the panoramic view, Jane liked her world a little less gritty.

Passing through Athena's Garden, a Greek restaurant located on the first floor, Jane decided to call home and check her messages before she went upstairs. She stopped at the bank of pay phones next to the elevator and slipped in a quarter, waiting as the line connected. Sure enough, she'd received three calls while she was out.

Tapping in her code, she listened as the first one replayed. It was Julia: "Jane? If you're there, will you please pick up the phone? We can't leave it like this. Jane . . . please! Just talk to me for a minute. I know I've made mistakes, but I love you. If that means anything, you've got to give me a chance to explain." Silence. Then, "All right, maybe you're not there. Or maybe you just don't want to talk right now. It's probably better that we have some time to cool off. It's just . . . I'm scared, scared that you'll never speak to me again, that I've messed things up so badly that we'll never be able to find our way back to each other. I guess all I can do is call you later. I . . . I'll . . . please, just remember the good times we've had. I'm just so *sorry*." The time of the call was twelve-fourteen.

The next call was also from Julia, this one shortly before two. "Jane? Are you back yet? I thought I'd try one more time to reach you. I just don't know what to do, how to make you understand. I'm supposed to be somewhere else right now, but I can't stop thinking about you, about what I've done." This time, her voice sounded less desperate, but far more depressed. "I deserve your anger—and your mistrust. But, if you're there, could you please just talk to me?" Silence. Then, "Okay, I'll leave you alone . . . if that's what you want."

Jane rested her head against the edge of the phone booth. The fury that had consumed her all morning had now subsided. In its place she felt the same weary depression that had permeated the last call. Julia's pain tugged at her, making her feel as if she'd gone too far. And yet nothing had changed, had it? Nothing but the heat of her own anger.

313

The third message was from Patricia. "Jane, hi. It's about two-thirty. I didn't leave a note or anything when I left this morning, so I thought I should call. I . . . hope you're feeling better today. I suppose it's no secret, especially after last night, that I'm not sorry you and Julia broke up. If you don't already realize it, I'm very attracted to you. And I . . . well, I've grown to care about you, too. Funny, it's usually the other way around for me. I sleep with someone first, and then I get to know them—or I don't. Usually, I don't. I didn't want to leave at all this morning, but I thought it would be best if I wasn't there when you woke up. You need some time to get your head straight. I'm at my parents' house right now. Mom has—well, she's kind of gone crazy. She locked herself in Dad's study and wouldn't come out. She's been drinking again. Dad threatened to break down the door if she didn't open it, so she did, and then when we weren't watching, she took off in her car. Dad's out looking for her now. I feel like . . . well, sort of like my whole world is crumbling and all I can do is watch. It's not just one thing, Jane, it's everything. I know your life isn't exactly calm right now either, but I thought maybe later tonight we could get together, just to talk. I feel like last night is still so unresolved—between us, I mean. I need to see you, but I'll understand if you can't. I'll call later."

Jane's mind was a jumble of conflicting thoughts and emotions. Should she get together with Patricia tonight or shouldn't she? She wanted to, but it probably wasn't smart, for many reasons, one of which was Julia. Jane realized all too clearly now that she still had feelings for her, though it would take a lot for Julia to repair the damage she'd done, if she ever could. Trust was a delicate mechanism, and once broken, it was almost impossible to repair. Jane wanted to be fair to both of these women, though she also wanted to be fair to herself. Her feelings for Patricia were nowhere near as deep and important to her as what she'd shared with Julia, but something was happening between them, something that intrigued her, and something she wasn't willing—given the current state of affairs with Julia—to ignore. Would it be wrong just to get together and talk?

Jane stood in the huge old hulk of an elevator as it rumbled slowly to the fifth floor. After knocking on Cordelia's door, she waited, looking both ways down the empty hallway. She had a key—just as Cordelia had one to her home—but didn't want to barge in without warning. Inside, Jane could hear disco music cranked up high, so she knocked again, this time louder and longer.

A few seconds later the music stopped, the door flew back, and Cordelia stood before her, a thin paintbrush grasped between her teeth and a black beret perched precariously on top of her head. "Ah," she said, pulling Jane inside. "Reinforcements."

"I'm not here to work," said Jane, taking off her jacket and tossing it over a chair. Glancing around the messy room, she took a seat on a fake Roman bench, a leftover prop from one of Cordelia's early Shakespearean productions at the Blackburn Playhouse. From the looks of the place, Cordelia had made some progress since Wednesday, but not a lot. Boxes were still piled high.

The loft itself was eighty feet long, with fourteen-foot-high ceilings, and with only a few exceptions—the bathrooms and the kitchen—it was completely open, no interior walls of any kind. The east-facing exterior wall held a series of floor-to-ceiling windows that provided the loft with its extraordinary view.

Cordelia picked up her can of strawberry pop and then sauntered slowly over to where Jane was seated, gazing at her with critical eyes. "You don't look so hot."

"I don't feel so hot."

"Anything you'd like to talk to Auntie Cordelia about?"

In spite of her mood, Jane smiled. "Maybe." She hesitated, then forged ahead. "Julia and I . . . well, we're having some problems."

"I know."

Jane looked up. "What do you mean, *you know?*"

"She called me."

"When?"

"A couple hours ago. She was looking for you and thought you might be here."

"And?"

"She told me what happened yesterday—about picking up her friend Leo at the airport, but giving you some story about how she couldn't make it down this weekend."

"Did she mention she lied about going to Boston last week?"

Cordelia tapped the side of her face. "Hmm. No. She omitted that little detail."

"How am I supposed to trust her when she lies to me . . . even about small things, stuff that shouldn't even be important?"

"I don't know, Janey." Cordelia sat down, then took a sip of her drink. "But I can tell you're really bothered by it. You don't look like you've slept in days."

"That bad, huh?"

"Yes, dearheart. That bad."

Jane looked down at her hand, touching the spot where Julia's ring had been. She'd taken it off this morning before her shower and hadn't put it back on. "I'm going crazy, Cordelia. I got so drunk in a bar last night that I barely remember what happened."

"*You* went to a bar?"

She nodded.

"Will wonders never cease? Did you do something . . . naughty?"

She glanced at Cordelia's eager face, then shook her head.

"But you came close."

"Sort of."

"With someone I know?"

"Patricia Kastner."

"Ah, the friendly neighborhood serial killer. Good choice, Jane."

"Come on."

"What? You mean to tell me you've proved her innocent since the last time we talked?"

"No, but—"

"You're human, Janey. You've got hormones just like the rest of us."

"Don't be patronizing. That's not what's happening. I simply don't believe she's guilty."

"Really?" Cordelia patted Jane's knee, then stood and climbed up the scaffolding in the center of the room where she was putting the finishing touches on a ceiling painting an artist friend of hers had almost completed—a rip-off of Michelangelo's *Creation,* though instead of God touching Adam's finger, in this new version, God was touching the white-gloved hand of Minnie Mouse. The painting covered the entire ceiling—one half very Renaissance, the other pure Walt Disney. It was *so* Cordelia.

Jane pushed off the bench and started to pace. "I had some bad news this morning. Earl Wilcox was found dead in his truck yesterday."

Cordelia stopped painting. "Jane, that's terrible!"

"I agree." She knew Cordelia would be interested in what she'd learned from Sergeant Ranfelt, but she felt suddenly weary of the whole situation. She just couldn't talk about it right now.

"You've got to be careful, Janey! Maybe you shouldn't stay at that house alone. What am I saying? Maybe you shouldn't be staying at that house at *all.*"

"I'm fine. Really. Nobody knows I've been helping Earl. And besides, I may not be alone tonight—at least not all evening."

"I see." One eyebrow rose. "Let me guess. First you're having dinner with Lizzie Borden. Next, John Dillinger and Ma Barker are dropping by—just to say hi, oh, and to show you their new machine gun. And finally, you've got plans to have a nightcap with Jack the Ripper—or Patricia Kastner, whoever's free."

"Okay. You've made your point."

"Have I?" She tipped her head back and added a touch of gold paint to the edge of an angel's wing. "I should find a nice, comfortable trunk and lock you in it."

Jane's head was beginning to throb. "Have you got any aspirin?"

"It's in a box labeled 'medicine chest.' "

"Do you have any idea where that is?"

"You have to ask?"

Jane glared at the mess, then held a hand up to her temples. "I've spent the last few weeks feeling confused—and I'm sick of it, Cordelia. I'm sick to death of feeling out of control, never knowing if people are lying to me or trying to manipulate me." She walked over to the windows and stared out at the river, her mind a whirl of sensations, most she couldn't even define. "I just want my old life back," she said finally, leaning against the glass, "the one that worked." A few seconds later, she felt Cordelia's arm slip around her waist.

"You're going to be all right, Jane. This will all get worked out."

"I don't know how."

"You know, it's difficult for me to see you like this." She took hold of Jane's shoulders and turned her around until they were facing each other. "You know I'd do anything for you."

"Sure."

"You're the best person I've ever known, Janey—the kindest, the most decent. And you're the dearest friend I've ever had. But you're flesh and blood. You hide that fact, sometimes, even from yourself. And then other times—" She looked Jane square in the eyes. "You're okay, aren't you?"

"Of course." She tried to squirm out of Cordelia's grip, but she wouldn't let go.

"You're not . . . you know, going to pull what you did right after Christine died?"

"What are you talking about?"

"The drinking."

"Are you saying I have a problem with alcohol?"

"No, but I am saying you abused it pretty badly for the better part of a year."

"I don't remember it that way at all."

Lifting her chin, Cordelia looked down her nose at Jane, then removed her hands. "All right. Fair enough. I'm not your mother—not that you couldn't use one every now and then."

"In case you've forgotten, it's not an option," said Jane, walking over to the door. The conversation was giving her an even worse headache and she wanted to leave. Grabbing her coat, she turned around with a fake smile. She knew Cordelia could see right through it. "Well, I guess I better get home."

"Of course, Janey. Just remember, you're welcome at Mount Olympus anytime—day or night."

Before she could open the door, Cordelia placed her body in front of it, blocking her exit.

"You have to promise me something before you go, dearheart."

"Or you won't let me leave?"

"Kinda looks that way, doesn't it?" She wiggled her eyebrows.

"What?" said Jane, trying but failing to hide her annoyance.

"That you'll have dinner with me tonight."

"Cordelia, look. I really just need some time to think. Between Julia and Patricia—and now with Earl's death—I'm a little off balance. I'll be fine, really."

"I have *no* doubt about that, Janey. But I've got to get away from these boxes for a while and we've both got to eat."

She took a deep breath, knowing it was pointless to argue. "Do you want to meet me at the restaurant?"

"Actually, I'd settle for a peanut butter sandwich, a glass of chocolate milk, and thou—at your house."

Jane shuddered. "All right. I'll fix us something. What time?"

"Seven sound okay?"

"You're *not* staying all evening." She gave Cordelia a quick hug and then added, "I know what you're trying to do, and . . . I appreciate it."

"I'm merely attempting to wangle a decent meal for myself at a price I can afford."

Jane smiled, this time, with a little more sincerity. "See you at seven."

36

On the way back to the house, Jane stopped at the supermarket to buy a few groceries. She wasn't exactly sure what she had in the refrigerator and knew that once she got home, she wouldn't feel like going out again. The weather was pretty chilly, but since she hadn't put the Weber away for the season, she decided she'd barbecue some chicken. Add a salad and some nice bread; Cordelia would have her supper, her conversation, and then Jane would send her packing. When Patricia called later, she still wasn't sure what she'd say, though most likely, she'd tell her, yes. Come over. They might as well talk.

After putting the food away in the kitchen and giving Bean his dinner, she checked to see if she had any mail. She stood for a moment on the front steps and watched a young man and woman across the street walk hand-in-hand to their car. As they drove away, she looked up and saw that the trees were almost bare of leaves now. And after last night's hard frost, the flowers were dying. She wondered what Julia was doing tonight, and if, at this moment, she felt as bereft as Jane did. Taking one last look around the neighborhood, she lifted a stack of letters from the mail slot and then shut the door and locked it.

On her way to the study, she glanced at a postcard from Beryl and Edgar, the first one she'd received. They were having a great time. They'd opened up Beryl's cottage in Lyme Regis, cleaned it thoroughly, and were now out looking for some new bedroom furniture. This was Edgar's first time in England and he wrote that he was enjoying every minute of it. Beryl said she was overjoyed to see her old garden again, and that her neighbor down the lane had done a fair job of keeping her vines and perennials alive, though still she had a lot of work to do to bring it up to her standards. Nothing was mentioned about when they would return. Jane was happy for them, and yet, after putting the postcard down, she felt strangely unsettled. She knew Beryl hated the winters in Minnesota. Was it possible they were planning to stay in England until spring—or even longer?

This wasn't a good night to dwell on it. She stuck the postcard inside the biography of Orson Welles she was currently reading, then sat down at her desk. The shattered glass from Julia's picture was still lying on the desk pad, right where she'd left it last night when she'd stomped out. Carefully, she brushed the pieces into her hand. When she looked down, ready to drop them into the trash, she saw the damaged frame with Julia's picture still inside it. Very gently, she lifted it back up and sat for a moment gazing at Julia's smile, wondering again what had gone wrong. She still loved this very beautiful woman, but was that enough? She was tired of feeling like her life was a train wreck waiting to happen. Funny, but she'd had that sense almost from the beginning of the relationship, though she wouldn't admit it. Placing the frame back on the desk, she wondered what else she'd been unwilling to admit about her life.

Jane sat for a long time just thinking. The house was quiet and dark. Bean was lying at her feet, snoring softly. When she finally emerged from her reverie, she saw that it was nearly five. She wanted to take a shower, and maybe even a short nap before Cordelia arrived, so she flipped briefly through the rest of the mail, intending to examine it more carefully later. She stopped, however, when she noticed a letter with no return address and a Des Moines postmark. Ripping it open, she discovered that it was from Earl—a letter scrawled in longhand on a yellow legal pad.

Tuesday night.

Jane: I'm sending you a copy of some information I uncovered—just in case something happens to me. I've never been particularly fatalistic, or easily frightened, but I realize now that I've been chasing a very dangerous person for the past few weeks. This is hard for me to admit, but for the first time in my life, I feel like I'm in way over my head. Unfortunately, I have no other choice than to push through to the end. The murderer, whoever he or she is, isn't going to let me live to a ripe old age with what I now know. If I don't catch him, he'll catch me.

Keep your nose clean, Jane, and let me take it from here. If something does happen to me, take this information and everything else you know straight to the police, but make sure they keep your name out of it.

Okay, here's what I found out. I've sent you a copy of Patricia Kastner's wedding certificate. She and Kevin Torland were married shortly after they moved in together. I've also talked personally with the lawyer Torland hired to help him sue Patricia for divorce. His name is written at the top of the certificate.

Get this: There was no prenup. Torland was about to take young Ms. Kastner to the cleaners. He was furious that she'd left him high and dry and was about to move back to Minnesota. And there's more. Patricia's parents didn't know about the marriage—at least, that's what Torland told his lawyer. Otto and Virginia made Patricia and Elliot swear on a stack of Bibles that if they ever got married, they'd first have the family lawyer draw up an ironclad prenup—just to prevent what Torland was about to do. Patricia was so hot to get married that she broke her promise. Consequently, she felt she couldn't tell her parents the truth.

So, here's what I'm thinking. Patricia Kastner had a compelling reason to want to get rid of Torland. He was about to drag her—and the rest of the family—through some very nasty mud. He had some other dirt on the Kastners, too. Virginia Kastner had a drug and drinking problem. Believe me, I doubt public humiliation is Virginia's bag. She would have hit the ceiling. And it would have all been Patricia's fault.

Next, that tip you gave me about Dr. Cyril Dancing—that was good work, Jane. I had a friend of mine in Mpls. do some more checking. My friend is pretty well connected in the psychotherapy community up there. He came up with something important. It seems, before Dancing died, he was bragging to a few of his associates about some X-rated video he'd taken of a lady friend—someone he was sleeping with. This was out of character for him, though at the time he was having a lot of personal problems. For years, his marriage had been unhappy. In 1986, he'd finally begun to act on his unhappiness.

I think it's fair to assume that, since Dancing didn't make a habit of sleeping around, we're talking about the one very specific woman, the one he was sleeping with before he died. And that points the finger directly at Patricia Kastner. She was undoubtedly the star of the movie.

Now, think about it, Jane. If Patricia's parents found out about her affair with Dancing and threatened to ruin his career over it, just for revenge, what if Dancing turns around and threatens to make that tape public? Or maybe he even made that tape, either in anticipation of something bad happening to him because of the affair, or after the fact, to save his ass. Whatever the case, we end up

324

with your basic Mexican standoff. Except, in this case, someone went tilt. The question is, who? Right now I'm leaning toward Patricia Kastner. If that's the case, since she's a friend of yours, you've got to be extra careful.

I'll mail this tomorrow morning on my way out of town. And I'll see you Thursday night. Maybe if we combine what you've learned with my information, it will throw some new light on just who we're chasing.

You should know, Jane, that I feel very guilty for getting you involved in this, even though I don't know what I would have done without your help. When it's all over, I promise, I'll take you out for a steak and a bottle of bubbly. In the meantime, remember: be careful!

Earl.

Jane stared for a few seconds at the marriage certificate, then dropped both papers on the desk, got up, and went into the kitchen, where she grabbed the bottle of brandy from the cupboard and poured herself a stiff drink. Her mind ached. What had Patricia been thinking to marry that guy? Had she loved him—and then murdered him? Had she made that video? Who the hell *was* Patricia Kastner?

Jane simply couldn't think clearly anymore. She was exhausted. She had to get some rest before she did something truly stupid. Taking the brandy bottle and the glass out onto the back porch, she sat in the rocking chair and watched the last of the day's light fade. She wished Beryl were here, just to talk, to make everything seem normal again. Not that it would help tonight.

After a few minutes, the alcohol started to do what she hoped it would. Since she hadn't eaten any lunch, it went right into her bloodstream, taking the edge off her emotions. Maybe she could even sleep for a while before Cordelia arrived.

Returning to the kitchen, she set the bottle on the counter. A fire seemed like a good idea. She could build it and then lie down in front of it on the living-room couch. Bean would like that, too. And then later, she could shower while Cordelia was getting the charcoal started.

Removing the pins from the back of her braid, she let her hair fall loosely around her shoulders. She turned off the light in the kitchen and walked through the darkened dining room into the living room. The brandy had settled her down, making her movements seem effortless. It was a welcome relief after the heavy depression she'd been carrying around with her all day.

She built the fire quickly and then sank down on the couch, unbuttoning her shirt so she could feel the heat from the flames on her bare skin. She just needed to turn the world off for a while. Leaning her head back against the cushions, she drifted to the sound of the crackling fire. She was so tired. Weary to her bones. She fell asleep sitting up.

A sharp noise woke her. Checking her watch, she saw that it was a quarter of seven. Damn. Cordelia was early. Rebuttoning her shirt, she walked into the front hall and drew back the door. No one was outside. Okay, she thought, shutting it and then leaning against it for a moment. Sure, she was feeling a little light-headed from the brandy, but she was pretty sure she'd heard something. She moved over to the stairs and sat down, stroking her temples and trying to make sense of it. Maybe she'd dreamed the noise. She'd been chasing someone down a long, winding corridor, jumping over pieces of furniture, knocking into stacks of empty boxes. As she thought about it now, she realized she was chasing Earl's murderer.

In that one moment, it all came together, like a crystal forming. She saw the face of his killer and knew the truth. Her eyes shifted toward the front windows as her mind began to race.

Something Elliot had said to her shortly after he'd moved into her third floor sprang to her mind. He'd explained that he just wanted to live quietly, write his books, and take care of the people he loved. But the only person Jane could see that he loved was

Patricia. And how was he taking care of her? A cold shiver crept down her spine as she contemplated the answer.

Earl had found one key piece of evidence. Kevin Torland and Patricia had been married, but Patricia clearly wanted out. Kevin was hurt and angry, and to pay her back he threatened to take her—and her entire family—to the cleaners. The day he died, Virginia Kastner had visited him, but Jane knew now she had nothing to do with his death. Neither had Otto Kastner, who was flying back from Aberdeen at the time. The only two people who could have sent Kevin Torland to his death were Patricia and Elliot. And while Patricia was no doubt scared by what Kevin might do, Elliot was the one who acted to prevent his sister from being hurt—as he had twice before.

Elliot probably saw himself as Patricia's protector. He constantly played with a hero theme in his children's books. *Danger Doug Saves the Universe*. Danger Doug was always saving someone. It was humorous, but it was also a metaphor. Sure, Patricia was in good physical condition, but she was small. Both Earl and Cyril Dancing weighed well over two hundred pounds. The fact was, it would have taken a man's strength to move all these unconscious bodies around.

But the final nail in Elliot's coffin came from what Abbie Kaufman had told her. Virginia Kastner might have been manipulative and two-faced, and Otto Kastner might have allowed himself to be pressured into becoming her emissary, the one responsible for encouraging Abbie to back away from Patricia, but it was Elliot and Elliot alone who delivered the physical threat—the same young man who was forever getting in trouble for his temper and his tendency to violence.

Jane might not have figured out all the specifics, and she might not be able to prove her theory to the police, but she knew she was right. And given enough time, they would discover how everything fit. The only real question remaining for her now was, Did Patricia know what her brother was doing?

Jane thought back to the conversation they'd had about moral philosophy—good and evil. Did Patricia see herself as Dr. Jekyll to Elliot's Mr. Hyde? Was that why she was so interested in the book? Jane recalled Patricia's saying something about Hyde having no real moral sense. He simply did what he did because he wanted to do it. But Jekyll knew the difference between right and wrong and at least, early on, could have stopped Hyde if he'd wanted to.

But he didn't. Could that be Patricia's story?

Feeling her head ache not only from lack of sleep, but with questions she still couldn't answer, Jane glanced into the living room and saw that Bean was no longer on his rug. Thinking that he was the cause of the noise, she walked back into the living room and headed into the rear hallway. If he'd knocked over the wastebasket in her study, something he occasionally did because he liked to eat paper, he could have cut himself on the glass. She should have cleaned it up right away.

Berating herself for being so thoughtless, she entered the room and looked around, but Bean was nowhere in sight. The wastebasket was just as she'd left it. So was everything else. The light was on next to the desk and the letter from Earl was. . . . She blinked, running a hand over her eyes to clear the cobwebs from her brain. Where was the letter and the marriage certificate? The envelope was still there, but the contents, the pages he'd sent were missing. She bent down to examine the floor behind the desk, but found nothing. As she straightened up, she heard another noise, this one directly behind her.

"Bean?" she said, glancing around.

That's when she felt it—a sudden blow that knocked her forward into the desk. She shut her eyes against the pain, then looked back, though she was too disoriented to focus on what was happening. As the floor rushed toward her, she groaned, rolling onto her back. She looked up at a face bending over her, and then, very slowly, watched it fade.

37

Cordelia stood on the sidewalk in front of Jane's house feeling like Mary Astor in *The Maltese Falcon,* pulled in too many directions—completely unsure where happiness lay. In Cordelia's case, however, it was more a question of appropriateness.

The third floor, where Elliot lived, was brightly lit, but the main part of the house was dark. Cordelia assumed that Jane had fallen asleep, and that was undoubtedly good. She needed to regain some of her normal resilience, and sleep was a big part of that. But back to Cordelia's dilemma. Should she ring the bell, or should she simply use her key and let herself in? She was already late. The elevator at Linden Lofts was teeth-grindingly slow. She'd had enough time to go through all five stages of grief while waiting for it tonight.

Making a carefully considered snap decision, a skill she was known far and wide for, she trotted up the front steps and pressed her key into the lock. Once inside, she could see a flickering light coming from the living room. She loved the smell of woodsmoke, especially on a fall night; it was the one amenity her loft lacked. Shutting the door softly behind her, she suddenly became aware of a series of odd, muffled sounds emanating from the back of the house. Thinking that perhaps Jane was in her study, she crossed into the living room and headed down the rear hallway.

The kitchen was at the far end, and when she squinted into the darkness, she thought she saw someone. "Jane?" she called, flipping on the hall light. Atmosphere was one thing, but total darkness was ridiculous. "I'm here. Sorry I didn't ring the bell, but I thought you were napping." She stepped cautiously into the kitchen and then stopped, surveying the room with one quick sweep of her eyes. When she saw the brandy bottle sitting on the counter, her brow creased with concern.

A moment later, she heard barking. "Bean?" she said, turning around. "Where are you?" She marched back down the hall and pushed the study door open. The light was on, but nobody was inside. Since Jane was generally a neat person, she was a little surprised to see the room in such disarray. Her gaze dropped to the floor, where a framed photo of Julia lay amid a jumble of papers and books.

Now she was getting worried. Racing back out to the front hall, she rushed up the stairs and switched on a light in Jane's bedroom. Again, nobody was home. She continued on down the hall to the bathroom where she could hear Bean not only barking, but scratching and whining. "Cordelia is coming, dearheart. Just hold your horses—or whatever the hell dogs hold."

As soon as she opened the door, Bean burst out of the room, charged down the hall, and disappeared down the steps. "Well!" she said, waving air into her face. She felt as if she'd just witnessed a cyclone. Her cats never behaved with such a tedious lack of manners, even in an emergency. She gave herself a moment to reconnoiter.

Why had Jane locked him up? Something wasn't right here, and Cordelia had a sneaking suspicion what it was.

She hurried back downstairs. Following the sound of Bean's whining, she entered the living room and walked slowly toward the fireplace. A sick feeling in the pit of her stomach told her that her instincts were about to be confirmed.

Jane was passed out on the couch, lying on her stomach, one arm dangling off the edge of the cushions onto the carpet. "Oh, no," she whispered, feeling an unwelcome sense of déjà vu.

The only light in the room came from the dying embers in the fireplace, but it was enough for her to see the empty glass. Picking it up, she sniffed it, then set it on the coffee table.

"Oh, Janey," she whispered, kneeling down next to her. "She's not worth all this. Nobody is." As she brushed a tangle of hair away from Jane's face, it all came back to her: the drinking. The anger. The terrible, inconsolable sadness. Perhaps Jane didn't remember that awful time as clearly as she did because she was unconscious during a good part of it.

The first year after Christine's death had been the worst. Jane didn't talk about it much now—perhaps she didn't want to admit how bad it was. Many nights Cordelia would arrive at the house only to find Jane just like this. Passed out on the couch, or sitting in a dark room, drinking and sobbing. Jane never let anybody in her family see her like that—only Cordelia. She maintained a brave front for the rest of the world, but in private, she was crumbling. And yet, over time, she had crawled back from the precipice and made a good life for herself. She was a strong woman, and had dealt with her problems, mostly alone. She needed people, and yet experience had taught her to be frightened of that need.

Stroking her face softly, Cordelia felt an intense pang of guilt. For years, she'd needled Jane about her lack of dates. It was meant to be playful, and yet maybe it was just plain stupid. When it came to relationships, they were worlds apart. Cordelia was a great believer in live and let live. She thought people were *way* too serious and *far* too moralistic. She was a free spirit living in a world of Calvinists. She'd had many relationships over the years, some good, some not so good, but all in all, she'd had a great ride. But with Jane, attachments came at a much higher price. Given her past, it was understandable. And that was just the point. Most people didn't realize how deeply she'd suffered over her mother's death, and then Christine's. Cordelia only understood because she'd watched it from a ringside seat. Not that Jane was stuck in the past, but those experiences had formed her and had left a very deep imprint.

"Janey?" she whispered, placing her hand on the small of Jane's back and shaking her gently. "Come on, wake up. We've got to get you upstairs. You don't want to sleep down here tonight, not unless you want to look like a paperclip in the morning." When Jane didn't stir, she shook her again, this time a little harder. "Janey?" She touched the side of her hair, wondering what she'd had to eat today, and how much she'd had to drink tonight. When she lifted Jane's hand, she felt something wet on her fingers. She quickly got up and switched on one of the living-room lamps.

"My God," she whispered, staring at the blood. She looked back at Jane and saw now that she had it all over her collar. She was still dressed in the same clothes she'd had on this afternoon—a red flannel shirt and jeans. What had happened?

This was no time for analysis. Cordelia picked up the cordless phone lying on the coffee table and dialed 911. "I need an ambulance right away!" she shouted to the woman who answered. She verified the address. "No, it's a friend of mine. I can't get her to wake up." She listened for a moment. "Yes, she's been drinking. She must have hit her head. What? Her pulse?"

She hadn't thought of that. She bent down and grabbed Jane's wrist. "Yes, I can feel it. How the hell should I know if it's strong? I don't go around taking people's pulses!" She waited while the woman told her to calm down. Then she answered a few quick questions. "No, there isn't a large amount of blood, but there's enough! Bigger than a toaster but smaller than a bread box. It's a joke, lady. How the hell should I know what you mean by *large*. What? No, I don't know how long she's been out. Maybe fifteen minutes, maybe two hours. Look, just send a doctor right away! A head specialist. A good one." In the light of the lamp, Jane looked very pale. "I'm frightened, all right? This doesn't happen to me a lot." She listened to the woman's reassurances. "Right. I'll be here waiting. Just make it quick."

Cordelia rode to the hospital in the back of the paramedic van. All the way downtown she stroked Jane's forehead and told her everything would be all right, but it was mostly for herself. Jane still hadn't opened her eyes or uttered a sound.

When they finally got to the hospital, Jane was rolled away on a gurney by two weedy-looking men in white coats. For all Cordelia knew, they were sanitation workers about to take her to a laboratory and turn her into Soylent Green.

After a brief examination, one of the emergency-room doctors—a Dr. McMichael—came out to talk to her, explaining that he wanted to run some tests. The longer Jane was unconscious, the more serious the injury to her brain might be. This was not the news Cordelia wanted to hear. The doctor said that after a skull X ray and a CT scan, he'd know more, but that wouldn't be for an hour or two. Right now, she was being observed closely and appeared to be in no immediate danger. For the moment, he recommended no visitors.

Cordelia found a pay phone and made a couple of calls. She left messages at Jane's brother's apartment and her father's house. It seemed that no one in the Lawless family was home tonight.

The idea of spending the next few hours sitting in a bleak waiting room worrying herself into a frenzy as she watched people with broken bones and bad gallbladders parade through the hallway was more than Cordelia could stand. Also, she had an uneasy feeling she'd forgotten to lock Jane's front door. Since there was nothing she could do here right now, she decided to make a quick trip back to the house. She could check the door and get her car, just in case she needed it later. Not that she intended to leave the hospital tonight. If someone tried to prevent her from seeing Jane, they would be in for one hell of a fight.

38

Cordelia arrived back at the house around nine-thirty. After paying the taxi driver, she raced up the front steps and checked the door. Thankfully, it was locked. Instead of returning immediately to the hospital, she knew Jane would want her to check on Bean. Cordelia wasn't sure when Jane would return home, and Bean, unlike her far more logically designed cats, had some rather pressing exterior needs. Maybe she should try to get that odd neighbor woman, the one who sounded like Marilyn Monroe and looked like Julia Child, to let him out in the morning and give him something to eat.

Entering the house, she stood in the front hall for a few moments and stared into the living room. The empty brandy glass was still sitting on the coffee table right where she'd left it. Never, ever again did she want to see a repeat of tonight.

Tapping a finger to the side of her chin, she set off to find Bean. She checked all his favorite spots downstairs, but when she didn't find him, she tried the second floor. She was on her way into Jane's bedroom when she saw a movement in the hallway. Switching on the overhead light, she discovered him wagging his tail at her playfully. "Come on, boy," she called, clapping her hands. "Let's go outside and destroy the grass." Instead of trotting toward her, he turned and scampered off in the opposite direction. "Hey, you little runt," she called, following him down the hall. Before she realized what he was up to, he'd pawed the door to the third floor open and raced up the steps.

"Bean!" she shouted, frustrated that he'd ignored her, and also more than a little surprised to find the door unlocked and ajar. She stopped for a moment at the base of the stairs and squinted up into the darkness. Even though she felt more than a little creepy, she still had to do something. She couldn't just leave him up there — or spend all night waiting for him to come down. If Elliot was asleep, or if he wasn't home, she could wait forever. It wouldn't do any good to call the little critter; not only did he have a mind of his own, but he was hard of hearing. She had no other choice. She had to go get him.

"Hello?" she called, taking the first two steps with caution. "Anybody home?" When she received no reply, she continued on up. All she wanted was to sneak in, grab the little runt by the scruff of his neck, and sneak out. Then she'd throw him outside, wait until he was done sniffing and spinning, and get the hell back to the hospital.

Reaching the top of the stairs, she peeked into the long, narrow room. The desk lamp was on, and so was the computer screen, but Elliot was nowhere in sight. That explained why Bean hadn't been bounced out immediately. Feeling more ill at ease with each passing second, she started her search. There weren't many places a dog could hide in such a small space.

As she passed by the desk, she heard him in the kitchen. "Get over here," she snarled. He was licking the base of a covered plastic garbage can. How *incredibly* tasteless. As she charged toward him, he scampered back into the living room and disappeared down the steps.

Oh, just peachy keen. Now when Elliot came home, as he no doubt would any second, she wouldn't have a plausible excuse for being in his apartment. Not that he didn't have some pretty fast explaining to do himself about why that door was unlocked. As she thought about it, her stomach became queasier and queasier. Why the hell had Jane rented her third floor to a member of that awful family?

She glanced at the computer monitor on her way back to the stairs, intending to take a quick perusal—just a tiny glimpse—and then bolt like hell for the door. But she stopped when she saw the word "Confession" at the top of the screen. Confession? The confessions of a psychic might make for some fascinating reading. Entranced by the very idea, she sank down into Elliot's desk chair and read:

Sgt. Engsdahl:

I know this isn't a legal document, but it's all I intend to leave behind. I want you to be the one to receive it. I guess, I just think you'll handle my confession fairly. I only have one request. Keep my sister out of it. She's the only person in this godawful world that means anything to me, and I don't want her hurt—any more than necessary.

I've killed four people. Connie Mayville. Dr. Cyril Dancing. Kevin Torland. And Earl Wilcox. Tonight, I attacked Jane Lawless in her home.

Cordelia felt a jolt of adrenaline hit her system. It only took an instant for the disaster to sink in. God, why hadn't she considered that? She was so sure she knew what had happened. Tapping in 411, she got the number of Hennepin County General, then waited while she was connected. Her hands were shaking, and so was every part of her body, but she kept focused. She had to. Jane's life was at stake!

A woman, probably a receptionist, answered. Cordelia demanded to talk to Dr. McMichael, stating that it was an emergency—a matter of life and death. After what seemed like a century, he came on the line. "Dr. McMichael here."

"This is Cordelia Thorn. My friend, Jane Lawless, was brought in a couple hours ago."

"Yes, Ms. Thorn." He sounded busy but concerned. "What's the problem?"

"Is she all right?"

"I believe she's in Radiology right now. She's still unconscious. Is that what you called to find out?"

"Yes. No! I have reason to believe that she's consumed a large quantity of alcohol and pills, most likely Valium. God, she could be dying! Can't you do something? Remove her stomach and squeeze it—whatever the hell you people do?"

"Calm down, Ms. Thorn."

"*Calm down?* A lunatic just tried to kill her!"

Silence. "I don't know anything about that, but we ran a blood screen on her when she first arrived. It showed no signs of tranquilizers, and only a minimal amount of alcohol."

"But I . . . I don't understand."

"I don't either, Ms. Thorn. Perhaps you should contact the police. In the meantime, be assured that we're doing everything in our power to help your friend."

"Good, that's good." Thank God she wasn't dying—or dead.

"As soon as the tests are done, we're transferring her to ICU."

"What's that?"

"Intensive care. We've got to monitor her closely. I'm afraid she's not out of the woods yet."

"Right," said Cordelia, feeling like an emotional yo-yo. Relieved one minute, terrified the next. After saying good-bye, she looked back up at the screen. She had so many questions racing through her mind, she didn't know how to even begin to sort them out. So she read on:

Jane would have been my fifth victim, but I was interrupted by a visitor and fled. As soon as Ms. Lawless is able to talk to the police, she'll confirm my guilt. I knew I might get caught one day, and I finally have. My one regret was Connie Mayville. While she was a horrible little girl, I didn't intend to end her life. It was an accident. I placed the cufflink in the dirt along with her body to incriminate my stepfather—just in case she was ever found. In many ways, her death paved the way for the other murders. I've performed the last three killings in exactly the same way—with vodka mixed with Valium.

I believe I have no other choice but to end my own life. I refuse to put my sister through the stress of a long trial. And I will not live out the rest of my days in prison. I could run, I suppose, but in many ways, this end is overdue, and will only close a circle that should have been closed a long time ago.

I offer no justification for these murders—other than to say that I had my reasons. I made a promise to protect someone I love, and that's what I've done. Beyond that, I will not comment.

Close this case, Sgt. Engsdahl. Don't let it drag on. Let the world think I'm insane and leave it at that. You and I—we know the truth. You see that truth every day, and I've lived with it most of my life. Anybody can be a killer. A father. A mother. Anyone. The killers out there aren't *them*—they're *us*. We only sleep at night by ignoring that fact.

Oh, there's one last point I should clear up. I'm not a psychic. I personally witnessed that young girl's murder at the Washburn water tower several weeks ago. At the time, there was nothing I could do to help her. I had hoped that someone else would discover her body and come forward, but when no one did, I couldn't stand the thought that she was there all alone. Some people *are* truly innocent—she was one of them. I knew if I told the cops the truth, with my background, I'd be a suspect in her murder. I'd be put under surveillance. I couldn't have that, so I lied. I also felt I might use this situation to my advantage with the police. I knew Jane might have to be eliminated, and if you all thought I was a good guy—on the side of the angels— I wouldn't be a suspect. I even thought I might offer to help you find her murderer.

And finally, I need to explain about the boy who killed his father. What can I say? I looked into his eyes and I knew. I never had one moment's doubt. I'd recognize that kind of hate anywhere, Sgt. Engsdahl, because it's another thing I've lived with most of my life. I looked at that boy and I saw myself.

Elliot Beauman.

Cordelia sat for a moment and stared at the flickering screen. For perhaps the second time in her life, she was completely speechless. And yet, she couldn't just sit here—she had to *do* something. If he was about to commit suicide somewhere, or already had, the police should be notified. So should his family.

Paging through his Rolodex looking for Patricia's phone number, she picked up the receiver and punched in the seven digits. After several rings a distracted voice answered, "Hello?"

"Patricia?"

"Yes?"

"Cordelia Thorn. I'm in Elliot's apartment. I don't know how to break it to you gently, so I'll just tell you. Your brother's confessed to the murders of four people."

"What!" A long silence. Then, "I don't understand? Put him on."

"I can't. He's not here. But he left a note on his computer. I just finished reading it. It's a suicide note, Patricia."

"No! He can't *do* that!" More silence. "Did he say where he was going?"

"I'm sorry."

"This is insane!"

"That about covers it. He attacked Jane tonight."

"What do you mean, attacked? Is she all right?"

"No. They're running tests on her at Hennepin County General."

"Oh God," she groaned.

Cordelia thought she heard a noise above her—a creaking sound coming from the ceiling. "Just a minute," she said, removing the receiver from her ear. Sure enough, the longer she listened, the clearer it became. "Patricia, I think I may know where Elliot is."

"Where?"

"Up on the roof."

"Go talk to him! Stop him from doing anything stupid. Tell him I'll be right there." She put her hand over the phone to muffle the sound of someone speaking to her in the background.

"I take it you're not alone," said Cordelia.

"No, I'm not. Look, don't waste another second. Try to keep him occupied until I can get there."

"Sure. But you better call the police."

"Just go!" said Patricia, rushing to get off.

Before Cordelia pushed away from the computer, she hit the print button and then waited a few seconds while two copies of the confession printed out. She knew Jane would want to see one, and also, she wanted to have a hard copy available for the police, just in case. Stuffing them into her pocket, she hurried to the door.

Once outside, she swiveled around and looked back up at the roof. Sure enough, Elliot was sitting next to the chimney, about twenty feet away. He was holding a liquor bottle in his right hand.

"Hey, Elliot?" Perhaps there was a proper way to address

someone in the process of committing suicide, but she didn't have a clue what it was.

He took several more gulps, then looked over at her. "Oh, *shit!*"

"That's not very nice. I, ah . . . thought we were friends."

"Jesus, Cordelia. Leave me alone."

"Why don't you . . . come back inside?" She glanced down at the ground, feeling her hands grow clammy and her knees go weak. For a moment, she was Jimmy Stewart chasing Kim Novak up an old Mission stairway.

He shook his head, then tipped the bottle back and drained it.

As he tossed it away, Cordelia watched it roll down the shingles and rattle to a stop in the eaves. Feeling an involuntary shudder, she forged on. "How . . . how many pills have you taken?"

"What's it to you?"

A hand rose to her hip. "I'm a detail person."

"Have you called the police?"

"Not yet."

"It doesn't matter." He seemed almost peaceful as he looked up at the stars.

"I read your confession."

"I assumed as much."

She could tell he was high, and getting higher by the second. "Why did you have to hurt Jane?"

No response. Instead, he tried to get up, but fell back against the chimney. Righting himself with some difficulty, he sank back down, then pulled the band off his ponytail and raked both hands through his hair. "I suppose she's talked to the cops by now. Is that why you came back here?"

"She's still unconscious."

He took that in. "That's weird. The others came around pretty fast."

"Well, Jane *didn't*." She couldn't believe she was having this tepid conversation with someone who'd harmed her best friend so badly. Anger swelled inside her. Why not just do what he asked? Go away and let him die. She was about to encourage him to do just that when Patricia burst into the yard and rushed toward the steps.

As she made it to the landing, she shouted, "Elliot, stop! You've got to listen to me!"

He covered his face with his hands, staying like that for several seconds, then eased back against the chimney and pushed up with his legs until he was standing. He was about to respond when he saw his mother come slowly through the gate into the backyard. "Oh, God," he moaned.

"She was at my house when I got Cordelia's call. I couldn't stop her from coming."

"Get her out of here!" he ordered. "Now!"

"Elliot, please," called Virginia. She seemed utterly transfixed by the sight of her son on the roof.

"Please *what,* Mother? Please don't do what Jay did? What do you care? The moment he fell off this roof, you checked out of my life."

"You don't understand a mother's guilt." Very slowly, she started up the steps.

"Don't you realize how *sick* to death everyone is of hearing about your guilt? Didn't you ever feel any guilt about abandoning *me!*"

"Elliot, I've made lots of mistakes, but I did the best job I could. Now . . . come down from there before you get hurt!"

"You shouldn't even call yourself a mother," he mumbled, taking a step away from the chimney.

"Elliot, don't!" shouted Patricia.

He ignored her, continuing to mumble. "I should have said that years ago. I didn't tell you something the other night, Mother—I guess I was too ashamed. But I might as well tell you now. Just so that when you flog yourself later with your booze and your pills, you'll have the whole story."

"Elliot!" cried Patricia, banging on the railing, "nobody's going to listen unless you come down."

"Fine. Go away. I never asked for an audience."

Virginia finally reached the top of the stairs. "I want to hear it, Elliot. I want to hear anything you have to say."

He gazed at her a moment, then passed a hand over his eyes. When he started speaking again, his voice was lower, his words slower and a little more garbled. "The night Otto made Jay drink that whiskey, he gave me a choice. I could stay upstairs with my brother, or I could come downstairs with him. Jay and I had made a sacred pact. It was the two of us against the world. We promised to protect each other—stick together. But that night I got scared. I left Jay alone. I broke my promise, and that's why he did it. I betrayed him. And I couldn't tell a living soul about it because nobody cared. On the day Patricia was born, I swore to myself on my life that I'd never make the same mistake again. If anybody ever tried to hurt her, they'd have to come through me first."

"Elliot, that's ridiculous," called Patricia. "You're not making any sense."

In the distance, Cordelia could hear a police siren, getting louder.

Virginia reached her hand toward her son. "Just come down. Give me a chance to make it up to you."

"It's too late." He tried to move away from the chimney, but stumbled and pitched forward on all fours.

"I'm going up there," said Patricia, hoisting herself up on the railing.

"No," said Virginia, seizing her arm.

"But he's going to fall!"

Elliot moved with some difficulty into a kneeling position. "I could have done this without the booze and the pills," he muttered, his voice listless, "but I didn't want to end up a vegetable like Jay. I want this end to be clean. Final."

"Elliot, stop!" cried Patricia, wiping her hand over her eyes.

She was jumping up and down, unable to keep still. "You're thinking like a crazy person."

"Maybe I am, but it's my life." Weaving to his feet, he brushed his hair behind his back. "I didn't want you here, Patty. I didn't want anybody here."

A squad car pulled into the driveway, its lights flashing.

Seeing the police, Patricia broke free of her mother's grip and started to climb up on the railing again.

Virginia grabbed her around the waist. "I won't let you go up there! You could fall."

"I have to try! For God's sake Mother, he's your son!"

"And you're my daughter!"

"But he's going to die if someone doesn't stop him!"

"I know," she wailed. "But I can't lose *you*. You're all I've got left!" She held on tight as Patricia tried to pull away.

Cordelia watched them in stunned silence. Shifting her gaze back to Elliot, she could tell he'd moved far away from them now. As he tried to stand, to position himself near the edge of the roof, he fought to stay alert. His movements were slow, deliberate, and very unsteady. Down on the ground, the police were rushing into the yard, shouting for him to stop.

At the last second Elliot made a great effort to open his eyes wide. Cordelia wondered what he was seeing, what he was thinking, and most of all, what he was feeling. Then, as Patricia shrieked for him to wait and Virginia held on to her for dear life, he raised his arms, dipped forward, and dropped headfirst into the backyard. The sound his body made as he hit the ground was surprisingly small.

Cordelia closed her eyes and looked away, feeling suddenly sick. When she got up the nerve to look back down, she saw that Elliot was lying in the grass near the lilac bushes. One officer was kneeling next to him, the other had run back to the squad car and was calling for medical help.

Patricia had already bolted down the steps and was at his side.

345

"We've got to get him to a hospital right away," she screamed. "He needs to have his stomach pumped."

Virginia and Cordelia remained on the landing.

"Aren't you going down?" asked Cordelia, feeling she was mere seconds from throwing up.

Virginia said nothing. Gripping the rail to steady herself, she sucked in a breath of air. "I watched one son die. I don't think I can stand to watch another."

An instant later, Cordelia heard an ear-splitting scream. Looking down, she saw Patricia on her knees, holding her brother in her arms, rocking him back and forth. "What's happening?" she called.

One of the cops looked up. "I'm sorry, ma'am. He's . . . not going to make it."

The police stuck around for several more hours, looking through Elliot's apartment, questioning everyone, taking photographs, and making several more hard copies of the confession. Eventually, Elliot's body was taken away in a van, and Virginia was whisked away by her husband in a Lincoln Town Car. Very little passed between husband and wife as he tucked her into the front seat. He kissed his daughter good night, and then asked her to call him in the morning.

Cordelia watched the scene play out from Jane's front door. Patricia had calmed down some, though her eyes were still red and swollen when she returned to the house.

"I have to go see Jane," she said, retrieving her keys from the dining-room table.

"I'm not sure that's such a good idea," replied Cordelia, leaning against the archway, her arms folded over her chest.

"You can't stop me. I love her."

"You hardly know her. Besides, I don't think the intensive care folks will care much about your *feelings*."

"She's in intensive care?"

"She's unconscious. *That's* what your brother did to her."

Patricia scrutinized her face. "But she's going to be all okay, right?"

"The doctor said she wasn't in any immediate danger, but nobody's talking about a prognosis just yet."

She continued to stare, then looked away. "Look, Cordelia, I can understand your anger. I'm angry, too."

"How appropriate of you."

"My brother was mentally ill. He had to be. He didn't know what he was doing. But it doesn't change what's happened between Jane and me."

"And what would that be?"

"She *needs* me, Cordelia. I need her." She started up the stairs.

"Where are you going?"

"I want to read that note my brother left."

"The police taped off the third floor. Nobody goes in or out without their permission."

She stopped and turned around. "When did they do that?"

"While you were helping your mother out to the car." Patricia looked so frustrated that Cordelia searched through her pockets until she found the copy she'd saved for Jane. "You might as well look at it, but I want it back."

Walking very slowly over to the dining-room table, Patricia folded herself into a chair. For the next few minutes she read silently, one hand clamped over her mouth. When she was finally done, she put the paper down and looked off into space.

Cordelia watched her with growing skepticism. There was something about Patricia Kastner's act she just didn't buy. This was as good a time as any to get it off her chest. "Did you tell the police the truth? You had no idea your brother had murdered Kevin Torland?"

She glanced at Cordelia, then pressed a thumb and forefinger to her temple. "What's the difference?"

Cordelia was aghast. "There's a *big* difference. If you knew, you could have stopped him! Jane might not be in the hospital right now."

"I . . . I never thought he'd hurt her."

"Patricia, he was a freaking time bomb!"

"Look, I didn't know anything for sure."

"I see. You just *suspected* he was a serial killer. No reason to get excited about something like that."

She shot Cordelia an angry look.

"So tell me. How *long* have you known?"

She looked down and mumbled, "A few months."

"And you did nothing about it?"

"What was I supposed to do? Turn him in? Bring up the subject while he was eating his morning Wheaties? 'By the way, bro, did you murder Kevin?' "

"You can save the attitude, Patricia. It may work wonders on Jane, but it doesn't cut it with me." Walking around to the other side of the table, Cordelia sat down. "What about Cyril Dancing?"

"What about him?"

"Did you suspect your brother killed him, too?"

She ran a hand through the back of her hair. "Yeah, I was starting to put it together."

"How inconvenient of you not to finish."

"You think I'm lying? For your information, I almost told Jane last night. We were playing a game—telling secrets."

"You like games, don't you, Patricia? But . . . let me guess. You never told *your* secret, did you?"

"No."

"Why not?"

"I was scared of what she might do. I needed more time."

"For what?"

"To talk to Elliot. To figure out the best way to approach him. Can't you understand, it was a delicate situation. And with Mother's drinking, and the police hounding my father about Connie Mayville's death, my whole family felt like it was in turmoil. Everything was out of control. Besides, I could have been wrong about Elliot. I mean, what would *you* do if you thought your brother might be a murderer?"

"I wouldn't lie to the police."

"Well, pardon me. I guess I'm not as smart as you are."

"We can debate that some other time."

"Look, Elliot was in trouble. I knew that. He's always lived on the edge. During that television interview last week, I thought he was either going to turn my father in for the murder of Connie Mayville or admit that he'd done it himself. I didn't want either to happen."

"You wanted him free so he could murder again."

"Of course not!"

"It seems to me he was cleaning up *your* messes. Everything he did was to your advantage. You could sit back and never dirty your hands. You were the energetic young businesswoman, wealthy, going places, and he was the oddball who lived in the background of your life, doing what you didn't have the guts to do yourself. You could remain pure while he did the evil deeds. Did you enjoy it, Patricia; get some vicarious thrill out of watching the dominoes fall always in the right direction?"

She glared, then shot out of her chair. "What are you saying? That I somehow controlled what my brother did? I don't need this crap. I loved him. He was a sick man, and I should have been able to help him deal with that sickness, but I failed. I'll live with that failure the rest of my life."

Patricia was angry, but Cordelia was angrier. Before she could reach the front door, Cordelia grabbed her by the arm and spun her around, pinning her against the wall.

"Get your hands off me."

"With pleasure, but first you've got to promise me something."

She tried to squirm away.

"I want you to stay away from Jane. She doesn't need someone like you in her life right now."

"What I do is none of your damn business."

"I couldn't agree more. But Jane is. Believe me, you don't want me for an enemy."

They stared at each other for several long moments.

When Patricia finally spoke, her manner had changed. Her confidence had miraculously returned. "I think the sensible thing to do is to let Jane make her own decisions, don't you? We're all adults. No one is coercing anyone." She smiled, and in a voice that was almost a purr, added, "Besides, you don't want me for an enemy either, Cordelia. Remember, there's an important vote coming up at the Allen Grimby in early January. My mother relies on my good judgment. I'd hate to think of you standing in the unemployment line come the new year."

39

Julia walked down the quiet corridor toward the nursing station, grateful that Cordelia had left, and even more grateful that she hadn't returned. As soon as she was gone, Julia had introduced herself to Dr. McMichael, explaining that she was Jane's primary physician. She'd even been able to examine her briefly, but had waited in the background, pacing the hallways, until the tests were done. Jane had finally been taken to a private room. It was almost midnight now, and Julia desperately wanted to see her, but first, she needed to check the test results.

Since their conversation earlier this morning, Julia had been beside herself with worry. She knew that Jane was furious, and also deeply hurt. Julia was thoroughly disgusted with herself that she'd been the cause of that hurt, but most of all, she was frightened. Lying to Jane had been the single worst mistake of her life, one she had to rectify. She'd assured Leo that she would stay in Grand Rapids for the weekend, that she wouldn't leave him at her house to deal with everything alone, but it was a promise she couldn't keep. She owed Leo her friendship, but she owed Jane something more fundamental: the truth—even if, in the end, Jane left her because of it.

By seven, Julia had reached the Minneapolis city limits. She drove straight to Jane's house, hoping that she'd find her at home. There was no use phoning ahead to say she was coming. She'd already left several messages on the answering machine—none of which Jane had returned.

As Julia was pulling into a parking space across the street, she saw Cordelia drive up. This was a complication she hadn't counted on. She and Jane needed time and privacy, especially for what she was about to say. Feeling thwarted but still resolute, she decided to sit in her car and wait. If she had to, she was prepared to wait all night.

Less than fifteen minutes later, a paramedic van, sirens blaring, turned the corner and stopped directly in front of the house. Julia watched from the car as Jane was wheeled out on a gurney. It took every ounce of self-control Julia possessed not to rush to her side. She didn't know what had happened, but deep down, she felt a growing sense that, one way or the other, she'd been the cause of it. If she was, she knew Cordelia wouldn't let her within ten feet of Jane.

When the paramedic van sped away, Julia followed. She had to know that Jane was all right. At the hospital, she stood around the fringes of the emergency room, making sure Cordelia didn't see her. She didn't want to get chased off before she found out what was going on. When she discovered that Jane was unconscious from an injury to her head, she was confused. She'd already glanced at the preliminary blood tests, but didn't feel that the alcohol in her system was enough to cause a fall. The cut just above her ear had been small and hadn't required stitches, but the internal injury to the brain, while hidden, could be far more serious. Once Jane was awake, she would be able to explain what had happened, and yet the longer she was unconscious, the more problematic her injury might prove to be.

Approaching the nurse on duty in ICU, Julia asked to see

Jane's chart, as well as the test results. Standing at the counter, she flipped through the reports, ending with Dr. McMichael's notes. Thankfully, there was no skull fracture, but the CT scan had detected bleeding. An evacuation had already been performed to relieve the pressure on the brain, but Jane would have to be watched even more closely now. As Julia closed the file, she realized her fears had been justified. This was no minor injury. Jane was in a coma.

Feeling as if something enormous and dark had just brushed past her, she continued on down the hall. She was operating on pure adrenaline now, mainly because she'd stayed up most of the night talking to Leo. Thankfully, as she entered Jane's room, she saw that her luck was holding. Jane was alone. Julia assumed her family would be arriving any minute, though since it was Saturday night, she might have a little more time. At this point, she was willing to take anything she could get.

Brushing a lock of hair away from Jane's face, she felt suddenly overwhelmed by an unreasonable panic. She was a doctor, trained for moments like this, and yet right now, her training failed her. What if Jane didn't wake up? Or even worse, what if she *did* wake up, but she was left with some sort of irreparable brain damage? Julia understood the possibilities in great detail. A coma wasn't an absolute indication of future problems. There was still a chance Jane could wake up and be just fine. Walking slowly up to the bed, Julia knew she had to hold on to that thought.

She lifted Jane's hand to her lips. She had so many regrets. The worst part was, she wasn't even sure Jane knew how much she loved her. At this moment, she wanted nothing more than to spend the rest of her life proving that love.

Standing by the bed in the silence of the hospital room, Julia made herself a promise. There would be no more secrets, no matter what it cost. If Jane gave her another chance, she wouldn't screw it up again. She couldn't let her fear—fear of Jane's contempt—dictate her behavior any longer. She would *make* Jane understand. There were reasons for what she'd done, compelling reasons. She was a doctor. She'd become involved because she wanted to help. Jane might not see it that way at first, but she'd come around. She had to. When Julia told her the truth about her move from D.C.—why she really wanted to set up a practice in a remote part of northern Minnesota—she had to trust that Jane would understand. And then they'd deal with the fallout, no matter how nasty it got.

"Please, sweetheart," she whispered, stroking Jane's hair, "you have to listen. I promise, I'll make everything right. When you're well, we'll talk. I'll explain everything." She searched Jane's face, hoping for a sign, *anything* that would tell her that she'd heard—that she understood. But there was nothing. In that one instant, Julia felt all the despair, the shame, and the longing she'd lived with for so many months come rushing out. She closed her eyes, crushing Jane's hand hard against her lips.

She stayed that way for several minutes—until she felt Jane's hand lightly squeeze her own. Looking up, she saw that Jane's eyes were open. At that moment, Julia felt such intense relief, she burst into tears. "You're going to be all right," she said, choking back her own emotion as she stroked Jane's hair again.

"My . . . head hurts," whispered Jane weakly.

"Just stay quiet." Julia knew the emergency-room doctor would want to see her right away, but she had to talk to her first. She might not have another chance to be alone with her for quite some time. "I've got so much I need to tell you."

Jane closed her eyes. "Not now, Julia."

"I know, I know. But you've got to listen to me for just one minute." Taking a deep breath, she began very slowly and gently, "I never wanted to lie to you, but what I'm involved in—what I have been involved in for many years—had to remain secret." She paused for a moment to see if Jane was comprehending. After assuring herself she was, she continued. "I moved to a remote spot in northern Minnesota to facilitate that secrecy. It wasn't that I didn't trust you, sweetheart, it's that I'd given my word as a doctor to keep what I'm doing private. Even from you. Leo, my oldest and dearest friend, is the one who got me involved in this in the first place. He's a good, kind man, Jane, and I love him very much, but not the way I love you. You've got to believe me. The reason I couldn't come down this weekend was because a mutual friend of ours is dying. He flew in from Jamaica on a private jet this morning. He's staying at my house right now. To be honest, I don't expect him to last the weekend. That's why I wanted to be there—to be with Leo and our friend, to help in any way I could. I was in Jamaica visiting this man when I lied to you and told you I was in Boston with my uncle. I'm sorry I had to do that, but up until now I've taken that promise of silence very seriously. This is a very delicate matter, Jane. And it's going to take some time to explain it all to you so that you'll understand."

Jane opened her eyes. "Why are you telling me all this now?"

"If I don't, I'll lose you. And that's too high a price to pay." Silently to herself she thought, *I may lose you anyway.*

Jane touched a hand to her temple. "I'm sorry, Julia, I'm trying to listen, but I . . . feel . . . sort of scrambled."

"You've had a hard knock on your head." Julia sat down next to her on the edge of the bed. "Do you remember how it happened?"

Again, Jane closed her eyes. "I can't remember anything."

"That's not unusual. It will probably come back to you in time."

"What hospital is this?" Jane blinked and looked around the darkened room.

"Hennepin County General."

"Have I been here long?"

"A few hours. It's Saturday evening—around midnight." Julia

could tell that Jane was frustrated by her mental sluggishness. "Just try to relax, okay?" She pushed the nurse's call button.

What Julia had failed to mention to Jane was that there could very easily be some danger involved in breaking her silence. But she would deal with that when the time came. Right now she had to concentrate on helping Jane get well. The fact that she was conscious was a positive sign, though if the bleeding hadn't stopped, she could still be in some serious trouble.

Jane gazed up at the silent television. "I'm tired."

"Just rest," said Julia, smoothing the covers over Jane's shoulders.

As she did so, a startled look passed across Jane's face. Trying to sit up, she said, "Julia? I—"

"You've got to stay still, sweetheart."

She dropped back against the pillow. "But I . . . I can't feel my left arm."

Julia felt as if an electric shock had passed through her body.

"And my left leg. It feels funny—kind of numb."

Julia moved to the end of the bed. Squeezing Jane's foot through the covers she said, "Can you feel that?"

"Yes."

"Try wiggling your toes."

Julia felt a small movement. "That's good. The loss of feeling is probably temporary."

"Probably?"

As Jane searched Julia's face, Julia hoped she couldn't read the worry in her eyes. "Look, your doctor will be here any second. You're going to be all right, sweetheart." Sitting back down on the bed next to her, Julia covered Jane's right hand with her own.

"You . . . won't leave, will you?" asked Jane, her voice unsteady.

"You couldn't get rid of me if you tried."

Jane attempted a smile, though it wasn't much of one. Looking down, she whispered, "I never stopped loving you." As she closed her eyes, Julia sat holding her hand, hoping with all her might that when all the crises were over, there would still be time left for the two of them to build a life together. What had once seemed so simple, so effortless and right, had now turned into a battle with no certain ending. Not that anything in this life was a sure bet. If anyone had learned that lesson, Julia had.